D1291670

The Krone Experiment

THE KRONE EXPERIMENT

J. Craig Wheeler

PRESSWORKS PUBLISHING, INC.
DALLAS, TEXAS

Pressworks Publishing, Inc.
P.O. Box 12606
Dallas, Texas 75225

ACKNOWLEDGMENTS

I am grateful for the valuable editorial help of Lucille Enix, Denise Brink, and David Hartwell. Special thanks go to Peter Sutherland and Linda Mills for reading and commenting on an early draft, to Hugo Bezdek for sharing insights into the workings of government agencies, and especially to my wife, Hsueh Lie, for her keen critical eye. Finally, I thank anonymous colleagues and their institutions who played host to me over several years, thus providing stolen moments in airplanes, motels, and restaurants, to add a few more paragraphs.

Library of Congress Cataloging in Publication Data
Wheeler, J. Craig.
The Krone Experiment.

I. Title
PS3573.H4325K7 1986 813'.54 86-3269
ISBN 0-939722-21-6

Manufactured in the United States
ISBN 0-939722-21-6

1 2 3 4 5 6 7 8 9 10

Dedication

For my parents, Peggy and G. L.

The Krone Experiment

Chapter 1

Abd Ar-Rahman was the first. The old shepherd leaned on his staff by the trunk of a gnarled thuja pine, trying to find shade. He gazed down the foothills of the Atlas Mountains to the snaking Oued Moulouya in the distance. The half-wild mouflan sheep clustered near the tree, cropping at sparse spring shoots of tough esparto grass. Ar-Rahman had the briefest impression of a noise overhead. As he raised his eyes upward, an unseen hammer blow sprawled him on his back in the dry North African dust. He was conscious of his infirmities and used to stumbling now, but this left him stunned and confused. As he gazed upward, a branch the thickness of his wizened leg cracked and sagged under its own weight like a broken arm. The bleating finally penetrated his stunned senses. He crawled to where one sheep had staggered and collapsed an arm's span from him, directly beneath the break in the branch. The animal was bleeding copiously from ragged wounds, one along its spine and one in its belly, as if it had been shot through. The old man watched in anguish as the sheep bled its life away.

Robert Isaacs tried to ignore the message from headquarters. He was enjoying himself, and did not relish facing whatever calamity had produced the summons. He kicked his fins and glided along the surface, peering through the sea-churned murk at the occasional brightly colored fish. An old tire caught his eye. He gulped air through the snorkel and plunged the six feet to the bottom. Grasping the outer rim, he tugged upward. The small nurse shark, startled from its resting place in the dark hollow of the tire, dashed for the safety of deeper water.

Isaacs smiled to himself. That's life, honey, he thought, somebody just kicked my tire, too. Surfacing, he swam to shore. After removing his mask and snorkel he balanced awkwardly, first on one foot, then the other, peeling off his flippers. He toweled himself dry, slipped into thongs, and crossed the narrow strip of beach. A spurt of traffic came along US 1, which separated the beach from Patrick Air Force Base, and he paused to let the cars pass. Immediately across the road was the blunt, brick sprawl of the Air Force Technical Assistance Center which had been his temporary base of operations. One last time his eye scanned the long line of obsolete missiles which stood sentry before the building. He crossed the road and turned left toward the clump of visitors' bungalows, resigned to packing and catching the next flight back to Washington.

A glorious spring morning greeted him the next day as he headed out of town toward Virginia. March was departing the nation's capital in its finest style, docile, but vibrant with new life. The break in his normal routine fresh in his mind, Isaacs tried to capture the pagan urge to rejoice by foregoing the usual morning radio news and by driving with the window open to the smell of dew-dampened trees. His hands guided the wheel of the compact Mercedes 380 SL semi-automatically as he followed his habitual route. He made the light on Canal Road and swung left onto Chain Bridge across the rocky narrows of the Potomac.

The light at the far end of the bridge stopped him. He glanced back over his shoulder at the distant spires marking Georgetown University. Fragments of breakfast conversation rushed back at him. Damned if I want to foot high tuition to some experimental college to help Isabel find herself, he thought. I can't expect a high school junior to be completely level-headed, but I don't understand Muriel's resistance to a high quality university like Cornell. Hell, it was good enough for us!

The light changed and he turned up Chain Bridge Road. The feel of the accelerating car regenerated his sense of well-being for a moment. Then the tunnel of trees blocked the free blue sky, and the physical ascent toward his destination drew his mind on a parallel course. Unable to focus on the quality of the morning and not wanting to dwell on domestic problems, his thoughts shifted more frequently to the concerns of his job. By the time he made the right turn onto the George Washington Parkway, he was concentrating on his priorities for the day. Top on the list was the emergency meeting at nine o'clock. Bad news, he mused. Scheduled that leave months ago, and they've got to haul me back. Whatever it is, the bastard's going to be an ulcer-buster.

Consciously attempting to quell that unpleasant turn of mind, he admired the fresh tan on the backs of his hands as they gripped the steering wheel. As a Major in the Air Force Reserve he served two weeks' active duty a year, a welcome relief from the tension in his position with the Central Intelligence Agency, Deputy Director of Scientific Intelligence. He thought back on the past ten days, chuckling to himself, recalling his postman's holiday. Intelligence officer at a beach-front Florida base, he thought, not a bad perk. The experience resonated with memories of his younger days of patient collection of raw intelligence data. In this case, however, there had been the lure of the beach and ocean and leisurely hours snorkeling to break the tedium. Those pleasant memories buoyed his spirits as he turned off the parkway toward headquarters.

He steered up the off-ramp, following it ninety degrees to the left as it crossed back over the parkway. A small jam of cars feeding into the headquarters entryway from the southbound ramp forced him to brake sharply to a halt. At the pause, his glance strayed up the green embankments to blooming stands of redbud and dogwood. The car ahead of him pulled right at the drive leading to the highway department headquarters. As he closed the resulting gap, he recognized the Fiat two-seater in front of him. It belonged to Alice Lavey, who clerked in his analysis section.

The Fiat accelerated through the gate in the high chain link fence and past the guardhouse. Isaacs did the same, receiving a curt nod from the guard on duty who sat scrutinizing the windshield passes. Isaacs detected a small smile on the guard's face which he presumed to be a remnant of the passage of the Fiat. Alice had a penchant for low necklines. He steered the car on up the winding drive and into his personal parking space. He grabbed his briefcase, checked the doors, locked the driver's side with his key, and stepped across the lot as he extracted and attached his photo ID.

"Good morning, Mr. Isaacs, welcome back."

"Good morning, Ralph. And it's a nice one, isn't it?"

"Sure enough!"

Ralph had been there on duty for fifteen years and knew virtually everyone in the Agency by sight. Isaacs idly wondered whether rotating the guard to insure ID's were more carefully examined would be better or worse for security. He crossed the lobby, skirting the great presidential seal embedded in the floor, and proceeded down the corridor. He climbed six flights of stairs, eschewing the elevator, pleased with the spring in his step which eluded many at forty-five, his reward for moderate consumption and frequent handball, not to mention miles of swimming recently. Continuing along the upper hall, Isaacs glanced at his watch and noted with satisfaction that he was right on time.

Whatever the subject of the meeting, as in any gathering of influential people, there was ground to be gained or lost. Isaacs tried to put the welfare of the Agency first and to avoid political infighting, but he had a talent for turning a situation to his advantage and protecting his flank when on the defensive. As he walked, he mentally sorted through the personalities who would be involved and the various hotspots which could be at issue. At 8:59 he stepped through the door of the top floor meeting room.

"You're late, Isaacs, take a seat!"

Brother! thought Isaacs, welcome back. He moved to an empty chair. The icy greeting had come from Kevin McMasters, the Deputy Director of Central Intelligence. McMasters, Isaacs' immediate boss, had been with the Agency over thirty years. He bridled at Isaacs' rapid rise in the organization and even more so at suggestions that Isaacs was a candidate for his position as DDCI.

Isaacs sat and glared at his hands clenched before him on the table, peripherally aware of the other principals. Next to McMasters at the head of the table was Howard Drefke, the Director of Central Intelligence. A recent political appointee, Drefke leaned heavily on McMasters in questions of internal affairs and spent most of his time on relations with the President and the National Security Agency. Across from McMasters, to Isaacs' left, was Vincent Martinelli. Martinelli was Deputy Director for Collection Tasking, responsible for making intelligence gathering assignments throughout the intelligence community. To Isaacs' right was Art Boswank, whose hearty air belied his clandestine role as Deputy Director for Operations.

A minute passed in silence which reverberated with

McMasters' reproach to Isaacs. Then Earle Deloach, Deputy Director for Research and Development, bustled in and took the last chair, across from Isaacs, next to McMasters, who nodded to him in greeting. Isaacs felt Martinelli nudge him and looked over to see him pull a quintessentially Italian face and roll his eyes skyward. Isaacs cracked a small smile of camaraderie. They both knew McMasters would overlook Deloach's transgressions even as he invented imaginary ones for Isaacs.

"Gentlemen," began Drefke, "I must report to the President. Let's summarize our situation please."

Martinelli and Isaacs exchanged another glance, Martinelli giving an abbreviated nod. Drefke was liberal with his references to the President, and Martinelli did a devastating takeoff in which they all came out "mah buddy, the President." This time Drefke was referring to his Commander-in-Chief.

"Isaacs has been absent for some time," interjected McMasters dryly, "perhaps you should fill him in."

You son-of-a-bitch, thought Isaacs, make it sound as if I was out chasing floozies on company time.

Drefke looked blankly at McMasters for a brief moment, his train of thought interrupted, and then turned to Isaacs. "Of course. The Russians went on Yellow Alert yesterday afternoon," he said curtly. "They activated troops, moved fifteen Backfire bombers to forward holding positions, and uncapped, uh," he checked the sheet in his hand, "seven missiles."

"Lordy," exclaimed Boswank, "they've hauled us through these dog and pony shows before. I've got the same question I had yesterday. How do we know they're not just feeling their oats?"

"We've just received word they've gone public with it, and they don't like an exposed position without good reason," replied Drefke. "They've walked out of the new disarmament talks in Geneva."

"Well, what the hell?" blurted Boswank. "They just convened a week ago."

"Exactly," said the Director, "it was in their interest, as well as ours, to give a semblance of cooperation to the talks."

"Why involve the talks?" Isaacs asked quietly. "Why choose that particular vehicle for protest?"

"That's just the point," said the Director, addressing himself to Isaacs again. "They now claim we have used some unorthodox new weapon on them. They made veiled references to it in Geneva, and then the whole team just walked out and caught the first Aeroflot back to Moscow. Not the faintest charade of continuing the talks. Caught our men totally by surprise, and the press in Europe was on them like a pack of dogs. That was late morning in Geneva, about four hours ago. The Washington newshounds will be in full howl by now, too."

"A new weapon?" asked Isaacs.

"Of course, there's no such thing, so we don't know what's caused them to be so upset. That makes the situation damned unstable. I just talked to the President. He had Ambassador Ogarkov in for a quiet evening chat last night. They talked for an hour, but aside from vague threats of retaliation, the President didn't get very much. Not even a tip about the walkout. We all know the Ambassador can be very cooperative in certain situations. In this case he's under orders to play a very tight hand. No question but that the Russians are running scared. The only substantive disclosure was that they think one of their carriers was attacked in the Mediterranean. They're hinting that some form of space-based weapon was directed at the carrier, igniting jet fuel tanks and causing quite a bit of damage."

"There's some basis for that," said Martinelli, leafing through a folder. "After our meeting last night, I put out a general call for possible clues as to what triggered their alert. We've got photos of their carrier, the Novorossiisk. One of the four Kiev class Protivo Lodochny Kreyser antisubmarine cruisers. Definitely a fire on board, day before yesterday. Pretty bad, but no reason to think it was anything but someone smoking in the wrong place. Until you mentioned it, I hadn't given it any particular attention."

"Why would they think they were attacked?" asked the Director.

"No clue."

"And what's this about space?" inquired Isaacs. "What did we have up? Presumably we had no aircraft in the immediate area, and they must know that."

"As usual, all our aircraft were maintaining a perimeter," answered Martinelli. "An SR-71 went over for these shots after the fire broke out. We have all sorts of space hardware up, of course, but nothing they don't know about. I can get that double-checked, but we seem to be clean. In particular, unless Defense has pulled a fast one on everyone, there's not a beam weapon in the inventory—lasers, particles, what have you—that's anywhere near ready to orbit. Hell, we all read *Aviation Week*; it's still years away."

"That's very strange then," Isaacs mused, "from space, in particular, not just from above. I guess that's why they're alarmed, given that they believe it. If we did have an operating beam weapon in space, the Russians would have good reason to be frightened. They know how potent those things can be; they invented them."

"Well, we can't have the Soviets running around with a panicked finger on the trigger," declared the Director. "We've got to get a handle on this and calm them down. What else, Martinelli?"

"The aircraft have been refueling in mid-air, they're still up. The best guess is that the missiles are targeted to the eastern seaboard. Boston down to Washington."

Drefke looked grim. "What about you, Boswank?" The Director looked down the table at him. "Your people turn up anything?"

A veil settled over Boswank's face, as it did whenever he had to directly discuss his men in the field. "Sir, it takes time to reach our people in deep cover. We should know in a few days what the real view is in Moscow. Our man in the admiralty can be requested to get us the damage report on the carrier. That may give a clue as to why they think they were attacked, and how."

Drefke was distinctly unhappy at the lack of concrete news. "A few days," he grunted looking around the table, "we could be dust in a few days. I've got to go to the President. What do I tell him we're doing? Waiting for some Russian turncoat to give us the time of day?"

Boswank winced uncomfortably.

"I want to know what the hell we're doing *now*!" Drefke demanded.

"There's the new ultraviolet camera and spectrometer on the FireEye satellite my team launched a week ago," said Deloach enthusiastically. "We could divert it to have a look at that carrier."

"We need that satellite where it is, Earle," said Isaacs, trying to keep the patronizing edge off his voice, "over the new industrial area in Siberia." Typical Deloach, thought Isaacs to himself; he'd look for the lost nickel under the street lamp where the light's good. Too bad he doesn't have the same sense for good intelligence he does for good hardware.

"The fire obliterated anything useful you could have seen on deck," added Martinelli.

"The satellite ought to be stationed over Tomsk," McMasters said with a hint of bitterness.

"We've learned everything we usefully can at Tomsk," Isaacs replied patiently. Isaacs was vividly aware that McMasters had developed the targets at Tomsk and that his ego was too tied up in them to grant that their usefulness was played out. He had not made a substantial contribution since. "We've been through the arguments in favor of Siberia in detail," Isaacs said, and you've resented every one I made, he finished to himself.

"Dammit, let's stick to the subject at hand," Drefke commanded. Isaacs nodded, chagrined at letting McMasters draw him in.

There was silence for a moment, broken by Isaacs.

"Surveillance of the carrier is useless, as Vince points out. The fire will have seen to that. We have to convince them we had nothing to do with it. They'll want more than Presidential assurances. We must figure out what happened to them, or help them find out for themselves. Nobody on the Novorossiisk itself, Art?"

"The Novorossiisk?" Boswank shook his head. "Sure, a few, but they're the worst for rapid feedback. We can't get to them until they return to Russia. We have to go through a Soviet contact, too dangerous for the source otherwise."

"Too dangerous?" Drefke asked rhetorically. "Danger is a paranoid with his finger on the button when someone pops a balloon. Your sources won't be worth much if this gets out of hand. Can't we get to them more quickly?"

"We could, sir," replied Boswank, "but if this blows over, we would have jeopardized a major component of our network. We must be very careful. In any case the earliest we could get to them would be when they put into port. We should hear from our higher source before that."

"None on the Novorossiisk have access to a radio?"

"No, sir."

"I don't suppose they would let us put an inspection team on board, as a gesture of cooperation?" asked Deloach.

"Out of the question!" McMasters was adamant. "They'd never allow it."

Isaacs nodded his assent, McMasters was on target there. "Art can take the most direct step. We need to know what's in that damage report to really understand their reaction, but that will take a little time. How about Ogarkov? Does he know the basis for the charges, and would he tell us? Can we find out how he was briefed, or are there any message intercepts?"

"Links to the embassy are some of the toughest to penetrate, of course," replied Martinelli, "but I'll put out a call for any intercepts that might give a clue."

Isaacs looked thoughtful. "This concrete event has grabbed our attention. What about related occurrences? Anyone know of anything that could possibly be tied to this, even indirectly?" The silence around the table answered his question. "Okay," he said, "that's a loose end that we can try to follow up. I'll put some of my analysis people on it, and if we come up with anything, Vince, we'll feed it to you."

Drefke leaned back in his chair. "I want all the stops out on this. I'll tell the President we expect the details of the damage report in a few days, but that's not good enough. We've given the President nothing to go on; all he can do is deny our involvement, and in the present crisis atmosphere that won't wash. We need a handle on this business, and we need it now. Martinelli, if you turn up even a hint that we could use as bait or as a prybar on Ogarkov let me know immediately."

Martinelli nodded, and scribbled a note on his pad, "Save boss's ass."

"Boswank," Drefke pleaded, "isn't there anything you can do with your d-," he caught himself, "with your networks?"

"I can put out a call, but I don't know much what to call for," Boswank replied curtly. "You tell me there's a carrier with a fire on deck. What am I supposed to do with that?"

Drefke stared at him a moment and then turned to Isaacs, "I'll also tell the President that we're doing everything possible to determine what happened to that carrier, and why the Russians suspect we are responsible. I expect your department to give us something to go on.

"Let me remind you," he glared around the table, "that until the Russians come to their senses on this, they are standing with the hammer cocked and the pistol at our head. It doesn't matter that we think they're mistaken. The present situation is very delicate and very dangerous, and it will remain so until we here in this room act to defuse it." He pushed his chair back, stood, and looked sternly around the table. Then he turned and left with a brisk stride. The others rose and filed out of the conference room.

Deloach tailed McMasters down the hall. Martinelli followed Isaacs and Boswank into the stairwell. "Well kid," he said to Isaacs, "looks like it's up to us to save the bacon again."

Isaacs smiled, then sobered, "This one is dangerous, Vince. Too unpredictable. Neither side really knows what's going on."

"True enough," put in Boswank, "but the DCI's got a case of first crisisitis if I've ever seen one. Damn, if he'd been around during that Austrian dustup he'd know what a crisis was. He's got something to learn about running networks, too." He shuffled through the door at the next landing.

Martinelli was silent until they reached the landing on his floor. "McMasters is really beginning to ride you. That's going to blow one of these days."

"I'm afraid you're right," Isaacs replied. "I'll try to keep a low profile, but he's so stuck on those outdated programs of his, and, of course, I have to cross him every time we recommend something more useful."

"Let me know if we can do some snooping for you." Martinelli pulled open the fire door and stepped into the hallway.

"And you let me know if you turn up anything that might be related to this carrier business." Isaacs continued down another floor and went through the door there. He strode rapidly down the corridor, grabbed the knob on the door marked Office of Scientific Intelligence, turned it, and went in.

Kathleen Huddleston had started in the Agency secretarial pool and worked her way up. She had been Isaacs' executive secretary for three years now and was as familiar with his character as she was with the ebb and flow of the workload in this odd business. She recognized his step and put on a smile of greeting as the door opened. As he entered, she read his mood with a practiced eye. The familiar figure looked preoccupied, but more relaxed than usual this morning. She took in the dark curly hair only faintly tinged with gray in front of slightly protruding ears. The ears themselves were pink from recent sunburn. The hawk nose rode above thin lips and strong chin. As usual, the eyes stood out, dark and penetrating, surmounted by surprisingly long, almost effeminate lashes. The lashes gave him a perennial boyish look despite the otherwise rugged face. Responding to her smile of greeting, the eyes crinkled, exercising a growing crop of laugh lines.

"Hi, boss, welcome back."

"Thank you, Miss Kate," he said with a mock bow, "it's good to be back."

"How was Florida? You certainly got some sun!"

He grinned more widely. "I did find some time for the beach. How have things been? Any excitement?"

"Nothing the DCI and I couldn't handle. You've just come from the meeting?"

Her voice hinted at a question that Kathleen had not quite intended. Despite security there was always scuttlebutt. They both knew that Kathleen was discreetly aware of many issues that were formally beyond her ken. Documents had to be typed, and with that responsibility came necessary access. Kathleen and her cadre were too bright not to put two and two together on occasion. In this case she had heard nothing and that had caught her attention and natural, if unwarranted, curiosity.

Isaacs perceived her questioning tone and the basis for it. The worse the emergency, the tighter the security. A grimace passed briefly over his face. "Yes," he affirmed, "I need you to set up a meeting with the crisis team at," he glanced at his watch, "ten-thirty."

Kathleen nodded and continued, "Bill Baris wanted some time. I suggested two o'clock and that seemed okay, unless you want to see him later this morning."

Lord, thought Isaacs, something in Africa again.

"This afternoon would be better," he said, confirming her judgment. "I have a present for you, just to keep you out of trouble." He plopped his briefcase on her side table, reached for his keys and unlocked it. He extracted and handed her a fat, black-clipped, typed manuscript. "These are the corrections for the Bulgaria report; I'll need it Monday morning." He enjoyed her mock groan, confident the job would be done quickly and exactly.

He stepped into his inner office, deposited his case and hung his jacket on the rack. Circling his desk, he cranked open the blinds to expose the blue sky and thickly treed surroundings. His thoughts passed briefly from the carrier crisis to the sunlit morning, to Alice Lavey's neckline, and back, and he turned as Kathleen entered with a stack of intelligence summaries and a steaming cup of black coffee.

He smiled "thanks" as he settled into his chair. She returned the smile, gave a breezy "you're welcome" and slipped out, closing the door. He waited until the door clicked, then leaned back and propped his feet on his desk. Bad for the posture and image, but good for concentration, he thought, as he reached for the bound folder stamped "Orbital Visual and Infrared Reconnaissance Survey—Top Secret" and arranged the coffee within easy reach.

He read quickly but thoroughly, skipping over familiar facts, pausing to sip coffee and ponder and assimilate new data. There was no question that the laborious analysis that had revealed the crucial infrared signal of the mobile launchers continued to be superlatively valuable. Each of the mobile stations had moved in the last week, and not only were the three new stations revealed, the movements of each of the old ones were uniquely determined.

Satellite identification was still proving a difficult task. The launchings could be predicted over a week in advance and followed simply. Once in orbit the reconnaissance net was sufficiently dense that each satellite could be tracked, but a few escaped classification into the offensive, defensive, or reconnaissance categories.

He finished the first report and started on the aircraft reconnaissance, continuing with desultory sips of his cooling coffee. The Chinese were beginning the reprocessing plant for their new reactor. The Warsaw Pact troops had interrupted their war games with the onset of the current crisis. He noted that two of the previously identified high-speed tanks in Poland had been reclassified as older, slower models.

He glanced at his watch as he finished with this report. 10:23. Time to start on the signal intelligence before his team assembled.

He read along, stopping at an item already covered in the other surveys, the Soviet low tonnage underground event at Semipalatinsk. The satellite photos had shown the surface activity involved in setting up the experiment, and the infrared trace had indicated when the explosion occurred. This report outlined the results of monitoring the data links, both those uncoded and those for which the code had been broken. The result was that the Agency experts knew nearly as much about the test as the Russian scientists who performed it.

The summary noted that the nature of the explosion was confirmed by the associated seismic signal. That statement caught Isaac's eye, and he stared at the ceiling momentarily trying to recall a related tidbit of information he had filed away. As usual, the seismic reference was added simply for completeness since the Agency was not directly involved with the seismic monitoring system. He snapped his fingers and leaned forward to punch the button on his intercom.

"Kathleen?"

"Yes?"

"Would you have—let me see, who might be available?—would you have Pat Danielson stop in just after lunch?"

"Yes, sir. Time for the meeting."

"Right." Isaacs swung to his feet and headed out of his office, flipping a goodbye sign at Kathleen. As he walked the short distance to his conference room, he began to sort out tactics for turning up clues to the fate of the Russian carrier. The meeting, frustrating and unproductive, lasted to noon and beyond.

Temper lengthened Pat Danielson's stride. Weasel! she thought. What garbage, lunch to discuss my report! Put a damn run in my stocking with his hangnail! She slowed her pace as she turned into the last hallway. How's a person to get any credit? He probably didn't even read it. Sure glad Isaacs is reasonable, knows I'm a woman, but listens. Hope this is good news.

When she entered Kathleen's office, the two women exchanged greetings. They were cordial to one another, but not close. Although they worked for the same man and Kathleen was only a few years older, the difference in their positions, secretary and professional, created a practical barrier. Kathleen waved the young woman into Isaacs' office and followed her with a quick eye skimming the details of dress, hair, carriage before turning once more to her tasks as the door closed.

Isaacs looked up as Danielson entered his office, her wide smile of greeting reminding him of his own ebullient mood on the way to work this morning, a mood battered but not yet dead.

"Good afternoon."

"Good afternoon, Pat," Isaacs replied. "Please sit down."

She seated herself in the chair across from his desk, a bit too tall and big-boned to be graceful, but with good control of her body, not gangly. Isaacs watched her sit and cross her legs. He caught a quick flash of a run before she reversed her legs to cover it up. He regarded her for a moment. Good worker, even disposition under everyday hectic conditions, but no real test yet. Some spine, but not bitchy. Attractive in a wholesome sort of way, wide face, high cheekbones, a vague sprinkling of freckles to complement the reddish tinge in her hair. His evaluation of her work did not depend on her appearance, but he was honest enough to admit he preferred a good-looking competent woman to an ugly one. She looked at him expectantly.

"How's your work going?"

"Fine," she replied, but he caught the hint of distress that passed over her face.

"I can't keep tabs on everything as much as I would like to. I called you because I have a small project I'd like you to take on, but if you're having some trouble, we have a chance to talk now."

"No, no trouble," she said quickly, then hesitated, and fixed him with a gaze. "My work is satisfactory, isn't it?"

"Very much so," he said seriously. "There's some excellent data coming from the new satellite; you're doing your part."

"Doing my part," she repeated quietly to herself. "May I say something?"

He nodded. There was something she wanted to get off her chest.

"I really like this job. I think I'm doing something to help my country." She paused. "But there are times when I wonder whether I'm getting due credit." She straightened up and adopted a sterner tone. "The fact is, somebody made a pass at me at lunch, and I'm still upset. I don't want to name names, but first he complimented my work too much, and then afterwards he said some unkind things."

"A superior of yours?"

"Well, yes, but I don't want to cause trouble."

"Sounds like you're not the cause. Tell you what. First, let me repeat, you are doing well. That's one reason I called you in here today. I'll confess I've heard that you're better than some who get as much credit, or more. I'll try to keep a closer eye on that. As we both know, you more than I, the Agency is still a man's world. No use pretending you won't have to work hard to get ahead. About this other thing, though, I won't brook harassment." He pointed a finger at her. "I want to know if that happens again."

Danielson nodded, but he knew she would not mention the subject again.

"So, can you handle another project?"

"Yes, sir, I can," she said confidently.

"Good." Isaacs leaned back in his chair and folded his hands across his stomach. "You know I just came back from my tour of active duty?"

"Yes, you were in Florida, I believe I heard."

"That's right, at AFTAC, the Air Force Technical Assistance Center on Cape Canaveral. Do you know what they do there?"

Her brow wrinkled. "No, I guess I don't."

"Do you know about the Large Seismic Array?"

She brightened. "A little. That's in Montana, isn't it? A collection of seismic detectors to monitor underground nuclear explosions and such things."

"That's right," Isaacs nodded, "among other things, AFTAC monitors the Large Seismic Array, other seismic detectors in a world-wide network, and a separate ensemble of underwater acoustic monitors. Basically, they maintain a surveillance system to complement the various aerial and satellite operations."

Danielson gave a brisk nod of comprehension.

Isaacs continued, "I was stationed in the intelligence section at AFTAC. I spent some time looking at data from the LSA and reports on the analysis of the data."

His tone altered slightly as he added an explanatory note. "The data's analyzed at the Air Force Cambridge Research Lab in Massachusetts."

"Anyway," Isaacs continued his narrative, "there was one little piece of information that piqued my curiosity. They've apparently picked up a repeated but very weak signal—only a careful analysis can pull it out of the noise—which has a period of about an hour."

Danielson raised an eyebrow, "Interesting."

"At first I thought it must be the shuffling of undergraduate feet during class change at the University of Montana."

Danielson smiled.

Isaac smiled back, "Unfortunately the signal is out of phase with the university. Still, such a period seems too anthropocentric not to be man-made, and yet no one I talked to came up with any plausible account of it. Worse yet, to my mind, no one seemed to have any inclination to follow up on it. It's probably not important, but it's the kind of item I like to put a tag on, so it doesn't cause confusion at a later date.

"I know you have heavy commitments on current projects, and this is not a crucial item, but I would like you to follow up on it. You'll have to get in touch with the people at AFTAC and the Cambridge Research Lab. You'll probably want to acquire some of the data tapes. I'll give you a list of the people involved and clear the way for you through channels, but beyond that you'll be pretty much on your own. Any questions about that?"

"Not until I talk to the people and learn about the system," Danielson replied. "I expect their basic signal processing techniques are similar to ones I use—computer enhancement?"

"There are some differences, but that was another reason I picked you."

"I'll have to learn something about seismology. That will be interesting."

"Very good."

Isaacs supplied the young operative with a list of contacts and suggested several reports which would help to familiarize her with the nature and operation of the Large Seismic Array. She made pertinent notes and then departed.

As Danielson closed the door behind her, Isaacs swiveled his chair toward the window and leaned back, staring out. Above the trees, hazy clouds had filled the clear morning blue. It would be muggy by now. He pondered the strange seismic data a few moments to no particular avail. Then another imperative broke his train of thought. Baris would arrive shortly to discuss developments in Africa. He glanced at his watch, groaned mentally, and squared up at his desk. An image of the fire-scarred deck of the carrier Novorossiisk filled his mind. Somewhere within that ship-bulk was the key to why we were toeing the brink yet again. He reached for the too, too thin file of notes from the morning's crisis meeting. In a few minutes he was totally absorbed in that project, straining to find a fresh approach. He took the strain home with him that evening.

Chapter 2

Yuan Li Tzu glanced toward the hated gaping mouth of the mine. His shift was due to make their descent into the depths, and he would be in trouble if he were late. He could not resist another careful reading of the letter from his father, mentally sucking from it all hints of hope. He paused and looked at his rough, scarred hands. They had once belonged to a talented and promising fourteen-year-old piano student in Shanghai. Then the cultural revolution descended. The Red Guards had labeled the piano a decadent instrument of the West. Yuan recalled the fear and bewilderment he had felt as he was banished to the copper mine in the high mountains near Tibet. He had spent over a decade, his young manhood, in bitter detention in the mine, sickly, torn from his family, his education, his chosen way of life.

Now this letter from his father gave the first ray of hope. A chance, still slim, that relatives in the United States could take advantage of the burgeoning political ties with China to free him from his slavery and to offer him a new life in a new country. Yuan's mind spun fantasies of escape as he carefully folded the letter and tucked it safely in a pocket of his tunic.

He arrived at the mine too late—the crude elevator had already begun its descent. As he expected, a member of the revolutionary cadre noted his tardiness and began to shout exhortations of devotion to the people and the party. Yuan suffered the tirade in numb silence.

As the elevator reached bottom, a small tunnel bored upward through the rock. The tunnel arced over smoothly and then headed downward once more into the depths of the earth. The plane of the arc paralleled the main horizontal shaft of the copper mine. The apex lay about forty feet above the shaft and twenty feet to one side. The small tunnel briefly existed intact. Then stress fractures grew outward from it, shooting rapidly down and across in multiple fissures through the mine-shaft weakened bedrock.

No one noticed the first cracks widening in the ceiling and wall of the shaft. Then small rocks crumbled down along with sifting dust. Several miners cried in alarm and men began to scatter in both directions from the weakened portion. The ceiling of the shaft released with a roar and the whole section of rock from the small recently bored tunnel to the mine shaft collapsed in, sealing off the mine with tons of rubble. Those few lucky enough to be on the upward side fled toward the elevator, help, and freedom. Scores of men in the depths of the mine felt the cold clutch of darkness and fear settle about them.

On the surface, a silent ominous shaking of the earth interrupted the diatribe from the party member. A faint rumbling sound rolled from the elevator shaft followed by the shouts of panicked men. After another moment the elevator creaked into action, cranking upward. The mining camp burst into turmoil.

Amid wild shouts and men scurrying in every direction,

Yuan turned and walked slowly back to his tiny dormitory room. There he sat on his mat, removed the letter from his tunic, carefully spread it out, and began to read once again.

God!

He had exulted then, reveling in the feeling of immense forces responding to his control, lifting him to a soaring state of grace like a surfer in the curl of a perfect wave.

Now crashing waves, forlorn and bitter, pounded him. He cradled the smooth butt of the small pistol in his palm and recalled with agony the feelings that had swept through him then, now so completely foreign. He drifted into a dream, back to that day of ecstasy. . .

He stood before the penthouse window and gazed at the sweep of the sleeping city of Vienna arrayed at his feet, the Cathedral of Saint Stephen and the Hapsburg summer palace alit with spotlights, suburban street lamps diffusing into the gloom of the dark woods beyond. He played again in his mind the complex themes, a fugue for the intellect only he could hear, now poised for the final resolution: the long hours of meetings, the frenzied stolen moments for his own work, the pills to keep it all going, and passionate interludes with the woman.

He knew that he had dominated the meeting of the International Atomic Energy Agency both by his fresh ideas and the force of his personality. He would help them in their pitiful stumblings to control the dirty monster they had created. What they did not suspect was that the true focus of his energies were the moments stolen for his own work, a vision that had become a reality in his mind only this evening, a reality that swept away as irrelevant not only all that they did in the meeting, but the concerns of a major piece of mankind.

He thought of the steps he would have to take to realize that which he now knew to be possible, the resources he would have to muster, the personnel to be assembled and, when necessary, pirated from competing efforts. As so often before, he could see the object of his desires take shape like a gigantic erector set, each element responding effortlessly to his will. He basked in the knowledge that he could do it on his own, with the power he already commanded. The world would bumble along unknowing until he chose to reveal his supreme accomplishment in its fullness. He felt the drug wearing off, but had no compulsion to renew the charge. No artificial aid could give him the feeling that presently coursed through his veins.

The view before him was replaced by one of time, spanning into the future, ten, a hundred, a thousand years—his name spilling as readily from a schoolchild's lips as that of Washington, Lincoln, as that of any resident of this proud city, Beethoven, Napoleon, Freud, as that of any scientist, Einstein. . .

"Paul?" The sleepy voice, muffled by covers and accent, came from the bed.

Silently, he continued to face the window, but his thoughts turned to her. What a delightful find she was. On top of everything else, what luck to come across this political fugitive at one of the parties scheduled to fill their evenings. Not only was she beautiful, a stimulating outlet for his more physical passions, but a consort guaranteed to tweak the maximum number of bureaucratic noses. The Russians were still smarting from her recent escape through Czechoslovakia with three male friends. He hoped that her promptly taking up with a well-known American scientist and lavishly sampling the best capitalistic delights Vienna had to offer would embarrass the hell out of them. As for his side, they would never be sure she wasn't a plant, and there would be shocked speculations about their pillow talk throughout the western security establishment. He chuckled to himself.

"Paul, it's nearly four a.m. Come to bed." Her voice was low, sultry, inviting. He heard the rustle of bedclothes and knew she was looking at him.

Neither could a woman give him the feeling that suffused him now, the intense mental orgasm of an earth-shattering idea come to fruition, but you can't make love to a concept. He thought ahead of the day to come. An hour with her now, to relax, a couple of hours' sleep, then a couple more to continue his calculations over breakfast before the meeting resumed.

He turned and walked softly across the dark room to the bedside. For a long moment he stood looking down at her, the covers pulled up to her chin, the halo of short black hair in stark contrast to the pillow. He could not see her face clearly in the faint city light reflected in the window, but he could picture the lovely contours of her face, the high slavic cheekbones, the sparkling eyes reflecting intelligence, a free spirit, and, deep within, an irrepressible sadness.

He reached for the covers near her feet and slowly drew them down, exposing her nakedness, the bed-warmth of her body palpable in the darkness. He leaned over and gently pressed his lips to the sweet angle where breast joins rib. . .

The desk before him came back into focus. The papers strewn across it screamed at him, confirming the feeling that had been in his gut for months, ignored. It had all gone wrong, disastrously wrong! Everything his career had stood for was demolished. Rather than emerging as mankind's savior, he had visited an incomprehensible horror on an unsuspecting populace. That he, of all people, could have made such an error!

He looked toward the fire flickering in the grate and lifted the pistol.

Maria Latvin glanced at her watch as she pulled the long serrated-blade knife from the drawer. 3:45 a.m. I can't keep him from working all night, she thought, but at least I can keep food in his stomach. She turned to the butcher block island in the center of the kitchen and carved two thick slices from the loaf of pumpernickel. She spread a healthy layer of Dijon mustard on the bread then carefully stacked interlaced layers of corned beef, swiss cheese, ham, turkey, and finished off with some lettuce. From somewhere in the quiet house she heard a sound, a muffled pop. She could not identify it, but the noise caused her to slip into a fatigue-driven reverie.

After six weeks of furtive, exhaustive trekking and hiding, they slogged through the snow, eyes fixed on the chain link fence topped with ragged strands of barbed wire. They were in a clear, unforested area, lightly patrolled since the approach was exposed. Then they heard that pop. A half kilometer away, a squad of Czechoslovakian soldiers aimed at them and more pops came. Their guides pointed at the place where the fence was closest and ran for the copse of trees and cover. Maria remembered her eyes almost frozen shut with tears of joy and fright during their adrenalin-charged dash through the drifts, hauling the ladder, planting it, scrambling up, leaping and landing. In Austria!

Austria. Vienna. Paul, sweeping her into a vortex that left her head and heart swimming. Now, two years of travel to places of which she had not known to dream, interspersed with retreat to this magnificent isolation, a feeling of freedom so strong it made her ache.

Paul. Strong, excited in his high moods, his energy drawing her like a magnet. The sudden, unexpected periods of despondency worried her, though, and this was one of the worst. She had learned to be patient. With time, he would bounce back.

She put a steaming cup of coffee on the tray next to the sandwich. She carried the tray through the living room, past the massive adobe fireplace and into the hall leading to the study.

"Paul, I——"

She froze in the doorway of the study, gripping the tray, knowing in an instant that it was all gone. She walked slowly across the room and set the tray on the edge of the desk. She looked at the familiar, handsome face, the thick brown hair laced with silver, the well-shaped head lolling against the back of the high-backed desk chair.

Then she forced herself to look at the small, neat hole a few centimeters above his ear. There was hardly any blood, but it was so dark, a bleak desolate pit that reminded her of all she had struggled to leave behind. The hole was in such an odd place. Not the temple, but higher, further back. Perhaps he had flinched, his spirit rebelling even as his finger tightened on the trigger. The small silver-plated twenty-two caliber pistol still dangled from his forefinger. Such a trivial weapon to still such a vibrant life.

A month ago he was fired with enthusiasm for this project which he had begun before they had met. He had been working on it in Vienna. Then the depression set in, ever deepening. Now something had pushed him over the edge. She examined the scattered pages on the desk. They were filled with incomprehensible calculations. What had the letters and numbers meant to him? she wondered. Which among them triggered this ultimate retreat? She felt what they meant to her—the end of a freedom too good to last.

In the stillness of the room, the faint flutter shouted at her. Her eyes locked on him. Yes!! There it was again! She knelt by his side, placed two fingers on his throat, and nearly fainted with relief at the weak irregular beat that massaged her fingertips.

At midmorning Isaacs concentrated on the report he had received from Baris the previous afternoon concerning new arms stashes in eastern Mozambique. The photographs were unmistakable, but the big question went unanswered. Whose were they? Baris' group had concluded they were not an unadvertised ploy by the Marxist government, nor did they belong to the active guerrilla movement. They seemed to mark a new force whose motives and intentions were a cipher. Boswank had to get somebody in on the ground.

A commotion in the outer office caught his attention. He heard Kathleen announce over the intercom and through the door as it crashed open, "Mr. Deloach to see you."

Earle Deloach raced across the room and leaned with his fists on Isaacs' desk, highly distraught, eyeglasses askew on his round face, a lock of normally slick-backed hair dangling over his temple. He passed a hand fitfully at the errant strand, causing more disarray.

"They've blown it up!" he shouted.

Isaacs rose quickly and circled his desk.

"Who's blown up what?" he asked as he closed the connecting door.

"My FireEye! The Russians! They blew it up!"

"Here, sit down Earle," said Isaacs, firmly. He guided Deloach by the elbow into a chair. "Now what are you talking about?" he asked, regaining his own chair. "Are you sure? What did they do?"

"One of their satellites—Cosmos . . . Cosmos 2112—from a couple of hundred miles away, must have been a laser. Didn't just fry a few circuits; we have photos from one of our other satellites. FireEye's gone! Vaporized!"

"Oh, damn!" exploded Isaacs, wrenched by a decidedly schizophrenic reaction. His gut knotted with the instant realization that this was the Russians' idea of a justifiable reaction to the Novorossiisk affair. The first step into the abyss of a new unknown mode of war. War in space. At the same time a quiet professional voice inside him gave grudging praise. Clever bastards, this voice said, the Cosmos 2112 was one of the recently launched satellites they had not been able to categorize. It had been camouflaged well. He had convinced himself that it was, after all, a recon satellite. A working laser! Well, they tipped their hand there, might be some profit to be had, anyway. Aloud to Deloach he said, "Why would they pick on FireEye? Because it's our latest?"

"Well," Deloach looked chagrined, "we decided to have a quick look at the Novorossiisk after all."

Isaacs leaned forward intently. "We?" But he already knew.

"Yes, uh, Kevin and I got to talking after the meeting with the DCI yesterday morning. No one seemed to have any ideas, so we thought it couldn't hurt to at least take a look. I had an orbit change worked up to minimize maneuvering fuel and we slid the orbit a little."

And afterwards, thought Isaacs, it would have slid to a station over Tomsk. That underhanded son-of-a-bitch!

"So you maneuvered over toward the Med," said Isaacs in a biting tone, "and the Russians chose to regard that as an aggressive act, and they raised the ante out of sight by blowing FireEye out of the sky with a laser we didn't even know existed.

"Good Lord, Earle! Do you know what you've done? Not only lost a seventy-seven million dollar satellite, but drawn us into a whole new kind of war we've been desperately trying to avoid."

"How was I to know?" Deloach cried, hysterically defensive. "We've looked at their carriers before, all the time."

"Hey, okay," Isaacs calmed his voice. "The Novorossiisk was special, but you couldn't know they would react this way. The important thing now is to prevent any escalation and to find out what really did happen to the Novorossiisk so we can defuse the whole thing.

"Earle, thanks for filling me in. The Director will want a meeting. We'll work it out." He rose and Deloach stood in turn.

"Okay," said Deloach with resignation, "but dammit, the gear on FireEye was a work of art. It's like losing a baby."

"We know that, Earle, but you can do it again. The next generation will be even better."

As Isaacs ushered him out, Deloach's mind was already turning over a couple of the sweet ideas he'd been forced to omit from FireEye when the budget was drawn. He could do it better and cheaper now.

Isaacs returned to his seat in gloom. This was bad all

around. They still did not know what had happened to the Novorossiisk. There would be strong quarters in the Pentagon plotting retaliation to the Soviet attack. And in his own nest, McMasters would be sending up smoke screens all over the Agency to hide his tremendous error. If the crunch came, Isaacs knew, McMasters would even sacrifice Deloach, his unwitting ally. That would be a tragedy. For all his faults, Deloach was too good at what he did best.

Two days later Isaacs sat at his desk, forehead cradled in his hands, intently reading the report before him. Every few minutes he would lower his right hand to turn a loose-leaf page and then replace it on his head, thumb to temple, fingers shading his eyes. Across from his desk, Vincent Martinelli sat, legs crossed, reading the same report. Boswank had done his job. The report, fresh from the translator, was taken directly from the file of the Soviet Admiralty. Isaacs finished first and leaned back gazing at the ceiling, mulling what he had read, waiting for Martinelli.

After a few minutes, Martinelli looked up. "What do you make of that? Sure as hell something more going on than a match in a gas tank. There's nothing in here about a space-based weapon, though."

"Someone higher up must have reached that conclusion after reading this," Isaacs said. "Let's see how the thinking may have gone. There is widespread agreement from the hands on the flight deck that there was some kind of noise, a hissing, growing in intensity, and coming apparently from overhead."

"That's no reason to think whatever it was came from something in orbit."

"Granted, but it is a peculiar precursor. I can't think of anything offhand to account for it."

"You've got me there."

"Then the fire breaks out," Isaacs continued, "apparently a punctured fuel tank and a spark."

Martinelli squinted in concentration. "I'd say the fire was incidental, granted one of them may have sparked the fire, but the punctures themselves are the odd bit."

"I agree and so, it seems, do our Soviet counterparts. Drilled is the word the translators came up with. A hole, a half a centimeter to a centimeter in diameter, right through the ship. No evidence in the first couple of decks because of fire damage, but from there on down, a clean little hole, right through every deck and out the bottom of the hull."

"That's the son-of-a-bitch, all right. Did you catch the reference to the sonar?"

"Ah, right, it's here on page—" Isaacs leafed through the report, "page fifty-seven. Sonar operator picked up a sudden strange signal just as the fire klaxon sounded and all hell broke loose.

"So," Isaacs continued thoughtfully, "you are Yuri Blodnik reading this report. What do you conclude?"

"Noise above," summarized Martinelli, "a hole drilled vertically through the decks, and a sonar trace below. I'd say I'd been shot." Martinelli dramatically clasped his hands to his heart and then thrust a pointed finger at the ceiling. "And the varmint what did it was up there!"

"All right, Tex," Isaacs smiled, "and just what were you shot with?"

Martinelli grew serious. "Not a conventional projectile. You'd need a hell of an explosive punch to penetrate all that steel, and then you'd rip things up, not drill any dainty little hole. If it's not an explosive, then it'd have to be a slug with tremendous velocity."

Martinelli could see the idea flare in Isaacs' eyes and spread across his face as his brow unfurrowed and his chin came up. Isaacs pointed a finger at him.

"A meteorite."

Martinelli stared at him and then slowly nodded in comprehension.

"The damned carrier was hit by a meteorite!" Isaacs exclaimed. "We've worried about them mistaking a large meteor for a nuclear explosion and launching a retaliatory strike. Now they get hit by a small one, a chance in a million, and they think it's a beam weapon."

"Damn, that smells right."

"We've got to convince the Soviets of that, particularly whoever decided a beam weapon was involved."

Isaacs reached for a pad and began to make notes. "We need to know who that person was, or what group, and how they think. Bureaucratic types? Someone in intelligence? Scientists? And, if so, government flakes or independent thinkers? We need evidence. What *would* a meteorite do? Can it do this? I'll set my team on that. We'll need a projectile specialist. Maybe there's some work in the labs, Los Alamos or Livermore. Too bad there's not more specific information here," he tapped the report, "on the nature of the punctures, stress on the surrounding metal, flaring at the rim. There should be contamination by meteoritic material, but that would require a specific metallurgical examination of a sample from around the holes. We've got to get them to do that.

"You get with Boswank and find out about the decision structure here. We'll do a report outlining the effects of meteorite impact, feed that to them through channels, and see if we can get them to look at those punctures in detail. If they can convince themselves, that'll be best. Great! We can move on this."

"Won't hurt to be quick," advised Martinelli. "I just got word about Drefke's meeting with the National Security Council yesterday. It went just the way you called it."

"The space shuttle?"

"Yep, the Joint Chiefs came out pushing hard for sending the shuttle after Cosmos 2112. Their arguments were almost a parody of what you predicted for Drefke day before yesterday. Can't let the Russkis get away with this, or they'll start picking off all our birds like sitting ducks. Got to hang tough.

And, of course, they're drooling to get their hands on the laser itself, do a little satellite vivisection."

"Damnation!" exclaimed Isaacs, pounding his fist on the desk. "Can't they see the danger of escalating this thing? The last thing the human race needs is a whole new way to make war! Good Lord! We have no idea where it will lead."

"Hey!" protested Martinelli. "You're talking to the wrong guy."

"Sorry," Isaacs slumped back in his chair, "but what a tragedy, especially if it's all an overreaction to a freak of nature. Oh, damn!"

He thought quietly for a moment. "Just what do they suggest? All we need is for the Cosmos to blast the shuttle as it approaches. No way we could keep that from the public. The President couldn't resist the war cries."

"Well, of course, they've been planning for just such a contingency all along. Apparently, as well as working on laser systems, the Livermore people have been working on defenses as well. They've designed a highly reflective, collapsible mirror specifically for the shuttle. It's been tucked in a warehouse for some time. The shuttle swings this thing overboard with the manipulating boom and positions it to reflect any laser blast as they close in. Just how they immobilize the satellite to get it in the cargo bay and bring it home isn't clear to me."

"Isn't it too big?" Isaacs wanted to know.

"In a sense, but the Soviets know how big the shuttle bay is. The satellite is basically the upper end of one of their big booster rockets."

Isaacs nodded.

"Apparently, they added some external gew-gaws specifically designed to make the whole thing too large to fit in the cargo bay. The idea is that the crew should take a torch to it with a space walk, cut it up into manageable-size pieces. In principle it'll fit."

"Great," exclaimed Isaacs with irony. "And when do they advise trying to attempt this insanity?"

"The next shuttle launch is in the middle of April, two weeks from now. That's what they're pushing for. The idea being, of course, to strike while the iron is lukewarm. They'd like to launch yesterday, but the shuttle isn't so flexible."

"Madness! And they think the Soviets won't then blow away one of our communication link satellites, Comsat or some such thing?"

"The argument is that Cosmos 2112 is the only laser they have flying."

"But we didn't know that until two days ago!"

"Tell that to mah buddy, the President."

"How's he leaning?"

"I didn't get any feeling for that, third hand, but the brass is pushing hard. They've pumped a lot of dollars sideways into NASA for the shuttle. They want to play with their toy."

"But they must have war-gamed this kind of thing."

"I suppose it can be contained in some scenarios."

"Yeah, in one percent of them. Vince, we've got to convince our side about this meteorite, too. That seems to be the only sure way to show that the Soviets had some justification and that we don't need to retaliate."

"You'll have to start in-house. Drefke will relay any report you write, but you know how his antennae are tuned to the White House. He's apt to take his cues from the President. And McMasters clearly won't be much help."

"That's a fact," Isaacs agreed. "That was quite a show he put on the other day."

"It was clearly his only tack. He had to really push the Russians as bad guys to keep Drefke from thinking too deeply about why FireEye was shifted in the first place. Now he's painted himself into a corner. He'll have trouble turning around and saying, well, maybe they're not so nasty after all, a little hasty with their death ray, but really not bad chaps.

"The other factor is," Martinelli continued, "that this meteorite idea and follow-up has to come from your group and his negative instincts won't allow him to embrace it with a lot of enthusiasm." The two men sat in silence for a moment, then Martinelli rose.

"I'll go see Art; we'll try to get some dope on the channels this report went through." Martinelli waved the document as a farewell gesture and paused.

"There's a bright side to all this, you know. If this trick with the shuttle backfires badly enough, we won't have to worry about getting our taxes done on time."

"Thanks a lot, Vince." Isaacs grinned at the black humor. "Silver linings like that I can do without."

Isaacs watched his friend shut the door. He began an outline of the questions to be addressed concerning the possible impact of a meteorite on the Novorossiisk. He would turn it over to his technical staff to flesh it out.

The preliminary report was ready late the next day, a rush job to which some thirty people had contributed in an intense surge of effort. It looked pretty good, plausible enough for a first pass. There were some troubling points. A meteorite would progressively disintegrate as it passed through metal walls. To go all the way through the carrier, a meteorite would have to drill larger holes than had been reported in the upper decks, and the holes should get smaller in the lower decks. It was not clear from the stolen Soviet report that that pattern was reproduced.

Isaacs downplayed such doubts in working over the final draft. He wanted to make as much impact as possible to forestall a decision to go after Cosmos 2112 with the shuttle. He relied on the state of emergency to go out of channels and took the report directly to Drefke. The Director was clearly impressed with the idea. Isaacs knew he would then show it to McMasters, but by then the original impact would have had its maximum effect. He would get the most positive response possible when Drefke in turn reported to the National Security Council and the President.

Korolev stirred at his desk, reached up and punched off the button on the neck of the gooseneck lamp, leaving the room to share the deepening light of dusk. He rose and moved to the window. From this upper floor of the Academy of Sciences building he could see a stretch of lights now winking on over Moscow. For years, no, decades now, he had stood at this window watching those lights at odd hours of the night as he contemplated some problem. How many there had been. Practical earth-shattering problems imposed by the voracious military: explosions, implosions, shock waves, *the* bomb. Later, intense radiation, hyper velocities, directed energy weapons. What did the Americans call them? Buck Rogers stuff. Lovely, basic problems. Microscopic, the innards of particles, and the innards of those in turn, and then of those. Cosmological problems, the wondrous workings of Einstein's mind on vast scales.

Tonight, a small but troubling problem. Some American was quick and thoughtful. He could see the mental play behind the words. Yes, the suggestion of a meteorite was bold, for all its obviousness. It was one of the first which had occurred to him as well. The author of this report had pushed it for all its worth, but he also knew the limitations. Korolev could read between the lines and see where the American had suppressed his reservations. What the American did not know were the results of the follow-up report which had come directly to him. The punctures were all wrong for a meteorite with enough impact to penetrate the carrier decks. There was no downward flaring, the holes looked drilled, not punched. They had done a metallurgical test; there was no meteorite material. The Americans had not yet stolen that report. It was no meteorite.

Although there were features that did not fit, a lack of heat searing, for instance, Korolev had been compelled to state that a beam weapon seemed the most plausible explanation. His superiors had demanded *some* hypothesis and he could think of no other. He had not anticipated that they would mistrust their intelligence so badly as to suspect that the Americans had leap-frogged them and orbited such a weapon.

What troubled him, beyond the still unexplained nature of the Novorossiisk event, was the sincerity in this report. He was convinced that the author would eventually come to the conclusion that a meteorite could not be involved, but this report was not a sham. The author pushed the meteor idea too strongly because he wanted it to be true. The whole tone told Korolev that the report was based on the secure knowledge of the author that the Americans were not involved with the Novorossiisk. That was the trouble. His government knew he had already considered and rejected the meteor hypothesis. They would reject the suggestion by the Americans. Could he convince them of the Americans' uninvolvement with the Novorossiisk based not on the contents, but on his sense of the motivation of the report on his desk? There would be much resistance. They were convinced the Americans were involved, somehow, and now there was the irrevocable act of the destruction of the American spy satellite. Korolev continued to stare out over the streets until the dusk faded to deepest black.

The first half of April slipped away as Isaacs spent two hard weeks probing the meteor theory. He called in projectile experts from around the country, and his top people visited various test sites. The harder they worked, the less likely the idea seemed. Boswank had traced the Novorossiisk report to one of the most respected members of the Soviet Academy of Sciences, Academician Viktor Korolev. That seemed a positive note, his reputation as a profound and unprejudiced thinker was well-established. Then at the end of the first week came the curt Soviet reply to Isaacs' report. A meteor had been previously considered and rejected. With Korolev's reputation behind that statement, and the increasingly negative results of his own team's study, Isaacs knew he was losing any power to influence events. To make matters worse, the Soviet reply was defensive and belligerent. It yielded no hint that they conceded the innocence of the Americans in the Novorossiisk affair, certainly no confession that they might have mistakenly overreacted in the destruction of the Fire-Eye. The only good news was that with the act of retribution the Yellow Alert had been canceled. The Backfire aircraft were returned to normal routine; the missiles recapped snugly; the troops redeployed.

Isaacs walked slowly down the hall from Drefke's office and punched the elevator button. The Director had just returned from the meeting of the National Security Council. Isaacs had read the result on his face. The shuttle was going up tomorrow. The crew was to disable the Cosmos 2112 and bring it back in the cargo bay. Or fry trying.

He got off at his floor and continued his thoughtful pace. He opened the outer door to Kathleen's office and was surprised to see Pat Danielson sitting there with an expectant smile and a pile of computer output and charts on her lap. The smile faded when she saw the heavy cloud on Isaacs' face.

"Is this a bad time?"

She detected Isaacs' quick visible effort to compose himself. His voice had a forced heartiness.

"Not at all." He smiled ruefully. "No worse than any other time. You have something important?"

She glanced down at the bundle of paper clutched possessively on her lap, and her voice carried an overtone of excitement.

"I think you're going to find your curiosity about this seismic signal justified."

Isaacs had to think for a second to recall what she was talking about. He was too preoccupied with the historical clash scheduled to take place over their heads tomorrow to give much attention to the task he had assigned her, but the little wheels had to be greased, just like the big ones. A little investment of his time would keep Danielson performing efficiently.

He crossed to the door to his office and held it open in welcome as she rose and bustled through. She deposited the material on his desk and took the chair across from him.

"It wasn't just a transient then?" he asked.

"On the contrary, the more we learn about it, the longer we can trace it back through the earlier data—several months' worth now." She pointed to the stack of paper. "Here's the latest output, hot off the printer."

He gestured outward with both hands, palms up, encompassing the output and the young woman.

"Shoot," he said, striving to concentrate on what she had to say.

"With a longer time base, more information becomes available. At first all one could tell was that the signal repeated itself. We had only a crude idea of the period and no notion of the location. We've worked very hard to obtain a better estimate of the period. The figure of an hour was an alias. The true period is somewhat less than ninety minutes. This update shows that we're beginning to get a handle on the location. Would you care to guess?"

Danielson did not usually play such little games, but came straight out with the facts. She thinks there's something special here, thought Isaacs. Aloud he said, "Undoubtedly, it's coming directly from the situation room in the Kremlin."

"Wrong, of course," smiled the young woman. She turned serious. "But you've hit on an important point. The first algorithms used in the signal analysis were based on the assumption of a static source, that the signal was coming from a single location. That assumption proved to be self-inconsistent and we abandoned it. When we allowed for the possibility that the source moved, things began to fall in place.

"I won't show you all the data, but look at these two clear

stretches when the background noise was low." Danielson unrolled a strip chart on Isaacs' desk. "See here, the signal comes from the vicinity of Egypt. Here, this is a week later, it comes from the mid-Pacific basin. That proves it moves. A more careful analysis hints, but doesn't yet prove, that the period is not due to a change in power at the source, but is due to a source of roughly constant power moving from one side of the earth to the other."

"A reflected wave of some kind," put in Isaacs.

"Perhaps," replied Danielson, "but not like any the seismologists have ever seen before. Any strong earthquake will set up reverberations which travel diagonally through the earth, but those die out quickly. Something continues to drive this wave—that's the mystery."

"So the actual energizing source might still be located in one place and the apparent movement is just due to the random bouncing of the subsequent wave."

"Possible," allowed Danielson, "and more comfortable, but the data still seem to suggest that the source is moving."

"How much energy is involved?" queried Isaacs.

"Well, of course, the power we detect depends on both the power at the source and the distance to our detectors. If we assume the source is, on the average, at the distance of one earth radius, about four thousand miles, then the seismic energy flux at the detector corresponds to a source power of about one thousand megawatts—big for a power station, but pretty small potatoes compared with all the seismic energy in the earth at a given time. Which is why the signal is hard to detect and analyze.

"Since we don't really know the nature of the source, it's difficult to associate an energy with it; that is, it could sit in one place and emit bursts of energy that reverberate, or it could represent a continuous supply of energy, as we believe. A ballpark estimate is the total energy liberated in one characteristic period, ninety minutes. In one period that would be about one percent of the energy of a one kiloton nuclear event."

"That's a maximum estimate, isn't it?" asked Isaacs.

"Yes, sir," replied Danielson, "within a factor of a few, given that the source is confined to the earth."

"One hundredth of a kiloton," mused Isaacs. "That's too small to be a nuclear device, and if the source is closer, the energy estimate only goes down. Still, if that amount of energy is being liberated artificially on the surface, we should be able to see other signs of it in the optical or infrared—somewhere.

"The most reasonable assumption," Isaacs continued, "is that this is some natural seismic event which happens to have a period of about an hour and a half, regular fault slippage of some kind."

Danielson raised a finger and opened her mouth to interject, but Isaacs interrupted her, "Unless, of course, you can prove the source is actually moving about.

"Obviously, I'm unconvinced this signal is anything but some sort of natural phenomena," Isaacs said, "but I am convinced we need to nail it down. Suppose you're right and it's not related to natural fault slippage somewhere, do you have any guess as to what it might be?"

"No. If the source is moving around in the earth as I think the data suggests, it's a total paradox. Fault slippage at different points on the earth shouldn't be correlated."

Isaacs leaned back in his chair, toying with a pencil. "A period of ninety minutes still sounds suspiciously like some artificial phenomena—keyed to somebody's time clock. If your positions are right, Egypt and whatnot, it's not a local man-made thing, but I'd like to make sure that is ironclad."

Isaacs sat up at the desk and gestured to Danielson with the pencil. "You had better make this a matter of some priority until it's resolved. We need to know the period, if it really is one, more accurately. If the period is not precisely defined, that's good evidence of a natural phenomenon. If the period turns out to be exactly ninety minutes, it will be a man-made event despite present evidence to the contrary.

"We need to know the location, whether or not it is moving around. When you have a location, we can look for some other evidence of its existence and nature. If it's seismic in nature, there should be some correlation with fault location and activity. Any other suggestions?"

Danielson paused a moment in concentration before she spoke. "No sense speculating without more data. It will probably be useful to get records from civilian seismic stations, universities here and abroad. We can look for correlations among events that would pass unnoticed in any single record. That should help with both the period and the location."

"That's fine," said Isaacs with a note of finality. "Let me know how this develops."

"Right," said Danielson, rising to leave, collecting the bundle from his desk. "We'll continue to monitor our own AFTAC data, and that may begin to pin things down. But it will take a month or so to acquire and analyze the civilian records."

"Okay, keep in touch."

"Yes, sir."

Isaacs watched the door close behind her. He stared at it, unseeing, as her problem diffused from his mind and his consciousness flowed out along tangled diplomatic channels. From his office to Drefke's to the White House. To Moscow. Academician Korolev. Why did he rule out the meteorite? What *had* happened to the Novorossiisk? What would happen to the shuttle?

Chapter 3

Major Edward Jupp went through the countdown procedure the way he had a hundred times in simulation and twice for real. His gloved hands played over the switches, and he responded to the voice of the mission control agent at the Consolidated Space Operations Center in Colorado Springs. His mind was on the gaunt, taciturn passenger in the rear seat. This was his first mission as commander, and he ached for a perfect flight. So what did they do but pull the mission scientists, and substitute this bozo, Colonel Newman, putting him in charge of a half-baked kamikaze mission to snatch a live Russian laser satellite. On the other hand, thought Jupp, they're giving me a chance to fly this sweet baby, new engines, high orbit capability; we'll see what she can really do.

He watched from the corner of his helmet visor as the boom swung away from the top of the liquid fuel tank. He could sense the billion cracklings as the liquid oxygen sucked heat from the mighty vessel, and he lightly fantasized again that he could smell its cool freshness. The hum of a thousand organs, electrical, mechanical, fluid, and solid sang their readiness to him. He listened to the countdown and felt the Pavlovian rush of adrenalin as the count reached "one." With "zero" the beast screamed its energy, first with the roar of the gigantic liquid fueled engines and immediately the answering call of the solid boosters, a triumphant Tarzan cry, hailing the defeat of gravity. And then, just as before, the miracle was repeated and they were on their way, lifting, twisting away from the gantry, the thrill of unbridled acceleration coursing through his body.

They kept to established routine for the first several orbits. The idea was not to tip their hand too early. Jupp knew, though, that the Russians would be watching them microscopically, anticipating precisely the move they now planned. The quiet passenger remained in his seat, not so much withdrawn as apparently oblivious to the activity necessary to establish a shuttle orbit. If he noticed that he was suspended head down two hundred miles above earth, he did not show it.

They switched to the briefing books for their revised mission, a mission they had studied and rehearsed for only a fleeting week. Only a week before that, the Russians had blown away a fancy new American reconnaissance satellite. Jupp was aware that the American military and intelligence communities had been in a retributive fury, little disposed to look past the surface act and examine the motive. The Russians, correctly or not, suspected a space-based attack on one of their carriers, and the recon satellite had shown an undue interest in the damaged ship. The Americans still did not have an operating laser in space. Now they knew the Russians did have one. The Americans wanted it. The shuttle would get it. Jupp had had only a few chances to discuss this change in plans with his copilot, Larry Wahlquist, but he knew Larry liked the whole thing even less than he did.

Jupp and Wahlquist stood facing the U-shaped console at the rear of the flight deck, their backs to the pilot's and copilot's seats and the nose of the shuttle, their feet anchored by velcro pads against the capricious lack of gravity. Each opened independent safety switches on opposite sides of the console, and then Jupp lifted a cover and thumbed a heavy toggle switch. They watched on the TV monitor as the twin doors on the large cargo bay swung open. Wahlquist fitted his hands into the manipulator controls. His gaze switched rapidly back and forth from the monitor screen to the rear window above the console which provided a direct view into the cargo bay. In the bay, the long, skinny, elbow-jointed manipulating boom came alive, an extension of Wahlquist's own muscles and nerves. He moved the boom to the only item in the large storage area. It was a cylinder twenty feet long and four feet in diameter. From the end of the cylinder extended a shaft that ended in a special fitting designed to be gripped by the manipulator boom. Wahlquist moved the boom to the shaft, then made the fine adjustments to align the clamp on the boom with the fitting. Slowly he closed the jaws on the clamp. Satisfied that the mating was exact, he threw a switch that locked the boom onto the shaft with an unbreakable vise grip. He threw another switch on the console and watched on the TV monitor as the tubular casing separated along its length and peeled back like a long skinny clam. He then used the boom to heft the shaft and hold it aloft, pointed straight out from the bay toward the earth below. Nestled along the shaft, cleverly and compactly aligned, were the segments of a mirror. At a signal, the many pieces would carefully unfold and arrange themselves like a gigantic polished umbrella, half again as big in diameter as the shuttle craft itself.

Jupp returned to the pilot's seat. They were in an orbit that carried them northward over China and Siberia, across the pole and down over the eastern seaboard of the United States. So far, so good. The shuttle, Cosmos 2112, and all other Soviet satellites capable of interference were monitored closely both from earth and from space. There was no sign of excess Soviet interest or activity. Shuttles did not usually adopt polar orbits, but they were not unknown, especially when a surveillance satellite had to be deposited in such an orbit. The mirror stayed folded against its supporting shaft to avoid adding premature confirmation to suspicions that must be growing.

The first tricky part was to close on the Cosmos, using the mirror for protection. The Cosmos was a long way out, in a parking orbit one day long canted a bit with respect to the earth's equator. In twelve hours it would swing from some distance north of the equator to an equal distance south, but at the same longitude since as the satellite completed a half orbit, the earth would complete a half revolution, maintaining the alignment. From the earth, the Cosmos seemed to drift slowly north and south, passing over a particular point on the earth twice a day. They would keep a maximum distance by going up in their polar launch orbit, at right angles to the orbit of the Cosmos. There was no place to hide in space from the weapon that shot beams at the speed of light, but at least aiming would be more difficult at greater distances.

To minimize direct ground-based surveillance by the Russians, they waited until they were over the west coast of South America headed for Antarctica and the Indian Ocean beyond. Then Jupp programmed the rockets to begin the meticulous ascent toward the Cosmos, which hovered near the spatial gravesite of its recent victim. They climbed in an open spiral, belly of the spacecraft up, the necessary orientation for ascent because of the preset angle of the rockets. They circled once every few hours at first while the Cosmos hovered near the northern swing of its cycle over the southern Urals. The time for an orbit lengthened as they rose until they were at an altitude slightly less than the Cosmos and also orbiting once in about twenty-four hours. They were high over

Panama while the Cosmos drifted lazily southward over Ethiopia.

Wahlquist had tried to keep the mirror shaft pointed at the Cosmos out over the wing of the shuttle as they ascended. This was difficult at first. Since they were upside down, the Cosmos was apparently "below" them where the boom did not extend easily. The heat resistant re-entry tiles might have offered some protection from the laser, but this was still a high vulnerability maneuver. As they rose, the necessary adjustments became minor. Their aspect changed little since, from their circular orbit, the Cosmos always appeared to be off their right wing. Nevertheless, Jupp could feel the tension rising in his copilot as time passed and still there was no activity from the Cosmos.

Once more, Jupp played lightly on the control thrusters until the nose of the shuttle pointed nearly at the Cosmos. The rocket thrust would now rotate their orbit until it aligned with that of Cosmos. The maneuver was a dead give-away, however, and Jupp strained against the static of his earphones to hear the warning he knew must be only instants away. He hit a button to engage an automatic sequence. The rockets surged, and then were quiet. He used the thrusters again to align them perpendicular to their new orbit. The Cosmos was now at eleven o'clock out his window as they hung upside down in the dark. Wahlquist adjusted the boom.

The computer signaled readiness for the next firing sequence. Jupp was reaching his finger toward the button when the voice came up over the scrambled radio channel, the standard conversational tone heightened with tension.

"Shuttle, this is control. We've got action here. Standby."

Jupp twisted in his seat to exchange a look with Wahlquist standing at the rear of the flight deck. He glanced at Colonel Newman who remained impassive.

"Cosmos has done a rotation and yaw. Alignment on shuttle suspected."

Wahlquist did not have to be told. He threw a toggle switch and pushed a button, and the mirror unfolded, a dainty weapon against the ravishing power of the laser on board the Cosmos. The shuttle could provide a shirt-sleeve environment, but they wore their suits for double protection. Now they closed and fastened the faceplates on their helmets, switching to the oxygen supply of the suits.

In their present orientation the mirror completely obscured their view out the front. Jupp felt a twinge of nerves. With the computer, he did not need to see where he was flying, but his fighter pilot instincts rebelled. For all his training with instrument flying and targeting, he still did not like to have his vision needlessly blocked.

They sat in silence for ten minutes. Finally mission control broke in.

"No further action, proceed with orbital sequence."

Wahlquist spoke without removing his hands from the boom controls.

"They've got a bead on us."

"I reckon they do." Jupp replied. "Maybe we're out of range. They know if they've guessed right we're only going to close on them. Maybe they're waiting to see the whites of our eyes. We've also given away our defensive strategy by popping the umbrella. They're probably working up their own tactics now."

Jupp reprogrammed the computers for the delay and fired the rockets. Wahlquist rotated the boom during the firing. Cosmos was now at ten o'clock out Jupp's window, and the boom and mirror shaft extended at almost right angles to the axis of the shuttle. They were particularly vulnerable because the mirror could protect the cabin or the tail, but it was not big enough to shield both when they presented their side to Cosmos as they now did. By previous decision, Wahlquist adjusted the boom forward so the crew was shielded. Jupp rushed through another programming sequence.

Too late!

No human could time the beam of energy that leaped from a portal in the Cosmos. No need to lead the target with this cannon, just point and shoot. Nor was there a mote of dust in space to mark its passage to any eye not in the line of fire. In less than a tenth of a second an intense beam of light crossed a distance greater than that between the poles of the earth and slammed into the upper tail of the shuttle.

The beam delivered heat but little impulse so there was only the faintest jolt and a tiny crackling carried not by the vacuum of space, but through the metallic walls of the craft itself. The three men in the cabin sensed the brief blue-white flare from the change in shadows and odd reflections, as if someone had struck up a welding torch out of their line of sight. The radio crackled to life as the man in the rear seat made his first overt move. With a single motion, smooth despite the constraint of his vacuum suit, he pushed a button on his wrist. To one side of his helmet visor, visible but not in his normal line of sight, the green luminous display of an electronic stopwatch leapt to life, its quickest digits whipping by at dizzying rate. He pushed another button and the display was once again that of a standard chronometer.

"Control to shuttle! Control to shuttle! Cosmos has fired. Repeat, Cosmos has fired! Are you hit? Come in shuttle."

The battle was on! Jupp felt a calm of adrenalin-charged tension settle over him. He rammed the control thrusters, slewing the craft around to present a smaller, tail-on target to the Cosmos, as Wahlquist adjusted the boom until the mirror shielded them in the rear. Then he responded in his best Chuck Yaeger drawl.

"Aaaah, that's affirmative, control. We have taken a hit in the aft section. We've covered our rear and are having a look now."

Jupp flipped a finger sign at Wahlquist who hit a switch to relay the image on the cabin monitor to the ground. Wahlquist adjusted the position controls on the boom camera and watched the image play awkwardly on the monitor until he was oriented and began to scan around. The boom extended directly to the rear so that the shaft lay against the right side of the tail with the mirror beyond. Everything seemed normal as he scanned across the base of the tail and then around the bay.

"Look higher up on the tail," growled Colonel Newman from the rear seat.

Wahlquist gritted his teeth, turning stiffly in his suit until he could see Newman seated behind Jupp. He glanced quickly at him and then for a longer instant at Jupp. He turned back and fingered the controls to tip the camera upward and then let out an audible gasp.

"Son-of-a-bitch," said Jupp slowly.

The upper third of the tail section was missing. A scorched crescent marked the damage, beyond which there were random ends of wires and shafts, and beyond them nothing, their intended connections vaporized. The lower part of the rudder that remained intact hung at a skew angle, its upper pinions blasted away.

"Aaah, you copy that control?"

"We've got it, shuttle. Evaluation is underway. Mandatory, repeat mandatory, shuttle, you must complete orbital adjustment with greatest speed."

"Roger."

Jupp nodded to Wahlquist who swiveled the boom so that the mirror was abeam them, clear of the rockets, but once again exposing their tail. Jupp played with the thrusters and rapidly fed data to the computer. He hit the rockets again, and they felt the thrust of the final burst that would bring their orbit into alignment with that of the Cosmos. When they finished the maneuver, they were orbiting directly toward the Cosmos, but going sideways, their side exposed. Jupp rotated the craft until they were pointing toward the Cosmos, and Wahlquist rotated the mirror to the front, protecting them to the maximum extent. They were behind and slightly below the Cosmos, but orbiting more quickly so they would slowly catch up. Wahlquist sticky-footed his way over and buckled himself into the copilot's seat.

At a critical point they would fire the rockets and rise into the higher, less rapid orbit of the Cosmos. In orbit, one could not simply fire rockets and catch up. You only went faster than the other guy if you were in a lower, quicker orbit. If you fired your rockets, you would be flung into a higher, slower orbit, a maddening reversal of fighter pilot instincts. If you wanted to go faster, you flipped ass over end and fired the rockets in the direction of your travel. Then you dropped into a lower orbit where your speed was higher.

They settled in to wait. The maneuver had taken fourteen minutes. In twenty-seven they would begin the final firing sequence that would raise them to within docking range of the Cosmos. Seventeen minutes had passed since the Cosmos had fired at them. Another six minutes passed in silence.

The intense white hot glow erupted in front of them, accompanied by static on the radio. Both Jupp and Wahlquist jerked, startled, in their seats. Newman punched a button on the wrist of his suit again, and a small satisfied smile creased his features.

"Shuttle, Cosmos has fired again! Please report!"

"Whoa, that one caught us by surprise. Scared the bejesus out of me. The mirror took that one head on, and it seems to be intact."

"Roger, shuttle, that's satisfactory. You may proceed."

Newman's voice croaked from the rear.

"The repetition time is twenty-three minutes and thirty-seven seconds, even a little slower than we guessed. We've got them now."

Jupp looked at him in the small mirror mounted above the window.

"Twenty-three minutes." He turned his head to see a count-down timer, and then looked back at the man in the rear. "We'll be in the middle of the final lift."

"They'll get one more shot at us. That can't be helped. But

if it's just before we close on the bastard, we'll have the maximum time to get in and get it disabled."

Jupp settled back into his chair and stared out the cockpit window at the thin mirror surface that shielded them from a fiery death. He understood the logic, but he was not at all happy about sticking out his chin and giving the satellite one more freebie punch.

They coasted in silence for five, ten, fifteen minutes. Without the obstructing mirror they might have been able to make out the pinpoint of light that was Cosmos 2112, hovering somewhere above and beyond them. Then as Jupp programmed the final burn, the radio crackled alive again.

"Shuttle, there has been a new development. This could be a problem."

There was a delay during which a mumbled conversation could be heard. Harsh whispers of troubled voices.

"Shuttle, the Cosmos has gone into a rapid rotation mode. We can't be sure but we suspect the purpose is to spread the next shot over the surface of the mirror."

"Roger, control," Jupp replied. "What's the matter with that? Doesn't that just lessen the intensity in any particular spot?"

"A little," came the concerned voice from the ground, "but more important is that it increases the chance that some of the power will fall in the interstices. The cracks between the mirror segments. The reflection will be imperfect there, a lot more absorption of energy, and the chance for some real damage. You'll be a lot closer, so the power will be more concentrated anyway."

"Copy that, control. What's the recommended procedure?"

"Shuttle, no change, repeat, no change in procedure." The voice lost some of its adopted authority. "Just a warning to be on the lookout. You're going to have to tough this one out. Fer Chrissake, shield your eyes!"

Just before beginning the burn they darkened their faceplates. Jupp set the automatic sequence and the rockets fired, lifting them methodically to their rendezvous. Jupp kept an eye on the clock. He sang out "twenty-three minutes," over the roar of the rockets. They closed their eyes and threw their arms over their faceplates. A minute passed. The rockets stopped. They floated in deafening silence for another minute. Somewhere just in front of them, at point-blank range, was the deadly Cosmos.

Finally, Wahlquist dropped his arms and turned again in his seat to look toward the man in the rear.

"Well," he demanded, "what's going on?!"

Without lowering his own arms, Newman could sense that Wahlquist had dropped his guard.

"No!" he cried. "Cover—"

But it was too late.

The beam seared out of the rotating satellite, sweeping rapidly but uniformly across the reflective face of the mirror, most of the power bouncing harmlessly off into space. The joint at the center where the mirror segments all came together reflected too little. It rapidly heated red then white hot. The laser pulse lasted only a moment, but as it died away a tiny hole was burned open, and the fading radiation passed through, racing to the shuttle beyond. There was insufficient energy to damage anything but fragile human tissue, but enough for that. Wahlquist had averted his gaze when the beam struck, but it did him little good. Wahlquist neither heard nor felt the impact on his face nor deep in the base of his retinas. He saw the flash, the last thing he would ever see. He knew that immediately and screamed his bitterness.

"AAAGH! I'm blind!"

Jupp lowered his arms and tried to turn to his companion. "It may be temporary."

"No, goddamn it! I know it! I'm blind!"

The cold voice cut in.

"Major, we must move quickly. If he's disabled, you must help me into my EVA pack. I've got to get out there now!"

"But he's injured!"

"We can't help him! We've got a job to do. And precious little time to do it in. Another shot like that and we're all fried. Help me with that pack. That's an order!"

Jupp unbuckled and pushed out of his seat with his left hand, keeping a grip on a handle in the armrest on his right so that he pivoted, floating toward his copilot. He steadied himself by grabbing the armrest on the other chair and stared into Wahlquist's sightless eyes.

"Larry," he said firmly into his helmet's radio, "you'll be in shock, take a pill and sit quietly. I'll be back in a few minutes."

Jupp gripped his friend's padded shoulder with gloved hand and then worked his way to the rear of the cabin using convenient holds in the deck. He dropped down through the hatch in the floor that led from the flight deck to the mid-deck. Newman was already disappearing into the airlock that gave access to the cargo bay. Jupp waited for him to clear the airlock then passed through himself. Newman worked his feet into special braces in the deck that would hold him as they fitted the pack, then he twisted sideways to reach the extra-vehicular activity packs fastened to the bulkhead. He unbuckled one pack and lifted it from the rack, passing it around behind him. Jupp moved in and adjusted the pack into the special braces at the rear of the man's suit and fastened the clamps. Over his headphone he could hear Wahlquist reporting his condition to mission control.

"Okay, Major," the Colonel growled when he was satisfied. "There'll be some changes in the plans. Their rotating craft complicates my work, but gives us an advantage. You get back into the cabin. The laser fires out the side, in the plane of rotation. As soon as you can make out the orientation, you move us to just below it. That way they can't take a shot at the shuttle without changing the plane of rotation. That's harder for them to do than shooting at a target anywhere in the plane of rotation, so you'll be out of the line of fire, and I'll be able to go straight up out of the bay. You got that, Major?"

"Yes, sir. I've got it," Jupp replied, striving to contain his resentment at taking orders on the ship he piloted.

"Okay. You holler when you're in position. I'll go in along the rotation axis; anywhere else, I'd get swatted away like a fly. I'll have to go without the umbilical. It'd get twisted like a spring as soon as I latched on."

"Without the umbilical?" Jupp's voice betrayed his shock. "If you lose your grip, get flung off, you're gone!"

"I know my job, Major. If I lose my grip, we're all gone."

Jupp looked at the stern face, barely visible behind the darkened faceplate, and then yanked himself into the airlock. He floated up through the hatch to the flight deck and worked his way to the seat and buckled in. A glance at the clock showed that four minutes had passed since the blast that had blinded Wahlquist. Perhaps twenty more until the laser recharged.

Jupp took a few seconds to orient himself and then let out an exasperated sigh. All he could see out the window was the back of the mirror. He had to move it, but the controls for the boom to which the mirror was attached were twelve feet away at the rear of the flight deck. You weren't supposed to have to fly and handle the boom all by yourself, he thought.

Wahlquist sensed his presence and reached out an arm, grabbing Jupp for reassurance.

"What's happening?"

"I've got to move the mirror and then do a little flying. With them spinning we can duck down under and hide from the laser."

"Listen, I'm okay now," Wahlquist said. "Talking with control calmed me down. I've got a good feel for that boom, and you can fly better if you're not jumpin' up and down. Why don't you tell me what you want done with the mirror, and I'll handle that part?"

It made sense; the mirror only had to be lifted out of the line of sight.

"Okay, buddy. You've got it."

Jupp unbuckled Wahlquist and floated him around the passenger seat and over the open hatch in the floor to the control panel at the rear of the flight deck. The rear facing windows that opened to the cargo bay were now an unnecessary luxury for his friend, Jupp mused as he planted Wahlquist's feet on the anchoring velcro pads.

"Can you get your hands on those controls?"

Jupp watched as Wahlquist felt around the control console in front of him. He fought the instinct to grab the sightless hands and guide them to the controls. Wahlquist found the recess after only a long moment and settled his hands around the reassuring familiarity of the controls. Jupp regained his seat.

"All right," he said, "lift the boom straight up ninety degrees."

He watched as the mirror lifted methodically from his line of sight. They were still upside down and as the view from the windows was cleared he could see the spectacular spread of earth out the tops of the windows.

"Okay, that's good," he said when the boom was overhead, pointed directly at the earth below. Straight out the nose was the blackness of space.

A clutch of panic seized him. Where was the Cosmos? It was supposed to be right there! Had the computers screwed up? Could they find it before it unleashed another hellish blast? He forced himself to think calmly. He triggered a thruster and put the shuttle into a slow roll. They had done ninety degrees when, thank god, there it was, out the corner of the window about three hundred yards away, a little above them. He continued the roll until they were "right side up" and the Cosmos was in clear view out the window.

"Now what," demanded Wahlquist.

"I've got the Cosmos in sight. We're about a hundred yards below it and a few hundred yards away. We're at twelve o'clock now," Jupp twisted around to smile toward his sightless colleague, "right side up, if that makes you feel any better."

Wahlquist appreciated the black humor. "Right," he replied with heavy cynicism. "Blind and weightless, it makes a shitload of difference to me."

"I'm going in." Jupp eased the thrusters again and the shuttle drifted forward. As he flew, he narrated to keep Wahlquist at ease.

"It's much like the sketches they showed us. Impressive looking brute. Big cylinder, just the upper end of the SS-18 booster. What did they say? Four meters in diameter, ten meters long? That looks about right. There's a booster rocket nozzle on one end, some sort of antennae on the other. That's the end pointed earthward now. It's got these four weird stubby wings. They stick out about two meters, and run the length of the cylinder, equally spaced around the circumference. I guess they're what we're supposed to lop off to get the thing in the cargo bay. The whole thing is rotating once about every, oh, ten seconds. I can make out thruster nozzles. There are four pairs of them at each end, midway between the wings. Each of the pair points in opposite directions along the circumference of the hull. There are a number of small ports and one big one, maybe a meter across, halfway along the cylinder between two of the wings."

Jupp was silent for a moment, watching the dark maw swing across his field of view. "I guess that must be the laser."

When Jupp saw the Cosmos disappear above the cockpit window, he hit reverse thrust and stopped, hovering just beneath it. He spoke into the microphone.

"Colonel, there it is. Good luck."

"I'm sorry, Major." The voice was ice. "I can't see it. You've got the mirror in the way."

"Christ!" thought Jupp. "Larry, can you move that boom on toward the tail?"

Wahlquist had not released his grip on the controls. Jupp strained to look through the overhead cockpit windows.

"Good, that's it," he said crisply when the boom was pointed at a forty-five degree angle toward the tail. He leaned over and worked the controls of the camera on the boom until he could see the Cosmos clearly on the monitor. They were drifting just slightly. He brushed a thruster to give a small opposing acceleration. Eleven minutes since the last shot from Cosmos.

A small figure appeared on the monitor, heading slowly but directly toward the antenna on the lower spin axis. A white plume shot briefly from the top of the backpack, then a shorter blast. The figure hovered next to the projecting antenna just below the spinning base of the Cosmos. An arm reached back and unsnapped a tool from the side of the pack. In a moment a torch flared brightly and was applied to the base of the antenna. The antenna fell free and drifted off.

"That should prevent any control commands," came the voice over the radio.

"He just cut the radio antenna off the bottom," Jupp informed Wahlquist.

"Now what's he doing?" Wahlquist's voice betrayed his fear and frustration.

"He's got the torch on again. He's holding it up to the bottom about eighteen inches from the center. I'll be damned. He's using the rotation as if the thing were on a lathe. Cutting a circle as slick as can be. I guess he'll try to cut a hole and then get inside to disable it."

"Wait a minute!" The pattern shifted, drifting. The torch went out.

"What is it!" shouted Wahlquist.

"Major!" came the curt command. "This thing is still alive. Must be an internal antenna. It's changing its pitch. Get your craft the hell out of the way!"

Jupp hit a thruster and backed the shuttle away and down. When it was in his line of sight again he could see the rhythmic puffs from its thrusters and see that the laser portal had already been slightly tilted down toward him. He began a frenzied game with the control thrusters, monitoring the Cosmos and keeping the shuttle out of the rotating, sweeping aim of the laser. He was not too busy to marvel at the actions of the diminutive figure that hovered around the massive contraption.

He watched the figure maneuver to the perimeter of the base of the Cosmos. An arm snaked out.

"What's he doing?" Jupp narrated to Wahlquist. "Slapping at it? My god, no! He grabbed it! He grabbed the nozzle of the thruster!" The figure was suddenly whipping around with the Cosmos, feet flung outward by the centrifugal force.

"He's got a hand on it, but I don't know if he can hold on. If he loses his grip and it slings him off, we may not get him back." A burst of white exhaust came from the thruster. "Damn! There it goes again! Wow! He's still got his grip! I guess the suit gives him enough protection from the peroxide jet." Jupp watched intently. "Oh, oh," he said. "They've slowed it down and it's tilted toward us again. They're still trying to draw a bead!"

Jupp concentrated on the controls again, moving the shuttle out of reach. When he could look again, Jupp saw that the Colonel had once more fired up the torch.

"He's hanging onto the thruster with one hand and using the torch on the sidewall about a foot above the thruster. I don't know how he's holding on, but that should be thin skin he's cutting there. Why's he doing that? Yep, there it goes."

A thin piece of the metal wall fell away leaving a hole about a foot across. The torch was released, dangling on its short cord.

"Now let's see, he's got a hole big enough for his hand. Yeah, he's reaching inside. Those edges will be sharp. He better not rip his suit! Okay, he's got a grip on something inside, a brace or something. He's hauling himself up. He's got a foot up, now the other. Oh, I see. He's standing on the wing."

"He's standing?" inquired Wahlquist, perplexed. "What the hell do you mean?"

"Well, he's got himself wrapped along the side with his head pointed in the direction of the rotation. That puts the flat surface of the wing under his feet, giving sort of an artificial gravity. There must still be quite a centrifugal force, but he's got some support.

"I can only see him about once every, oh, about every twenty seconds now, the thing has slowed its rotation as it's maneuvered here. From our vantage, he's moving from left to right, clockwise if you look up from below. He's got the torch back and is poking it into the thruster nozzle. Ah, yeah, that'll fry the nozzle and the works inside. Now he's doing the opposite nozzle of the pair. He's cutting another hand hold. He's near the bottom end of the cylinder. There's another thruster at the top; he's going for that."

Jupp watched as the man held on with his left hand and reached over as far as he could with the torch in his right hand to cut another hole. There was an awkward moment as the torch was released, and the change of handholds was managed, right hand into the old hole, left into the new one. That maneuver was repeated again so that the figure was holding on only with his right hand and had moved to the left. After a brief fumble the torch was retrieved from where it spun outward at the end of its tether, and yet another hole was cut. Repeating this pattern, Newman made his laborious way along the side of the Cosmos, pausing a couple of times to direct the torch into small ports that could be easily reached. Whatever sensors had peered out from within were now blind. Electronic eyes in exchange for the human pair in the shuttle. Newman was almost at the other end, at the second pair of thrusters, when his cold voice came again.

"Major, are you out of the line of fire?"

"Yes, sir—"

"Then make sure *your* eyes are goddamned covered!"

The laser! Jupp had not been watching the clock in his

fascination with the laborious climb up the face of the Cosmos. He barely had time to throw his arms up over his faceplate. The laser port was between the protuberance Newman stood on and the one that followed in the sense of rotation. The timing was immaculate. The laser flared as the rotation swept it in the direction of the shuttle, the vast surge of energy passing several hundred feet above the shuttle. Jupp slowly lowered his arms and looked at the clock. About twenty-four minutes between shots, just as before. The remaining thrusters flared on the Cosmos, and it slowed and slewed again, a little erratically Jupp thought, the effect of the destroyed thruster pair. Hurriedly, Jupp eased the shuttle into a new safe position.

"Everything all right?" Wahlquist wanted to know.

"Yeah," replied Jupp, "we were out of the line of fire, but I shouldn't have lost track of the time. He's torched the upper pair of thrusters. Now he's leaning over and cutting a hole in the top edge of the wing projection. Another one in the hull just above the wing. Oh, man! He's using those holds to lower himself down toward the next wing, dropping back against the rotation from our point of view. It's not working! The centrifugal force throws him out. It's a little too far; he can't get a foot straight down!

"He's hauled himself back up and is lying prone on the wing, reaching way down to cut another hole in the hull."

Jupp was silent for a few moments.

"It's a foothold! He's hanging down again and has a foot in that new hole. He's down; he's got a foot on the other wing. He's got a hand in the foothold, both feet down. He made it! Damnation! That clown is good!"

Newman applied the torch to the thruster pair near him and then began to cut holds and work his way toward the pair of thrusters to his right at the bottom end of the long cylinder. Midway along he came to the large ominous port that housed the laser. It spanned the distance from his belt to his throat as he paused before it and reached for the torch.

The satellite had rotated the port away from them and Jupp felt more than saw a brief glow. Over the radio they heard what might have been the start of a scream, but the lungs that were attempting to drive it vanished, and the sound came out a choked sigh.

Jupp watched in horror as the satellite rotated, now in seemingly infinitely slow motion. Before the laser port came into view he saw the legs, thrown off by the centrifugal force. Legs, ending at the waist of the suit, twisting slowly off into oblivion, followed by a piece of the backpack with the torch still dangling from it. The next stubby wing swept by and he could see the remaining ghastly tableau. The left hand was still wedged into one of the freshly cut hand holds. The arm led to shoulders, another arm, the head above, but nothing below, the torso blasted cleanly away. The truncated assemblage, flung centrifugally out from the side of the satellite, rotated slowly out of view.

Jupp felt an intense nauseous sweat break out on his forehead and sweep down through his body. He breathed deeply to keep his stomach. Finally he realized Wahlquist was screaming at him.

"Ed! Ed! For god's sake what happened?! Ed? Answer me!"

"The laser," he finally croaked. "It went off when he was right in front of it. He's gone."

"What do you mean went off? It couldn't have been time."

"No. No, you're right," Jupp looked at the clock. "It could only have been about twelve minutes." He lay back in his seat. "Maybe it was triggered prematurely somehow. A trip device, some signal from the ground. Not full power, but enough to kill a man. I don't know. But it sure happened. God!" he exclaimed as the laser port and the remains of its victim swung into view again.

"We've got to get out of here!" exploded Wahlquist, near hysteria.

Jupp thought for a moment, his head spinning, rationality almost out of grasp. Then order settled in, years of training asserting its influence.

"Larry! Listen to me!" He spoke sternly, commanding his copilot to calm down. "We can't go down."

"We've got to!"

"Listen to me! We can't take a shot from that laser. A direct hit and we've bought it. I can't fly and position the mirror at the same time. You can't see where to put the mirror, and it probably won't give us much protection anyway, damaged as it is. Besides we came up here to do a job. A damn good man just got killed for this mission. We've got to see it through."

"I'm blind, goddamn it. I'm no good. Are you going to take that thing on single-handed?"

Jupp was silent a moment, then answered.

"Yes. But you can help. I'll get into it and disable the power. Then I'll tell you where to guide the boom so we can grab on and tuck it into the bay."

"You're out of your gourd!" protested Wahlquist. "What happens when you're out there and it takes aim and blows the shuttle away? And the damn thing is spinning; that's a tough job with the boom, even if I could see!"

"Three of the eight thruster pairs are out of commission. It probably can't maneuver well. That gives us a margin. I'll have to kill the rest. And if you can't maneuver the boom, then you'll have to pick me up, and I'll do it. Hey, I know this is no picnic, but we can do it! We've got to do it. What we can't do is waste time talking. I've got to get us in position under the Cosmos, and then you've got to come down and help me with my backpack."

Jupp knew it was necessary to get Wahlquist moving, give him something to do so he wouldn't work himself closer to panic. He had to remember that, desperate as he felt, he could at least still see. Wahlquist would be just that much closer to cracking up. These thoughts spun through his mind as he worked the thrusters and brought the shuttle up under the Cosmos, scarcely conscious of his actions.

He unbuckled and floated back to where Wahlquist stood. Ignoring his protestations, Jupp guided Wahlquist to the hatch in the floor and watched him drop through. Then he floated down himself. The two of them squeezed into the airlock and then out into the cargo bay. Jupp made sure Wahlquist was on a short tether. He detached a second backpack from its rack and gave it to Wahlquist. It took them several minutes of fumbling to get it attached, but Jupp could sense Wahlquist growing more assured as he let his training take over and worked the familiar catches, buckles, and straps by feel. Jupp helped him into the airlock, then detached the tether and watched him disappear through.

In their orbital minuet, they had tipped so that now they were not aligned with the earth beneath them. The fierce blue line of the earth's horizon made a cockeyed angle over one of the bay doors. Jupp looked up at the menacing hulk of the Cosmos spinning its grisly cargo a hundred feet over his head. His body felt encased in electric ice. He stared at the Cosmos, and then decided on a plan. He had to move before he thought about it too deeply. He selected and attached a tether. He reached for the thruster controls that extended forward on an arm from the backpack, gently fired the bottom thruster and rose up out of the bay.

The tether stopped him opposite the middle of the Cosmos. He watched the spinning craft carefully, calculating how long it would take him at full thrust to cross the void. He used the tether and his thrusters to line up precisely with the laser port, the easiest point to grab hold. Then he pointed himself headfirst at the Cosmos. He got himself as steady as he could and then detached the precious tether. The movement rotated him slightly. He resisted the impulse to grab for the security of the tether and used the thrusters to realign himself. He thought it would take about ten seconds, half a rotation time.

He watched the laser port pass from his left to his right, one stubby wing, another.

NOW! he screamed silently to himself and hit the thruster at the bottom of the backpack, producing a long continuous jet.

He accelerated toward the equator of the spinning cylinder. Another blunt wing passed. Too slow. Too slow!

Then the next wing passed, and he could see the port. He was almost there. But the port moved on. He had to get there before the next wing swept by, leaving him to crash into the smooth side, nothing to grip. Too close. Too close!

He was moving in rapidly, the crucial wing swinging toward him, right at him! He threw out his left arm, fending off the rotating wing, deflecting himself toward the laser port, menace and salvation.

The swinging appendage crashed into his arm, sending a jolt up through his shoulder. A moment later he collided headfirst with the hull of the Cosmos. The wing swept him around as the momentum of his impact rolled him into a ball. The force of his thruster kept him against the hull for a moment, but then he dizzily felt as if every force of nature were working against him. The centrifugal force of rotation tugged him inexorably outward, away from the hull. He extended his legs, and the thruster began to push him up along the hull, away from the laser port. He killed the thruster, but could feel himself tilting outward, falling away from the hull. He pushed against the stubby wing and lashed out desperately with his right leg, kicking along the hull until he felt the ominous opening of the laser port.

Only a few minutes had passed, but scarcely a few more had been enough to kill. He simply prayed that he would not somehow trigger a similar blast. He felt the upper side of his boot catch over the rim of the opening, his toe extending inside the port. The friction gave him some anchor, but his upper body tilted away, still at the mercy of the centrifuge.

A hand reached out, and he grabbed at it without thinking. Only after a moment of relief did he realize in horror what it was. No time to think, his boot could slip at any moment. He pulled frantically against the centrifugal force—grabbing hand, forearm, shoulder, then reaching beyond the helmet to grab another handful of suit near the other shoulder. He was too busy to look, too frightened to look, but he caught a glimpse of gaping mouth and eyes staring in perpetual shock. He stuffed his hand into the torch-cut hole, searching for the grip to share with a dead hand.

There! A reinforcing bar! Got to—Finally the infinite sinking relief of a secure handhold.

As he grabbed the fixture within the hole he became aware of the shaking of his leg from tension and too much adrenalin. Sewing machine leg, the rock climbers called it. He forced himself to breathe calmly for a moment. He could not wait for long. He was aware of his appendages as never before. His whole consciousness split and flowed to his left hand wedged against the dead one, gripping some frame member, his right foot, hooked upward, straining to keep a purchase on the rim of the deadly laser port. Would he trigger it? What if it goes off? Is his foot out of the way, or will it be seared from his leg? The terrible centrifugal force, pulling, pulling him away from the side. How did *he* do it, one-handed, with the Cosmos rotating twice as fast?

Jupp tensed his stomach muscles and slowly drew his dangling left leg in against the outward tug of the artificial gravity. His foot bounced against the hull, and then he slid it downward, trying awkwardly to keep it against the hull until he could reach the stubby wing. It was like hanging from the ceiling and trying to stand on the wall. Finally, he could feel the surface of the wing. There was some friction on the sole of his boot, precarious but precious support against the outward tug.

Slowly, he released his toehold on the laser port. He twisted suddenly, his left foot slipping on the wing. A surge of panic, primordial, fear of falling, ran through him. He forced himself to have confidence in his hand grip and got his left, then right foot planted on the wing. Now the rotating wing offered a floor under his feet, an artificial gravity giving some security against the perilous outward component.

He reached backward for the torch, every move awkward

and twisted as if he were on a rapid merry-go-round. He grasped the torch in its clamp on the backpack. He dropped it! The torch slung out to the end of its tether. He grabbed the base of the tether and pulled it around in front of him, extending his arm, letting the tether slip through his hand until he could almost reach the handle of the torch. Then he worked his gloved fingers in cumbersome rhythmic fashion, inching along the tether and onto the handle until he had a firm grip. He pressed the button and the torch sprang to life, a flaring blue ally.

He worked the torch in a loose U shape two feet across below the laser port. The torch sliced the thin metal easily. The chunk of side wall fell away and he could see inside the Cosmos for the first time.

He saw that he would not be able to get through the hole. The bracework for the laser mount obscured the way. He shuffled his feet aside and cut another U extending to the left of the first. As the next piece fell away, he felt his perch shudder. To his right, he could see the cloud emerge from one of the undamaged thrusters. The Cosmos was maneuvering again! He watched as the rotation carried him around. Yes! They had tilted down slightly toward the shuttle. He had to get inside!

Two heavy braces blocked the new hole. One ran along the side and provided his handhold in the smaller hole above. The bars resisted, but the torch did its work.

He replaced the torch in its clamp and reached inside the freshly cut hole, seeking and grasping one of the bars supporting the laser. Then he released the grip of his left hand and withdrew it from the upper hole. As he did, the Colonel's hand came loose as well. The head bumped his and the hand slapped against his faceplate, a farewell pat, as the remains swung off into space. The sudden movement jolted Jupp again and he froze motionless for a long moment until he felt the thrusters shift the Cosmos once more.

Rapidly, he crouched and snaked his left hand in for a

grip. He pulled himself inward. God, it was dark! He needed the lamp, but could not release a grip to get it. He pulled again and inched inward but then stopped. Now what giant solid hand blocked his further movement?

The backpack. It was caught on the severed brace. He might cut a hole big enough for it, but there was probably no room in the confined innards of the satellite. Cool daring descended on him. He had come too far. He adjusted his position until his grip with his left hand was as firm as possible. He transferred the torch and a lamp to fasteners on his suit. Then he began to release the straps and catches with his right hand, working awkwardly but methodically at a job meant for more than two hands. The partially freed backpack swung out tugging on the straps, fighting release. At last he had it. He held onto the final strap for one moment and then let go without a backward glance to see the mechanism spin off to join the severed body in eternity.

He twisted slowly one way then the other, testing for freedom, finding a contortion that allowed motion. He grasped for new handholds and worked his way in headfirst.

Finally! He could feel his feet clear the opening and planted them on the bracework surrounding the hole through which he had entered. He stood, the centrifugal force at last a friend, feet on the wall of the huge cylinder, head toward the center. He found the lamp and flicked it on. The laser loomed alongside him, a huge enclosed box. There was room to maneuver, if just barely, a technician's access space. Elsewhere, equipment, snaking cables, wires, and pipes packed the interior of the satellite.

Now what, Mister brave guy commando? a cynical voice asked. You going to destroy this thing with karate chops?

He felt the satellite shift again, and through the frame around him could sense the flow of peroxide to the jets. Peroxide. The tanks must be somewhere. Could he puncture one with the torch and put the jets out of commission without blowing himself up? He scanned around and could not identify the tanks. They could be anywhere; why wasn't he briefed for this?

Power! If he killed the power, he would stop both radio commands from the ground and the laser. He played the lamp again and located a cable the thickness of his arm coming from the rear of the laser. That had to be the main power supply. He followed the cable around the hull to the point where it disappeared into the bulkhead that had been behind him as he faced the laser.

Stenciled lettering caught his attention, just out of the reach of the lamp. He swung the light and froze. He dimly felt the involuntary release that flowed down the relief tube of his suit. He didn't read Cyrillic, but there was no mistaking the purple and yellow international symbol for radioactivity. Of course, he thought, no solar panels, the thing has to be powered by a nuclear reactor, and no room nor need to shield it in space.

I'm a dead man. The words echoed in his mind as he swung to work. He started with the large cable from the laser, severing it with the torch. Sparks flew, arcing the gap he cut, but he felt no glory in the fireworks, only a grim determination. Then he methodically cut every other cable he could reach from his confined space that might carry electrical power. As he proceeded he could feel the cessation of certain hums and vibrations of which he had not been consciously aware. If it was killing him, he was killing it.

When he could find no more cables intact, he backed out of the hole very slowly so as not to catch his suit. When only his upper torso remained inside, he hooked an elbow around one of the laser braces so that he had a firm hold that would not tire his hands. The centrifugal force tugged his legs straight away from the satellite.

"Larry?"

"Oh, thank god!" Wahlquist's relief came to Jupp as a palpable force over the intercom. "I wanted to call you but was afraid to spoil your concentration. Control is frantic. I cut them off from you too."

"Sorry, it must have been rough on you just sitting. I think I've disabled it. I cut the power lines."

"Control says it's probably nuclear powered. Did you go inside?"

"Yeah, I had to, but only for a little while. I'm fine."

An extended silence echoed with Wahlquist's doubt. Then he spoke.

"Now what?"

"I sure want to get back home. How'd you like to play catcher?"

"How's that?"

"I had to jettison the backpack to get inside. I want you to jockey the bird around where I can just jump into the bay. Can you do that?"

Jupp heard the forced bravado.

"If you can pitch it, I can catch it."

"Great! Are you at the controls?"

"Yep. I've been feeling around; I'm into it. Talk to me."

"You're about forty-five degrees from my plane of rotation. This polecat was trying to get you in its sights again, by the way."

"Thanks, podnuh."

"Anytime. Let's start simple. Give me a little port roll to get the plane of your wings perpendicular to my rotation. Not too much. Smidgen to the right. Wait'll I go around to get another good look. Just a hair to the left. Okay, that looks pretty good. We'll tune it up later. Now let's see if we can get a parallel lateral shift to the right. You want to hit the front and the rear left thrusters by just the same amount. No. Too much nose! You're moving but spinning. A little right nose! Now some right rear. Let me get my bearings, I can only see you once every twenty seconds. You're still drifting. Give me just a light brush on the right. A little more. Okay, let me watch again for a minute."

Jupp had realized throughout this exercise that they would never get a perfect alignment, with Wahlquist having no direct visual feedback. They might stop the spin of the shuttle, or the drift, but to get them both stabilized at once was asking too much. He could maximize his chances, but he was still going to have to hit a moving target from a merry-go-round. And he was the projectile.

He spent a few more minutes with Wahlquist until they seemed to have the drift minimized. The shuttle passed before his eyes once every twenty seconds, its open bay yawning a welcome to him. The craft hovered a little below him but had a slight upward drift. It was also in a slow clockwise spin from his perspective. He planned to push off from the Cosmos when he faced at right angles to the shuttle. His inertia from the spinning satellite would carry him sideways toward the bay. The problem was timing. Even if the shuttle were perfectly stationary, he could release too soon and be thrown past the tail; too late and he would sail helplessly past the nose. He could increase the target angle by bringing the shuttle in closer, but then there would be too great a chance of collision.

He waited until the shuttle was pointed with its long axis along his plane of rotation so that he had the best chance of landing in the bay. He worked his body around until his feet were under him. He crouched on the side of the Cosmos and held onto a brace with one hand behind him, like an ungainly swimmer about to begin a race. He waited a minute, three more revolutions, and then as he saw the tail of the shuttle come into view to his extreme left, he pushed off.

He immediately sensed his error, and the panic of falling gripped him again. He had concentrated so hard on timing his leap to the rotation that he had not paid enough attention to pushing straight off from the side of the satellite. He had pushed himself slightly upward, exactly the wrong thing to do with the shuttle a little below him. He felt as if the shuttle were drifting downward, even as he rocketed toward it, arms and legs flailing wildly in ungrippable space. He began to tumble, and as he caught occasional glimpses of the shuttle, he could see the edge of the bay drop below his inexorable path. He steeled himself to see the shuttle float by, his last connection to humanity fading in the vastness of space.

The blow nearly took his breath away, a surprising painful rap from his left shoulder blade to his right kidney. As he bounced back, he caught a twisting view of the bay rotating in his line of sight, and then a pole. He spread-eagled, reaching for his life. His left arm and leg hit it; he swung his right arm around, reaching, clawing, grabbing, hugging. And then he was still, legs tightly wrapped around the manipulating boom, his arms clasping it to his bosom. He closed his eyes and listened to the pounding of his heart, racing as never before. The sweat ran stinging rivulets into his eyes, clinched though they were. At last he opened them and looked around. The clamshell door. He had missed the cargo bay, but had collided with the edge of the extended door. He looked at the boom immediately before his eyes. Had it not been for the plastic barrier of his faceplate, he would have kissed it.

He tried to speak, choked, and then tried again.

"Larry?"

"You okay?"

"I'm home. Don't go away; I'll be right in."

"Hot damn!"

Jupp shinnied his way carefully down the boom, and using handholds in the bay, made his way to the airlock. He rotated through and nearly collapsed with relief at being back within the confines of the familiar shuttle cabin. He drifted up through the hatch. Wahlquist was standing next to the pilot's seat, waiting for him, his faceplate up, listening intently, compensating already for his lack of sight. Jupp floated to him and without thinking grasped him in a bearhug. Wahlquist was surprised for a moment, but then responded in kind and the two figures stood for a long moment locked in a cumbersome space-suited embrace.

Finally Jupp felt control return. He held Wahlquist off at arm's length.

"Okay, buddy, we've got work to do. Let's bag that bird and get out of here."

He guided Wahlquist to the copilot's seat and then settled into the comfortable familiarity of the pilot's seat. He jockeyed the thrusters and loved every response of his craft. He loved his eye-hand coordination, and he loved the total absence of the terrible repellant artificial gravity that dwelt on the object out his window.

He maneuvered the shuttle until it was beneath the Cosmos once more, craning to see through the window over his head to position the boom. When he was satisfied, he moved to the boom controls at the rear of the flight deck. He released a catch and watched the life-saving mirror drift off to join the other detritus of their mission. Then he raised the boom until it was just beneath the Cosmos. He flipped the switch that set the rotatable stanchion on the end of the boom spinning and with it the payload interface claw. Monitoring the picture from the camera that spun with the claw, he adjusted the speed until the image of the bottom of the Cosmos was fixed, the claw rotating at exactly the same speed. He then closed the gap to the Cosmos and thrust the claw up into the open wound where the bottom antenna had been. He could feel the shuttle rock as the spinning claw sought a purchase on the satellite and transmitted small torques through the stationary boom. He could see the claw span a frame member and he locked it on.

Now for the tedious part. He had to slowly decrease the speed of the claw. Too fast and he could snap the boom or the brace in the Cosmos with equally disastrous results if the spinning satellite should collide with the main span of the boom. As he decelerated the tremendous angular inertia of the Cosmos, it was transferred to the shuttle, setting it spinning. Jupp called orders to Wahlquist who operated the thrusters to remove the spin.

An hour later the Cosmos and the shuttle were one in motion. Jupp slowly lowered the boom until the Cosmos was just out of the bay, the jury rigged wings that had abetted his entry blocking the final nesting. With some reluctance he floated back down through the hatch, passed through the airlock, and stared once again at the hulking satellite. He anchored a tether to his suit, pulled a torch from the rack and affixed it to his belt.

He started on the structure with which he had first collided. His skin crawled to see the gaping hole of the laser port, and its smaller, ragged companion where he had found his first grisly hand-hold. He was too fatigued to do more than a butcher job, but it still required fifteen minutes to sever the blunt structure and shove it off into space. He continued around, doing two more in three-quarters of an hour. He was bone tired. He floated back to the deck of the bay and scanned the remains. He was sure he could position the thing to one side of the bay so that the final wing would fit. God help them if it bounced around during re-entry. He hung up the torch, detached the tether and slipped back through the airlock.

More careful manipulation of the boom brought the Cosmos into the bay, the remaining wing just clearing the hinges where the port clamshell would close. He hit the switch and watched the doors swing shut on their captive with the relief of a beleaguered traveller whose suitcase finally closes. He journeyed once again into the bay and secured the huge bulk as well as possible with various cables and clamps.

For a final time he floated up onto the flight deck and buckled himself into the pilot's seat. He programmed the computer and they began the descent to near earth orbit. He suggested to Wahlquist that he discuss with mission control the best mode of re-entry with an evaporated vertical stabilizer, tilted his chair back, and slipped into a heavy sleep.

He awoke fighting the sleep, caught in a fear that if he did not arouse now he never would. He could sense without opening his eyes that the booster was not firing. They were in parking orbit.

"Back in a minute," he told Wahlquist, as he pried himself out of his chair. Down on the operations deck he stripped off his gloves and undid his helmet. He went to the medicine cabinet and washed down a couple of benzedrine tablets. Wouldn't do to sleep through re-entry.

Back in the pilot's seat, he listened intently to Wahlquist. They had immediately concluded that a routine landing at the Cape was out of the question. Emergency crews were assembling on the dry lake expanses of Edwards Air Force Base in the Mohave. Part of the vertical stabilizer was still intact and the guess was that it would provide sufficient stability during re-entry. The problem was that maneuvering in the atmosphere would be severely hampered. They could make some gentle turns with judicious use of wing spoilers, but without the rudder a proper coordinated turn was impossible. Not a job for computers, no programs were written for laser-blasted equipment. Jupp had to fly. He'd known that as he fell asleep, and as he had pawed for the stimulant.

His senses were keen as they did the final burn to start their descent. They began in standard orbital orientation, upside down, rockets pointed in their direction of travel. The rockets thrusted and they dropped into an ever lower, ever faster trajectory. As they entered the atmosphere, they flipped over to the normal atmospheric configuration, nose forward, tiled belly down into the heat. Jupp immediately felt the vibration. Something was wrong with the damaged tail. The mangled remains of the rudder still clung to the lower portion of the vertical stabilizer. The vibration grew to a teeth-clattering shudder. Jupp felt a cool wisp of irony amidst his fear. They would die now together, the shuttle and the Cosmos, after being through so much.

His mind raced, scenes of childhood, his technician's sense wondering what would give out first, a wing come off, a rupture in the hull? Then in a heartbeat it was gone. The shorn rudder succumbed to its own lack of aerodynamic perfection. The tremendous heat of re-entry ablated and then finally swept it away.

They came out of radio blackout only fifty miles off course. Jupp applied a little spoiler. Not the most perfect turn, his flight instructor would have washed him out had the ball drifted that much in training, but they were back on course. There were the chase planes. God, they were lovely! There was the strip. No graceful turns for position, they were going right down the pipe.

He was going to miss the painted center stripe by a quarter mile, but he couldn't worry about that. Without the capacity for a coordinated turn he could not risk a destabilizing crab this close to the ground. A bit too hot, too. Can't be helped. Flaps down. Gear down. Nose up, drop the forward speed as much as possible. Wasn't this strip supposed to be long? Isn't that the warning marker? Nose higher, ease her down. Now, nose down, even her up, here we go, flare, flare! Down, bounce, down, *down,* DOWN!

Jupp heard the ground crew swarm over the craft. He began the post-flight shutdown, responding automatically to prompts from ground control. We're down, he thought. We made it. We brought the son-of-a-bitch back. I should feel happy. I *do* feel happy. He looked over at Wahlquist. Below the sightless eyes was a wide, relieved grin.

Then he felt the first grip of nausea.

Chapter 4

Rhein Haartvedt hurried along the narrow, dirty street in the fading light, trying to place his carefully polished shoes in the least distasteful spots, his thoughts eddies of conflicting currents. He badly wanted to give this speech, his maiden public stand against apartheid, but conflicting images of past and future crowded his mind. The knowledge tore at him that the way of life which had nourished him, and which his loved ones loved, must be destroyed. He pictured his father: tall, stern, and unyielding, fair in his own way, but blind to the screaming inequities of their system. He imagined his family—father, mother, two sisters—shocked, hounded, uprooted, deprived of their privileged existence, and he felt the pain they would feel at his perceived betrayal.

He paused in a rutted intersection and looked again at the crude map Roy M'Botulu had scrawled for him. Roy was wise, witty, urbane. Unbelievable that he came from this place. Rhein tried to ignore it, but the repulsive poverty and ignorance radiated at him from every angle. To subjugate someone like Roy was a crime of monstrous proportions, but was it conceivable that these people could ever be raised from the squalor in which they mired themselves? As a child, he knew in his heart that it was wrong that all the faces at the table should be white, all the hands serving, black. Roy had carefully fanned that flame of disquiet, had shown him the depraved depths of the sin of man against man. He believed those words, had made them his own, and wanted to fight for Roy's cause, but the quiet passions of a coffeehouse were not reflected in the dim reality surrounding him now. Could these people really rule themselves?

A greater question, could they rule Rhein's people? Irrationally, his mind filled with an image of his mother in all her refinement banished to one of these hovels, serving some filthy hag with a scrawny child stuck on one teat. Rhein shook his head, banishing such thoughts. If Roy could rise above this, so could others. For the hundredth time he mentally ran through the opening lines of his speech, which were carefully memorized Swahili. According to the map, the small meeting place was just a block away, around the corner. Roy would be there to give him strength.

He peered in the dark and stepped with his left foot over a puddle. As he placed his foot on the other side and leaned forward to design his next step, he felt strangely heavy, and then he was dying.

Something shot from the puddle, shattered the femur of his extended thigh near the pelvic joint, and ripped a hole in his upper leg. Then, because he was leaning, it penetrated again at the bottom of his rib cage, blew a thumb-sized hole in his aorta, and punched out through the base of his neck, nicking his ear.

Rhein collapsed forward heavily, his hips in the puddle, his face in a pile of day-old dog shit. He struggled to turn his nose from the stench and felt the fetid water seep into his trousers. He blinked his eyes open and saw a small, fat-bellied child staring at him from a doorway. A dark circle narrowed his vision until all he could see were the eyes. White eyes. Strangely sideways. Roy's eyes. I'm dying Roy. Trouble for Roy. I'm sorry. Roy.

Maria Latvin held the hand of the figure that lay with swaddled head against the crisp whiteness of the hospital bed. She could feel the pressure of his hand, was sure he knew she was there.

She looked through a faint mist of tears at the gray, sixtyish man who stood on the other side of the bed. Until the—accident, she had known Ralph Floyd only vaguely as manager of the operations at Paul's laboratory.

"What are you asking of me?" she asked plaintively. "How can I do this thing?"

"Someone must care for him. You've seen that he responds to you. There are many people that depend on him, now we must depend on you."

"But he needs medical help. I can not do that."

Floyd looked at the man standing quietly behind Latvin's chair, stethoscope draped around his neck.

"Dr. Crawford has done all he can for him here at the lab in terms of immediate medical attention. His body is healthy. He is just not in complete control of it. We need someone to look after him, while we seek expert consultation for his remaining—problems."

"But shouldn't he be taken somewhere, to a city, to a big hospital?"

"There are many complications, my dear. He is the head of a large complex structure, far more than this lab which has been his recent headquarters. Much of this complex runs on its own without his day to day intervention or control." Floyd shrugged. "But if he should die, there would be many problems. The situation is even worse in his present state—alive, but not competent to run his affairs. If that news should become general knowledge, the result would be chaos. You must keep him, care for him, while we seek to restore him to full health."

Maria Latvin looked deeply into the eyes of the older man. She did not know his true motivation. Was he merely trying to maintain order in a difficult situation, or did he have deeper desires for control of this complex of which he spoke? She felt the pressure of the hand in hers again. She owed this man much. Here was a chance to hold to him, and to the life she had come to love so deeply, a bit longer.

Somebody stood up and turned on the room lights. Isaacs jerked his head up from the photograph he had been studying. In his bleariness he had not realized that the bright Sunday afternoon sun had faded. He scanned the accumulated disarray of their four-day marathon and looked out the window of the conference room. He tried for a long moment to figure out what time it must be from the purpling of the evening light. He finally remembered to look at his watch. 8:38. Eastern daylight. God, was he tired.

He thought back to the return of the shuttle, the Cosmos laser satellite. Could that have been three weeks ago? Now April was gone, spring replaced by the summer heat of early May.

The Russians had immediately gone into overdrive to put up another satellite. The laser had been delivered from the development site at Saryshagan to the launch site at Tyuratam four days ago. Isaacs' Office of Scientific Intelligence had worked around the clock to monitor the transition and the operation at Tyuratam.

Isaacs looked again at the photograph from the K-H 11 Digital Imaging Satellite. He had been trying to discern some clue to the nature of the box of electronics sitting on the gantry next to the rocket. Now he looked at the technician who squatted next to it. From three hundred miles up the photograph only showed a fuzzy image of the top of the man's head, his back, the tops of his thighs and his right arm extended to a knob on the electronics. I bet that bastard's tired too, Isaacs thought to himself. Isaacs knew the man well, as well as one ever could by studying the flat two-dimensional creatures that inhabited these photos. They had picked him out from the first photographs taken a month ago at Saryshagan by the un-slavic mop of curly hair that occupied the rear half of his balding head. They had taken to calling him Curly. Isaacs was amused at the odd resentment he had felt when Boswank finally got a make on him, identifying him as plain old Fyodr Rudikov. Fyodr was a subterfuge, an alias. His real name was Curly.

Curly had arrived last Thursday at the launch site at Tyuratam along with the laser components. Since then Curly had been working sixteen-hour days, just like Isaacs' team. The launch of the new laser could be as soon as next month. Curly was on the front line down there, beating himself and his crew to greater effort. In this room, in the bowels of this building, and in many others, thousands of American intelligence people focused on the same event. When would the launch be? What were the capabilities of this new laser? Could it be stopped? Should it be stopped? Would it strike? Where? Were there defensive measures?

Isaacs shoved his rolled cuffs further up his arms, then raised his arms in a stretch over his head. He looked at the bedraggled group around him. Martinelli sat with one of his aides in a circle of coffee cups and cigarette butts. They were sorting the latest pile of useful photographs culled from the reams that poured in from a host of satellites. Bill Baris huddled with Pat Danielson at the far end of the table. Bill had isolated the crates which housed the laser components from among the bewildering array of associated rocket parts. The task now was to glean every scrap of information they could as the relevant crates were unpacked and their contents incorporated into the rocket.

Danielson ran liaison with the computer. When Baris

found some shred of evidence in a portion of one photograph, Danielson or one of her cohorts would dash off to retrieve that part of the photo from the computer memory and run it through a panoply of analysis routines, reducing noise, heightening contrast, pulling this feature then that from data, until they could do no more. Then they would move to another photo or call to Martinelli to order up a new one, concentrating on whatever feature seemed likely to be particularly illuminating. The Russians knew they were being spied upon. When they could not avoid exposing a piece, they would sometimes move it about at random, specifically to foil analysis teams. Then Isaacs' group would race to see if they could relocate the missing component, all the while searching for new clues.

Boswank had gone off to attend to other concerns. Several of his deputies remained, continually updating a list of target material amenable to investigation by clandestine networks on the ground. They conferred often with Henry Sharbunk, the representative from the National Security Agency, where a similar emergency operation progressed.

Isaacs looked again at the box Curly was operating on. If it held a power supply, as Baris maintained, what would that tell them? How the hell could they learn anything useful if they didn't know what it powered? He had a strong urge to shout down at Curly, to force him to turn his face up, so he could see him, talk to him. Demand to know where he intended to install that box, what it would do.

He snapped out of this fantasy when he felt a gentle hand on his shoulder. He looked up into Kathleen's eyes. She was deeply somber. He looked down at the note in her hand and took it from her. His chest constricted and his stomach felt a wince of sympathetic nausea. He had been expecting this, but he sickened anyway. Ed Jupp was dead.

Isaacs dropped his head onto his hand, replaying in his thoughts a fortnight of increasing agony. He had never met the man, but followed the progress, through messages such as these, as his hair fell out and the pain turned his guts to liquid fire.

Isaacs finally looked up at Kathleen and nodded to her. She gave his shoulder a brief, hesitant pat, and then left.

Isaacs finally cleared his throat and raised his voice above the hubbub of muted conversations.

"Excuse me!" He waited until he had their attention. "I just got a note from Walter Reed Hospital. Major Edward Jupp died an hour ago from radiation poisoning."

Everyone in the room lowered their eyes from Isaacs and did little things with whatever objects lay immediately in front of them.

"It's late Sunday. None of us have seen our families in a while. We've accomplished a lot in the last few days, and this rocket's not going anywhere," he gestured at the photograph of Curly before him. "Let's break and get a good night's rest. We'll hit it again tomorrow."

A riffle of shuffling and glances passed around the table. Despite the fatigue, putting down such an all-consuming task was not easy. Finally Martinelli spoke.

"Damn good idea. I came just that close to ordering up a new photo of the grounds in my coffee cup." He turned to his aide. "Let's just leave these in the piles as we have them," he pointed at the stacks of sorted photographs. "Lord knows there'll be a fresh batch tomorrow." He got up and stretched.

Slowly the other groups around the table began to arrange their material so that they could pick up again in the morning. They filed out one at a time, disoriented by the need to cease the intense effort and think of home and rest.

Isaacs sat staring at the top of Curly's head. He finally realized that everyone had left but Danielson. She moved over and sat down next to him.

"I'm sorry about Jupp," she said, her voice throaty. Isaacs nodded and looked at her, not quite seeing. Finally she spoke again. "Do you have enough energy to give me some advice?"

Isaacs rubbed his eyes with the palms of his hands and

worked his shoulders. "I can try." He gave her a wan smile. "I have this vague feeling I'm not at the peak of efficiency."

Her voice was apologetic. "I'm sorry to trouble you, but I have a conflict. Maybe you can help me resolve it. I've been spending a fair bit of time on that seismic signal you asked me to investigate. I had to drop that when this rush came up, of course. The problem is the people I've been working with at the Cambridge Research Lab. They know I've got an emergency down here, but they don't know what or how severe. They've assembled seismic data from a lot of universities and apparently feel there is significant new information in it, more thorough coverage. They've been pressuring me to go back up and work on it, as I originally promised. I don't quite know what to tell them. Should I tell them to put the whole thing on indefinite hold? Should I try to get up there for a little while if we can see a break here? I'm not sure how I should respond, but I don't think I should just keep putting them off."

Isaacs thought for a moment. His pleasant days in Florida seemed another era, another world. "We're going to be at this until the launch, a month, six weeks, several months if they get hung up somehow. Then a different show once it's in orbit. On the other hand, we're over a hump here in terms of sorting the procedures at the launch site." He looked at her intently. "Baris has been particularly pleased with your work, by the way, thinks you have a real flair for isolating important ingredients in the photos."

Danielson smiled in pleasure.

"That means you're especially valuable to us on this project, but we can't keep going with the intensity we have the last four days, and shouldn't have to. If you took a break to do something else, you might come back fresher. How would you feel about that?"

"I understand how crucial this effort is, but I'm just one member of the team and I'm still fascinated by this seismic thing." She looked at him, searching his eyes. "I'd hate to see it dropped."

He pushed back in his chair. "Let me talk to Baris. See if he thinks he can spare you. We'll have a better feeling of developments by midweek. Maybe we can work in a break for you."

"Thank you. I'd like that. I'll hold the Lab at bay and check with you later in the week."

She rose and left the room at a surprisingly fresh pace. Isaacs picked up the picture of Curly between his index and middle finger and sailed it gently to the middle of the conference table, a thousand dollar frisbee, one of several hundred stacked around the room. He checked that the door was locked on his way out, bid good evening to the security guard posted outside, and headed for his office, picturing a tall drink and cool, soothing sheets.

Sometime after lunch in the middle of May, Pat Danielson paced down the long central corridor which carried her through the multi-numbered interconnected buildings of MIT. She barely recalled catching the ride from the lab in Lexington into Cambridge. With little sleep in the last three days, she felt the hollow tension of deep fatigue. Atop that fundamental, like frosting on a cake, rode the giddy feeling of accomplishment that accompanies an intellectual breakthrough. That feeling provided the motive force that directed her numb legs to maintain a reasonable pace.

She crossed the main lobby decked with illustrations of ongoing student projects and pushed out the door. Pausing at the top of the steps, she blinked in the hazy sunlight. After gazing a moment at the busy traffic on Massachusetts Avenue, she leaned back against one of the tall fluted pillars and closed her eyes. Her head buzzed with the lack of sleep.

A brazen honk snapped her eyes open. She stood for a moment trying to sense if she had actually fallen asleep on her feet. Then she focused on the cab parked on the far side of the street. She gave a quick salute to the driver and proceeded down the steps where she stopped to push the walk/wait button. As the flash of red and yellow lights signaled a halt to the flow of traffic, she crossed to the taxi and climbed in the rear from the driver's side.

The driver cocked an ear and Danielson mumbled, "Airport—Eastern shuttle."

On the plane she tried to practice what she would say to Isaacs. Every time she began to assemble her excited thoughts into coherent English sentences, the words would drift and dissolve as her brain fought to sleep. Back in her office in the Langley headquarters she dropped her briefcase on her desk and, still standing, punched the phone for Isaacs' office.

"Yes, Miss Kate?" Isaacs fingered the intercom in answer to the buzz.

"Pat Danielson, sir. On the phone."

"Put her on the line," Isaacs said, reaching for his telephone. "Hello, Pat? Isaacs, here."

"We've completed the analysis on the periodic seismic signal," Danielson reported. "We've got something big, but I don't know what." She sounded excited, only an occasional slurred word indicated fatigue.

Isaacs looked at his watch. "It's four-thirty now, do you want to talk this afternoon, or wait until tomorrow?"

"Well, I thought you might not be free until tomorrow, but I'd rather get it off my chest. That might help me get some rest tonight. I've lived with the computer here and at the Cambridge Research Lab the last week and haven't had much sleep. I could at least give you the bottom line, then we could go into detail tomorrow sometime, after I've had a good night's sleep."

"Okay, come on up." Isaacs buzzed Kathleen to show Danielson in on her arrival and cleaned his desk of the latest summaries concerning the new Russian laser being readied for launch at Tyuratam.

Danielson arrived two minutes later. She looked haggard, but an intensity burned in her eyes. She dropped into the proffered chair, took a deep breath, and held it momentarily before exhaling slowly through pursed lips.

Isaacs waited for her to compose herself. Danielson's mind spun with the reams of data she'd lived with over the last few days as she endeavored to decide where to begin.

"It's not a surface effect," she blurted out. "In places we can clearly track it from the mantle to the core. It then seems to head on back to the surface. A scattered wave would have an attenuated amplitude. This grows in strength as it leaves the core and passes into the mantle."

"Does it move between two fixed points?" inquired Isaacs, already calculating the surveillance apparatus that could be used once a location was specified.

"On the contrary," replied Danielson, destroying that train of thought. "At first it seemed to move around randomly although confined to certain latitudes. It's too weak to follow continuously and it seemed to be taking arbitrary trajectories.

"I racked my brain trying to find a systematic effect that would tie all the data together. I only hit upon it late last night and finished working it out this morning. The path is fixed all right, but not to the earth."

Isaacs' brows rose slightly in surprise. He didn't speak but fixed his gaze on Danielson as he waited for her to continue.

"At first I thought it always pointed in the same direction with respect to the sun. Not at the sun, but at a fixed angle to it. But that wasn't quite it, so I tried a position fixed to the distant stars and that fits like a glove, as nearly as I can tell."

"Aaah, wait a minute," Isaacs leaned forward on his desk and clasped his hands. "Run that by me again."

"Okay," Danielson pointed her left index finger at the ceiling and moved her right index finger in a circle around it, pointed at the floor. "As the earth rotates exactly once on its axis, marking a sidereal day, a given point on its surface will fall on the line of motion we have determined," she moved her right finger back and forth past her left, "and a fixed distant star will be directly overhead once more. Because of the earth's motion in orbit around the sun, the interval between times when the sun is directly overhead, the solar day, is four minutes longer. Sidereal time represents a more basic inertial clock, uncomplicated by the orbit of the earth, and that is the time this phenomenon keeps."

"Let me get this straight," said Isaacs. "You're claiming that this motion is fixed in space? Just as the axis of the earth's rotation points in a fixed direction, towards Polaris?"

"Absolutely." Danielson gave an assertive nod which caused a curl to slip down on her forehead. She pushed it back with a gesture that suddenly recalled her femininity to Isaacs, but continued at a professional clip.

"Something moves on a line through the center of the earth. It always comes up near thirty-three degrees north latitude, goes down through the center of the earth, and comes out again at thirty-three degrees south latitude. Then it goes back to the center and comes out once again at thirty-three degrees north latitude. But since the earth rotates and the direction along which it moves is fixed, it never comes up at the same point twice."

The woman's fatigue receded as she endeavored to elaborate her argument. She jammed a slim finger onto Isaacs' desk. "Not only is this trajectory independent of the rotation of the earth on its axis, it's also independent of the motion of the earth around the sun. We have good data now spanning three months. In that time the earth has moved one quarter of the way around the sun in its orbit, an angle of ninety degrees. Yet the seismic trajectory has pointed to the same direction in space, a point somewhat to the north and midway between the constellations of Gemini and Cancer. If you extend the line of motion through the earth's center and out the other side, it intersects the sky at a point just south of the constellation of Capricorn."

Danielson leaned back and looked out the window over Isaacs' shoulder, as she sought an analogy.

"It's as if there were a string tied at two opposite points in space, Cancer and Capricorn, and passing through the center of the earth. That string intersects a different point on the earth's surface every second as the earth rotates, but the direction in which the string leads is independent of the rotation of the earth on its axis or its revolution in orbit about the sun."

Isaacs and Danielson stared at each other and then diverted their gazes to random points in the room. Danielson, convinced of the certainty of her conclusions, nevertheless abandoned herself to retracing mentally the steps she had taken over the last few days. She hadn't the mental energy presently to contemplate the impact of her efforts. Isaacs' thoughts took two tracks simultaneously, trying to absorb the significance of the raw conclusions just presented and beginning to catalog the possibilities for weakness or errors in the analysis leading to those conclusions.

When he spoke, Isaacs took a middle ground, that of attempting to elicit key facts. "Tell me more about the nature of the signal itself. How close to the surface does it get? What other characteristics does it have?"

Danielson leaned back and massaged her eyes with thumb and index finger while she replied, "Pinning down the position at a given instant is difficult because of the weak signal." She removed her hand from her face and looked intently at Isaacs. "Our latest estimate of the period is eighty and a half minutes, give or take a few seconds. We don't get a signal from the mantle, but then we pick it up as it proceeds back toward the core. There is also difficulty in estimating the propagation velocity without accurate positions, but it seems to pick up speed as it approaches the core of the earth. That is crudely consistent with the behavior of an ordinary sound wave since the sound velocity goes up in the hotter parts of the core. That's about the only thing it does like an ordinary seismic wave."

"You say that it goes right through the center of the earth?"

"That's right. It goes down on what seems to be a straight line, then proceeds straight out to the opposite surface, always on a line pointing midway between Gemini and Cancer. As I said, it doesn't behave like a wave in the sense that a wave gets weaker as it proceeds. This may get weaker going down, but it gets stronger, if anything, on its trip up. Then, as far as we can tell, the next cycle is identical."

Isaacs thought a moment. "So the net power in the signal isn't changing."

"Right again. It seems as if the strength of the signal only depends on where it is in the cycle, and that the power is the same cycle after cycle."

Isaacs paused, then asked, "Do you see any way this could be artificial? Man-made?"

"Not without a position fixed on the earth's surface," replied Danielson.

"But it seems not to be a normal seismic phenomenon?"

"Too many of the properties are strange, particularly if the path is fixed in space and not with respect to the earth."

"Could there be some tidal effect? A collective action of the sun and moon?"

"I don't see how. There's no obvious way to trigger such an event. In any case there seems to be no connection with the position of the moon which has orbited several times without changing anything while we've monitored the data. Still, we're dealing with something strange here, so possible subtle or indirect tidal effects should probably be explored."

Isaacs fixed his gaze on the tired young woman in front of him. "I think you're right; you're onto something peculiar," he said slowly. "Why don't you go home and get a good night's sleep. Come in tomorrow and we'll go into your evidence in detail."

Danielson smiled abashedly, acknowledging her fatigue

once more. "Fine. I'll see you tomorrow morning." She rose and let herself out the door.

Isaacs leaned back and clasped his hands behind his head, staring at the ceiling. He quickly decided he needed more information. A detailed discussion with Danielson tomorrow might show some flaw in the analysis. That was unlikely, however, despite the strange nature of the situation, considering the careful work Danielson usually produced and the sophisticated computer analysis groups on which she relied. But more information or no, this problem required expert consultation to begin even to categorize it.

He leaned forward and punched the intercom. "Kathleen?" When she responded, he said, "Get in touch with Martinelli. I want a one kilometer resolution photomontage of everything within ten degrees of thirty-three degrees north and south latitude and a first order scan for anything out of the ordinary. I don't know specifically what to look for."

Isaacs then leaned back and contemplated the situation. After some time he realized that he was imagining an extraterrestrial civilization beaming a mysterious ray at earth from some point in space. He shook his head ruefully as he put Danielson's problem out of his mind and retrieved the Tyuratam summaries from his desk drawer.

Chapter 5

Hot, late afternoon air rustled through the kibbutz. Duma Zadoc cautiously flipped a switch and smiled as the old water pump started up with a functional din, rewarding her afternoon's efforts. She wiped a forearm across her forehead, replacing sweat with grease, and kneeled to her final task. Methodically, she began to cinch down the bolts of the pump housing, a diametric pair at a time to ensure even pressure. She cringed as the first of the fourth pair turned too easily and the head of the bolt sheared off. With an uncharacteristic show of disgust, she threw the wrench down. The bolt head popped loose from the jaws of the wrench and rolled crazily across the floor. Duma stood up with hands on hips and watched with dismay as droplets of water began to seep from the seal near the broken bolt. As she tried to decide whether to attack the lodged remains of the bolt this afternoon or wait until tomorrow, a strange noise suddenly rose above the sound of the clattering pump. It came from the nearby orange grove, a mixed roar and hiss.

Terrorists! thought Duma and the image of her mangled infant flashed before her eyes. Thirty-five years as a sun-toughened sabra gave her the instincts to react coolly and quickly, quelling any hint of desperation. She raced from the pump house for the alarm. She punched the button starting the klaxon's howl, then ran the forty meters to the attack shelter and stood at the door assisting the children and then older kibbutz members who streamed inside.

Despite the sound of the siren and the hubbub of voices, Duma kept an ear tuned to the original sound. She had realized that there was something unorthodox about it. Unlike an incoming mortar round, this noise had gotten quieter and there had been no deadly, thumping explosion.

She wandered away from the shelter toward the orange grove. She heard the noise again, faint but growing in volume. Although the sound sent a chill down her spine, something told her there was no immediate danger. She squinted up toward the direction indicated by her ears, but saw no sign of the source. She followed the indicated trajectory as the noise reached peak intensity and then vanished. At the same time she saw a puff of dust arise just beyond the barbed wire fence of the compound.

Duma crawled through the fence and paced back and forth in the area where the dust had kicked up. She half expected to find an unexploded shell casing. Instead, she saw absolutely nothing. Puzzled, she crossed the fence again. As she headed back into camp, she waved an "all clear" sign at a compatriot, and the klaxon faded away. She decided the broken bolt in the pump housing could wait for another day.

Two more weeks were absorbed in the intensive routine of monitoring developments at the Soviet launch site at Tyuratam. Isaacs spent rare moments with Danielson discussing the seismic project. There seemed to be no flaw in Danielson's analysis, but they could not contrive a reasonable explanation for her data. The photomontage of the suspect latitudes provided by Martinelli showed nothing of interest. The routine was interrupted by a phone call.

Isaacs hung up the telephone and glared at the opposite wall of his office. He clinched his teeth, rhythmically rippling the prominent muscles over his jaws. The call had been simple. Kevin McMasters' secretary requested that Isaacs report to the office of the Deputy Director immediately. The secretary's voice was briskly formal, as that of the second in a duel, announcing his man's choice of weapon. It suggested the black mood of the official who had given the order. Isaacs instantly recognized the root of the problem; indeed, he had expected the call. His bid to eliminate two more of McMasters' outmoded pet projects had succeeded. McMasters could not counter Isaacs' arguments, but he would find some way to strike back, his vindictive urge whetted by defensiveness over his role in the fate of the FireEye satellite and the orbital confrontation to which that had led. Isaacs had no clue to McMasters' target, something not immediately subject to objective scrutiny, but he was certain that the ploy was about to begin.

He stood up and faced the window for a moment, hands clasped behind his back, unconsciously rocking up and down on the balls of his feet. Then he turned abruptly and walked briskly out of his office.

"I'm going to see McMasters," he announced to Kathleen.

She nodded, confirming her deduction.

Isaacs used the stairs to ascend two flights and then paced a long hallway and half of another before turning into the suite of offices commanded by the Deputy Director for Central Intelligence.

The secretary looked up at his arrival and arched an eyebrow.

"He'll see you in a moment—won't you have a seat?"

Without the protective anonymity of the telephone receiver, she seemed pleasant and proper, giving no hint of reflected animosity.

Isaacs replied, "Thank you," curtly, but remained standing, fidgeting tensely. For five minutes his irritation grew, but then he made a strong conscious effort to calm himself. Obviously, McMasters designed this childish trick, requiring him to cool his heels, to put him in a rash state of mind. He drew a deep breath and let it out slowly, glanced at the secretary and settled into a chair.

In the next ten minutes he catalogued most of the projects which commanded his direct attention. Tyuratam continued to be the central concern, particularly planning sessions to suggest strategies when the launch occurred. He glanced at the calendar on his watch, June 2, seven weeks since the first laser was destroyed and the Soviets had begun their crash program on the second. Launch was anticipated in two or three more weeks. Surely, there was no ground for attack there where everybody was pitching in on the common goal. They had not spent time on Mozambique and still remained uncertain about the origin of the arms cache. Could that be a weak point? Their lack of progress on some back burner problem? He attained a controlled state of mind, yet was unable to fathom where McMasters would elect to apply pressure.

The intercom on the secretary's desk buzzed, and he heard the low fidelity rattle of McMasters' voice though he could not make out the precise words.

"He'll see you now."

This time Isaacs caught a note of excitement, a school child announcing a fight on the playground. Despite the imminent confrontation, Isaacs found this droll. He maintained a serious face as he opened the door to McMasters' office, but just before he stepped through he looked back over his shoulder and gave the woman a broad wink. To his satisfaction, this incongruous act on the part of a respectable, if beleaguered, high official of the organization caught her by surprise. Her eyes widened and her mouth dropped open slightly. Isaacs closed the door behind him.

Several steps took him to McMasters' desk in the middle of the spacious room. The DDI sat erect, but with eyes focused on a folder on his desk. A hint of pot belly spoiled his medium build. At fifty-nine, short, wavy, salt-and-pepper hair covered his head, the waves shorn short on the side. His face was an elongated rectangle, with pale green eyes that receded into the surrounding folds, giving no access. His aquiline nose suggested the refinement evident in his comportment. He had a habit of holding his chin high so that he literally looked down his nose at people to whom he spoke.

Now he raised his gaze to Isaacs and spoke in a measured, cultured voice, "What—is—this—bull—shit?"

The epithet was delivered slowly, poisonously, reinforced by the contrast to his excessively proper demeanor.

"Sir?" Isaacs said, taken aback despite himself.

McMasters picked up the folder in front of him and gestured with it.

"With the fate of this nation and the free world at stake, you have deliberately chosen to squander the time of yourself and others and the resources of the Agency in an absurd wild-goose chase after earthquakes that follow the stars! We are not here to do astrology, Mr. Isaacs."

Isaacs caught a glimpse of the folder. It was labeled QUAKER, the code name for the strange periodic seismic signal. His mind whirled and locked like a magnetic computer tape searching for the appropriate data strip. He felt a certain relief. He was involved in a number of areas of immediate importance where McMasters' interference would have been disastrous. Apparently, those were safe for a moment. Yet McMasters had chosen shrewdly. Isaacs would be hard put to objectively defend his interest in the bizarre seismic signal which Pat Danielson continued to study when she could spare the time from Tyuratam. There was not the slightest hint that it represented a danger in any way. Nevertheless, his career-honed instinct warned him that to neglect the signal with its true nature still unknown would be foolhardy.

He started in a calm tone, "That signal is unprecedented, I . . ."

McMasters interrupted him coldly.

"We operate in an environment awash with information, some of it unprecedented and most of it trivial. If we are to maintain our precarious hold on freedom, we must be ruthless in our drive to focus on the crucial and ignore the rest. This is no time to idly follow pet fancies. The monitoring of seismic signals is not even this Agency's business. I must question your competence in choosing to mobilize the resources of the Agency to chase such a chimera."

The bald personal attack on his judgment stirred Isaacs' anger. Tension crept into his voice.

"Sir, we are in full agreement on our goals. We must select the important elements from a flood of information, but my record demonstrates that I am effective in doing just that."

He had stressed the "my" and McMasters' ears tinged with red at the riposte.

Isaacs extended a vigorous forefinger at the report on the desk and continued, "There is something profoundly disturbing about this seismic signal. Of course, there is a chance that it is insignificant, but I don't believe that is the case. I believe we must pursue this thing until we understand it."

"You *believe?*" McMasters spoke with anger and mockery. "On what basis? Is there a clear and present danger to the nation?"

"Not clear and present. You can't expect . . ." Isaacs began hotly.

"Is there any hint of the slightest bother to anyone, anywhere?" McMasters interrupted.

"Not yet, but . . ."

"Your concern for this trivial matter is foolhardy."

Isaacs suffered the second interruption and gritted his teeth.

McMasters continued, "You occupy a position of great authority and the Agency can ill-afford such lapses. I order you to desist totally in your pursuit of this matter. I will draft a memo summarizing your ill judgment. If there is any repeat performance, I will be forced to place that memo in your file and report your case to the Director."

Isaacs recognized this as part bluff. His record was good and McMasters could not impugn him recklessly to the Director without endangering his own position. Still, the Director's reliance on McMasters for advice on internal affairs was well-known. McMasters, in turn, used his favored position adroitly. Isaacs was aware that McMasters could influence the Director in a manner which could damage Isaacs professionally and, worse, could interfere with important Agency operations.

Isaacs gestured with his hands at hip level, tense fingers spread, palms facing each other, an aborted, instinctive reaction to his desire to clutch and shake the object of his frustration.

"For god's sake!" he shot. "You're taking me to task for doing my job the best I know how."

"Perhaps your best is not good enough," McMasters replied sharply.

Isaacs raised his arms and eyes toward the ceiling in dismay. Then he brandished a weapon-substitute finger at the older man.

"We both know the real reason for this confrontation," he said, louder than he intended. "The root of it is not my competence, but yours. You're irritated because I managed to scuttle some of your outdated programs."

"Don't raise your voice to me," McMasters responded with surprising volume. "My competence is not the issue here, whatsoever."

Outside in the anteroom, the secretary smiled slightly. To this point the conversation within had been entirely muffled. The latter outbursts did not carry clearly through the soundproofed door, but their tone was clear. The two distinguished gentlemen were, indeed, at each other's throats.

As if aware of this monitoring, McMasters lowered his voice, if not the level of his irritation. He continued, glaring at Isaacs.

"Your suggestion borders on insubordination. You are not improving your position."

Isaacs, on cue, lowered his tone.

"This discussion is ridiculous. We both want what is best for the Agency. You know I acted in good conscience when I argued against your programs. You are doing neither us nor the Agency a service by threatening to interfere with me in general and a potentially critical area in particular."

"I am threatening nothing," McMasters responded. "I am simply carrying out my assigned duty which is to see to it that the Agency functions in the most efficient possible manner. I am putting you on notice that your unilateral authorization of worthless projects and disrespect for this office will not be tolerated. I repeat you are to terminate the operation regarding this insubstantial seismic phenomenon."

Isaacs calculated quickly. He was in a no-win situation, with no chance of talking McMasters out of his vindictive position. He had little beyond his intuition to justify the effort he had authorized to understand the queer seismic waves. The expenses involved were small, but still a finite drain on Agency resources. He did not want the project to come up for a full-scale Agency review as McMasters could easily arrange. In such a case he would be forced to rank the seismic project below a goodly number of others. Even the Director, through no malice, was likely to suggest a "compromise" in an effort to quell disagreements among his subordinates. His best hope would be to lose only the seismic project and prevent McMasters from lopping off any other projects. He would be no better off than now, but the disagreement between himself and McMasters would have been aired widely, and that could only lead to other trouble. He had little practical choice but to accede to McMasters.

Isaacs stared down at the man before him.

"All right," he conceded, "both of us stand to lose if you insist on dragging our personal disagreements before the Director, but I won't risk Agency programs being gratuitously interrupted for the sake of exposing your machinations."

"You'll abandon your investigation of this seismic folly?"

"Yes."

"You understand that this is an order carrying the full authority of my office?"

"Yes, dammit!"

McMasters eyed him for a moment, then snapped, "You are dismissed."

Isaacs promptly whirled and strode out of the office. He resisted a temptation to slam the door behind him. The secretary half expected another wink. Instead he treated her to the sight of his back as he crossed her office and disappeared down the corridor.

In his office, Kevin McMasters wrote a brief note to his secretary, attached it to the file before him and dropped the file in his "out" box. His gaze lingered on it, and he smiled a small, self-satisfied smile.

That afternoon Pat Danielson was one of a handful of people to receive the following memo:

> Due to a reordering of priorities, active investigation connected with operation code name QUAKER will terminate effective immediately. Please act promptly to deliver to central inactive files all material relevant to Project QUAKER which is in your possession.

It was initialed by Isaacs.

Danielson reread the two sentences with confusion and disappointment. She still had no inkling of what caused the strange signal, but she was captivated by it and had spent long hours wrestling with it. Only yesterday she had spoken briefly with Isaacs about it. They had expressed their mutual frustration that no solution had been devised, but his interest showed no sign of flagging, and he had expressed satisfaction with her work. Stunned by the surprise terse note, she was now assailed with doubt. Was her enthusiasm for the project misplaced? The signal a trivial curiosity? Even worse, was it through an inadequacy on her part that progress toward understanding had come to a halt?

Without pausing to analyze the propriety of her actions, she logged off the computer, slammed her notebook shut and strode off toward Isaacs' office, the memo crumpled in her hand.

Kathleen looked up in mild surprise when Danielson appeared in her office and announced stiffly, "I'd like to see Mr. Isaacs."

"He's in the middle of a conference call. Do you want to wait until he finishes to see if he has the time? It may be fifteen or twenty minutes."

Danielson was taken aback by the roadblock.

"Oh, well, yes. Yes. I would like to wait," she finished in a strong voice. She looked around and sat briskly in one of the office chairs.

Kathleen recognized the wrinkled memo. After a moment, she nodded at it and spoke in a friendly tone.

"Is that the problem?"

Danielson looked at the slip of paper. She sat back in her chair and brandished the memo at Kathleen. "It was such a surprise. I'm a bit upset."

"Not my place to stick my nose in," Kathleen said, "but I can give you a little insight. That's nothing against you."

"I'd like to think so, but I've done the most work on it, spent every spare minute since I got back from Boston, and to have it canceled . . . I was afraid . . ."

Kathleen leaned on her forearms. "Do you know about the tiff between Mr. Isaacs and McMasters?"

"There's some scuttlebutt. I haven't paid much attention to it," Danielson smiled in self-deprecation. "I don't operate in that league."

"Who does?" Kathleen smiled in return. "But sometimes some of us get caught up in the battles." She turned serious. "For some reason McMasters has it in for Isaacs. Bob, Mr. Isaacs, is always having to tiptoe around him. It's too bad. Mr. Isaacs can be pretty ferocious when he's worked up, but he really is very sweet."

"I've enjoyed working with him," Danielson admitted. "He takes everything very seriously, but he's reasonable."

"Well, he won't toady to McMasters, and McMasters took a dislike to him early on. I don't know the details, but McMasters is behind the cancellation of that particular project. As I say, it's nothing personal against you, I'm sure."

"I'd like to believe that."

"Do you still want to see Mr. Isaacs?"

"Yes," Danielson said thoughtfully, "I think I still would."

"Well, you're welcome to make yourself at home, but I've got to finish this briefing paper."

"Oh, please go ahead."

Kathleen turned back to her keyboard. Danielson watched her fingers rap the keys and then began to think about Project QUAKER. The project fascinated and haunted her. She also wanted very much to please Isaacs with her performance. How frustrating to do your best, she thought, try to gain some appreciation and be thwarted by something beyond your control, in this case interference by McMasters, some high muckety-muck I haven't even met.

She recognized the cord of tension, strong and familiar, the ambition to go her own way played against the need to satisfy another authority figure, no stranger at all. She slipped into a reverie, her thoughts drifting to her childhood, dim memories of the tragic, premature death of her mother in an auto collision with a drunk. Her father, a chief petty officer in the Navy, giving up the sea he loved to take a desk job, trying to be both father and mother, while she tried to be wife and daughter.

She had worked hard to do well in school, at first to protect him from further disappointment, but then more to satisfy her own drives. She had been only dimly aware of the degree to which he lived his life through her, of her irrational guilt that his situation was somehow her fault, of her own repressed resentment that she had to be strong for him, that she could never, for even a brief moment, set all her burdens on his broad shoulders. In hindsight, she saw how the seeds had been slowly planted for the bitter row that still tainted their relationship years later, despite their love for one another.

She was finishing high school and planning to join the Navy as he wished, but she aimed for, insisted on, sea duty. He wanted her to follow his path, but was too tradition-bound to countenance women on shipboard, particularly his own kin. Years of repressed feelings erupted. He called her headstrong and ungrateful for his years of sacrifice. "It's not my fault that your wife died," she shouted in return, and suffered immediate remorse.

In the aftermath of their fight, she had spurned the Navy and gone to UCLA to study engineering. Now she found the work for the Agency stimulating and enjoyed the notion that she played an important, if small, role in the strategic balance of power in the world. Still, during those low points like the present, she could sense her father looking over her shoulder.

Her head snapped up as Isaacs' voice came over the intercom.

"Yes, sir," replied Kathleen, glancing at Danielson. "Do you have time to see Dr. Danielson? She's waiting here."

Isaacs appeared quickly in the doorway.

"Pat, please come in." He held the door for her and gestured her to a chair. "I'm sorry that was so impersonal," he pointed his chin at the note still wadded in her hand. "I was too busy to get around, and it did have to be in writing anyway."

"I didn't mind that," she lied a little, "but I was shocked."

"It was sudden, a decision from upstairs." Isaacs looked at the young woman, wondering how much of the real problem he should reveal to her.

Danielson searched for words that would not seem too bald an appeal for approval.

"I couldn't help wondering, if I had made more progress, if I had isolated the source of the signal, would that have kept the project alive?"

Isaacs spoke thoughtfully.

"Perhaps. Unfortunately, we can't answer that, since we didn't find the source." He noted the look of discomfort that passed over her face and hastened to add reassurance. "Please don't feel responsible for this. You did some very good work to get as far as you did. You can't blame yourself for getting bogged down. It turned out to be a problem with no simple resolution, and you had lots of other things to do the last two or three weeks."

He disliked the tone of those words. By weaseling around the real issue, he made it sound as if she might shoulder some blame for not working quite hard enough or being quite bright enough. He sighed mentally. If this young woman had a future in the Agency, she might as well learn the ropes.

"Pat, let me level with you. Unless you had showed that this was a new Russian weapon aimed at the Oval Office, the project would have been killed. The decision really had nothing to do with the project itself. It was strictly politics."

Danielson was relieved to hear these words from Isaacs, but as her potential guilt feelings receded further she found anger in their place.

"But that's so unfair! I worked hard on that project. Why should it be canceled?"

"Maybe not fair, but logical in the scheme of how things really work around here."

"I don't understand."

"If you want to get things done, you have to fight for what you think is right." He pointed a finger at her. "Just as you're doing right now."

She met his gaze straight on. He continued.

"The fact that I use the word fight means that somebody

holds opposite views, and they're going to be fighting back. I push for what I think is right and get pushed back. You lose some skirmishes to win the battles. I'm sorry that this skirmish was particularly important to you personally."

Danielson glanced at the closed door to Kathleen's office.

"I guess I see."

Isaacs was quick on the uptake.

"Kathleen told you about me and McMasters," he stated flatly, then laughed gently as Danielson looked surprised. "Kathleen knows everything that goes on around here. I would have been disappointed if she hadn't bent your ear a little out there.

"McMasters is old school, losing his touch and very defensive about it. I've had to challenge him on occasion and he doesn't like that. Frankly, I don't think he likes me. He may resent the fact that my grandfather wore a yarmulke. Who knows? The feeling is fairly mutual. In any case, let me give it to you straight out. He killed Project QUAKER out of spite because I killed some of his projects. Simple as that."

The fire was in her eyes again.

"I don't think that's so simple. I think it's wrong."

"Wrong. Yes, I think it was wrong, too, but you're not looking at the bigger picture. If I let McMasters get his way here, I can get other more important things done more efficiently."

"But I don't see how he can get away with this—this obstructionism."

"For one thing he's not a total loss. He's effective at keeping up the day to day affairs of the Agency, as long as tricky strategic questions aren't involved. If nothing else, he keeps the Director from meddling in the details so we can get our job done. We all have our strengths and weaknesses."

"But how can you write QUAKER off as unimportant. Doesn't it worry you that we don't know what that signal is?"

"You misunderstand me. I am worried about that signal. I'm sorry as hell McMasters canceled it. But we don't really have any proof that it's important. That's why he picked it.

And there are other projects of proven merit that can proceed without his interference."

Danielson sat, looking angry and unconvinced.

Isaacs wondered how much of her reaction was righteous indignation and how much resentment at not being allowed her own way on the project. Did she betray some inflexibility in the face of interference? She would have to learn to get along if she wanted to move up.

"How did you come to work for the Agency?" he asked.

The change in topic and tone caught her off guard.

"I beg your pardon?"

Isaacs folded his hands and leaned on his forearms. "I was thinking about your future in the Agency. That got me to wondering what brought you this way in the first place."

Danielson gave him a long look, wondering what was on his mind. She did not reveal her inner thoughts often, but as her boss, maybe Isaacs had a right to be curious about her underlying motivation. He did seem sympathetic. She was in a mood to talk and succumbed to that.

"It's funny you should ask." She relaxed back in her chair and looked at her hands then up at Isaacs. "I was thinking about that while I was waiting.

"Like anyone, I suppose I had a mixture of emotional and logical reasons. I had a desire to serve my country. My senior year I interviewed a bunch of Orange County firms, and the Agency, mostly out of curiosity. They ended up offering me a stipend to go to graduate school and a job when I got my degree. That appealed to me." She laughed briefly. "If some of my fellow graduate students at Stanford had known I was funded by the Agency, they would have gone wild."

"Hot bed of radicals, eh?"

"Well, you know, that's the time of life for feeling that way. I guess I was raised differently."

Isaacs leaned back in his chair. "It's been a long time since I looked at your file. You were raised by your father, if I remember correctly."

"Since I was five. My father has been a big influence on me, for better or worse. He was Navy. I suppose the Agency is my way of carrying the flag."

"Nothing wrong with that. We're all here for that reason in one form or another." He regarded Danielson for a long moment.

"Do you plan to make a career in the Agency?"

"I haven't any thought of quitting."

"Not the same thing. Right now you're down in the trenches, working hard, trying to please everyone."

Danielson wondered if he had been reading her mind as she had daydreamed in the outer office.

"You have three choices," Isaacs continued. "You can continue doing what you are doing. You can move up. Or you can do something else. You ought to think about it. The Agency would love to have you right where you are, hard working, productive, underpaid, forever. If you want to get out of that slot you need to set your sights.

"I've been watching you. Your work on Tyuratam has been first rate. You didn't crack QUAKER, but your insight about the trajectory would have escaped a lot of people. That showed a rare gift for breaking out of established channels of thought. You have the talents necessary to get ahead. I'd like to see you do it. But it's a big challenge."

"I'm not sure what to say. I appreciate your support. I do have some vague ambitions," she laughed quietly. "But I haven't been actively coveting your job."

Isaacs smiled with her and thought about the special toughness of mind needed to get ahead in the Agency. He wondered whether any woman could make it in this male bastion. Pat Danielson had some of the necessary qualities. A patriotic upbringing and a workaholic nature got her through graduate school, brought her here, and kept her here. Did being an only child of a single parent give her that extra edge, or portend a problem as yet unseen?

This time it was as if Danielson read Isaacs' mind.

"I know I have a built-in handicap," she said. "I don't see a lot of women in charge around here."

Isaacs nodded thoughtfully.

"No woman has ever risen to the level of a Deputy Director. You couldn't hope to in less than a decade even if you were the President's daughter-in-law. But if, as a woman, you have any desire to aim at that level, you'll have to be particularly resourceful at setting your goals and working toward them."

He leaned up on his forearms again.

"You wouldn't be crazy to decide there are better things to do with your life."

"Better things," she mused. "I haven't found anything better."

Isaacs picked up a pencil and fiddled with it. He looked up at her. "Nor anyone?"

Danielson understood his line of thought and found it irritating, despite her original willingness to get a little personal.

"If you don't mind my saying so, that's a bit chauvinistic. Are you worried someone will turn my head, and I'll run off to the suburbs to make babies?"

"I'm sorry. It does sound that way. But even if I denied my culpability there are people in the Agency who will raise that kind of argument. Fact is, they'll hit you both ways. If you don't get married, they'll suggest there's something wrong there."

"So I need to snap up a quick husband and continue to labor in the trenches until the powers that be, present company excepted, stamp me with the seal of approval." Her irritation waned to be replaced by bemusement. "Somehow, even with all the emphasis on security, it never occurred to me that the Agency would have any interest in my love life. They don't check up, do they?"

"No," Isaacs laughed. "Not without special cause. They turn up a few tidbits of everybody's past during the security check. Yours couldn't have been too sordid; you're here."

Danielson wondered if Allan was in the file. Allan with the blond hair, golden tan, easy smile. Peter Pan with surfboard. He was probably still on the beach.

Isaacs detected her pensive look and switched gears.

"I've managed to get off the point. I just wanted you to know that I think you have a future with the Agency, if you want to work for it. One thing you'll have to learn is that hard work alone isn't all there is. You will always have to do a little getting along by going along. The art is to make the most judicious choice of what to give and what to get. I had to make a hard choice with QUAKER. I hope we'll find that I chose correctly."

Danielson looked at him seriously. "I appreciate your taking the time to talk with me like this. I'll try to give some thought to exactly where I'm heading."

"If I can give you any more bad advice," Isaacs smiled, "give me a call."

Danielson smiled good-bye and let herself out. Despite other pressing duties, she spent the remainder of the day glumly divesting herself of any involvement with Project QUAKER. She gathered up a number of files and voluminous personal notes. The better part of an hour was required to transfer several analytical computer programs and extensive sets of data onto master storage tapes and to delete all active files from the computer memory. Despite Isaacs' attempt at explanation, she drove home that evening thinking that she knew what a miscarriage would feel like.

That same evening Isaacs sat in his living room looking at, but not perceiving, the early evening television news. He loosely supported a half-consumed drink on the arm of the sofa where beaded moisture slowly soaked into the velveteen. The coaster on the side table went unused. The cook made final preparations for dinner and from upstairs the bass from his daughter's stereo carried subliminally. The townhouse perched over a two-car garage off a steeply sloping

Georgetown street. Inside it was furnished in a refined, tasteful way. In his wry moods Isaacs estimated he could afford between a quarter and a third of it. The person responsible for the lion's share came bustling in, discarding her purse and jacket. His wife, Muriel, was a dark-haired, slender woman, attractive, although a bit long in the face. She had some money of her own and, more important, a successful, politically oriented law practice.

She came in alternately damning a recalcitrant senatorial aide with whom she was forced to have dealings and crowing over the successful completion of another case in which an out-of-court settlement had saved their client the embarrassment of a court appearance. She elaborated on these developments in a keyed-up, stream-of-consciousness flow as she mixed herself a drink at the bar and sat alongside her husband. As she chatted, Isaacs half-listened, nodding and responding with appropriate monosyllables on occasion. Muriel realized he was down and covered for him for awhile, but finally inquired.

"You're quiet tonight. How was your day?"

Isaacs smiled tiredly at his wife, then looked down at his drink. He sat up and tried belatedly to brush some of the collected moisture off the sofa arm.

He smiled again, more genuinely, at his gloomy forgetfulness.

"I shouldn't let him get under my skin. McMasters outflanked me this afternoon. A petty move on his part, but I had to put aside a potentially significant project which is only in the early stages. One of my young people was pretty disappointed. She'd put a lot of good work into it."

"Can't you go over his head?"

"No, it's not that kind of thing. He put me on the spot before enough evidence was in to make a rigorous case. That's one thing that bothers me, though. Now we won't know. If it is serious, it'll catch us by surprise later."

"I don't suppose you can continue surreptitiously?"

Isaacs chuckled.

"You've got too many clients who spend their lives going back on campaign promises. No. It would be hard to do and hell to pay if I got caught. He gave me an order as a senior officer. Even if it's stupid, I'd be putting my job on the line and jeopardizing a lot of programs of proven importance. The Director would rule against me unless I had an overwhelming motivation for my insubordination."

Muriel grinned and raised her glass in a mock toast. "So you're going to eat it?"

He returned the gesture.

"I can assure you I've already done so in my most humble and cooperative way."

Chapter 6

The USS Seamount, out of Pearl Harbor, sailed steadily toward the Bering Sea carrying a cargo of sixteen nuclear-tipped missiles. Her blunt hull cut cleanly through the water at four hundred fathoms, maintaining a steady twenty-five knots.

Lt. J. G. Augustus Washington sat at the controls of the sophisticated computerized sonar, his consciousness merged with the surrounding sea, as it would be eight hours a day for the next three months. Half his mind tuned to the sounds coming through his headset and to the green glow of the twin display screens in front of him. He automatically registered the turning of the screw on a distant Japanese tanker bound for Valdez, a school of whales somewhere to the west, and the anonymous squeals, rattles and clicks which characterize the undersea world. The other part of his mind wandered to his recently ended shore leave, to his wife. His quarterly sessions at sea were rough and lonely for a young woman married only a couple of years, but if she couldn't be home in Little Rock, Hawaii was not bad duty for her. At least blacks were not the bottom of the heap. There were always the native Hawaiians. And their reunions—oooeee! Almost worth three months of nothing doing. He swore it would be another two weeks before he would even begin to think about sex, then recognized that he had already succumbed and laughed softly to himself.

He began to form an image of his woman standing on the bed in the moonlight, naked and spread-eagled over him when the angry boiling broke forth from the earphones. Tension seized his gut and left his heart pounding. He jerked upright in his seat, his eyes fixed on the brilliant dot on the right hand screen that passively recorded incoming signals. His gaze whipped to the left screen which registered the reflection of the active signals the submarine emitted and saw only the faintest reading.

"Holy Christ!"

His exclamation cut through the cabin, violating the hush of routine.

"What have you got?" inquired the duty officer, moving to his side.

Washington's eyes remained fixed on the screens before him. He reached to flip on the external speaker and the bizarre hiss filled the cabin. He hit another switch and the right screen shifted to the target doppler indicator mode. Offscale! He twisted a knob.

"Somethin's comin' at us like a bat outa hell! Five thousand—shit! No!" He looked at the right screen again. "Coming on four thousand meters already—goddamn! I can't even get a reading on it. Closin' fast. From directly beneath us! And I can't even see it in active mode! Sucker must be *small!*"

"That's absurd," retorted the officer, "nothing moves that fast," but his ears heard the noise and his eyes read the screens; his shaken voice belied the conviction of his words. He stepped quickly to the ship's phone.

Washington began expertly to assimilate the flow of information from the panel before him. He switched the left screen for a brief moment to the target noise indicator display and mumbled to himself, "white noise, no sign of a screw frequency." He switched the screen to the target data and track history mode, fed from the computer memory. "Now at three thousand meters," he sang out. The noise from the speaker grew steadily. The knot in his stomach tightened with each fraction of a decibel. He reached to turn down the volume and spoke over his shoulder.

"It's not coming right at us. It should pass us about eleven hundred meters off the port bow."

The duty officer repeated the message to the captain.

They listened, unmoving, as the sound peaked and then diminished slightly with a perceptible change in pitch. Washington noted its passage through the ship's depth level, headed for the surface.

Abruptly the noise ceased, to be replaced with an almost painful silence as saturated ears tried to adjust. Active dials lapsed into quiescence and the bright blip on the screen disappeared. Washington swiveled in his chair to exchange wide-eyed looks of surprise with the duty officer who reported once more to the captain.

Washington returned his attention to his instruments. Ten, fifteen seconds went by. Slowly he turned up the sensitivity of the device and the volume on the speaker and earphones. Only the routine sounds of the sea issued. After twenty-five seconds the duty officer still stood with the phone clamped in a sweaty hand, but others in the cabin began to shuffle in relief. Washington increased the gain a bit more and concentrated his trained ear to detect any hint of abnormal sound. He systematically switched display modes but found no clue to the thing that had just assaulted them.

With the suddenness and impact of a physical blow, the cabin filled with the sound again. Washington shrieked, ripped off his earphones and slapped a palm over each ear. He slipped off his chair and knelt in a daze of confusion, his body pumped with adrenalin, his ears ringing with an intense hollow echo. Several figures rushed to the sonar console. Two friends bent to Washington. Someone fumbled, then found, the volume control. The frightening hiss dropped to a muted roar and the duty officer was left in the new quiet, shouting hoarsely into the phone.

The noise dropped gradually, and then just before it faded below a perceptible level it ceased abruptly once more. Silence fell in the cabin, broken only by the chatter of the sonar and the quiet moan of the man who remained on the floor, rocking gently, his hands over his ears and his eyes squeezed shut.

Several days after the cancellation of Project QUAKER, Isaacs played a closely fought game of handball with a friend and colleague, Captain Avery Rutherford, one of the senior officers in Naval Intelligence. Rutherford was three years older than Isaacs, but in excellent shape. They split the first four games and went to a tie breaker on the match game. Isaacs scored once and served at game point. After several volleys, Isaacs took a shot in front court. Calculating to catch his opponent off guard, he hit the ball softly to the front wall, but it went a bit too high and gave Rutherford time to cover it. With Isaacs in the front court, Rutherford played a favorite shot which came off the front wall as a lob calculated to land in the rear corner, a troublesome left hand return at best. He then retreated rapidly to center court just behind the service area to await the return, hoping to hear the satisfying silence of a missed shot.

Isaacs knew the other man's tactics, however, and backpedaled furiously to cover most of the distance to the left rear corner before the ball left the front wall. This gave him time to plant his feet firmly, eye locked on the descending sphere. The ball bounced on the floor, then off the back wall, nicely clearing both it and the side wall. Isaacs made the shot at hip level, putting into it everything his weaker left hand could muster. The ball rifled cross court, just missing Rutherford's left knee. It struck almost dead in the corner, the front wall a fraction of a second earlier than the right, two inches above the floor. It skittered once and then meekly rolled across the court to bump gently into Rutherford's toe.

The sudden denouement caught Rutherford by surprise and he just stared at the ball. Then he scooped it up and turned.

"Damnation, Bob, that was a hell of a shot!"

"Thanks," Isaacs grinned. "Amazingly enough, that's just what I wanted it to do."

They played two more games for exercise, but without quite the fire. Isaacs took the first by a comfortable margin, Rutherford the last.

After the game, they left sweat-sogged piles of gym clothes in front of their lockers, grabbed their towels and stepped into the steam room. They sat on the bench and rehashed their play, each enthusiastically recalling the other's good points and mixing in an occasional soft-pedaled critique.

They fell silent for a couple of minutes. Then Rutherford swiveled his head and looked at his companion.

"Do you mind a little shop talk, off the cuff?"

Isaacs leaned back against the wall, his eyes closed.

"Of course not, what's on your mind?"

"Well, we've had scattered reports of a strange acoustic phenomenon, sort of an underwater sonic boom. This thing's been kicking around. Nobody's done anything about it because no one knows what to make of it. I just wondered whether it might ring a bell with you?"

"No," said Isaacs lethargically, "I haven't heard anything

about it. We've been up to our ears counting screws and bolts in Tyuratam, waiting for them to launch the other shoe. Some kind of explosion?"

"No," Rutherford shook his head and pinched some sweat out of his eyes, "it's not localized like that. Something seems to be moving through the water, making a hell of a racket as it goes. It comes from the ocean bottom and apparently disappears momentarily at the surface. Then, it reappears and proceeds back down to the bottom."

"Some kind of missile, torpedo?"

"Seems like it, doesn't it? But there's no indication of any launching craft. Besides this starts from really deep down, miles."

"How about an underwater volcano, maybe spewing out blobs of lava, or rocks?"

"There's probably too much drag in the water for that to be possible, but I'd give some credence if the reports were from one spot. They're not, though. They're from all over the globe. Several from mid-Atlantic shipping lanes, a few near Japan, a couple from the Sixth Fleet in the Med, one south of Madagascar, another in the Sea of Tasman between Australia and New Zealand. The latest one came from a sub north of Hawaii, that's why it's on my mind. A particularly close call, poor bastards thought they were being attacked. Anyway, the thing seems to hop all over."

The men fell silent. Rutherford leaned over to examine a chipped nail on his big toe. Isaacs had not really been concentrating on the conversation. Now snippets of it rolled around in his head. Suddenly, a surge of adrenalin went keening out of his belly and through his body. His eyes snapped open and, despite the heat, he felt as if someone had just raked a large icy comb down his back.

He sat up and faced Rutherford who still bent over his foot.

"Those reports you just described, they seem to be either

north or south of the equator, about equal distances." He tried to keep his voice casual.

"Oh yeah, I forgot to mention another curious feature. This thing appears at random times, but always near the same latitude, sometimes north, sometimes south."

"Thirty-three degrees."

Now Rutherford swiveled his head in surprise.

"Hey, friend, you've been holding out on me!"

Nervous energy drove Isaacs off the bench. "Nothing like it," he said intently, "just slow to make the connection." He paced the small room randomly, oblivious to his steamy surroundings, his mind racing. "Good lord, in the water, too! What the hell does that mean?"

Rutherford had witnessed his friend's bursts of intensity before and, failing to understand what had set him off, watched bemusedly as Isaacs moved about, his cock flipping drops of sweat and condensed steam at each sudden turn.

Isaacs stopped in front of him.

"Up to last week we were analyzing the seismic equivalent of your phenomenon. Something's moving through the earth, generating seismic waves."

He sat suddenly next to Rutherford and continued.

"I had some of my people keeping an eye on it, even though we didn't know what to make of it."

Then he was thinking out loud.

"The seismic data only told us what was happening in rock. I convinced myself that whatever it was was confined to the earth's crust, that the seismic waves were its essence. Now you tell me something about it continues into the water." He shook his head. "I don't like it. I don't like this at all.

"Listen, we've learned some things you apparently haven't stumbled onto yet. This thing is always there, and very methodical. It just goes back and forth, back and forth, always on the same path through the earth." He waved his arms. "And then out into the ocean! Shit! No reason to think it doesn't continue into the atmosphere! No telling how far it goes."

He leaned back against the wall. "Our problem is that McMasters scuttled our operation, claimed it wasn't Agency business." He paused for a moment. "Damn, it's hot in here! Let's go someplace where we can do a little serious talking. Better make it your office, since the subject is officially 'verboten' on my turf."

As Rutherford steered his staff car through the prerush hour traffic, Isaacs explained animatedly how his interest in the seismic signal became aroused during his duty at AFTAC. He then outlined the progress Danielson had made, culminating in her conclusion that the phenomenon followed a trajectory fixed in space. They finished the drive in silence while Rutherford ruminated on this new information.

A half hour later they entered Rutherford's office. Rutherford ordered up the Navy file on the acoustic phenomenon. He sat behind his desk while Isaacs remained standing, rocking nervously on the balls of his feet. Rutherford spoke first.

"Boy, I'm really having trouble absorbing this. I had a notion of a random, infrequent occurrence, and now you describe something punching through the surface like clockwork, every eighty minutes or so. I guess I still don't get the picture. Tell me again how this fixed motion works."

"Let me use this globe," Isaacs said as he lifted a fancy relief model of the earth off its shelf and put it on Rutherford's desk. He grabbed a pencil and held it pointed toward the surface of the globe, about a third of the way above the equator. "The thing always moves along a line, like this." He moved the pencil in and out, parallel to itself, "Zipzip, zipzip. But as the earth turns," he spun the globe slowly with his free hand, "the thing always comes up in a different place." He tapped the pencil rhythmically as he spun the globe, each tap hitting it an inch further on than the last.

"Let me see that," said Rutherford, reaching for the pencil. He held it alongside the globe so that he could project it in his imagination into the center of the globe. Then he moved it back and forth along its length as he spun the globe slowly, eraser to the northern hemisphere, then point to the southern, eraser to the north, point, south. "Okay, I think I get the picture, but what could possibly do that? Through the center of the earth? Jesus Christ!"

He jerked his head up as a knock sounded at the door.

"Come in."

An aide came in bearing a file folder.

"Bob, Lieutenant Szkada. Lieutenant, Bob Isaacs, Central Intelligence."

Isaacs nodded at him.

"Sir." The young man placed the folder on Rutherford's desk.

"That'll be all," Rutherford said to him with a note of paternalism.

"Yes, sir." The lieutenant turned and left.

"Sharp young man, that," Rutherford confided. "My right arm." He pulled the file toward him. "Let's see what we have here." He extracted a list of reported detections and handed it to Isaacs. Rutherford leafed through the corresponding write-ups, looking for ones that were not hopelessly sketchy.

As Isaacs scanned down the list of sonar reports, he let out a loud exclamation.

"I'll be damned!"

"What?"

"One of life's little ironies. Several of these reports are from the undersea arrays of acoustic monitors."

"Sure, we have those babies all over, bound to pick up something like this. So?"

"That system is also operated by AFTAC. The whole ball of wax was right under my nose, both seismic and sonar data. I'm kicking myself, I was so hung up on the seismic signal propagating through the earth. I had my people trying to put together a puzzle with half the pieces missing."

Isaacs threw the list on the desk and pulled a chair around beside Rutherford. They spent fifteen minutes checking the time and position on earth for each of the reports and converting that data into a projected position on the celestial sphere, to see what stars were overhead. As near as they could tell, it was always the same patch of stars. All the sonar events fell on the path predicted by the seismic data. Trying to estimate whether the influence was precisely at the phase which brought Danielson's seismic signal to the surface was more difficult, but the evidence they had seemed damning enough.

"So what did you say you are doing about all this?" Rutherford wanted to know.

"Not jackshit." Isaacs described his skirmish with McMasters.

When he finished, Rutherford inquired, "Can't you get McMasters to reopen the file, now that you have this confirmation from our data?"

"I doubt it." Isaacs frowned in concentration and rubbed his prominent nose. He got up and paced the room. Post handball thirst nagged at him. He wished he had a cold beer.

"You've told me something new. The source of energy driving the seismic waves somehow proceeds into the ocean. That banishes my lingering suspicion that we were dealing with an ordinary, if highly regular, seismic phenomenon. But we're no closer to understanding what's really happening. Without a more substantial change in the situation, McMasters would stand to lose face if he backs down. I've got to have something beyond the fact that this thing is amphibious before I can go back to him and convince him to reopen our investigation."

He crossed the room twice more, thinking.

"He's right that there's no obvious reason to consider this

Agency business. But dammit! It's got to be somebody's business."

Rutherford rubbed his chin. "Is this thing dangerous?"

Isaacs stopped pacing and faced the man seated at the desk. "Not clear, is it? Whatever it is, it makes a lot of noise that travels through rock and water. But noise alone doesn't make it dangerous." He resumed his pacing.

"The scary part is that *something* is moving through that rock and water, making the noise. We haven't the faintest idea what. That doesn't make it a threat, but it sure as hell makes me nervous!"

Rutherford leaned forward on his desk, watching Isaacs perform his epicycles. "Listen. Your seismic data were ideal to track this thing over large distances coherently and establish that it moves along a fixed direction. But with your hint of where and when to look, our sonar detections should give a higher precision. We could put a ship right on top of it and find out what we're actually up against."

Isaacs sprawled stiffly in a chair, as if he might leap out of it again at a moment's notice. "Actually, we could do something like that on land, too, if McMasters hadn't tied my hands," he responded. "You're right, though, you're in a position to proceed, and I'm not.

"There is a practical point," Isaacs continued. "As it stands now, you don't formally have enough information to move on your own. You need our knowledge that it behaves in a systematic way."

Rutherford nodded his assent.

"But I can't give it to you officially because of this roadblock McMasters has thrown up."

Isaacs smiled and leaned forward in his chair. "I think you're going to have to wake up in the middle of the night with a sudden insight. Your past brilliant record would presage such a breakthrough."

Rutherford gave an exaggerated "aw shucks" gesture. "Actually, it might be better if it didn't come directly from me. McMasters knows we're friends, and he might fit things together and give you a hard time for leaking information. I think I can handle it so that one of my associates has the inspiration."

The two men grinned at one another and then lapsed into a contemplative silence. After several minutes, Rutherford stirred and walked over to a window and looked out.

He turned and asked, "What in hell are we getting into here, Bob?"

Isaacs returned his look, unspeaking.

Rutherford continued, "I keep coming back to the fact that this thing is locked to a fixed direction in space. That must be a crucial hint. And the fact that it moves easily through solid earth and miles of water. What does that mean?" He turned to the window again, anxious to express disturbing thoughts, but subconsciously unable to face his friend at the same time.

"You know the image I get? A beam. A beam of some kind, focused into the earth and playing back and forth."

He turned suddenly, angry at a situation that departed so profoundly from his experience, forcing him to strange, uncomfortable extrapolations.

"Damn it, Bob, you know I'm a hard-nosed, practical man. But don't we have to face up to the idea that something is out there? Doing this to the earth?"

Isaacs ground his right fist into his left palm. "I confess, Av, when I first heard about the selective orientation in space, I found myself toying with such a notion. I put it out of my mind as idle fantasy. Now I don't know. I do know the more I learn about this thing, the more scared I am."

Avery Rutherford stood next to the captain of the USS Stinson and gazed out across the ocean as it reflected the early morning sun. Rutherford delighted at being able to spend these long days of mid-June where he loved to be the most. His job was challenging and important, but it kept him behind a desk far too much. He had grown up in boats of all sizes in the waters off Newport and the only time he felt fully alive was at sea. A hectic week had been required to feed Isaacs' hint to his aide, Szkada, then to work up a plan and arrange for the ship, but it was worth it. Rutherford felt great!

The captain barked commands as they closed on the chosen position. Finally, the trim craft lay dead in the water, and they waited and watched and listened. The ship, a Spruance class destroyer, was designed for intelligence work and bristled with sophisticated tracking and detection devices. At last, word came up from the sonar room that their target had appeared, moving incredibly rapidly, headed for the surface in a scant thirty seconds. Rutherford gritted his teeth and trained his field glasses on the water a thousand yards away where they had calculated the influence would reach the surface.

The sonar data were automatically fed into the ship's computers to plot the trajectory. He listened to the tense messages on the intercom from the sonar room, the voice clipped, rapid, hurrying to keep up with something moving too fast. The new prediction showed the point of surfacing to be several hundred yards further from the ship than originally estimated, but still very close. Ten seconds. Rutherford felt a knot of tension as beads of sweat grew on his forehead. He tried to keep his mind neutral, but an image kept intruding, that of a ray guided by an unseen hand. He could sense that ray arcing through space like nighttime tracer bullets, then cutting a swath through the earth.

Over the intercom came the tinny squawk as the sonar operator counted down the time to contact with the surface:

"Five."

"Four."

"Three."

"Two."

"One."

Rutherford held the binoculars tightly to his face, the magnified image of the water welded in his brain. He braced himself for the shock, either physical or mental.

"Zero."

Nothing.

Absolutely nothing happened except for a small splash at the margin of his field of vision. Then he blinked and even that was gone. Faintly over the water a strange hissing carried, but that, too, quickly faded.

Rutherford and the captain exchanged amazed looks.

The captain punched a button on a console.

"What have you got?"

"Nothing, Captain, it's gone," came the negative reply.

He turned to Rutherford.

"If it's like the Seamount event, sonar should pick up something going down after some delay."

Rutherford nodded.

The sonar man had been alerted not to increase the gain on his instrument in the interlude.

Again came the faint hiss. Rutherford raised his glasses too late to see a second rise of spray some distance from the first splash.

"Whup! There it is!" came the report of reacquisition from the sonar room. They listened as the relayed reports followed the acoustic noise to the sea bottom far below.

Rutherford spent the next two hours in the computer room overseeing the analysis of the tapes of the sonar signal. His examination of the previous underwater events suggested to him that the phenomenon did not move along precisely the same line. This data supported that view. There was a certain erratic behavior superposed on the basic fixed direction of motion. They would never be able to tell exactly where and when the surfacing would occur. He thought to himself, so your aim's not perfect, you bastards, and took some satisfaction in that.

The estimate of the next nearest surfacing was refined on the computer and Rutherford reported that to the captain. After some discussion they agreed that for all the furor underwater, whatever it was seemed to lose potency at the surface. They agreed to get as close as possible to the next event. The destroyer headed for a spot about a hundred and ninety miles west which, in a little more than twenty-four hours, would fall along the right path at the proper phase so that the phenomenon should approach the surface.

They arrived in late afternoon and spent the remainder of the daylight hours cruising the area obtaining comparison data on the sonar background and checking for anything which could represent a precursor to the expected event. There was none.

Rutherford turned in early. He spent a restless night and dropped into sound sleep only shortly before daybreak when a young crewman awakened him.

Two thousand miles west of where the Stinson made slow circles in the mid-Atlantic, Robert Isaacs roused from a troubled sleep, carrying his dreams with him. He was watching the tops of the heads of figures as they roamed the flat terrain of satellite photos. One figure tried to turn its face upward to be recognized. Isaacs could feel the strain of its effort, the head swiveling backward, the forehead tilting upward, upward, upward, but never enough to reveal the face.

Then, there—Not a Russian! Rutherford!

Isaacs jerked awake, staring at the ceiling, his pulse racing. His twitch disturbed Muriel. She snuggled over to him, cupped a bicep in her hand, and pushed her nose into his shoulder.

"You all right, honey?"

"Uumph. Just a dream." He turned toward her and threw a comforting arm over her hips. Soon she was breathing deeply again. He lay awake, slowly relaxing back toward sleep. Rutherford. . . Ship. . . Water. . . Sonar. . .

The Novorossiisk!

This time he sat bolt upright. No dream. Dear god! How could he be so dense? The Novorossiisk was so long ago, succeeded in his attention by the attack on FireEye, the shuttle mission, the feverish developments at Tyuratam. But this had to be it! The Novorossiisk had been in the Med, near thirty-three degrees latitude. The Seamount had reported something going up and something going down. Rutherford had radioed the same behavior yesterday. The Novorossiisk had reported something going down. Why not up? Lost in the shuffle? Who knows? Must check that out. Was the Novorossiisk in the right place? Check that out. Oh goddamn, Rutherford said he was going to sit right on it!

He rolled out of bed.

"Bob?"

"I think Av Rutherford is in danger. I've got to make some calls."

"Do you want me to get up?"

"No, that's crazy; you've got to be fresh in court at nine."

He pulled on some sweatpants in lieu of a robe and fumbled out the door to the stairs. In the kitchen he blinked in the glare as he tripped the light. He punched the familiar number into the phone, missed the next to last digit in his bleariness, swore, and punched it again. He requested the night radio operator to call him on a secure line. As he awaited the call, he grabbed a note pad and tried to figure out if the Novorossiisk had been right on Danielson's magic trajectory. He was still too befogged and the numbers too cumbersome. But it was plausible. Too plausible! This thing they chased not only moved through the earth and oceans, it punched holes in ships!

As he stared at his scribbled notes on the pad, he slowly became aware of the smell of fresh coffee permeating his nostrils. He looked up to see Muriel fetching cups and saucers out of the cabinet. She caught his mixed look of guilt and irritation that she should be up tending to him and headed him off.

"I can use an early start, too. I need to polish my strategy."

Her husband still looked disgruntled.

"Besides," she continued, "if I beat my minions in to work on a Monday morning it will fire them with such defensive zeal that we'll just blow the opposition out of court."

Isaacs smiled wanly at this image and rose to hug her from behind.

"All right, counselor, you win. Let's have some coffee."

He broke off his embrace suddenly at the sound of the telephone, whirling to grab it in mid ring. He sat and hunched over the receiver as if to make it part of him.

"Hello? Yes?" He repeated a sequence of code numbers. "Right. I want you to patch a call through the Navy. Top Priority. For Captain Avery Rutherford on the Destroyer USS Stinson. It's on patrol in the Atlantic. Yes, I *know* what time it is. What's a satellite link for? It's two hours later on that ship. Yes, I understand, but this is extremely urgent." He glanced at his watch. 4:38. Nine minutes until contact. "Yes, I know you will. Yes, immediately please. Thank you."

He hung up the phone.

"Problem?"

"Not in principle, it's just that our vaunted instantaneous satellite communication net is designed to function from various war rooms, not from cozy Georgetown kitchens."

He lapsed into tense silence, glancing at the coffee pot, his watch, the phone. Time dragged slowly. After an excruciating interval, the coffee maker stopped gurgling, sighed its readiness. He looked at his watch for the tenth time. 4:40. Seven minutes. How long would it take to move the ship if they did get through? Several minutes? When would it be too late? He did not look up when Muriel put the coffee in front of him. He took a few sips and then watched it steam away its heat, its life force. 4:44. Three minutes, probably too late, anyway. He felt ill.

The phone rang. He jerked the receiver to his ear.

"Mr. Isaacs?"

"Yes!"

"I've got the Stinson. They're looking for Captain Rutherford. Will you hold on?"

"Yes, of course. He'll be on the bridge."

Isaacs could hear the operator relay this message to the radio man on the Stinson. Then he spoke to Isaacs again.

"Bit of a crunch there, sir. They seem to be in the middle of an operation."

"Yes, I know."

There was a long pause.

"Sir?" The voice sounded worried.

"What is it?"

"There seemed to be some kind of ruckus there, and then I lost contact."

"You what?"

"I'm sorry, sir. I lost contact with the Stinson."

Isaacs remained silent a long moment.

"Sir?"

"Okay. Try to get them back. Call me when you do."

"Yes, sir."

Isaacs hung the receiver on its wall cradle and then slowly lowered his head onto his hands. Seated next to him, Muriel reached a hand to his bare shoulder, her face drawn with concern.

The sea lay calm and the rising sun burned along the gentle swells.

The routine of the previous session repeated. Rutherford took a position on the bridge and stood checking the liquid crystal digits as they swapped on his watch. As the time counted down to scarce minutes, an orderly stepped onto the bridge.

"Captain Rutherford?"

Rutherford swiveled to face the young man.

"Yes? What is it?"

"Sir, you have a call on the radiophone."

"I can't take it now! Tell them if it's important to hold on for a few minutes."

The orderly sensed the tension and stepped back against the bulkhead to watch as Rutherford turned to scan the ocean. Within seconds of the predicted time, the sonar room reported.

"Here she comes!"

Allowing for the inaccuracies in the calculations, Rutherford had stationed the ship precisely at the point where surfacing was most probable. Those inaccuracies plus the intrinsic meandering of the position convinced him they would be very lucky to be within several hundred yards of the event. He hoped they would be able to see something to help clear up the mystery.

"Coming straight up! Right underneath us!"

Just so, ruminated Rutherford. At great depths, small lateral offsets in position were difficult to detect. On his watch, the minute digit shifted up by one. Ten seconds.

"Two thousand meters!" squawked the sonar room link. "Uh, Captain? It's still headed right for us!"

In a corner of his mind, a thought began to dawn on Rutherford. Maybe they had been too brash, forsaking a second distant observation. Our measurements aren't exact, he thought, the thing does wander a little erratically. How confident can I be that our best estimate is *wrong,* that it will surface nearby, but not *exactly* where I predicted? What if the small random motion just offsets our position errors and we are correct by blind luck? Even worse, what if many periods are required before the random motion causes an appreciable change in the position of surfacing? Suppose over the small time span since the last event there has been negligible change and my predictions are precisely correct?

He wanted to be nearby, but, with a sinking feeling he knew he did not want to be exactly on the point of surfacing.

The sonar room began the final countdown. There was no time to move the ship anyway.

"Five."

"Four."

"Three."

"Two."

"One."

"Ze—"

Chapter 7

A small hole appeared in the thick plate of the hull just to the port side of the keel. A disturbance winked through the fuel oil stored in the large ballast tank shaped to the hull. Brief instants later similar holes were created in the top of the fuel tank and then in the floor of the engine room. In the next moment a deep score ran across the shaft of one of the four large General Electric gas turbines. A crack sprang out from this defect augmented by the huge centrifugal force, and the multibladed shaft went careening like a rip saw toward the turbine casing as yet another hole penetrated the ceiling of the engine room. On went the succession of holes as if on a rising plumbline, through decks, furniture, equipment, until a last long gash ripped through the floor of the helicopter pad.

"—ro!"

The damaged turbine exploded, filling the engine compartment with high velocity titanium-blade shrapnel and burning fuel. Weakened by the small incident hole, the floor buckled under the disintegrated turbine. Flame leaped down along the vapors leading to the fuel tank. After the briefest hiatus, the fuel tank exploded. The force of this release was directed upward along the rising line of perforations. The penetrated structural members gave way, and a violent stream of shredded metal and superheated gas blew a cavity upward into the guts of the ship. The explosion also tore like a rocket into the surrounding water. In reaction, the destroyer listed rapidly and severely to starboard. As the ship pendulumed back to port, water rushed into the new gaping hole and splashed upward following the path of the blast into the ship. Great portions of the upper midship sections filled with water. The ship was rendered top-heavy. As it rebounded, its natural capacity to right itself was destroyed, and it carried on over. In the space of a minute the Stinson capsized, floating bottom up, the ragged hole in the hull aimed at the sun, narrowly above the horizon. A handful of men survived. Avery Rutherford was not among them.

That evening, still numb from loss, Isaacs stared at the draft of the memo he had carefully composed. He was reticent to commit himself to writing, but he could not just go bursting into McMasters' office and demand that Project QUAKER be reinstated. McMasters would never hear him out. Instead, he had put all the arguments he could muster into the memorandum. McMasters would not want to read anything from him, but he *would* read it, out of self-defense.

Memorandum
To: Kevin J. McMasters,
Deputy Director of Intelligence
From: Robert B. Isaacs,
Deputy Director for Scientific Intelligence

Subject: Connection between the loss of the USS Stinson, the Novorossiisk, and Project QUAKER

On June 14, the Navy Destroyer USS Stinson was lost at sea while on a mission indirectly related to our now inactive Project QUAKER. The circumstances bear marked resemblance to those involving the Soviet carrier Novorossiisk. In this memorandum, I set forth the case linking the USS Stinson, the Novorossiisk, and Project QUAKER and call for the immediate reactivation and vigorous prosecution of Project QUAKER.

Isaacs pictured McMasters resisting the urge to scrunch the memo into a ball and toss it in the can.

As you will recall, Project QUAKER produced evidence for a source of seismic waves which moved in a regular pattern through the earth. The trajectory of this motion is fixed in space independent of the rotation of the earth or its motion in orbit around the sun. The source of seismic waves always approaches the earth's surface at 32° 47' north longitude. Approximately forty and one-quarter minutes later it has passed through the earth and approaches the surface again at 32° 47' south longitude. It then returns to the northern hemisphere nearing the surface at a position about 1170 miles west of the previous location of surfacing, due to the rotation of the earth in the intervening eighty minutes and thirty seconds.

One day later, the source of the seismic signal will return to the surface about 190 miles west of the point where it surfaced at nearly the same time the previous day. The source of the seismic waves has approached the surface about 2000 times since it was first detected. Because of the incommensurate motion of the seismic source and the rotation of the earth, however, the probability of the source returning to the surface within even a few miles of any previous point of surfacing is very small. Despite the underlying regularity of the motion of the source of the seismic waves, the effects manifested at the surface will be perceived to be highly irregular.

Isaacs paused at this point. McMasters presumably knew the basic facts and he did not want to overdo here nor delay getting to the meat of his argument, but he felt compelled to summarize the issues to provide a context for the pitch to come. His mind whirled with details which he would have added for someone who *wanted* to really know what was going on, but he pictured McMasters' sneering scepticism and decided for the fifth time that this was the best he could do.

I have learned through informal sources

Ha! Let the bastard chew on that one, thought Isaacs. He'll discover that Rutherford was on the Stinson and dig like a dog to find some proof I violated his stricture. Well, let him dig! I don't confess to any active role for either me or the Agency, so he'll stew, but there's not much he can do. Except summarily reject the proposal. Damn!

that the Navy has sonar data which correlate with the motion of the seismic source. The source of the seismic noise apparently

Apparently. He pondered whether to leave that word to honestly portray the possibility, remote to his mind, that the strong circumstantial evidence had not been rigorously confirmed, that there was no case in which both seismic and sonar detectors picked up the signal of a single event to prove they were related. McMasters might seize on such a subtlety. Isaacs sighed and opted for honesty.

proceeds into the ocean. The source of the sonar signal goes to the surface, ceases for about forty seconds, then proceeds back to the ocean bottom. There is a strong presumption that the source of seismic and sonar waves is in the atmosphere for those forty seconds. The seismic and sonar waves generated by the source of energy propagate over great distances, contributing to their detectability. The lack of above-surface confirmation suggests that the effects there are very localized.

Now for the pitch, if he hasn't set fire to it by this time.

To conclude from the evidence that the phenomenon is innocuous at the surface would be a grievous error. The fates of the Novorossiisk and the Stinson show that this phenomenon is destructive and must be understood and eliminated.

The Stinson was on a mission to investigate the sonar signals which are the counterpart of the seismic signals tracked under Operation QUAKER. On June 13, the Stinson witnessed the rising and falling sonar signal from a thousand yards, with no appreciable surface effect. An associated hissing noise was reported. On June 14, it was stationed directly on the path of the rising sonar signal. The ship exploded, capsized and sank with the loss of all but 23 of her crew of 259. Fragmentary evidence from the survivors suggests that the fuel tanks exploded.

I believe the facts show that the Novorossiisk suffered a similar fate. The Novorossiisk was at 32° 47' when the incident occurred. Within the accuracy of our records, she was at a location that would have been in phase with the rising of the seismic/acoustic phenomenon. A hissing noise was reported on the Novorossiisk before the fires broke out. A sonar signal was reported afterwards.

The similarities between the Stinson and the Novorossiisk events and the relations to the signal of Operation QUAKER are too striking to be coincidence. There is every reason to believe that the phenomenon that made the holes in the Novorossiisk and triggered the fires on board had a similar, but unfortunately more destructive, effect on the Stinson. This phenomenon also generates the signals studied under Operation QUAKER.

The present facts are disturbing enough. Men have died,

equipment has been destroyed and we have drawn closer to war. Even more troubling is that the underlying phenomenon is completely without precedent, and its nature totally unknown. In our present state of ignorance we may have no inkling of the true magnitude of the problem that besets us.

We must take immediate action to discover the nature of this phenomenon. I strongly recommend two steps. One is the reinstatement of Project QUAKER and the enactment of similar projects in all relevant agencies of the government. The second is to communicate these findings to the Soviet Union to forestall the developments which have succeeded the Novorossiisk event. In this regard, I recommend a query to the Soviets regarding the detection of a rising sonar signal just prior to the Novorossiisk event. Confirmation of this prediction would help to convince the Soviets of the innocence of the United States in the Novorossiisk affair and tie together more firmly the disparate phenomena described here.

When he finished reading the draft, Isaacs stared at the last page, his eyes defocused, straining with his mind's eye to see where this attempt would lead. Despite himself, his mind filled with an image of Rutherford, those last seconds, desperately trapped in the submerged bridge. He shook his head and rose from his desk. Something fearful was at work here. McMasters had to free his hands to go after it. Kathleen was gone for the day. He unlocked a cabinet and placed the clipped sheaf of paper in the front of her work file.

In the parking lot he unlocked the door of the car and half-tossed his briefcase into the passenger seat. He sat behind the wheel a moment, feeling like driving, but with no particular place to go. Finally, he wheeled out of the lot to the rear exit from the grounds, past the guardhouse and down the long leafy lane. He turned right on Route 123, but the traffic heading into McLean was still fairly heavy, the driving unsatisfactory. He joined the throng on the beltway headed north. He took the first turn-off after crossing the Potomac and headed home, still frustrated and deeply troubled.

A week later, Isaacs stood with his back to the wall, away from the early Sunday crowds beginning to fill the Air and Space Museum. He came here sometimes for the pleasure of it, sometimes to think. This was a thinking time. His eyes caressed the old F-86 Sabrejet. It was his favorite craft in the whole place. The first grace of swept-back wings and tail. The captivating curve of the intake maw, surmounted by the subtle outward swell of the radar housing, a puckered lip to kiss the wind. With none of the venomous dihedral of today's fighters, the Sabrejet gave him the profound feeling of inner peace that came from witnessing perfect design.

He could not hold it. The peaceful feeling slipped, shattered and fell away from him. Rather than despoil his favored icon with secular thought, he wandered back toward the main rooms. Starting with the loss of Rutherford and the Stinson, the last week had been horrendous. Just like a roller coaster, Isaacs had known what was coming as the chain ratcheted him toward the top, but that did not keep his stomach from leaping as the dizzying fall began.

The Soviets had completed preparations at Tyuratam and launched their second laser flawlessly at midweek. The President immediately put the armed forces on full alert. Around the world, attack submarines encircled Soviet flotillas and Russian and American aircraft flew sorties eyeing one another on radar. A hundred hair triggers waited for the slightest pressure.

Drefke had returned from the NSC meeting nearly hysterical. Hysteria may have been the only sane response. Myriad alternatives sifted, the President had chosen the one he felt most appropriate. Specifically targeted to the task. Limited enough not to demand full-scale war if implemented. Stark enough to be impossible to ignore. The US spelled out its position in graphic detail to the Soviets at all diplomatic levels. If they used the laser, retaliation would be swift and sure, treaties to the contrary notwithstanding.

Isaacs stood looking up at the Mercury capsule. Is this where it began? he wondered. Or maybe with his Sabrejet out in the far wing. Or, over there, with the Wright brothers. Or with the goddamned wheel! He gritted his teeth in despair and frustration and wandered up the stairs toward the Saturn booster. The new plateau of crisis had made him easy pickings for McMasters. He reached in and felt the letter from McMasters folded in his jacket pocket. Coincidence. No proof. Crisis. No time. The fool! McMasters couldn't, wouldn't see the truth. Of course the Agency was in overdrive, with no resources to spare. But the root of the crisis was not in the White House, or even in the Kremlin. It hurtled through the earth, a sly unknown enemy that had us at each other's throats. If the world proceeded to nuclear holocaust would this thing care? Would it continue to sift through the seared rubble?

Isaacs followed the crowd into the auditorium and sat, his eyes blitzed by the recorded history of the air, his mind in its own warp. Subconsciously, he had known it would come to this. His alternatives were sorted and handed up to him even as he read the letter from McMasters. Someone had to focus on this evil in the earth. He had to go it alone. His career, his rapid rise to authority, all his hard work, seemed like a fragile bird in his hand. So easily it could die, or fly away. But what alternatives did he have? To watch the world careen to disaster? A disaster that might be forestalled if only they knew the true origin of this thing? He thought of Muriel, her successful career built on the precarious sands of political influence. If he failed, were found out, disgraced, she'd have a lot at jeopardy as well. They would go down together. Would they go down together? Would they *be* together? Would she forgive him for sacrificing her to a cause of which she was ignorant? What of his daughter? How would she take the news of her father's ejection from the Agency for willful violation of policy? What would she think of a father in a unique position to stem the rush to war who lacked the courage to act? Disgrace or the prospect of nuclear war. Could there be any real choice?

One step at a time. He fumbled his way out of the auditorium, the aisle sporadically lit by the flashing screen. He pulled up his steep driveway twenty minutes later and stared for a moment at the house, picturing the occupants, before getting out of the car. As he closed the front door behind him, he could hear the perpetual music from Isabel's room and the rustle of paper from the front room, Muriel digesting the Sunday Post. She looked up as he came in.

"Hi!" she said cheerily. "Have a nice drive?"

He sat on the edge of a chair next to her. "I worked some things out."

She sobered at his look.

"I need to talk to you. Can you get some clothes on? I'd just as soon get out of the house."

"Well, sure." She pinched at the lapels of her robe. "I'll just be a few minutes." She gave him a perplexed look and headed up the stairs. Five minutes later, he heard her knock on Isabel's door and announce they were going for a ride.

"My hair's a mess. We're not going anywhere in public are we?" she asked as he joined her in the hallway.

"No, you look fine. I just want to find a quiet place to talk."

In the car he headed them toward the Naval Observatory grounds and found an empty turnoff where they could park. He turned off the ignition and looked out over the rolling lawns.

Muriel broke the silence.

"This is a little frightening, you know."

"I am frightened," he said with a shy grin. He half turned in his seat to face her. "I'm about to take a big step. I've never involved you in Agency business, but if I miss my footing here, it could be very bad."

"You know I trust you."

"You trust a guy who has always played by the rules. I have to break some rules now."

"Maybe I shouldn't know."

"According to the rules you shouldn't. That's one of the rules I need to break. I can't go into this leaving you in the cold."

"It's got to do with Avery, doesn't it?"

He nodded. "You read about the alert?"

"What there is to read," she said, befuddled. "Rumors of a full alert, unconfirmed by the White House. Official mumblings about routine training exercises."

"And you remember my last dust-up with McMasters."

"Humble pie."

"They're all tied in together. I don't have to tell you the details, but I need to sketch it for you, to explain what I'm going to do.

"There's some influence moving through the earth. We picked it up by seismic signals, microscopic earthquakes. Avery stumbled onto it by sonar signals. We have no idea what causes the noise as it goes, but, whatever it is, it moves back and forth through the earth. No one seems to have noticed it above the surface, but Avery was on a mission to investigate that, and I'm convinced it sank his ship."

"It? You mean you have no idea what sank a ship?"

"That's right. Incredible as it seems, there's something deadly out there, down there, and we have no clue to what it is. Last spring a Russian aircraft carrier was damaged in a mysterious way. All the evidence points to the same phenomenon. The carrier was in the right place at the right time to have run into this thing. They blamed us, thought we had some mystery ray. They zapped one of our spy satellites with a laser satellite; we snatched their laser with the shuttle."

"Oh, yeah." Muriel wagged a finger in memory. "There were some reports of skullduggery with the shuttle. Someone high up sat on that one very hard."

"Right. Well, it's continued to escalate. The Russians have launched another laser. That's led to the alert." He paused. "I know you realize that this is all confidential, but what I'm going to tell you next, you really have to regard in the strictest confidence. If it gets out, then the whole works go down the drain."

"Don't tell me."

"This is the crux. You won't understand my motivation otherwise."

"It seems pretty clear. Something strange is going on. You've lost a good friend to it. We and the Russians are at odds over it, without even knowing it. That neanderthal McMasters has blocked your way, and you're going to defy him by continuing to dig when he has forbidden you to. If he catches you, he skins you and makes a gift of your tanned hide to the Director, no matter the motivation."

Isaacs smiled. "An admirable summary, counselor. You're right. It was the investigation of these seismic signals that McMasters squelched. I appealed to him last week, but with this alert on he just slapped me down, got to tend to the business at hand. The problem is, of course, that I think the business at hand is the outgrowth of this mystery noise. We must understand that."

"Then go after it."

"If I'm wrong, or if I'm found out mucking around before I can come up with incontrovertible proof, I'll be kicked out, disgraced. I'm worried about your position, about what Isabel would think. It wouldn't be worth the risk if all that was at stake was my concern for what happened to Avery."

"No, not just for a personal question," Muriel agreed, "but other men have died. This thing sounds dangerous on its own, even if it didn't lead to lasers and shuttles having at it in space."

"Muriel, men die all the time, and we and the Russians are always involved in some skirmish or other, some of which I can influence, others I can't. The stakes are a lot bigger here."

She looked thoughtful for a long moment. "Okay, tell me if you have to. But for your sake, not mine."

"We launched a nuclear device this morning. It'll track the laser. If the laser is used, we explode it."

"Oh, Bob. Oh, my god. What would the Russians do?"

"Who knows? That's just the worry. What would we do if they used a nuclear device against us in space? We'd retaliate somehow. Two things frighten me. That unknown thing in the earth, and the knowledge that we're as close to the brink as we have ever been."

"Bob, this is insane. You have the key to defuse this, and only McMasters in the way. Can't you go to the Director? Go to the President, for god's sake!"

"I have a pile of circumstantial evidence, no real proof. I think that with some thought and work the connection can be established, but doing that in an open fashion, never mind with the full-scale interagency cooperation that's required, is just what McMasters has blocked. If I get myself sacked, then I really am useless. Somehow, I've got to assemble a stronger case so I can circumvent McMasters. And I've got to do it in the midst of this goddamned full-scale alert, when they want to know everything that's happening, and why—yesterday."

She reached over and touched his arm. "Bob, you do what you have to do. Take me home."

He started the car and drove, barely seeing the road. He slowly realized that he had, besides Muriel, two possible allies. Maybe there was hope.

Korolev sat at his desk and stared at the incredible document in his hand. It was postmarked from New York, a simple attempt at subterfuge. Naive? Or sophisticated in its attempt to hide in plain sight? The fact that this letter was mailed to him just like any other piece of scientific correspondence that he received regularly from colleagues world-wide appealed to him greatly. What was the chance that this piece went unscreened by the authorities? Small, regrettably.

What a delight to see his confidence in this American vindicated. In the letter he confesses to pushing the meteorite idea, even as his confidence waned. Here is a man of conscience, trying honestly to struggle with forces beyond his control. How clearly he sees the disaster that has followed like night the day from the damage to the Novorossiisk.

And what a bizarre case he has compiled! A seismic signal that traverses the earth every eighty and one half minutes. The Novorossiisk in the way. This destroyer of theirs also in the path, and sunk! Could we have such seismic data? Korolev sighed. Probably far inferior, and locked in tight bureaucratic compartments. Could he pry it out? What an effort to ask of an old man. Expend much of the capital of his prestige in an effort like that. But this Isaacs fellow had now neatly forced his hand. He must try.

What a nice touch, the straw on the camel's back that would force him into action. Why, he queries, did the Novorossiisk not report a rising sonar signal? Ah, the subtleties of Soviet militarism. Isaacs must know that we do not keep tapes of sonar signals. There would be no point, without the ready computer power to analyze them. Our records are in the memories of men and the written page. What Isaacs does not know is that one of those memories was erased. The sonar man, not so far from retirement, had finally worked his way up to chief sonar officer on the Novorossiisk. No one was surprised at the heart attack that felled him. Until now, no one had questioned why his collapse had preceded the emergency, the fires on the ship. His second had taken over and had heard the descending signal. What had the first man heard that instigated his attack? Isaacs had asked a key question. Korolev was convinced he knew the answer.

Two problems. Could the disastrous chain of events be broken? From the Novorossiisk to the FireEye, the Cosmos, the shuttle, the new Cosmos, and now this evil new device of the Americans. Did this linkage have a momentum of its own that could not be stopped? Could he make a case that would cause his government to defuse the issue, to look to the common problem? If he could get independent evidence, beyond this document, to whom would he turn? Who in his stolid, conservative government would respond to this outrageous tale?

And what was this common enemy? This motive force within the earth, that punched holes in ships, and frightened men to death? What could be so omnipresent and yet so surgically precise that death can come and go and leave scarce a trace?

Korolev wrote a word in heavy blunt pencil in the margin of Isaacs' letter: TUNGUS.

On the following Saturday the precious morning slipped away, but Pat Danielson still wore her nightgown and robe. She had worked late the night before, responding to the crisis atmosphere that gripped the Agency, trying to monitor and anticipate the Soviet response to the orbiting nuclear device. She was due back by two in the afternoon. Now she kept that tension at bay by methodically devouring the morning paper. The condominium ads had caught her attention. After a brief stay with friends of her father upon her arrival in Washington, she had moved into the present high-rise apartment. She shared the rent with her roommate, Janine Corliss, a secretary in the FDA, an amicable arrangement, but looked forward to the independence and tax advantage of owning her own dwelling and had nearly accumulated a down payment.

A key rattled in the lock and Janine came in clutching a tennis racquet and a handful of mail, sweaty from an early match with the young lawyer from down the hall. She threw the mail on the coffee table and extracted one piece. She walked down the hallway and into Pat's room and tossed the letter on the stack of discarded newspaper sections.

"A letter for you."

She bustled into her own room and then into the shower.

Danielson picked up the envelope and examined the address written in a strong hand. She ran through her brief list of friends, unable to place the writing. She opened the envelope and looked at the terse message in surprise:

Pat,

Please meet me at the Olde English Pub, 87412 Wisconsin in Bethesda tomorrow (Sunday) at 3:00 p.m. Please do not mention or show this note to anyone.

Bob Isaacs

Danielson read the message three times quickly and then stared at it. They had ample opportunity every day of the week, and then some lately, to discuss Agency business. She had spent a half hour with Isaacs the previous Wednesday and their interchange had been routine, although he had been more preoccupied than usual. The message was so oddly clandestine; that wasn't even their branch of the Agency. That it represented the prelude to some romantic entanglement seemed preposterous. Not that it couldn't happen, but there would have been some other clue. She thought back to their conversation after the cancellation of Project QUAKER. The question of her social life, or lack of it, had come up. Had she sent him some kind of false signal? Had she misread him so badly? He seemed straightforward and sincere, but how could you ever tell what people were thinking?

Whatever its motivation, the request put her on the spot. She realized after some reflection that she would keep the appointment, but knowing she would have a few more hours off tomorrow afternoon, she had accepted a rare date for a concert at Wolf Trap. How did Isaacs know she wouldn't be working? Easy enough for him to check the roster, she supposed. Anyway she would have to break the date. The easiest thing would be to claim that something had come up at work, but especially if it were true, that would violate the spirit of Isaacs' request for discretion. Maybe Janine would get sick, and she would have to stay home with her.

Janine came into Pat's room dressed in her robe and wringing her hair in a towel. Danielson recognized that to ignore the note would be the best way to arouse her roommate's interest. She waved the letter by one corner and then tossed it into the wastebasket.

"An insurance salesman, begging me to call him and compare policies when my auto insurance comes due. Apparently, a struggling independent who can't afford his own stationery."

Janine shrugged.

"Well, he shows initiative. Maybe you should call him up and check him out."

Danielson grinned. She felt she had pulled off her little lie, but her pulse pounded with the effort. She recalled the polygraph test which had constituted part of her screening for the Agency position, glad not to be hooked up to it now.

Janine plopped down on Pat's bed and began to comb her hair.

Isaacs sat in the back of the bar where the afternoon sun barely penetrated from the opaque plastic panels in the front windows. He had debated the alternatives: to meet in a crowded place where strangers would take no note, but where the probability of a chance acquaintance was higher; or to pick a quiet spot where the bartender and the few patrons might have some vague memory of their presence, but their chances of being recognized together were near zero. He opted for the latter.

Isaacs dawdled over his drink, feeling alternatively morose, angry, and expectant. He recalled his attempt at fatherly advice to Danielson and felt the sting of irony. This was not the way to get ahead in the Agency. He smiled with relief when the door opened, revealing her silhouetted in the doorway. He was grateful that his confidence in this competent young woman had not been misplaced. The thought also passed through his mind that his goal could have been personal, rather than the business at hand, and she would have responded the same.

Danielson stood for a moment as her eyes adjusted from the sunlit afternoon. She instinctively peered toward the darkest area of the room and saw Isaacs arise from the booth. As she strode to greet him her senses were alert to his manner and carriage. His smile was warm, but did not quite reach his eyes, which looked troubled. He clasped her hand firmly, maintaining his grip just a fraction longer than necessary before giving it a last small pump and gesturing her into the seat.

"Thank you for coming," he said.

Before she could respond the bartender had rounded the bar and sauntered to their table. He glanced at Danielson and raised an eyebrow toward Isaacs.

"Will you have a drink?"

"Well, it's early, but it is hot out. I'll have a gin and tonic."

The bartender nodded and lackadaisically retraced his path.

"I hope I haven't inconvenienced you, springing this on you. I know you have precious little time off these days."

"I did have a date this afternoon."

"I'm sorry. I tried to give you a day's notice. I'm afraid I haven't played the dating game in quite a while."

Danielson raised an eyebrow. Was he playing it now?

"I did try to pick a time when I thought you'd just be relaxing at home."

"I might have been, but this afternoon's concert happened to fit my schedule. Anyway, I told him my hay fever had flared up, and I couldn't face either sitting in the grass sneezing or doping myself silly with antihistamines. I got a rain check for next week at the Kennedy Center, safely inside and air-conditioned. Now if I can just get the DCI to let me off—."

Her voice trailed off, her real question left floating in the air. Isaacs sensed her reserve and grinned nervously as the bartender arrived with her drink. He put down a fresh coaster, then promptly soaked it as he deposited the glass too abruptly. Danielson started to take a sip, but the coaster stuck to the bottom of the glass. She looked on with mild surprise as Isaacs unpeeled the coaster, reached for the shaker, and shook some salt on it. He gestured at the coaster. She placed her glass down and then lifted it. The coaster stayed nicely in place on the table. She took a sip, then raised her glass in an abbreviated toast. Isaacs nodded his appreciation. After a moment a serious look settled on his face.

"I need to talk to you about Operation QUAKER."

Danielson smiled wryly to herself. She had been right; romance was a preposterous notion. Aloud she said, "I find myself pondering it on occasion." She glanced around the bar. "Do we need to meet here to beat a dead horse?"

"Circumstances have changed. I think it's imperative that Operation QUAKER be revived." Isaacs looked down into his drink and then up at Danielson. "I need your help, but the political roadblocks still exist so there are risks." He smiled briefly. "That's the reason for this skullduggery today."

He leaned forward and spoke intently.

"Let me explain what has happened."

Isaacs described his relation with Rutherford, the naval operation that had ensued, and its connection to the Novorossiisk. He gave a brief, professional description of the fate of the Stinson and her crew, but Danielson felt his pain. She sensed that his personal loss spurred him on in this venture. She asked herself how much of his renewed enthusiasm for Operation QUAKER was a reaction to his grief, how much a need for retribution against McMasters, and how much a cool objective decision that he alone must shoulder the responsibility.

"If you're right about the Stinson and the Novorossiisk, then the whole situation we're caught up in now," Danielson looked around and lowered her voice even further, "the Russian satellite and our, uh, device, stems from whatever is causing the seismic signal."

"That's my reading."

Danielson leaned back in the booth, her mind swimming, trying to assimilate all that Isaacs had said. "This damage," she mumbled, almost to herself, "how could the seismic signals I was tracking possibly sink a ship?" She looked directly at Isaacs. "What could this thing be?"

Isaacs shrugged his shoulders and looked pained.

"I've asked myself that over and over. I don't have a single rational suggestion. Only a profound vague fear."

"Could it be a Russian weapon of some kind? But why would they use it on their own ship? An accident? And why would they blame us? Bluster to cover up?"

Isaacs shook his head again in worried fashion. "My instincts tell me the Soviets aren't behind this. They really don't understand what happened to the Novorossiisk. Everything else has followed naturally, god forbid."

"Then who?"

"Who? What? No answers."

Danielson was silent for a moment, thinking.

"What is the Navy doing about it? It was their destroyer that was lost."

"The Navy is continuing its surveillance, but sporadically and from a great distance. Of course, they're on full alert as well, so the energies of any of their brass who could make some constructive decisions are focused on what they see as the immediate problem—trying to monitor everything in the world that floats and flies a red star.

"There's a self-defeating dichotomy in their approach. They don't really know what happened to the Stinson and won't officially admit any direct connection to its mission. And yet, they're afraid there was some direct cause and won't commit any ships or equipment to close surveillance. As it stands, they aren't learning anything new, not even establishing in their own minds that this thing is definitely dangerous."

"But you think it is."

"I'm convinced of it."

"What you suggest is so totally inexplicable, maybe coincidence is the only reasonable explanation after all."

"There's the slimmest chance that I'm overreacting to some outrageous coincidences. But I think the situation must be resolved one way or another. I'm certainly convinced that the present hiatus is unacceptable. Someone must take steps to determine what is really happening here."

"Can't you go back to McMasters and appeal to him to reopen the file on its merits?"

"I tried that. I drafted a long memo setting out the case. It only succeeded in getting him more angry. He suspects I had some role in the Navy's interest, but can't prove it. In any case, he's clever enough to turn it around on me. He made an issue of the fact that there is no proof that the loss of the Stinson was not coincidence and that the Novorossiisk was not, after all, sunk, and hence that there is still no evidence that anything important is going on, much less for a connection between the two. I sent him the memo, what, eleven days ago, the day before the second laser was launched and we started this whole new loop. So he also gave me a healthy dose of 'Don't you know there's a war on?', ignoring my argument that the issues are one and the same. He also maintains that since the Navy now has some official interest in the phenomenon, there is no reason for the Agency to duplicate the effort."

Danielson toyed with a small puddle of spilled tonic on the table, tracing a random pattern with her finger. She looked up.

"AFTAC is still collecting the seismic data—and sonar data from the undersea network, from what you say."

"That's right," confirmed Isaacs, "but the Cambridge Research Lab stopped analyzing this particular signal, once we terminated our official interest in it. The AFTAC sonar data would help to pin down accurate positions, but since I didn't have enough sense to make the connection, there's been no analysis of it whatsoever. By rights the Navy should at least be studying the AFTAC sonar data, but from what I can tell, they're not."

"So all the data are piling up," Danielson summarized, "but no one is looking at them."

"True. And we can't get at it. None of this is official Agency business, so a special request through channels is necessary—and McMasters has that approach effectively blocked."

Danielson concentrated. "There are the data we gathered before the halt came. But that's all in the inactive file. I didn't save anything out."

Isaacs punched a finger into the table. "I think we must start there. I'll have to camouflage my request, but I can get some of that retrieved without it necessarily coming to McMasters' attention. Particularly if you can give me an idea of the few things, data tapes and such, which would be of greatest use.

"The problem," he continued, "is that I can't do any of the analysis. I'm rarely directly involved with raw data and computer analysis any more. If I were to go anywhere near that data on a regular basis, McMasters would be on my back immediately. Any kind of blowup is apt to foreclose the investigation completely."

"On the other hand," Danielson looked at him coolly, "I interact with other data and the computer on a routine basis."

Isaacs returned her level gaze. He knew he did not need to spell out the situation for her further.

Danielson lowered her eyes to the damp spot on the table again. Isaacs watched her averted eyes and noted the crinkling between her brows. When she looked up there was a hint of mischievousness and triumph on her face.

"I can do it! I can add a couple of subroutines to my

fourier transform package. Then I can read in and print out the seismic data interspersed with the results of other projects at intermediate stages when no one routinely examines the output but me. The chances of someone noticing without going through step-by-step would be very small."

"I'm sure you can do it. The question is whether you should and will. If we're caught at it, your job could be at stake. I would take responsibility for giving you the order, but that might not be sufficient. I'm asking a great deal of you."

Danielson paused. "Do you really think we can do any good? We can rehash the old data, but if that's all, can we accomplish any more than the Navy?"

Isaacs suddenly pounded his fist onto the table and then hunched in chagrin as the bartender looked up in their direction.

"We can think!" he whispered intensely. "The Navy is sailing in circles, no one is really trying to understand what is going on!"

He relaxed and put his hand momentarily on hers. "There's no doubt we'll be at a handicap. This analysis by subterfuge will be far less efficient and useful than the way we proceeded before. But we can use our heads on the data at hand rather than hide from it. Any effort at analysis will be preferable to the fiddling which is going on now. Our Rome is up there in orbit," he glanced at the ceiling, "and it could burn any minute."

Danielson looked at him. She concluded that he acted from a variety of motives, but that the overriding one was a deep concern to prevent the escalation of the conflict with the Soviets by understanding what was happening to the earth. She could not readily accommodate the notion that she might personally affect global power politics, but she keenly felt the need to come to grips with the mysterious motions in the earth that she herself had coaxed into rational form. Could the alignment of the Stinson and the Novorossiisk with the trajectory she had mapped out be only a coincidence? To believe that would be so easy, but, like Isaacs, she could not do so. The alternative was horrendous to contemplate, but impossible to ignore. Whatever drove the seismic signal, killed. What bizarre, implacable thing plagued them?

She recalled her notion that Isaacs might have had some romantic motive for this meeting. A wave of embarrassment burst upon her. How trivial that notion was compared to the fearsome reality.

The idea of violating a directive both fascinated and terrified her. She nodded at Isaacs, and he leaned back in satisfied relief.

Jason, he thought to himself. The next step is to call Jason. Aloud to her he said, "Next weekend is the July Fourth holiday. I'll have to ask you to keep it open. We may have to take a trip."

Chapter 8

Nancy Wambaugh pedaled down the sidewalk on her bike. School was out for the day, and the crisp air and warm winter sun of late June felt good in her windblown hair. Sometimes the teacher made her do things in the first grade she didn't like, but she was delighted with the lesson she had learned today. Her daddy had taught her some time ago to recite, sing-song, where she lived— "Newcastle, New South Wales, Australia." When she was too young to be ashamed, she would put a little curtsy at the end, pleased at her father's big smile. She had always loved the image in her mind of a new castle, full of princesses and good things, but today she had learned a new grown-up thing about it. She had learned to spell it, and it made a little poem! As she pumped, she sang,

"N, E, W, C,"

Left foot, right foot, left foot, right.

"A, S, T, L, E,"

Left foot, right foot, left foot, right.

Wham!

Nancy landed on her right elbow and cheek, feet tangled painfully in the pedals of the bicycle. She sucked in her breath from the shock and then wailed as she looked at the blood that began to seep from the long scrape on her arm. She scrambled away from the bike and looked around, hurt and angry. She was sure her older brother, David, had bumped her off the bike with a pillow, that's what it had felt like when the bike tumbled, like when they had pillow fights and David knocked her down. She put her fingers to the sting on her face, and they came away bloody. She screamed louder.

Her cries drowned the hiss that rose above her head. The raucous whisper returned some distance away as Nancy ran toward home.

"MOMEEEE!"

McMasters' head snapped up from the report he was reading at the sound of the intercom buzzer.

"Yes, what is it?"

"Alan Mirabeau, from the computer section, is here to see you."

"Umm, ah, yes." McMasters leaned back in his chair in anticipation. "Send him in." McMasters watched as the earnest young man peered around the door and then walked to his desk.

"Sir? You asked for me to monitor requests for certain files?"

"Indeed."

"Well, a request did come this morning for some of the inactive files associated with Project QUAKER. Here's a list of the files that were requested."

McMasters leaned forward to take the proffered sheet.

"The files were transferred out for about an hour, then written back in and deactivated again."

Long enough to transfer their contents to any active files, McMasters mused. He glanced over the list. They meant nothing to him, and everything. "Who requested this?" He knew, but he wanted to hear.

"It was a written request, sir. Signed by Mr. Isaacs."

Mirabeau was nervous. He had dreamed of a chance like this to interact with the upper echelons, but this was not what he had envisioned. He wanted terribly to please McMasters, but not at the expense of getting in trouble with Isaacs, another member of the ruling circle. He had not realized that McMasters' seemingly routine and innocuous request was going to put him in the position of spying on Isaacs. Every fiber of his being was attuned to sensing the desires of his superiors and satisfying them. He was in agony at the thought that he could not please one of these men without incurring the displeasure of the other.

"Can you put a trace on this material?" McMasters put a finger on the list in front of him.

"But it's been deactivated again," Mirabeau protested, but then the light of understanding spread over his face, and his admiration for McMasters increased. "Oh, I see. You think a copy was kept out."

"Precisely," McMasters replied.

The young man concentrated for a moment.

"The file names will have been changed, so a search for them would be pointless. There is no simple way to search for this material, but I can do a sampling of running jobs to search for particular combinations of data and instructions that occur in these files."

"I want to know when this material is used, and by whom," McMasters demanded.

"Yes, sir."

"That's all."

"Yes, sir." The young man headed for the door.

"Oh, Mirabeau."

"Sir," he replied, swiveling quickly.

"Not a word of this to Isaacs, or his associates."

The young man smiled with relief.

"No, sir, of course not, sir." That solved his problem of divided allegiance. Now he was acting under direct orders. He gave a brief bow toward McMasters and then shut the door behind him.

Saturday morning Isaacs paced up and down in front of the check-in counter at Dulles. He felt unmoored, detached from the bearings that had given him stability for almost two decades of his career. He was desperate to get on with this quest, but awash with anxiety over the risks he was taking, risks he had convinced Pat Danielson to share. And now she was late. He stopped to look at his watch and glance down the passageway toward the main terminal. He fought down the urge, born of frustration, to blame her tardiness on her womanhood. She didn't deserve that. She was too good, too responsible. She'd have some good excuse. He clinched his fist on the handle of the slim briefcase he carried and resumed his pacing.

He prayed that some glimmer of understanding, some hint of where to turn next, would come from this hurried unauthorized rump meeting with Jason. He feared that it would prove nothing but a scamper out onto a limb, with McMasters grinning, sharpening his saw. He rethought the steps he had taken, the precautions. He had done everything practical to minimize the chance that McMasters would stumble onto his resurrection of Project QUAKER, but the old bird was canny, there was no way to be absolutely sure. He jumped when the hand grasped his arm. He turned to see Pat Danielson's flushed, excited face.

"Bob—Mr. Isaacs."

His irritation at her faded with the relief of her arrival and the infectious sparkle in her eyes.

"Right the first time."

"Bob." She touched his arm again, still animated. "I'm sorry I'm late, but I've found something. I got up early to look over my calculations and then lost track of time."

"We've got a couple of minutes. Let's—Here."

Isaacs looked around, then took her carry-on bag and led her to a vacant waiting area. As they sat, he inquired in a low voice, "What have you got?"

"A prediction, I guess," she almost whispered, leaning toward him. "I've been running my programs since Wednesday, checking the position and phase of the signal. I can guess with fair accuracy where the signal will come to the surface each cycle.

"The question that has been preying on me is the sinking of the Stinson. That means something destructive can happen when the signal comes to the surface. So I asked myself, why aren't there reports of some destruction on land?"

"I wondered the same thing," Isaacs remarked. "One possibility is that much of the path falls along areas of relatively low population density. Maybe most of the time no one notices. Another factor is that we don't really know what to expect. Sporadic reports of strange events could easily be overlooked in the undeveloped countries, even here in the United States."

"Exactly," nodded Danielson. "But occasionally the phenomenon should surface in a region of high population density. That would increase the probability of someone noticing something."

Isaacs raised a quizzical eyebrow.

"Four days from now, it should come up in Nagasaki about 11:13 in the morning local time," said Danielson flatly. "That's 9:13 Wednesday evening, our time. And nineteen days later, July 26, it will surface in Dallas about midnight."

Isaacs leaned back and looked at her.

"How well can you pinpoint the location?"

"There are uncertainties in the period and location from

the seismic data alone, but those are big, sprawling cities. I am reasonably sure there will be a surfacing somewhere within their boundaries."

Isaacs turned to look out of the window, staring past the airplanes arrayed on the tarmac.

"Would it help you to have some of the Navy data?"

"Yes, sir, even just one or two recent high precision locations would allow me to calibrate my curves. We might be able to pin down the site within. . ." She paused to think. "Well, maybe a few hundred meters to a kilometer."

"I may be able to get that," said Isaacs intently, returning his gaze to her. "It's very short notice, but I may also be able to get some satellite time to monitor the area in Nagasaki." He mulled the chances of contacting an agent in Nagasaki who could make an on-the-spot observation, without tipping his hand to others in the Agency.

"Okay, Pat, that's good work. When we get back, I'll try to get some of the Navy information so you can refine your estimates."

"Aren't you going to have to tell McMasters, to issue a warning to Nagasaki?"

"We're still on shaky ground here. I'm hoping we can gain enough information on the Nagasaki event that we can go above board in time for Dallas. And with luck, this trip to Jason may give us some insight into the whole mess."

Danielson looked uncertain, but then their flight was called and they had to queue up to board.

During lunch on the plane, Danielson queried Isaacs about the nature of the group with whom they would meet.

"These people who serve on Jason—how are they selected?"

Isaacs paused to swallow a bite of gravy-swathed grey meat.

"Well, they operate under the auspices of the Secretary of Defense as you know. They're quite autonomous though and select their own members. The idea is, I suppose, that they themselves are the best judges of whatever arcane talent is required to participate in a general-purpose think tank.

They receive the standard security clearance, but the hard part is getting elected—a single no-vote eliminates a prospective member."

"They don't have any particular training at defense work?"

"No, they're just required to be the very best in their chosen area of science."

"How many people are we talking about then?"

"Thirty some. But we'll only see a small group of individuals who may have some particular expertise to bring to our problem."

"So all these great brains spend their summer vacations worrying about whatever problems are dished up to them."

"That's about the size of it."

"And they always meet in the same place—this Bishop's School?"

"Generally, yes. The grounds of the school are cloistered and secure. And, of course, La Jolla is a very congenial place to be in the summer. I believe some members rent houses in town, but most of them move right into the dorms. They're converted into combination living and working areas. I guess I see the sense to it. You take a bunch of very bright people and make them comfortable in an environment where they can concentrate and interact without interruption. In any case, it seems to work. Jason has a long record of developing significant ideas and cracking hard problems."

"I'm sure." Danielson poked at the food on her tray. "I find it an ironic mix, innocent little Episcopalian school girls during the school year and great scientists weighing the fate of mankind during summer vacation."

"I suppose," Isaacs replied.

"If you don't mind me asking," Danielson continued, "I'm curious as to how you could set up a meeting with them so quickly. I would have thought there were all sorts of channels to go through."

"Normally you're right," Isaacs assented. "Another piece of the tightrope we're walking. I've dealt with them before, through those official procedures. I took the chance of calling Professor Phillips; he runs Jason now, a pleasant fellow, I think you'll like him. I hinted at the emergency and let him know this was something informal, something I am doing on my own recognizance, on a weekend like this. Of course, I couldn't come right out and tell him about McMasters' prohibition. We'll have to trust his discretion. I'm pretty sure Phillips is okay. I don't know the others personally. We'll just have to hope."

He cast her a worried glance.

"Pat, I am concerned about this trip. I hate exposing us, you in particular, but we need some help, some idea of what's going on." He poked at his green beans then went on. "Frankly, even without the risk, I always have mixed feelings with these people. Individually and collectively they're very bright. They have an excellent track record for making progress on seemingly intractable problems, like ours, and the fact that they do serve on Jason gives us something in common, I suppose. But I can't help thinking they're still academics. The fact that they choose that sort of life, rather than committing themselves to the front line like some of us are compelled to do, means we have a different mindset. A basically different view of the world, life."

He shrugged.

"I think I understand," Danielson said. "I guess I'm pretty nervous meeting with them for another reason, but it's related. I've never had to do any Agency business in public, outside of Langley, except for that liaison with the Cambridge Research Lab, but that was just work. Now I've got to try to explain what I've done, what I've been thinking, to professional scientists, trained sceptics. It's a little frightening."

He looked her seriously in the eyes.

"You know your stuff," he said confidently. "Don't worry on that account."

A passing stewardess eyed their trays. They concentrated once more on the food before them. After lunch, Danielson extracted her case from beneath the seat in front of her and reviewed her notes one more time.

At the San Diego airport Isaacs called ahead to announce their arrival, then they picked up a rental car and got on the freeway headed north, passing between steep hillocks on either side. Only the tang in the airstream through a partially opened window gave evidence of the nearby Pacific. They turned off the freeway and headed uphill to the west. The crest brought a panoramic view of a sweep of coastline to the right, broken in mid-arc by the jut of Scripps pier. To the left the town of La Jolla snuggled around the hillside and down to the sea. In another few minutes they turned into the gateway of the Bishop's School for Girls, nestled a short distance from the commercial center of La Jolla.

As they got out of the car, Wayne Phillips called to them. Isaacs and Phillips greeted one another with refined congeniality. Phillips, a Harvard physicist, was, at 68, the senior member and current head of Jason. Like many of his generation he had nurtured his career both in physics and in defense-related matters on the Manhattan Project during World War II. A contributor to a wide variety of fields, he was best known for his work on nuclear physics which had earned him a share of a Nobel Prize.

His physique conceded something to age, but Phillips' rangy build still extended to nearly six feet. His thick grey hair was balding, but not exceedingly so. The lock of hair in the middle of his forehead gave the effect of a high rise widow's peak. His longish face displayed kindly blue eyes underscored by pronounced bags. Phillips had come from a monied eastern family and had been raised in style. Although he was among the most highly respected of his colleagues, he had long been regarded as a pariah by some members of his family for not devoting his life to the disbursement of the extensive family trust funds.

Isaacs introduced Danielson to Phillips and they chatted as

they moved off down the walk and into a nearby building. Danielson warmed immediately to the physicist's courtly manner which belied his aggressive intellect.

They entered one of the dormitories. The bulletin board in the foyer bore outdated reminders of the school-term occupants. Freshly scattered around were announcements of classes and various activities. In a lower corner, neatly aligned but yellowed with age, was a detailed list of covenants applicable to proper young school girls.

Phillips gestured for Isaacs and Danielson to ascend the stairway which led from the foyer. At the top they paused while Phillips caught up with them and led the way down a hall. At midpoint he stopped, rapped once on the door, then turned the knob and stepped back to usher them in.

The furnishings of the room they entered looked all out of place. After a moment's reflection, Danielson realized that it was a regular dormitory room converted for the summer into an office. The beds had been removed and replaced by a large serviceable desk which stood against the left wall, littered with papers and books. A comfortable old sofa had been shoehorned in beneath the windows opposite, and along the right wall stood a roller-footed portable blackboard. Next to the blackboard a partially opened door revealed a compact lavatory. Extra chairs were placed randomly, adding to the sense of clutter.

Two men sat on the sofa. Isaacs recognized one as Ellison Gantt, the distinguished seismologist from Caltech who had been instrumental in planning the large seismic array. Gantt had receding grey hair and wore dark framed glasses. His jowls and chin were beginning to sag. The two men rose and Phillips introduced them. The other was Vladimir Zicek from Columbia, one of the world's experts on lasers. Danielson was unsure she would recognize Gantt if she were to bump into him on the street later; he looked like so many other grey, middle-aged men. In a coat and tie he could have passed anywhere as a business executive. Zicek was more distinctive.

He was rather small in stature with sharp features and hair combed straight back from his forehead. There was a friendly twinkle in his eyes and his polite continental manner appealed to her.

Phillips addressed Gantt.

"Ellison, you're our host here today. Would you mind assembling the others?"

"Of course. Let's see—it's Leems, Runyan, Noldt, and Fletcher, isn't it?"

"That's right," acknowledged Phillips.

Gantt moved into the hallway. Phillips offered Danielson a seat on the sofa, which she took. She realized it put her in full direct view of each new arrival, and she watched with amusement as they filed in over the next several minutes. Each reacted with various degrees of surprise to find an attractive female in the retinue.

Isaacs remained standing, fidgeting at the delay which would be barely excusable by regimented CIA standards. They were all assembled in a few minutes, however. Isaacs conceded even that was admirable for a bunch of prima donna college professors.

Phillips courteously introduced each new arrival and Isaacs checked them off against the files he had studied. Carl Fletcher and Ted Noldt arrived together. They were experts in high energy particle physics, Fletcher, a theorist from Princeton, Noldt, an experimentalist from Stanford. They both were in their middle thirties, friends from graduate school. Fletcher was of medium height with shaggy brown hair. He had quick dark eyes set in a square face with the gaunt, tanned cheeks of a long-distance runner. Noldt was a bit taller, but blond and pudgy. A crooked grin and glasses gave him the look of a good-humored owl.

Harvey Leems, a solid-state physicist from Berkeley, followed in a minute. Leems was tall and bald. His thick, rimless glasses diminished his eyes and contributed to a sour look. He greeted Isaacs and Danielson with a quick nod.

Gantt returned lugging a slide projector and screen which he proceeded to arrange. Last to arrive was Alexander Runyan, an astrophysicist from Minnesota. Runyan's rawboned frame ran three inches over six feet. Danielson watched him come through the door and stop to be introduced to Isaacs. He was wearing a T-shirt that showed a slight paunch, cutoffs, and flip-flop thongs. He moved slowly, almost shambled, but Danielson sensed in him an energy that could be quickly galvanized. A dark beard going salt-and-pepper, particularly at the sideburns, covered a face she thought might be handsome if she could see it all. He turned toward her then, gave a look of surprise and delight and whipped off the glasses he'd been wearing. He stepped across the room and introduced himself, shaking Danielson's hand and giving her a warm smile. His eyes were light grey or green, hidden in a perpetual sun squint that melded easily into his smile. He squeezed between Danielson and Zicek on the sofa. There was an exchange of knowing looks among the scientists. If there were an attractive woman in the crowd, Runyan would be at her side pouring on the charm.

Phillips moved to the small, clear area before the projection screen which Gantt had placed in front of the lavatory door.

"Gentlemen," he began, "we are pleased to welcome Mr. Isaacs and Dr. Danielson from the Central Intelligence Agency. They have an interesting problem to set before us. It's not on our formal agenda, but I've promised Mr. Isaacs we'll lend what insight we can. They'll present us with some details and then lead a general discussion to explore the nature of the situation. Mr. Isaacs."

"Thank you, Professor Phillips," Isaacs began, looking around the room. "I want to thank you all for giving up your Saturday afternoon on such short notice. As you will see, we are dealing with a problem so foreign to our experience, that any hint of how to proceed will be most useful."

Isaacs spent ten minutes giving a general but concise review of the surveillance role of the CIA and the parallel operation in AFTAC with particular stress on the capabilities of the Large Seismic Array and the undersea acoustic monitors. He also described the role of the Office of Scientific Intelligence in guiding and interpreting the surveillance missions. He then turned the floor over to Danielson.

Although nervous, Danielson had maintained her demeanor while watching the group file in. Butterflies struck in earnest, however, as she listened to Isaacs. She was intent on giving a professional presentation. She knew intellectually that she was well versed in her subject, but her emotional reaction was tainted by the knowledge that she, as a woman and an engineer, was about to stand up before an audience of male physicists considered the best in their fields.

As she stepped around next to the projector, she was vividly aware that the all male group was equally conscious of her sex. Her voice broke slightly as she began, and she spoke her first few introductory sentences at a low volume which scarcely carried over the faint traffic noise from the window.

"A little louder for those of us who are hard of hearing, please Dr. Danielson."

The admonition came from Phillips, but it was delivered with a warm supportive smile. Danielson heartened and her tone strengthened. She turned on the first slide which drew her attention away from the audience and to her subject matter. Soon she was caught up in the precise intricate web of analysis which, through her deep involvement, was an extension of her own personality.

Danielson's reading of her small audience was largely accurate. Before she began to speak and establish some grounds for an intellectual bond, the instinctive response was to react to her as a female. Not a man in the room failed to run a glance from her softly curled hair down to trim ankles and back and say to himself, "not your standard CIA type" or variations on that theme. There was a communal embarrassment and the reinforcement of some prejudice as she began so softly, but by and large they were a sophisticated and open-minded group prepared to relate on an intellectual level. Once Danielson got involved in her subject, she commanded their attention, and a growing respect. When she reached her major point, that the seismic signal kept sidereal time, time with the stars, there was a muffled commotion of gestures and excitedly whispered comments that told Danielson that she had established the desired rapport with her audience.

When Danielson finished, Ellison Gantt spoke from his seat in the swivel chair at the desk.

"This is a very strange situation, but let me say for the information of my colleagues that Dr. Danielson seems to have a good command of the basics of seismology in general and the nature of the Large Seismic Array in particular. I'd like a chance to study the data she's presented in more detail, but at first sight I have to concur that the signal's a genuine one. I've never seen one like it. It's certainly not the result of normal seismological activity."

Danielson knew Gantt by reputation. She was pleased by his gesture of support.

Harvey Leems spoke up from his seat near the door. "Do you have other independent evidence of the existence of this phenomenon—something other than this seismological record, that is?"

"Yes, let me speak to that," replied Isaacs. "The seismic data is crucial because it told us that something systematic was occurring and led us to look for corroborative evidence. That's the other half of the story."

He gave a quick smile and nodded at Danielson. As he rose, she took his chair which was more convenient than the sofa. The remnant state of intense nervous involvement with her own presentation persisted. Several minutes passed before she could concentrate adequately on Isaacs' remarks. Isaacs outlined the associated sonar data and the behavior it portrayed. Whereas the seismic signal was lost in the mantle, the sonar signal proceeded along the extrapolated path to the ocean surface, disappeared for about forty seconds and then retraced its path to the ocean bottom where the seismic signal was picked up once more.

"On the basis of such data," Isaacs continued, "about three weeks ago a Navy destroyer was sent to investigate a site of the predicted surfacings. At its first station it recorded and relayed a signal typical of the one I just described. It then took up position near a second predicted point of surfacing."

Isaacs paused and looked around at his audience. "Our data is incomplete, but at approximately the predicted time of surfacing, the ship exploded, capsized and sank. Two hundred thirty-six of the crew were lost."

Most of the men to whom he spoke stared down at their hands or off to various spots in the room. Only Leems and Runyan kept their eyes on Isaacs.

"There's some evidence that the turbines exploded. There's no proof that the sinking of the ship was related to its mission, but the circumstantial evidence and other events suggest to me that that possibility must be strongly considered.

"We have seen in hindsight that a related event probably occurred to the Soviet aircraft carrier Novorossiisk last April. It was in the Mediterranean on the trajectory Dr. Danielson described and at the right time, as nearly as we can tell. Something punctured a small hole through it vertically a few millimeters to a centimeter across and triggered extensive fire damage. There was an associated sonar signal. We suggested a meteorite, but the Soviets rejected the idea; we're not sure why. In any case, that event began an escalating and very dangerous conflict with the Soviets. We needn't go into that here, but to say that the Soviets mistakenly blamed us for the damage to the carrier. Besides direct physical damage, ignorance of the true nature of this phenomenon threatens us with other indirectly related, but very real perils."

Isaacs paused and scanned around the group.

"It's imperative that we understand this phenomenon for

its intrinsic menace, and to contain this related confrontation with the Soviets."

He looked at them again, satisfied he had made the point.

"To summarize the picture we currently have, then," said Isaacs, "some influence moves along a line fixed in space. It travels through the earth or the ocean where its passage can be detected with seismographs or sonar, respectively. It seems to reverse just above the earth's surface and then return on a parallel path. There is evidence that this influence is responsible for puncturing a hole several millimeters across through solid steel. And there is every reason to think that it is something that is an immediate threat to life and property and, indirectly, to our political stability."

Leems had listened carefully to this extended reply to his first question and raised another.

"If this phenomenon is as dangerous as you indicate, why haven't there been widespread reports of damage? If it really surfaces regularly, that's about eighteen times a day somewhere on earth."

"I agree that's a point of interest," replied Isaacs, "and Dr. Danielson has had another important insight in that regard which she just told me about this morning. We think the answer is that, for the most part, the damage is of a curiously limited nature, and the locus on the earth's surface passes through relatively sparsely occupied territory. You've noticed, I suppose, that we are very nearly on the track here in La Jolla. From San Diego the path stretches across the southwest United States, where there are few people, although it does pass through Dallas/Fort Worth. The southeast United States is also not too densely populated. The nearest big cities to the path are Macon, Georgia and Charleston, South Carolina, both somewhat to the north. From there the path goes across the Atlantic, intersecting Africa south of Casablanca then cutting across North Africa and into the Mediterranean. It passes through the Middle East, but again misses the big cities, going south of Haifa and Esfahan. From there it goes across Afghanistan and Pakistan and through the Himalayas. The path cuts through the heart of China, but misses major population centers. If there were incidents in the rural areas there, as for many of the other affected countries, we might very well hear nothing of it. The path intersects Nagasaki and then proceeds across the Pacific. The story is very much the same for the locus in the southern hemisphere. Lots of ocean, relatively little population density.

"So I suspect most events go unobserved, and that many which are observed go unreported. The probability of a surfacing twice in the same place is small. To any single witness it would be an isolated event with little meaning.

"What Dr. Danielson has pointed out is that the seismic signal should come up within a region of high population density occasionally, increasing the chances of observing some associated phenomena. She predicts that the trajectory of the seismic wave will intersect a position within the city of Nagasaki this coming Thursday, July 8, Japanese time. On July 26 a similar event should take place in Dallas."

"Well, you clearly want to put some observers at those sites," said Leems, coldly. "Aren't you jumping the gun, talking to us now without that data?"

Isaacs stared at Leems for a long moment, then replied in an equally cool tone. "As I said, the predictions were made after this trip was scheduled. I'm hoping the events which have already transpired will give you some clue to tell us what to look for."

"Well, what about this business of sidereal time then; what do you make of that?" asked Gantt, attempting to head off Leems' negativism.

"That's one of the crucial issues we would like to raise with this group," Isaacs replied to him. "The timing seems to be so special that it must be an important clue, but we haven't been able to utilize it. Perhaps we could get some comment now from you." He swung his hand in invitation around the room.

"Well, Alex—what the hell?" Gantt turned to address Runyan on the sofa.

Runyan scratched his thick beard. "I'm working on it," he replied in a testy tone overlaid with humor, picking up the cue from Gantt. There was a general chuckle. "The sidereal time would normally indicate an extraterrestrial source. That seems outlandish in this context, but I guess we should kick it around. I deduce we're under attack by an extraterrestrial army stationed on Alpha Cancri aiming tachyonic earthquake beams at us." The chuckles turned to guffaws. Isaacs smiled wryly, recalling his own fatigued fantasy.

Noldt asked, "How about a Jupiter effect? Is there an alignment of planets that would cause a tidal or some other effect which would be associated with a fixed direction in the sky?"

"Jupiter effect?" Isaacs queried and Gantt turned to answer him.

"The Jupiter effect is supposed to be a terrestrial upheaval associated with an alignment of the great planets every two hundred years. One version has it that this alignment causes solar storms which eject particles affecting the polar atmosphere. Associated changes in air pressure are supposed to trigger earthquakes."

"I don't believe any of that," Gantt went on, "and have even more difficulty seeing how it could enter here. The regular tides should swamp any such effect. I suppose this might be a resonance of some kind, but it would have to be completely unprecedented."

"Where's Jupiter now?" asked Runyan. "Would you have noticed a change due to its motion over the time base you have?"

Isaacs deferred to Danielson. "Jupiter is about forty degrees away from the direction we're talking about," Danielson replied. "That may not mean anything if a resonance is involved. A preferred direction that's a mean of the moon and the sun and Jupiter might be involved. Over the last three months the earth has moved far enough to rule out a preferred direction with respect to the sun, but Jupiter moves more slowly. I'm not sure we could rule that out."

"Jupiter would have moved through two or three degrees," Runyan stated, having done a quick mental calculation.

"That's a shift of over a hundred miles along the earth's surface," Danielson replied. "If that's the case, we can just about eliminate the possibility of alignment of the trajectory we see with the position of Jupiter."

Runyan continued thinking out loud. "The twenty-three degree angle of the earth's equator with respect to the ecliptic is purely random—there's no other solar system or astronomical connection—ruling out the accidental location of Polaris. A fixed angle of thirty-three degrees with respect to the earth's equator means even less. This thing has to be basically terrestrial. And yet sidereal. I'll put it back to Ellison. What the hell?"

"How do you know the Russians aren't behind this somehow?" Leems asked. "It seems like some kind of beam technology could be involved, and they invented the techniques. A satellite could be rigged to fire at a precise point in orbit so that it would look as if it always fired from the same position with respect to the stars. As Alex just said, terrestrial, but sidereal. They might do such a thing just to throw us off the mark. I point out that the eighty minute period you report is very close to the time for a satellite to orbit the earth."

"That's short, though, Harvey," said Runyan. "A satellite takes closer to ninety minutes."

"Use an array of satellites then." He turned to Isaacs. "You have checked the location of Russian satellites, haven't you?"

"No, that hadn't occurred to me—"

"I'm sure you'll remedy that oversight at the first opportunity," Leems interrupted.

Isaacs gritted his teeth and Danielson came to his defense. "But that doesn't make any sense," she said. "Why would they use any such weapon on their own ship? And wouldn't we know if they had some technique for generating seismic tremors deep inside the earth?"

"I don't suppose we know everything the Russians are up to," said Leems with a patronizing tone. "Perhaps they shot their own ship to embroil us in the very scandal you alluded to."

Danielson leaned back in her chair, her face flushed. Isaacs shook his head slowly.

Quiet fell on the group momentarily, then Fletcher spoke. "Alex, you were joking a while ago, but it got me thinking." He looked around at his colleagues. "Apparently, none of us can propose a natural explanation to account for the evidence presented: the seismic signals, the sonar signals, the suggestion that something is boring small holes through the earth itself. I can't buy Harvey's suggestion that it is some Russian plot. There are too many weird aspects. I think we must seriously consider another possibility. Suppose that we aren't dealing with either a natural or a man-made phenomenon?" A deep silence filled the room. "Suppose there is a, well, an external intelligence behind this?"

The silence continued as Fletcher's words probed a queasy, sensitive spot in each member of Jason. Trained as scientists, they sought to explain the world around them with the simplest rational extension of previous knowledge, but each knew their knowledge had bounds, limits. Each knew the rules of the game could be changed and their carefully honed intuition would be of little use. Each looked for and craved a simple solution, but each knew there was a chance, however small, that Fletcher could be right. They could be facing a situation so fundamentally different than anything they had encountered previously that their training and experience could be meaningless.

"Are you suggesting that there's an extraterrestrial intent behind these occurrences?" asked Phillips. His tone was incredulous. There were mutterings of dissatisfaction around the room.

"None of us here are UFO fanatics," pressed Fletcher, "least of all me. But we all know you can't prove a negative; we can't prove other intelligent civilizations don't exist. We know there are a few standard cliches concerning how such civilizations are to be discovered, radio emissions and all that. But I convinced myself long ago that guessing at the character of an extraterrestrial civilization by extrapolating the human condition is an exercise in futility. We have no basis for estimating the sociological and cultural evolution of an alien society even if we all obey the same physics.

"All I want to do is to raise the possibility. If we can rationally rule it out, or develop a preferred alternative, then so be it."

"It doesn't make sense," proclaimed Ted Noldt. "If there were an intelligence at work, we should be able to discern a purpose. What we've heard about here, holes drilled through ships, is no benign attempt at communication. It's certainly not overwhelmingly destructive either, an overt act of aggression. What could the purpose possibly be?"

"That's just my point," retorted Fletcher. "You're not asking a question of physics, but one of motivation. I submit we're unlikely to fathom any but the most transparent of motives—as you said, peaceful communication or war. The true possibilities are limited only by our imaginations. Suppose they're prospecting? Suppose we're seeing the effect of some probe and our existence here is totally immaterial to them? We could be like an anthill which is accidentally in the way of a geologist's test well as he searches for oil. Your first reaction was to think they must be for us or against us. Maybe they don't give a damn.

"Or maybe it's a test," Fletcher continued, trying to think of unorthodox possibilities. "Maybe we're dealing with a bunch of extraterrestrial behavioral psychologists who just want to provoke us in a certain way and study our reactions." Fletcher looked from man to man, defensive but determined to make his point.

"How can we possibly know what their purpose is? I certainly don't."

Ellison Gantt then spoke up. "I think Carl feels backed into a corner. Let me take a different tack. I agree with him that we should at least consider this possibility, and that an attempt to fathom motives may be premature. Suppose we assume for the moment that some influence is being beamed at us from a fixed point in space. Is there any way to determine what that influence is and where it's coming from? Could it be something with which we are basically familiar, like a laser or a particle beam?"

"I can speak to that. In fact, I'd been mulling over that very question," said Vladimir Zicek, his speech hissing with East European sibilants. "Any orthodox beam device would have a different signature than what has been described here. That is, one can imagine boring a hole from one side of the earth to the other with an exceedingly powerful beam, but one of the characteristics of the present phenomenon is that for half the cycle it goes from north to south, but on the other half it proceeds in the opposite direction. No external beam can do that. A beam must always propagate away from its source."

"Hmmm, perhaps not a beam in that sense then," said Fletcher thoughtfully. "What if some focusing principle is involved? A diffuse source of energy which is brought to a concentrated focus along a certain path. Maybe the source of energy isn't along the line of the trajectory, but transverse to it."

Fletcher lifted an imaginary rifle to his shoulder and strafed back and forth a few times. Several of those along his line of sight flinched involuntarily. Fletcher stopped squinting through the sight.

"Maybe a neutrino beam?"

There were several loud voices raised in simultaneous assent and dissent. A general hubbub ensued.

Wayne Phillips sensed that it was necessary to assimilate all that they had heard and called for quiet.

"Perhaps this is a good time to take a break for refreshments," he said. "Let's resume our deliberations in half an hour."

Against a rising background of chatter, the group stood, filed into the hall and down the stairs to a room where coffee, tea, and some cookies were set out.

Phillips escorted Isaacs and Danielson as they queued up. He made a small ceremony of preparing a cup of coffee for Danielson, ensuring she had the desired ingredients, a couple of cookies, and a napkin. She thanked him and then moved off by herself, motivated partly by a desire to be alone to contemplate the afternoon's developments and partly by a suspicion that Isaacs and Phillips would appreciate a chance to converse privately. She stood by a window looking over the parking lot and the playing field beyond, cradling her cup and saucer and munching on the cookies.

"That's crazy," she heard Leems' voice rising disdainfully over the chatter. "All the more reason to look to satellites in orbit, one to fire one direction, and another to fire a return shot in the opposite direction. That would solve Zicek's objection."

A bit later she made out Runyan in a more conversational tone.

"——good idea, Carl, couldn't hurt to have astronomers look in that direction. Very deep photographs taken with telescopes on Mauna Kea and in Chile. Who knows what we might see. Maybe I'll call some friends, see what they can do."

Runyan, speaking to Carl Fletcher and Ted Noldt, lowered his voice to a conspiratorial level.

"In fact, the first step is to make sure I have the precise coordinates."

He winked at them and crossed over toward where Danielson was standing, his thongs flapping on the floor. Fletcher leaned over to whisper to Noldt.

"Doesn't take him long, does it?"

Noldt smiled into his coffee and shook his head.

As Runyan approached her, Danielson finished her last cookie and wiped her fingers awkwardly on the napkin which she held under the saucer. The gesture attracted Runyan's eyes to her waist where she held the cup. Out of habit, his gaze continued down her legs and then back past her breasts to her face which was in profile to him. Taking pleasure from the innocent voyeurism, he stopped at arm's length from her.

"A pretty little problem you've posed for us here."

Danielson turned, a reflex smile of recognition brightening her face. She took a sip of cooling coffee and glanced out the window before replying.

"I thought we were on to something significant from the beginning, but I have to confess I don't know what to make of some of the ideas we just heard." She faced him again. "Beams from outer space. Could that possibly be true?"

"What do you think?"

She laughed lightly, chiding herself.

"I suppose that somewhere in the back of my mind that possibility had been flitting around since I first discovered the fixed orientation in space. I've been refusing to recognize it because it seemed so outrageous. Now it's been dragged out into the open. It still seems outrageous, but not unthinkable."

"I suspect most of us feel the same way," he returned her laugh and laid two fingers on her forearm, a small intimate gesture. "But we're taking a break here. Tell me about yourself. How did you get into the intelligence game?"

Danielson looked down at his hand. The fingers were those of a craftsman, large and gnarled, ungainly to look at, but capable of deft, intricate movement. She raised her eyes to his face and enjoyed the way his grey-green eyes reflected a sense of humor and well-being.

"Not much to tell—" she began.

While Runyan entertained Danielson with small talk, Isaacs and Phillips discussed the developments of the afternoon and their options for the remainder of the day. Isaacs was not pleased by any of the ideas he had heard. Phillips suggested gently that they should allow the brainstorming to continue until they either ran out of ideas or found one on which there was some consensus. They were interrupted by a woman who announced a phone call for Isaacs. He raised his eyebrows at Phillips and followed the woman out.

He returned several minutes later and headed for Danielson, his face grim. He interrupted Runyan in the middle of a funny story, and addressed Danielson.

"There's an emergency," he said brusquely. "We've got to get back to Washington."

As Danielson looked at Runyan with uncertainty, Isaacs turned to Phillips.

"I'm very sorry, but we must go. Something has come up. I'm grateful for your time today."

"We're happy to be of service, of course. Your problem has intrigued us, and I'm sure we'll continue to discuss it."

"I hope you will. I'll be in touch as soon as I can."

Isaacs hustled Danielson around as they gathered up their things and escorted her to the car.

He drove quickly in great concentration for several minutes until he was sure of his course. Then he glanced at her.

"That was Bill Baris. The Russians have made their next move. They've surrounded our nuclear satellite with a pack of hunter-killer satellites."

"What will they do?"

"Not clear. Baris has called the crisis team for this afternoon to try to get the basic facts together. We'll meet again first thing tomorrow morning and try to anticipate them. If they hold off that long. Damn! McMasters will wonder where the hell I am."

He drove in silence again for a while.

"That was a very good presentation you gave today," he said, keeping his eyes on the road. "You convinced them we've got a real problem. And thanks for coming to my defense when that bastard Leems got on my back."

"This can't really be a Russian weapon, can it?" she asked.

"Sure doesn't smell right to me, but we should check satellite locations just as Leems said."

Danielson began to contemplate how she could obtain and sort Soviet satellite positions. They were quiet the rest of the way to the airport.

There were problems getting their reservations changed. They spent an hour and a half in the terminal amid crowds that prevented any discussion of their mission. Danielson could tell Isaacs was tense and fretful. The visit with the Jason team had been intriguing, but inconclusive, and the move of the Russians had caught him up short. If he had been in Washington he would have assembled the crisis team, not left it to Baris. Danielson sympathized with the anxiety she knew Isaacs felt. CIA officials had a right in principle to their free time, but they had better be on the spot when an emergency cropped up, never mind off on another coast suborning Agency policy. Danielson felt exposed herself.

The only seats they could get were several rows apart in the crowded midsection of the red-eye flight. Jet lag and strain caught up with Danielson. She napped most of the way. Isaacs was trapped between a talkative matron and a young mother, squirmy babe in lap. He stared grimly ahead through the whole flight, trying in his fatigue to think.

Chapter 9

Jorge Payro grabbed another piece of sheet metal off the palette behind him. He fed it carefully into the machine, checking the alignment, then stepped back and yanked the lever triggering the hydraulics. The press crumped down, folding edges, slicing off the extra metal. Jorge raised the lever, pulled the formed piece off the platform and worked around the edges with his file to remove the worst of the burrs. He placed the partially formed object on the conveyor belt. Somewhere down the line, after more cutting, stamping, drilling, painting, and fitting, the part would emerge as the top of a washing machine. Jorge turned for another flat sheet. While he worked he thought of his date for the futbol game that evening. One of the teams from Buenos Aires was coming to play Rosario. Rosario was good this year; they had a chance. Jorge was excited by the prospect of a victory. He was also excited by his own chances with Constanza. Particularly if they won, everyone's passions would be running high.

He pulled another piece off the press and tackled it with his file. He put it on the conveyor, then did a double take, and yanked it off again. He held it before him and stared in amazement. There was a hole in it, about the size of his little finger. He had not noticed that when he picked up the sheet. He looked at the stack on the palette. No holes there. How could he have missed such a thing? He set the damaged part aside, picked up a fresh sheet, and maneuvered it into place. He pulled the lever. The press dropped a little, but then jammed, groaning.

Jorge slapped the lever off. He threw the switch that shut the machine down completely, raised his safety goggles up onto his forehead and stared. The upper jaw of the press was skew in its framework. Jorge stepped forward and craned his neck to look up at the underside. His eyes widened. There was a hole in the massive piece of steel. It was drilled through, just like the damaged part he had just removed. From somewhere higher up in the works of the machine, a steady stream of fluid seeped down. Jorge removed a glove, ran a finger through a drip and sniffed. Hydraulic fluid. This machine is in bad trouble, he thought to himself as he wiped his finger on his overalls. He pulled the sheet of metal from the press and was not completely surprised to find another hole in the bed of the machine. He ran a finger around its clean edge and bent to peer down. He couldn't see but a fraction of a centimeter in, but he bet it was deep, maybe all the way to the floor. He stuck his little finger into the hole up past the first knuckle. He couldn't imagine what could have caused such a thing.

Jorge pulled off his other glove, threw it next to the first, and went in search of his supervisor.

It was 7:30 a.m. Sunday morning, July 4. Isaacs had not slept on the flight back from San Diego and then had spent an hour on the phone catching up on the Russian deployment of hunter-killer satellites and making arrangements for this morning's meeting. He'd gotten three hours of troubled sleep and nursed a splitting headache.

Isaacs scanned the packed conference room. Twenty-three people were more than it held comfortably, but he had called for everyone in his crisis team to bring their aides. This would speed dissemination, give the young people exposure, and encourage them to participate directly. He did not want any bright ideas languishing in the face of an unprecedented confrontation with the Russians. He began as the last chair was filled.

"I'm sorry to have to call you in on a holiday. This may be the Soviets heavy-handed idea of irony, but they're threatening us with some real fireworks.

"You know that the Soviets launched an operating laser and used it to destroy the FireEye satellite which had recently been placed into orbit last April." You don't know why, though, he thought. He caught Pat Danielson's eyes on him from where she sat in a rear corner looking remarkably alert despite their late flight. She returned his gaze steadily until he looked on around the room and continued. "The US appropriated that laser satellite with the shuttle, but the Soviets launched another. The US response was to put a small atomic device in orbit near the laser. The device is specially shielded with a reflective coating, difficult for the laser to penetrate. There are also heat sensing circuits that will trigger the device if the laser is used on it. The Soviets have been informed of this. We have promised to detonate the device if the laser is used.

"They have now made their countermove. They've surrounded the two satellites with a pack of six hunter-killer satellites. These contain only conventional explosives, but they're powerful enough to neutralize our nuclear device. The concern is that the protective circuits will not respond to a blast wave. The Soviets are betting, or bluffing, that we are vulnerable to the hunter-killers.

"Our task is to anticipate the intelligence gathering operations that will be necessary to map out their tactical possibilities, and our appropriate responses. As of forty-five minutes ago, the Soviets had not tried to aim the laser, but they could force the issue at any moment."

Isaacs signaled, the lights were dimmed, and a slide projected at the end of the room. The people sitting too near the screen shuffled their chairs around and craned their necks.

"This was taken from one of our KH-11 satellites from about 5,000 miles," Isaacs continued. "The laser satellite is the cylinder at the tip of the yellow arrow. You can make out some details on it if you look closely, and, of course, the image can be reprocessed to bring them out. The small spot at the tip of the white arrow is our device."

"What's the actual spatial separation there?" a voice asked.

"About two hundred meters," Isaacs replied. "The effective range of the device is much greater, the proximity was chosen mainly for psychological effect. You'll notice that our device is located along the long axis of the laser satellite; the laser fires out the side. The small dots at the tips of the six shorter yellow arrows are the hunter-killers."

"That's an odd configuration they're in," said Bill Baris from somewhere down the table. "Unless there is a funny projection effect, they seem to be in two groups of three and closer to the big laser satellite than to ours. Why would they do that? Won't they do themselves as much or more damage as they do us?"

There was a silence for thirty seconds, then a sudden voice.

"Shaped charges! I'll bet they're shaped and specifically aimed away from the laser and toward our device."

There were murmurs of agreement, then Baris again.

"We'll need some close-up photos to see if the hunter-killers have distinguishing features and if there is a pattern in their orientation that suggests they are aimed. I bet we find they're positioned so that any recoil will miss the laser. We'll need ground intelligence concerning their manufacture."

Another voice. "If we assume they're shaped, we can work out the spread angle of the explosion from the positions they've been deployed in, assuming they're all designed to hit us and none to damage the laser."

Isaacs listened to this interchange with the satisfaction he always took when the ideas began to flow in one of these sessions. He had worked hard to assemble this crew and rarely failed to admire their performance. It was a good thing someone could think this morning. His mind was numb.

"How did we get in this fix?" someone inquired. "Surely we saw the hunter-killers converging?"

"The Soviets play good chess," Isaacs responded. "They know how to use their pawns. They correctly anticipated our dilemma as they moved the first one up. We had promised to fire the nuke if the laser were used. But it's a very different story to fire the first nuclear device in space in a generation when neither the laser nor even the hunter-killer is actually used, just repositioned. I think there was also a failure to realize that the heat sensitive circuits might not be triggered by an explosion until extensive physical damage was already done. In any case, once they had bluffed the first one into position, adding others wasn't much different."

"We could up the ante," someone suggested. "Put up another nuke at a greater distance, but still in kill range. If the hunter-killers take out the first, we take out everything left with the second nuke. And we lay down an ultimatum. Use one or both nukes if any hunter-killers approach the second."

Isaacs made a couple of personal notes to augment the record of the session which would be transcribed and stored in computer memory. "The President may not want to escalate in that direction," he replied. "Let's see what else we can come up with."

"What's to keep the Russians from putting up their own nuke?"

"They may be trying to keep some lid on this in their own way," answered Isaacs. "But that's clearly one of their options.

Let's come back to that and see if we can map out what would drive them to it."

"How fast are those hunter-killers?" a new voice asked. "Can the nuke be scooted somewhere else before they can respond? For instance out of their range, but still within nuclear range?"

Another voice answered. "Tough to outrun an explosion."

"Yeah, true," the first voice answered thoughtfully, "but at least you would be putting the pressure on them to make the first overt move."

"Maybe," came the second voice, "but if you force them to blast the nuke, they may figure they're already committed and start using the laser on everything else in orbit."

Isaacs had the projector turned off and the lights back on. Around the room, people sat erect from the postures they had assumed to peer at the slide.

"Let's talk some more about the options of the Soviets," Isaacs requested. "What are they apt to do?"

"Well," said Baris, "they could fire a charge over our bow, so to speak, if the charges are shaped and the explosion can be directed, just a little sabre rattling without changing the status quo. Or they could go for broke, zap us with a hunter-killer then use the laser with impunity. Or they could just fire the laser, betting that we won't use the nuke even if the laser is actually used. Hunter-killers don't do them much good then, but there is some chance any explosion would trigger the nuke, and they may not want to risk that.

"Come to think of it," Baris wagged a finger, "maybe they would want to try exactly that, just go ahead and use the hunter-killers. If the nuke goes, they have us for using atomics in space. If we chicken out, they have free use of the laser and our vaunted nuclear threat comes to nothing. Just the kind of pitiful giant posture they like to trap us in."

Baris scratched his head as he thought. "If that's their most obvious move, then we just force them to it if we try to move the nuke out of range of the hunter-killers. That seems to me to be the question. Will they risk our wrath and perhaps a nuclear explosion by using the hunter-killers, or just sit tight? Do we use the nuke without direct provocation, or try to horse it out to a greater distance? Or do we just sit with them and sweat blood?" He stopped and looked around the room for a reply.

The discussion continued for an hour and a half. They continued to produce ideas, filtering out the unproductive ones, refining and developing the good ones. A priority list of intelligence targets was constructed and assignments handed out. Isaacs finally called a halt so that all could turn to their individual tasks.

The next day, Monday, Isaacs finally found some time to pursue his personal agenda. He'd promised Danielson more data to refine her predictions of the upcoming event in Nagasaki. Now he looked across the desk at the young Navy lieutenant. Philip Szkada had been placed in nominal charge of the Navy's surveillance of the strange sonar signal. Although the day was officially a part of the three-day holiday weekend, he had agreed to meet Isaacs in Rutherford's old office.

"It's a pleasure to see you again, Mr. Isaacs," said Szkada. "I guess the last time was when you came to visit Captain Rutherford just before—just before—." His face took on a heavy pinched look. "It's still difficult to believe he's gone. By all rights I should have made that trip, but he insisted on going himself."

He was silent for a moment, then met Isaacs' gaze.

"What can I do for you today?"

"You know that Avery Rutherford was a good friend of mine. I'm interested in his death for both personal and professional reasons. When we spoke over the phone at the time, you indicated uncertainty as to whether the ship's sinking was related to its surveillance mission, but that the surveillance program was downgraded afterwards. I was hoping to learn more about the circumstances and the mission."

"There's not too much to say. In fact, under the shock of the moment, I may have said too much. From reports of the survivors and some scattered physical evidence, it appears that the ship's turbine exploded. There's no firm reason to conclude that the fate of the ship was related to her mission."

He paused and made a tent of his fingers. He cleared his throat before continuing.

"The mission itself is a confidential Navy investigation. With all respect, sir, I'm not sure you have a need to know."

Isaacs expected and admired that response. He would have demanded it of his own subordinates. He could not accept it, however. He turned the tack back to the personal issue.

"You said you should have been on the ship. Avery wasn't the sort to pull rank unnecessarily."

"No, sir, he wasn't. But in this case I had worked out the ideas that were the basis of the mission. I expected to go."

"Avery had nothing to do with the planning? Strange then that he should have involved himself in that way."

"Well, of course, we discussed the mission. Some information had been kicking around and I managed to make sense of it."

"Avery had no role in that?"

"Not really. Some things just fell into place for me after one of our discussions."

Szkada paused and looked thoughtful.

"He did ask me some leading questions. With the pleasure of seeing it fit together, I didn't give much thought to the actual process that brought me to the conclusion."

He looked up toward the far wall over Isaacs' right shoulder. Isaacs remained silent, reading the workings of his face. He saw the frown lines disappear, to be replaced by arched eyebrows and a look of mild surprise. After a moment another idea hit him and he leaned forward and locked eyes with Isaacs.

"He fed me the idea, didn't he?"

He pointed an index finger at Isaacs.

"And you gave it to him!"

Isaacs admired this perspicacity, even somewhat belated. No wonder Rutherford had spoken highly of him.

"Lieutenant, I sent my best friend to his death. I want to know what killed him."

"Mr. Isaacs, I really can't help you. I presume you already know what the mission was."

Isaacs wanted to make it easy for him.

"You're monitoring a sonar signal that moves on a trajectory which is fixed with respect to the stars."

Even having deduced Isaacs was aware of the mission, the frank statement startled Szkada. Isaacs continued.

"We have some seismic data showing the same behavior. In case you're curious," he smiled, "the idea of the fixed trajectory actually came from one of my people, a counterpart of yours in the Agency."

"You must know all I do then," Szkada commented. "I don't have the authority to push for a full investigation here, so we're just in a monitoring mode. We've learned nothing new. Perhaps we could collaborate," Szkada suggested, "with an official request from the Agency."

Isaacs cut him off with a raised hand.

"Lieutenant, we have a similar problem. Our mission has been officially shelved, partly because my superior knows that your superiors are nominally continuing the investigation. I want to say that I am here unofficially today.

"Let me ask you," Isaacs looked intently at the young officer, "do you think the ship's destruction was related to its mission?"

"I think we should be doing a lot more to find out."

"I believe I have a way to open this case up. I'll handle it in the Agency and if it doesn't work out, I don't want you involved. Your data is intrinsically more accurate than ours. I can't ask you through channels, but if you could give me the most precise values you have for recent sonar data, times, and locations, I may be able to exploit them in a way which is satisfactory to us both."

Szkada contemplated the man across from him for some time.

"I'll show you the numbers we have. You copy what you want on your own paper in your own handwriting. And good luck."

Isaacs nodded his acceptance of these terms and reached in his portfolio for paper and pen. Enough time, he thought, to get this data to Danielson before the crisis team reconvenes. He could sense the presence of the hunter-killer satellites orbiting, Damoclean, overhead. For the moment, at least, the thread still held the sword aloft. He knew Danielson was stealing moments from the hectic press of other duties to analyze the positions of Soviet satellites to check for any correlation with the seismic signal. He wondered whether she were having any luck with that. He needed to see Martinelli to arrange surveillance of Nagasaki, only two short days away, but that would probably have to wait until tomorrow.

Vincent Martinelli came around his desk to greet Isaacs, his doughy face lit with a smile.

"Bob, how are you? Sit down." He motioned Isaacs into a chair and sat in an adjacent one.

"What did you think of the President's decision to hang tight? Guts ball, huh?"

"So far, so good. I guess that makes it a wise move. We discussed the possibility that the Russians would take out the nuke and go for broke with the laser, but the more we talked, the more it seemed like their actual goal was to establish their right to orbit a laser, free of our interference, and that they would hold to the status quo. The President bought the idea that they didn't want an overt escalation any more than we did. But you're right, it took some nerve to just let the nuke sit in the range of those hunter-killers and wait it out."

"What's it been?" Martinelli glanced at his watch. "Sixty-odd hours since they were launched. As long as nobody nudges the trigger on one of those hunter-killers, we have a truce."

"Looks like it."

"So other than that, how are things in the think tank? Seems like we haven't had time to chat since that damn Russian carrier caught fire."

"Things are fine, Vince. But I was hoping you could improve them by taking a couple of pictures for me."

"Sure, anytime. That doesn't require a personal visit."

"I would like coverage of an area in Nagasaki near the bay, tomorrow."

"Tomorrow! Jesus, man, you know it takes a week at top speed to get a request through the priorities committee."

"I know that, Vince. That's why I'm here. All I need is one hour of your flex-time, but I need it tomorrow. There's no time to go through channels."

"It would help to clear it through McMasters, at least, even on an informal basis."

Isaacs was silent for a moment.

"I hoped that wouldn't be necessary."

Martinelli contemplated his visitor. He had known Isaacs to work around McMasters before, but not in a matter like this when consultation with him was explicitly mandated.

"This is important to you?"

"Vince, I think I'm on to something that may help explain the Novorossiisk event and get us out of this whole mess it has led to. I can't prove it yet. I need more evidence, including your photos."

"You want to tell me what it is?"

"You'll be sticking your neck out as it is if you do this. I think we should leave it at that."

"And you need to steer clear of McMasters?"

"He's got me between a rock and a hard place. The less said about that the better for now, too."

Martinelli let out a sigh. "Let's see whether what you're asking is even feasible. You have the coordinates?"

Isaacs withdrew a small sheet of notepaper from his pocket and handed it to Martinelli.

"I'll check with the scheduling office. Hang on a bit."

Martinelli left Isaacs in the office. Isaacs rose and paced the floor. He severely disliked involving Martinelli in this way. He could not even be sure the photos would be useful, but some steps had to be taken to reduce their level of ignorance. He wanted to bring to bear as many means as possible. He had cabled the consulate in Nagasaki and arranged for an observer to cover the area, hinting at the possibility of some political turmoil. Again he was operating out of channels since his office was not directly responsible for covert intelligence. He had gambled that any request from central headquarters would elicit a cooperative response and had apparently been correct.

Martinelli returned in a few minutes.

"The satellite time is tied up tight. There're troop movements in southern China, near the Vietnamese border. On the other hand, we'll have a U-2 flight returning from the same area at about the time you want. I can't give you an hour, but maybe we can get him to save a few frames in his magazine and circle Nagasaki for ten minutes. Any longer and the Japanese will get suspicious. We're allies, remember. They don't appreciate us taking spy pictures of them. At least we try to be subtle about it," he grinned.

"Ten minutes is cutting it very close. But if it's ten minutes spanning that time," Isaacs pointed at the slip of paper in Martinelli's hand, "that may do the trick."

"We'll see what we can do."

"Thanks, Vince, I owe you one."

"Wait till you see if we get anything."

Isaacs spent most of the next twenty-four hours as he had the last, in the frenzied analysis of Soviet signal intelligence, searching for clues that the deadlock in orbit might be broken. Danielson had used Szkada's sonar data to refine her estimate of the several block area in Nagasaki where she predicted the seismic event would encroach on the city. Isaacs had cabled the revised information to the consulate and passed it on to Martinelli. Martinelli had confirmed that they could get some aerial photos of the area.

As Isaacs headed home Wednesday evening he was concentrating on the upcoming event in Nagasaki, only a few hours away, a little after eleven in the morning Japanese time, July 8, allowing for the International Dateline. Would they learn anything useful? And, if so, for god's sake what? What were they dealing with? He replayed in his mind the interchange in La Jolla. Russians? Extraterrestrials? Damn it all anyway! He failed to notice that he had been following the same dark sedan all along MacArthur Boulevard nor did he notice the limousine that pulled in behind him as they neared Georgetown.

The sedan pulled into the quiet narrow street Isaacs always took to get home, and Isaacs followed. Part way along the block the sedan braked, and Isaacs also did so mechanically. The sedan's back-up lights came on, and it reversed to within a few feet of Isaacs' bumper. He felt a momentary hint of irritation at the delay and then looked back over his shoulder, preparing to back up himself to give room. All he saw was the hood of the limousine. At the same moment, someone opened his door and he jerked around with surprise.

A tall figure in a dark suit was silhouetted in the doorway. The man bent down, revealing a broad-featured face that was vaguely familiar.

"Mr. Isaacs?" The voice was slow, working methodically with an alien tongue. "Mr. Zamyatin would like a word with you."

Mr. Zamyatin was it! Isaacs' eyes followed those of the man back to the limousine. Colonel Grigor Zamyatin was well known in the Agency as the head of the KGB station in the capital, a position that gave him immense power throughout the country, not to mention his own homeland.

Isaacs fixed his eyes on the man again, recognizing now the face from the Agency file on the embassy staff. Yegor Vassilev, a "secretary" in the visa section.

"Zamyatin be damned," he said with some heat. "You can't accost me like this on a public street in my own country!"

"Please, Mr. Isaacs," Vassilev replied in a placating tone, "Mr. Zamyatin said to mention Academician Korolev."

Isaacs stared. What the hell did that mean? It was on the record that Isaacs had submitted the report suggesting meteorite damage to the Novorossiisk. A report that Korolev had rejected. But this forced liaison was unlikely to have arisen from such an interchange. They must have intercepted his personal letter to Korolev. Resignation mingled with a strong dose of curiosity drove Isaacs out of his seat. Could Zamyatin conceivably be turned to an ally in this bizarre situation?

As he stepped onto the pavement, Vassilev mumbled, "I will operate your vehicle," and slipped behind the wheel of the Mercedes.

The rear door to the limousine opened and Isaacs stepped in and sat. Someone outside closed the door, and a deep hush settled into the interior of the car. In a moment they began to move ahead gently.

A half block away an anonymous tan Oldsmobile Cutlass was parked in a driveway. The driver lowered the compact camera he had been using and spoke softly into a microphone. He watched as a van from a Georgetown appliance store pulled around the corner and closed to within a half a block of the limousine. He then backed out and headed in the opposite direction.

In the limousine, Grigor Zamyatin reached across, extending a hand.

"Mr. Isaacs," he said in a carefully developed Midwestern accent.

Isaacs, examining the neatly combed grey hair, the friendly peasant face, the shrewd black eyes, hesitated a moment. Then he took the hand in a firm grip. No sense insulting the man before the cards were on the table. He felt some protest was deserved, however.

"Colonel. I trust you have good reason for this bit of piracy. You could get me in quite a jam. The Agency frowns on unauthorized clandestine meetings with the opposition."

"Come, come, Mr. Isaacs. I think you will agree we need a quiet, frank chat, man to man. Surely you would not want me to make an official request for an audience. How would you explain that to your Mr. Drefke—or to your Mr. McMasters?"

Damn! thought Isaacs, even the KGB knows he's on my back.

"In any case," said Isaacs, "here we are. What's on your mind?"

"Your role in the Novorossiisk affair, Mr. Isaacs. Simply that."

Isaacs looked at him silently.

"You wrote a very persuasive memo concerning the possibility of a meteorite striking the carrier. Your premise had already been considered, tested, and rejected. Nevertheless, your sincerity, if I may use that word, made a deep impression on Academician Korolev."

Zamyatin watched closely as he used that name. He saw a slight lifting of the chin. He faced straight ahead and continued.

"You have probably guessed that we are aware of the contents of your personal letter to him."

"What I don't know is whether he even received it," said Isaacs, attempting to take the offensive. "I've had no reply."

"Oh, he received it. Indeed he did." Zamyatin glanced sideways at Isaacs. "He has referred to it in some very high circles, and some lowly ones. I myself recently had opportunity to discuss it with him."

Isaacs ignored the feigned modesty.

"You might be interested to know," Zamyatin continued, staring ahead over the shoulder of the chauffeur, "that your letter played a small role in recent events. As you are very aware, an unfortunate series of circumstances has followed from the attack on the Novorossiisk. The decision of your President to confiscate the Cosmos 2112 was a terribly unfortunate and provocative act. His response to our launch of Cosmos 2231 perhaps even more so. These events have taken on a life of their own. The Soviet people do not lightly regard an attack on the sovereignty of our Union, whatever the motivation."

Zamyatin shifted his gaze to fix on Isaacs.

"But the Soviet people also have a deep concern for truth and justice."

And the Russian way, thought Isaacs, despite himself. Could all this be an elaborate ruse, he wondered, to further masquerade Soviet complicity in a scheme he could barely fathom?

"If your country were blameless in the case of the Novorossiisk, this is a mitigating circumstance to be considered in any action we might take during subsequent events," Zamyatin continued.

"Academician Korolev has argued strenuously, using your letter and report as evidence, that your country knows nothing of the attack on the Novorossiisk. This was a factor in the decision not to escalate our response to your recent provocations."

But what does your country know about the Novorossiisk

that you're not telling me? Isaacs asked silently. He chose his words carefully.

"If that is true, then I won't deny some satisfaction. But this rendezvous was not arranged for my pleasure."

"No," Zamyatin agreed flatly. "There is concern at the highest levels in our government to understand the fate of the Novorossiisk. We have gathered some fragmentary evidence of our own for this curious signal you described to Korolev. I am authorized to ask you some questions, that we can better understand the situation.

"Many of my colleagues reject your story. They are convinced of the culpability of your government beginning with the events on the Novorossiisk. They demand to know what you did to the Novorossiisk, and why you, personally, were selected to propagate such a rooster—pardon me, cock and bull story, eh?—about mysterious effects in the earth."

"Lord deliver me from fools of all persuasions," Isaacs blurted, throwing his hands up in exasperation. "Look," he said heatedly, "I have no proof to give you, but I do give you my word of honor. No one in my government has a clue to what happened aboard the Novorossiisk—or the Stinson, I remind you. But it's the thick-headed idiots in your government and mine who can't see the true threat here who are leading us close to catastrophe."

"Sir! Sir!" Zamyatin held up a hand in protest. "Let me stipulate that I personally accept both your word and that there is a more subtle problem here to be understood. We must know the position of your government. What is being done to clarify this matter? What have you learned?"

"Precious little," Isaacs replied in disgust. "If it were otherwise, do you think I would write that letter to Korolev?"

"But if the situation is as mysterious and potentially serious as you say, surely it becomes the center of a major investigation?"

Isaacs looked closely at the Russian. Careful, he cautioned

himself. If the Russians aren't responsible, then, properly cultivated, Zamyatin could prove useful, as Korolev apparently had been. What irony to find allies in the Soviet camp even as the confrontation overhead escalated. He must have some hint of the problems with McMasters, but now was not the time to take this man fully into his confidence, not when he could not extend that confidence to even his close friends in the Agency. He shifted to face Zamyatin more squarely and spoke with sincerity.

"There is a basic problem here. I see a dangerous pattern I don't understand. My government is not behind it and neither, I'm convinced, is yours. But to launch a full-scale investigation requires hard evidence, and that is lacking. I have certain plans to gain more evidence, but I don't feel at liberty to reveal them."

Isaacs paused to collect his thoughts. Zamyatin watched him carefully.

"Look," said Isaacs, "I know the real reason for this meeting. You would have received any hard facts as a bonus, but you're really here to take my measure face to face. You're asking yourself, is this really a man who is carrying on a legitimate crusade outside official channels?"

This time it was Isaacs who caught the narrowing of eyes that said he hit home.

"There is nothing else I can say to convince you at this point; you'll make up your own mind. But if you decide to believe me, hear this. We face a common, unknown danger. Whether I succeed or fail in my efforts, it's to your advantage to push your own investigation in any way you can. Listen to Korolev. He'll know what to do."

Zamyatin studied Isaacs' face carefully for a long moment. Then, still holding his gaze, he gave a small motion with his right hand. The limousine immediately braked to a gentle halt.

The Russian extended his hand again. His voice was polite, but cool.

"Good-bye for now, Mr. Isaacs. And good luck."

Isaacs pumped the hand once and let himself out. As he closed the door to the limousine, Vassilev pulled up behind in his Mercedes. Isaacs paused for a moment with his hand on the handle of the limousine door. Then he responded with uncharacteristic spontaneity to an inner voice. He yanked the door open again and leaned down to peer in.

"Yes?" Zamyatin was startled.

"Nagasaki. Tonight. 9:13."

Isaacs slammed the door and strode rapidly back to his own car. Vassilev saw him in and shut the door behind him. Isaacs threw the car into gear, then pulled quickly out and around the limousine, causing Vassilev to step back out of the way. Isaacs looked about him, recognized where he was, and headed for his house a few blocks away.

The appliance store van cruised slowly across the intersection behind the limousine. It turned at the next corner, accelerated to normal speed, and headed away from the site of the rendezvous.

Chapter 10

Masaki Yoshida leaned on his taxi horn in frustration. He had free-lanced for the CIA for several years. He expected to know only a minimal amount about operations to which he was assigned, but the description he had received from his contact yesterday was the most ill-defined he had seen yet. He was supposed to cruise a several square block area of warehouses near the harbor and keep an eye out for some unspecified form of trouble.

His contact had said nothing about the jam of cars and trucks which crowded the streets and loading docks, making it nearly impossible to move. He had spent five minutes edging the last half block. Earlier he had maneuvered his cab up onto the sidewalk only to find a truck unloading and blocking his way. It had taken him ten minutes to force a gap in the creeping traffic and return to the street. He sounded the horn again. There could be a riot a block away, and he would not know a thing about it!

Immediately ahead of the erstwhile CIA agent were two cars and then an open bed truck which blocked his view on down the street. As Yoshida leaned out the window in an attempt to see past the truck, the asphalt of the road between the truck's front wheels buckled downward slightly and a small hole appeared in the center of the depression. A hole was pierced in the bottom of the oil pan just as the third piston advanced on its exhaust stroke. Then, as if by the action of a ragged drill, a gash ripped the base of the piston rod where it joined the crank shaft. The rod cracked and the piston flew unimpeded up the cylinder. Another series of holes appeared in the block, the head, the air filter, and finally in the thin sheet metal of the hood, all aligned with those in the asphalt and the broken rod. The piston ruptured the engine head atop the cylinder, then punched a second, larger hole in the hood. The piston and fragments of engine arced thirty feet over the road before crashing loudly into the galvanized steel wall of a warehouse. The mortally wounded engine shuddered to a stop with the shrieking sound of twisted, grinding metal. Hot water shot through the upper hole in the block, filling the engine compartment with steam. This in turn billowed out of the seams, the hole ruptured by the piston, and in one dainty vertical stream. Beneath the motor a pea soup green mixture of oil, water, and antifreeze poured out of the hole in the oil pan, collected in the underlying dent in the pavement and then slowly drained down the hole in the middle.

With his head out the window, Yoshida clearly heard the explosion as the piston blew and saw it rifle into the warehouse wall. Forgetting his mission, he rammed the shift into neutral, let out the clutch, and hauled on the parking brake. He ran to the truck and yanked open the driver's door. The man inside sat stupefied, but apparently unhurt. Yoshida stepped up and helped the man out and over to the sidewalk.

The truck driver sat on the curb and in a reaction to shock, began to jabber his innocence of any wrongdoing.

Yoshida attempted to calm him and then noticed a stinging in his eyes and burning in his lungs. His first reaction was to glance at the truck. Then he whirled as he heard a shouting tumult behind him. A hundred yards away drivers were pouring out of their cars, and people were running frantically in both directions from a warehouse on the other side of the street. Many held handkerchiefs to their mouths or covered their eyes.

As Yoshida had been helping the driver from the truck, a window had shattered in the skylight of the warehouse. Below, an array of large cylindrical storage vessels held chlorine gas. Almost instantly, twin punctures appeared in the top and bottom of the cylinder directly beneath the skylight.

Jets of bilious yellow-green gas shot toward the ceiling and mushroomed out onto the floor. Within seconds a heavy layer of gas blanketed the warehouse. In a small office at the rear of the warehouse an employee was roused by the sound of cascading glass. He stepped out and was immediately assailed by the billowing fumes. In a panic he charged for the front door, his way blocked save for aisles among the huge containers. He tripped and fell, the pain of contact with the floor causing him a sharp intake of breath, a poisonous draft. He regained his feet and stumbled to the door, flinging it open and collapsing on the walk outside in a spasm of coughing. The dense gas flowed out the door and seeped around the choking figure.

Down the street, Yoshida could not identify the particular agent that assaulted his eyes and lungs, but he reacted to the shouts of *gas!* He joined the fleeing crowd racing among the stalled cars and trucks toward fresh air.

Thursday morning Isaacs raced into the office. There was a cable. Something *had* happened in Nagasaki! The reports were vague, fragmented. A gas leak. One person dead. He didn't know what he had expected, but not this tantalizing irrelevancy. It was the right time and place; it had to be connected. But what did a gas leak have to do with their strange signal? Was there some puncture, like the Novorossiisk? He stole some moments with Danielson, and they agreed they had to concoct some way to get more information on the specifics. What had leaked? How? He felt a rise of panic. He needed time to think, to assimilate this, to plan, but there was none.

He returned to the mass of data culled from the signal intercepts of the Russian laser and hunter-killer satellites. He was supposed to be thinking like a Russian, anticipating them, but his mind was swimming with thoughts of Nagasaki when Kathleen put through the call from the Director.

It froze him to his chair, an ice storm raging through him. He had been found out!

They knew everything. QUAKER. Nagasaki. Somehow McMasters had gotten onto him.

He was to report to the Director's office at nine the following morning. His hand shook as he replaced the phone on the hook.

Isaacs fought to quell the churning in his bowels. He had not been so angry and frightened at one time since he'd been hauled before the principal in the third grade. He and a friend had been throwing rocks during recess, in violation of one of the strictest rules. His friend had broken the window, but he had run, leaving Isaacs to be caught with a stone in his hand. This was no schoolyard prank, however; this was the big time. He turned the knob and entered the room.

The Director of Central Intelligence motioned curtly for him to take a seat across from his desk. Isaacs did so, avoiding the venomous green eyes of McMasters who was already stationed at the opposite corner of the desk.

"Mr. Isaacs," Drefke began. "I can't express how shocked I am at the charges that have accumulated against you." He spread his hand on the folder on his desk. "A man of your status and record. This is not petty malfeasance. I don't want to overreact, but some of your recent behavior could be regarded as verging on treason."

This word brought a wisp of smile to McMasters' lips.

Drefke opened the file and scanned down it. "Unauthorized use of restricted computer data. Unauthorized consultation with Jason. Unauthorized access to field agents. Unauthorized use of photoreconnaissance facilities." He looked hard at Isaacs, then clenched his fist in frustration. He wanted to work with the President on global issues, not to be involved with awkward disciplinary questions. Why had McMasters let these internal affairs get out of hand? What the hell did Isaacs think he was doing?

"Good Lord, man," he spoke aloud. "Do you realize that on this basis alone I have virtually no choice but to ask for your resignation? And not just you, but Deputy Director Martinelli and this woman, uh, Danielson? They've conspired with you. Have you any idea of the turmoil in the Agency if I'm forced to let you all go?"

Isaacs started to speak, but his voice caught in his throat.

"What's that?" demanded Drefke.

Isaacs tried again. "I said you can leave Martinelli and Danielson out of this. I coerced them."

"You may want to leave them out now, but it's too late," McMasters' voice was cool and smooth in his victory. Isaacs refused to look at him. "They allowed themselves to become involved. They must suffer the consequences."

Damn my eyes, thought Isaacs. Danielson was bad enough; her low status is some protection since I can say I ordered her. But I shouldn't have involved Martinelli. Photos from the U-2's altitude relayed from a special scanner by satellite link showed virtually nothing useful anyway.

Drefke had his hand over his eyes, looking inward to struggle with the enormity of the final issue.

"How could you," he removed his hand to stare at Isaacs in

pain and anger, "how *could* you meet with them, the head of the Washington KGB, for chrissake, to reveal the President's tactics in the confrontation over the new laser in Cosmos 2231? What could possibly induce you to sell out? To put the whole future of our control and use of space in jeopardy? And in such an obvious way?"

"Have you been one of them all along?" McMasters asked calmly.

Drefke glared at him and Isaacs exploded. "No! God-damnit! I'm not one of them! I've sold out nothing! You don't understand!"

"Understand?" asked McMasters quietly. "We have the interchange with Zamyatin on tape. It's quite damning."

Tape! So the bastard had me under surveillance, Isaacs thought. He continued to speak to Drefke. "If you recorded that session in his limousine then you know that whole crazy episode was Zamyatin's idea."

"The recordings are incomplete for technical reasons," McMasters purred, "but there was enough to show your perfidy. You failed to report the contact. There is nothing to suggest you were not a willing accomplice in this conspiracy. We have only your word for that."

"But you *have* my word," Isaacs shot the oath at McMasters, looking directly at him for the first time. McMasters stiffened, but could not summon the strength of mind to voice a contradiction.

Isaacs used the opening.

"Sir," he addressed Drefke, "you said yourself the meeting with Zamyatin was an absurd way to sell out. Surely it's obvious that if I were really cooperating with the Soviets, I wouldn't do so in so stupid a fashion?"

Drefke gave a small nod. He didn't understand, but he knew that if a man like Isaacs turned, he would be damned difficult to catch. He certainly would not be hitching rides with the local KGB to exchange tidbits.

Isaacs continued, "I won't deny that my actions precipitated the meeting, but it was all Zamyatin's idea. He didn't think I could or would respond through official channels. Whether he thought or cared that I would be in hot water if he snatched me off the street, I don't know.

"If you will hear me out, I would like to try to explain. You recognize that my recent behavior is not only at odds with Agency policy, but also with my own record and methods. We are all involved in some very odd circumstances. These peculiar circumstances have forced me to extreme lengths. I think the peril was confirmed two days ago in Nagasaki, but we still don't understand—that's the major problem."

"Ah, Nagasaki," Drefke leaned back in his chair. "Perhaps you can tell me what the hell went on there."

"I can tell you the background. The details are in this memo."

Isaacs extracted an envelope from his pocket and pushed it across the desk to Drefke.

"Mr. McMasters has a previous version of it."

"Oh? I wasn't informed of that."

"In my considered opinion," McMasters said uncomfortably, "Mr. Isaacs has constructed a tissue of fantasy. What little merit there was to the case was not Agency business. I did not and do not believe there was any rationale to violate Agency regulations in the manner summarized there." He nodded at the file on Drefke's desk.

"I see," said Drefke. He didn't, but he was beginning to.

"Mr. Isaacs, may I ask why you did not proceed according to regulation if you had some concern?"

Isaacs looked him squarely in the eye.

"I was ordered not to."

"By McMasters here."

"That's correct."

"His request was ill-considered and inappropriate to the function of the Agency," McMasters said stiffly.

"Mr. McMasters is your superior," Drefke said to Isaacs.

"Yes, sir."

"You not only disobeyed him; you violated a number of Agency regulations to do so."

McMasters relaxed a little. Precisely so, he thought.

Drefke regarded the two men before him, sensing the tension between them. McMasters ran a tight ship on internal affairs. That freed Drefke to concern himself with the large issues. Isaacs had risen rapidly with an excellent record. Two such men could come to legitimate disagreement on occasion. In this business, McMasters was acting true to form, but Isaacs' behavior had been bizarre, completely out of character. Was Isaacs' aberrant behavior to be stopped short and penalized for the greater good of a smooth-functioning Agency, or did he actually see something that McMasters, the narrow-minded authoritarian, couldn't perceive? If McMasters were right, Isaacs was a damnable nuisance. If Isaacs were right?

"You were going to tell me about Nagasaki," Drefke said to Isaacs. McMasters shifted uncomfortably.

"This all goes back to the Soviet carrier, the Novorossiisk," Isaacs said.

"The Novorossiisk?"

"That's right. You know what followed from that. An escalating conflict in space."

"If you're implying all that has been Agency business, I'm quite aware of the fact, thank you," said Drefke drily.

"But you don't know what happened to the Novorossiisk. What started it all."

"No," Drefke said slowly. "But does it matter now?"

"It matters for two reasons. An understanding of the origin of these affairs may help put a cap on them. And what happened to the Novorossiisk may be the greater question."

"Greater than nuclear or beam warfare in space?" Drefke asked incredulously.

"Ridiculous," McMasters said, backing him up.

"I have no proof yet, but I'm sure Nagasaki and the Novorossiisk are closely linked. Nagasaki is another clue to the ultimate problem. The current danger is the unknown. The Soviets feel that, too. They don't know what happened to the Novorossiisk either."

"Why did Zamyatin pick on you anyway?"

Isaacs paused. This could be crucial, if it weren't already on the tapes.

"I wrote a letter to Academician Korolev," Isaacs said, "describing my fears about the Novorossiisk."

"You what?" Drefke almost shouted.

"Oh, for god's sake," McMasters blurted simultaneously.

"You've got to see we're on the same side on this one," Isaacs protested.

"But you can't go discussing Agency affairs with the top brains in the Kremlin!" Drefke said, exasperated.

"According to Mr. McMasters, this wasn't an Agency affair," Isaacs said.

"Well, any security matter then," Drefke said, but he calmed down, granting Isaacs the point.

"I felt something had to be done," Isaacs persisted. "I sent a memo to Korolev similar to the one I gave Mr. McMasters, outlining the series of circumstances that led to my concern. Zamyatin saw that letter. I told you they're still worried about the Novorossiisk. That's what we talked about."

"You talked about the Cosmos 2231 and our nuclear deterrent," McMasters said meanly.

"Only briefly, and in a completely different context from what you'd like to believe," Isaacs snapped. He turned to Drefke.

"Korolev has used my letter to argue that we did not initiate the Novorossiisk business. Zamyatin told me that my letter convinced the Soviets to keep a cap on the confrontation over the Cosmos. That's all we said about it. And Zamyatin did most of the talking."

"So they're worried," Drefke said.

"Yes, they are."

"You still haven't told me what exactly happened at Nagasaki."

"Pat Danielson assembled a variety of data which has shown that some force or influence is moving through the earth in a very regular way. I think that influence damaged the Novorossiisk, sank the USS Stinson which was sent by the Navy to investigate the phenomenon, and did the damage in Nagasaki."

Drefke started to speak, but Isaacs continued intensely.

"We don't know what's going on; that's what frightens me. That's what has caused me to do all these things you think are so crazy. But this thing is dangerous. It's real. It's predictable. Pat Danielson predicted where and when there would be damage in Nagasaki. She has predicted a similar fate for Dallas in a little over two weeks. This thing, whatever it is, will keep on causing death and destruction until we determine what it is!"

Isaacs leaned back, spent.

Drefke tried to absorb this diatribe. He didn't understand at all. But Isaacs was either sincere and committed, or he was insane. Could his insanity be contagious, caught by the Russians? What the hell was going on? Was this a good man gone around the bend? Or was here an issue of great magnitude on which he could truly serve his President? He would have loved to kick the whole thing to McMasters, but he perceived that, in ways he did not yet fully comprehend, McMasters was part of the problem. Besides, the involvement of the Russians smacked of truly global issues, not simple internal bickering. The only good decision now was no decision.

"Mr. Isaacs, I don't understand all that you have been trying to tell me. Not by a long shot. And the fact remains that there is a *prima facie* case against you for violating Agency regulations as well as good common sense." He paused and picked up Isaacs' memo.

"But I think perhaps I should read this document of yours before deciding what to do about you and the others."

The tone of dismissal hung in the air for a long moment until Isaacs and McMasters finally shuffled their chairs and got to their feet. There was an awkward moment at the door as they each tried to ignore the other, which prevented signals as to who should go first. Finally, Isaacs stepped back and gave a brief gesture. McMasters charged through. Isaacs waited until McMasters passed the outer doorway and then slowly closed Drefke's door behind him.

Drefke got up and walked to the window. He looked out for a long time, hands clasped behind his back. Then he took his seat and pulled the typewritten pages from the envelope Isaacs had left him. He began to read.

Robert Isaacs resigned himself to the fact that the situation was out of his hands. Under the terms of his partial suspension awaiting the outcome in Dallas, he could not engage in policy decisions, so for the next two weeks he busied himself with routine things neglected in the recent press of events. To his relief the confrontation with the Russians cooled. The fragile status quo held. On the final weekend before Dallas, he arranged for his daughter Isabel to stay with a friend and convinced Muriel to spend the time with him sailing on the Chesapeake.

Pat Danielson spent the two week period in an agonized limbo. She, too, went about her duties, but the upcoming event which would profoundly affect her career was never very far from her mind. Some mysterious force would push through the earth six hundred times, she mused, while she chewed her nails, waiting for it to hit Dallas. In a way, she was glad that Drefke had explicitly forbidden both Isaacs and her from going to Dallas, as well as from exercising any other connection to Project QUAKER. She recognized the great likelihood of futility, but knew that if the trip were not proscribed she would have gone to Dallas to try to see something, anything, that would give a clue to the force which would erupt there.

On the final Saturday she dragged her roommate, Janine, on a prolonged shopping trip and then to a movie. Sunday she could not shake the doldrums and spent the day in fretful listlessness. Monday evening she went to bed early, but tossed in a restless, unsatisfying sleep. Something in her kept time, and she later found herself wide awake, staring at the ceiling. Without looking at the clock she knew that it must be nearly one a.m. An hour earlier in Dallas it was about to happen. She continued to stare in the darkness, straining to project herself into the scene. What would she see? What would it do? She felt completely halted in that prolonged state of painful anticipation, but then the alarm pulled her up from a deep sleep. She pried her eyes open. The world still looked the same.

"You ever been to Dallas before?" Glen Wilson asked his partner in a subdued voice.

The two men walked slowly, purposefully, down the street, eyes catching every facet of the subdued activity.

"Me? Nah," replied Sam Spangler. "Unless you count changing planes in the airport. You ever ride those little trolleys?"

"Um. Yeah, couple of times. Kinda fun at first, no driver and all. Irritating, though, when they stop for no apparent reason."

They skirted a disheveled old man, slumped asleep against the wall, legs sprawled onto the sidewalk, brown bag cradled in his lap.

"I was just thinking," Wilson continued, "I've seen a few boots and hats, but except for the fact that it's damn awful hot, it's hard to tell where we are. I mean, look at this. Bars, strip joints, porny flicks. The only women you see that aren't hookers are with some guy hustling 'em off somewhere else. Just a little seedy piece of anywhere, USA."

"You're right about that," Spangler agreed. "They do move a lot of produce through here in the daytime, I guess." He flicked a rotting cabbage with the side of his shoe. It rolled up against the barred storefront. Behind the bars were partitioned tables waiting the next day's yield.

"You're also right about the heat. Feels like I'm wearing a blanket. Told you we should've gone native, jeans and T-shirts. Would have fit right in and been a damn sight cooler than these suits."

"Hey, better than that," Wilson shot him a quick smile, "I coulda dressed as a wino and sat around taking it easy and you coulda come in drag and walked the streets 'til something happens. You might've made a few bucks."

Spangler smiled back and swaggered a few steps. They reached a corner and turned to cross the street, waiting for the light. Wilson looked up at the buildings around them. The tallest ones of the main commercial area were a few blocks away. Around them, the buildings ranged from two to ten stories in height, the upper stories mostly dark as midnight approached. Once across the street they turned and headed back in the direction from which they had come. Wilson glanced at his watch.

"Five minutes?"

Spangler nodded confirmation. "Beats the hell out of me how they can know where something is going to happen, and when, to the second, and not know what. Screwy damn assignment."

They walked on in silence, checking their watches more frequently as the assigned time approached, unconsciously walking more slowly, watching more carefully. Finally they stopped. Wilson noticed the digits on his watch which indicated seconds as they flashed to zero-zero, signaling the onset of the final minute during which the unspecified, but potentially dangerous event should occur. He tried to simultaneously register the numbers on the watch as they swapped places, second by second, and the urban visage around them. Thirty seconds later, he realized he had been holding his breath as he strained for any clue. He stared at the watch and exhaled, more loudly than he had intended.

The sound of his released breath mingled with and covered the onset of a strange whistling roar. The two agents glanced suddenly at one another and then turned to look down the street, trying to fix the location of the noise. It seemed to rise rapidly above the buildings.

The roar diminished, to be replaced by a hoarse cry. In the

middle of the next block a man emerged onto the sidewalk and stood there, his frantic screams tearing the night.

A hole appeared in the concrete foundation of the basement of the Poodle Lounge. Twin punctures followed in the keg of beer immediately above it. As the pressurized brew began to spurt a frothy spout, another hole was ripped in the floor of the bar. Chaos ensued there as the quiet atmosphere was split by the sound of smashing glass shelves and bottles, as if someone had suddenly taken an ax to the racks behind the bar. As the bartender spun to stare in disbelief, a new hole had already been drilled in the ceiling above his head.

Upstairs at Crazy Lil's they played out the quiet midweek evening. The smokey room was dominated by a small oblong stage surrounded by seats for patrons. At the four corners of the stage were pillars which supported a canopy with mirrored undersurface and ruffled trim, the whole thing a grotesque parody of an old four-poster bed. Along one wall a screen was mounted for entr'acte movies. Opposite were a pair of coin-operated pool tables. At one of these, a tough-looking pair played eightball, studiously ignoring the woman working on the stage.

The audience was sparse. Three young cowboy-types in boots, jeans, and carefully sculpted straw hats. One of these boasted an unlawful eagle feather, the emblem of little britches rodeo days, not long past. A few bored salesmen sat each by himself, their common predicament being insufficient grounds to bring them together. The only spirit came from two stray out-of-town convention goers. One of these had just crooked a finger and gestured with a dollar bill. The dancer had interrupted her gyrations to pause in front of him, pelvis outthrust, as he worked the bill under the strap of her g-string. That position was one of precarious balance and left her unprepared for what happened next.

She felt as if the floor were suddenly thrust up under her, as with the rapid rise of an elevator. She fell backward heavily onto the stage. As she tipped, a large ragged gash was torn along the length of one of the four canopy posts. The post snapped and splintered. Deprived of symmetrical support, the mirrored canopy sagged and then twisted as the remaining three posts tilted in unison.

The dancer stared upward in numb shock and saw her image grow. With a burst of panic she realized the canopy was collapsing upon her. She flung her arms over her face and shrieked. The men seated along the perimeter recoiled frantically as chairs and bodies went sprawling. The young cowboy with the eagle feather made an aborted move toward the woman, but he was too far away. The canopy crashed down putting an abrupt end to her screams.

The bouncer-cashier-projectionist, who had been sitting on a stool by the entrance attempting to read a paperback western in the dim light, dropped the book when the first post splintered and stood as if paralyzed, watching the collapse of the canopy. In the stillness which followed, he took a few tentative steps toward the stage. All he could see of the dancer was one leg. A shard of mirror the size and shape of a pizza slice was embedded in her thigh, its shiny surface obliterated by a pulsing gout of arterial blood. The man paled, raced for the door and clattered down the stairs toward the street shouting hysterically.

Across the alley and down the block rose one of the taller buildings in the neighborhood. It was vacant save for a janitorial staff scattered over several floors. As the patrons of Crazy Lil's joined the hysterical employee on the adjacent street, a small tunnel was punctured in the rear corner of the building where the left side and rear walls joined. This tunnel proceeded rapidly but methodically down through the wall passing with equal ease through concrete and reinforcing bars.

A minute or so passed uneventfully, then fractures began to radiate from the tunnel into the surrounding concrete. The building settled slightly, amplifying the unequal distribution of stress along the wound and increasing the rate of fracturing.

Inside, in a corner of the building, a weary man guided a buffing machine slowly back and forth. He stopped suddenly as he felt a shift in the floor. The unguided buffing machine dug more heavily on one side and skittered away from him. He grabbed for it and quickly shut it off. He stood, listened and felt through his feet the barely perceptible vibrations of rupturing concrete.

He shuffled out of the office into the hallway. He stopped and felt with his feet again and sensed nothing.

"Hey, Harold!"

A young man working with a mop on the floor at the far end of the corridor looked up.

"C'mon down here. There's sumpin' funny goin' on."

The old man led the younger one into the office and stood him in the corner. They stared at one another as each felt the minute vibrations emanating from the weakened corner. Suddenly, a portion of the rear wall sagged a quarter of an inch. A jagged crack raced from the corner of the room to the windowsill. The window glass shattered; some pieces fell inward; others made the longer plunge to the alley below.

Harold shouted.

"Hey! This mother's comin' apart!"

He raced for the door. The old man followed him in a lumbering jog.

"Harold, you're faster than I am. You get upstairs and warn the folks there. I'll head down."

Harold spun to a stop and stared hard at the old man. After a long moment he nodded and pushed through the exit door into the stairway and headed up three steps at a time. The old man followed him and two-stepped downward.

A block away, Glen Wilson and Sam Spangler had joined the crowd which stood a discreet distance from the man who had run, shouting into the street. Now the man was pacing nervously about, mumbling incoherently. Patrons of the strip joint babbled to one another or to passers-by about what had happened. People from the Poodle Lounge below anxiously explained their disruption to whoever would listen. Wilson tried to absorb these several conversations at once. As they had crossed the street, he had heard the returning echo of the whistling roar which had preceded the commotion. The sound had vanished in an ill-determined direction, but he also listened for some repercussion.

Finally, he heard the muted crashes as large chunks of masonry began to break away from the other building, crashing into the alley. He grabbed his partner's arm and led him off down the street in the general direction of the sound.

As they reached the nearest intersection, they heard from around the corner the terrifying roar as the rear quarter of the building gave way. Portions of the rear and side walls peeled away to expose the multilayered innards of the building as if it were a large misshapened doll house.

The two agents froze at the corner until the noise died away and then walked to the alley and peered down it toward the ruined building. Even in the dim light they could see the huge pile of rubble reaching above the second floor, torn chunks of concrete interspersed with crushed office furniture. Soon they were joined by others from the crowd in front of the strip joint.

The agents edged out of the crowd. Wilson began to start back toward the bar, but Spangler gestured in the opposite direction, and they continued on around the block.

They passed in front of the damaged building. The only sign of disturbance from this aspect was the group of a dozen or so janitorial workers who huddled nervously in the street, some talking loudly, many standing silent, a few still conspicuously clutching their brooms and mops.

The agents continued on around the block. Back on the first street they returned to their car. A squad car was parked in front of the strip joint entrance. From a distance, the wail of approaching sirens could be heard. The crowd had grown. They got in the car. Wilson put the key in the ignition, but paused before he turned it. He looked at his partner.

"What in god's name do you suppose that was?"

Spangler was slumped down in his seat, staring straight ahead.

"Beats the living hell out of me. Never seen anything like it."

"This ought to get headquarters lathered up. I have a feeling the boss was hoping nothing would happen, but now they're going to want some physical evidence. From that collapsed building for sure, probably in that bar, too. I hope the locals don't go mucking around and mess something up. No sense talking to the beat cop over there, but it's not our business to go higher up. I hate to play dumb bunny, but I guess we need to call home for orders."

"I need something," Spangler growled. "Jesus!"

Wilson cranked the key and headed for the motel room they had rented out toward the airport.

Four days later, on a waning Friday afternoon, Vincent Martinelli hosted Isaacs for a celebratory drink. He put the bottle on the little bar built in behind his desk then swiveled in his chair and hoisted his double scotch and soda.

"L'chaim!"

The turning point in Nagasaki flashed in Isaacs' mind.

"Kampai," he said, returning the salute.

"Well, son-of-a-bitch, Bob," Martinelli said. "Maybe old man Drefke's not a complete knucklehead after all. For a while there I thought I was going to have to look for a new career, Kelly Girl or some such thing."

Isaacs grinned. "I'll tell you it was a relief to me when he agreed to read my memo. Up to that point he could easily have just said screw it and tossed the lot of us out."

"Seriously," Martinelli said, "I appreciate everything you did to save my butt."

"For god's sake, Vince, I got you into it."

"I'm a big boy, I knew what I was doing. I appreciate you going to bat for me."

"Well, I shouldn't have gotten you involved. I'm relieved we got out okay." They both stared into their drinks, a little embarrassed by this open exchange of gratitude.

Then Martinelli strove to recapture the spirit of celebration. "So how is friend McMasters taking all this?" he inquired in a jovial tone.

"He's sulking."

"Couldn't happen to a nicer guy."

They both chuckled.

"It really backfired on him," Isaacs mused. "Not only did he not get me booted, but now Drefke's made the whole investigation top priority and put me in charge. That's really going to hurt him."

"I don't suppose it's too much to hope that a little luster's gone off his star?"

"My reading is that Drefke still appreciates his ability to run internal affairs, but he sees him in a different light now. McMasters had some rationale to argue Project QUAKER wasn't agency business, but his forbidding me to work on it and then having me shadowed don't look too hot in hindsight."

"Ah, another toast then. To the future Deputy Director of Intelligence." Martinelli raised his glass to Isaacs.

"C'mon, Vince," Isaacs protested.

"You know it's true."

Isaacs was pleased, but embarrassed again. He recognized the timetable for his promotion had probably accelerated.

"So what's happening in Dallas?" Martinelli inquired.

Isaacs laughed, glad to change the subject.

"You wouldn't believe the confusion out there. Your basic case of conflicting authorities. The city cops are all over the place. The governor, and more importantly, his chief financial backers, are all from Dallas. They feel personally attacked, so the governor's got a squad of investigators from the state intelligence bureau on the spot. That's already enough to piss off the locals and make for a general madhouse because nobody in those outfits has any idea what it is they're supposed to be investigating. Then we get into the act and that really stirs up the pot.

"I wanted to send in a few of my people on the quiet, but by the time Drefke made his decision to go ahead the place was swarming with the Texas troops. Drefke decided we had to follow the letter of the charter: no internal investigations.

"So we contacted the FBI and they sent a team of investigators. We told them what sort of information we want, but not why. We're sitting on that till we better understand what's going on. One of the things this accomplishes is to get the local FBI special agent riled up, first because he's got these out-of-towners descending on him, and worse because he knows they're working for us, not even for the FBI."

Isaacs chuckled again.

"To complete the confusion, the local cops and the state police have been ordered to cover up the FBI involvement and to absolutely avoid any hint leaking out that the Agency is interested. I doubt that will be totally hushed up, but it's got them in a pickle."

"Wow, real circus then," Martinelli laughed. "I've got to sympathize with the local cops. If I've got the picture right, they've got the formal public responsibility for the investigation, but can only go through the motions while the spooks crawl in and out of the woodwork."

"That's about it," Isaacs said. "Actually, we need to help them develop some cover story. They really are in a bind."

"So are you learning anything in the midst of all this chaos?"

"A bit. We sent a team to check the site in Nagasaki. We had less trouble with the Japanese government than we've had with Texans." Isaacs shook his head in amusement. "The physical evidence is very similar in the two cases. I put that in my preliminary report. That's what convinced Drefke to let us all off with that bit of wrist-slapping today and give me the green light."

"Another?"

"No thanks. I've got to get home. This whole thing has been tough on Muriel. I promised her a nice quiet dinner out."

"Fair enough." Martinelli grinned, but then a serious look settled over his eyes. "I read that copy you sent me earlier this week of your original memo outlining this mess. Frankly, I lost some sleep over it. Can you explain to me what the hell's really happening?"

Isaacs shook his head wearily. "I'm relieved we're off the hook and the investigation can go ahead full throttle, but the truth is I'm scared. I don't know what we're up against. There's something damned serious going on."

"So what's the next step?"

"We've got to get better heads than mine working on the clues. Pat Danielson and I had a brief consultation with Jason back in our underground days, three weeks ago. We're headed back there on Monday. I'm not sure anything will come of it, but we have some fresh evidence from Nagasaki and Dallas, and I can't think what else to do."

"Well, good luck. Have a quiet weekend, will you? And my love to Muriel."

"Thanks, Vince."

Isaacs drained his glass and headed home.

Chapter 11

Pat Danielson was home. Her relief had turned to elation during Drefke's lecture to them the previous Friday afternoon. As he droned on in somber tones, she slowly realized that he was not only reinstating them, he was granting Isaacs full authority to pursue Project QUAKER. She had invited Janine out to one of their favorite spots and had gotten gaily tipsy before dinner. Returning to the apartment, she had succumbed to a spontaneous urge and called her father in Los Angeles and made plans to spend the weekend with him.

She enjoyed it immensely, being back in the small house so flooded with childhood memories, now gently nostalgic in her buoyant good mood. She and her father took walks down familiar sidewalks, the cracks in them so much closer together than when she had played hopscotch along them. They talked long and avidly, sharing experiences past and present. More balm on the wound in their relation, now nearly invisible. Long Beach and the ocean were only two miles away. She spent Sunday afternoon on the beach, alternately body-surfing, jogging, and soaking up the sun, a teenager again. She rediscovered the simple pleasure of sitting on the seawall and watching the world go by—sunburned throngs on bicycles, roller skates, skateboards, even a few ordinary pedestrians, all in constant motion up and down the miles of beachfront sidewalk. She thought a lot about Project QUAKER and their scheduled meeting with Jason to renew their consultation. She thought about Alex Runyan. She looked forward to seeing him again.

Late Monday morning, she flew down to San Diego and met Isaacs' incoming flight. By early afternoon, they were back in Ellison Gantt's room closeted with the same members of Jason. Both Wayne Phillips and Alex Runyan had greeted them on their arrival. Runyan, again in shorts, T-shirt, and thongs, had attached himself to Danielson, escorting her with friendly chatter up the stairs and to a seat on the comfortable, slightly frayed sofa next to the portable blackboard. She had self-consciously enjoyed the attention. Now she looked around noting with amusement the tendency for people to resume the positions they had previously established, even three weeks before, some instinctual territoriality, she supposed. Noldt and Fletcher sat in the same chairs, next to the sofa. Noldt's round face beamed as he greeted her again. Fletcher had just come in from a run on the beach, his dark lean face still flushed and his hair wet from a shower. Gantt was again seated at his desk, looking as grey and undistinguishable as ever. Zicek and Leems came in. Leems scowled and took the chair by the door, but Zicek smiled and joined the pair on the sofa.

Phillips and Isaacs remained standing by the door until Zicek was seated, then Phillips spoke. "Gentlemen, you remember Dr. Danielson and Mr. Isaacs and the novel problem they brought to us before. There have been a number of developments, among which is the change in status of this situation. They came to us informally before to seek what wisdom we had to offer. Now they are here on highest priority official status. I urge you to listen carefully to their new information and to address this problem with all the acumen at your command. I've no doubt that when you have heard the latest developments you'll need no further goad from me. Mr. Isaacs."

"Thank you, Professor Phillips." Isaacs clasped his hands behind his back and looked around the room, last and longest at Harvey Leems seated close to his left side. "You'll recall that Dr. Danielson had predicted that our regular seismic, sonar signal was to impinge on Nagasaki on July 7 and on Dallas July 26, just a week ago.

"For Nagasaki we stationed a ground observer in the area and obtained high resolution aerial reconnaissance photographs. At about the predicted time, a chlorine tank in a nearby warehouse sprang a leak. A workman in the warehouse was killed by gas inhalation, and a number of others were hospitalized with lung damage. The tank was punctured with two holes approximately a centimeter in diameter. A vertical line through these holes was aligned with a similar hole in the concrete floor. The hole appeared to extend into the subsoil beneath the foundation, but there is a high water table and moist soil obliterated any sign after a few centimeters. The skylight above this line of holes was broken out. In the street we found a truck with its engine blown. There were signs of odd damage to it, but it had been moved and we can't determine with certainty that there is a connection. The aerial survey photos showed nothing."

"While you're on that point," Runyan interrupted. "I had some astronomical colleagues take photos of the points in space the signal seems to travel between. Same result, zip."

"I see," said Isaacs. "That's interesting." And maybe not too smart, he thought to himself. If they had found something, a big goddamn cat could have been out of the bag.

"In Dallas," he continued, "the details were different, but the overall picture was the same. Two buildings were damaged. In one, there is a hole roughly a centimeter across from the roof down through the basement. Again, evidence for penetration into the subsoil, but in Dallas it was too sandy to support the tunnel, or whatever it was. Once again there was a death, incidental, but related. A young woman was crushed when a structure collapsed on her."

"How's that?" asked Noldt, his owlish face screwed in concentration.

"Well," Isaacs paused, "this was a two-story place with a bar underneath and a strip joint upstairs." He gestured with his hands flat, one above the other. "The woman was, uh, dancing upstairs. This tunnel, or whatever it was, weakened a support structure on the stage and it collapsed on her."

"I see," said Noldt, sitting up straighter in his seat, a little embarrassed.

"A hundred meters away," Isaacs continued, "the rear quarter of a seven-story building gave way and collapsed into the alley behind it. In this case, fortunately, no one was injured. The cause of the structural failure has not been positively determined, although some pieces of masonry show elongated gashes which bear similarity to the holes in the concrete floors in the other damaged buildings in Dallas and Nagasaki. Two agents in the area reported hearing a whistling noise of some kind. Their impression was that it receded up from the bar, and one of them thinks he heard it again about forty seconds later, prior, he believes, to the collapse of the building. There is no question now in my mind that this thing, whatever it is, causes physical damage, and that it was similar effects that damaged the Russian aircraft carrier, the Novorossiisk, and sank our destroyer, the Stinson."

"You say," remarked Zicek, "that this phenomenon seems to have gone up and then down in Dallas, in consonance with your feeling that something goes back and forth in the earth."

Isaacs nodded.

"I remind you that I remarked before I didn't see how any

beam could do such a thing, reverse directions. That feeling seems to be reinforced with your new evidence."

"Wait a second, now," Leems broke in. "What about satellite locations? I need to be convinced that more than one source isn't involved somehow, one shooting one way, one, the other."

"I checked that," Danielson responded to him. "There are hundreds of Soviet satellites in orbit. Occasionally, there was a marginal coincidence of position with a single event, but no pattern that could explain all the incidents we know of. And no case when two satellites lined up on the trajectory simultaneously on opposite sides of the earth to account for the reversal of direction."

She looked down and brushed a piece of lint from her skirt and then looked back at Leems.

"I also tracked all US, European, and Japanese satellites, with again the same null result. Nothing currently in orbit can account for what we have seen, even discounting the question of what the technology could be, something that could propagate through the earth."

Beside her, Alex Runyan smiled lightly, taking pleasure in her neat parry. Leems scowled more deeply, but did not respond. After a long quiet moment, Danielson leaned around Runyan to address Zicek.

"Excuse me, Dr. Zicek, but there's another thing that I'm not sure came out clearly just now. The marks that we've investigated, the holes in the concrete, look very clean. There's no sign of a great release of energy, no blackening, no melting or fusing of the material. Perhaps that makes the situation more confusing, but there's no indication of explosion or burning which you'd expect of radiation from a beam of energy. It looks more like the material was drilled out; it's just gone."

The group of scientists fell silent, thinking. Fletcher and Noldt muttered to one another.

The idea hit Runyan like a physical blow. Suddenly he was

encased in a suit of armor from neck to groin, three sizes too small. He stared at Danielson, and she returned his look, her right eyebrow arched quizzically.

Runyan felt as if he were balanced on a vertex. He sensed the grip of forces of which he had been unaware until moments ago. Danielson's words had lifted a curtain to reveal the crest and the chasm yawning immediately before him. Random moments from his career flashed out of his subconscious, and he perceived them as stepping stones that had led him inexorably up to this teetering edge. He had no choice but to take the step that would send him plummeting headlong down the other side.

He knew the antagonist. He knew the mathematical structure of its bones and sinews, its space-time stretched tight on this frame. He knew the roaring cauldron deep inside which marked the boundary where knowledge stopped, but from where new beginnings would inevitably arise. He knew the men and women, past and present, who had pieced it together in their imaginations, fragment by careful fragment.

But this was not imagination. This was not mathematics. This was the most delicate dreams of the intellect come real in nightmare fashion. And that reality changed everything. Everything.

He had an urge to close his mind, as if by sealing off the thought he could seal the abyss, but he knew it was there. A dynamic, hurtling, all-consuming void.

"Do you have a pen, some paper?" Runyan whispered hoarsely to Danielson. He was scarcely breathing.

Danielson rummaged in her purse and produced a pen and a small airline cocktail napkin she had salvaged on the flight down.

"I only have—" she started to say.

"Fine," Runyan breathed, grabbing the pen and napkin, "that'll do."

He pressed the napkin onto his bare knee and began to scratch symbols and numbers on it, oblivious to the uncertain, dispirited conversation in the room. Danielson was confused by his action, but could feel a new tension radiating from him. She had trouble following the discussion. Even though he was completely ignoring her, she felt partially mesmerized by Runyan's newly focused intensity. She found this intensity, contrasted with a potential for warm amiability, strangely attractive.

Runyan was uncertain how much time had passed when he finally drew a long breath and let it out slowly. He handed the pen back to Danielson and locked eyes with her for a long moment. Then he stuffed the napkin into a pocket of his shorts and waited for a break in the discussion. At an appropriate point he poked a finger up.

Phillips nodded at him. "Dr. Runyan. You have a thought?"

Runyan lapped his fingers together and leaned forward, forearms on his bare knees. He pressed his thumbs in opposition, looked down at his hands and then up toward Phillips. His terrible conclusion was inescapable. Now he had to lead his colleagues down the same path.

"Let me see if I can speak to what is bothering all of us," he said slowly and reflectively. "We've been unable to account for any extraterrestrial source, natural or artificial. The fact that we're dealing with something that has a fixed direction in space suggests an origin out there." He jerked a thumb toward the ceiling. "But the basic phenomenon occurs within the depths of the earth." He jabbed a long forefinger toward the floor. "It only comes to the surface periodically."

Danielson sat tensely on the sofa, partially turned toward Runyan, watching his eyes and mouth as he spoke. The words were neutral enough, but seemed darkly ominous to her, a cold vapor filling the room.

"Incredible as it seems," Runyan continued, "I think the conclusion we've been avoiding is that there is actually something inside the earth, something moving around through the earth, triggering seismic waves and tunneling holes as it goes."

He glanced sideways at Danielson, his eyes crinkled by a faint smile. "I don't remember whether it was Sherlock Holmes or Nero Wolfe who argued that one should throw out every impossible explanation, and the remaining one, no matter how improbable, must be the truth." The smile faded. "I've done something like that in my own mind and reached a conclusion, but it's bizarre, and I don't want to prejudice you with it yet. I'd like you to follow this line of reasoning and see where you think it leads."

Runyan seemed to be sitting calmly, looking around at his colleagues, but Danielson happened to glance down at his feet. His toes were curled around the end of the thongs, gripping them, pale splotches on the knuckles contrasting with the tanned skin.

Across the room, Isaacs was staring at Runyan, mentally groping, trying to grasp the implications of the scientist's statements. The quiet was broken by Fletcher who sat up straight in his chair and muttered, "Oh, Jesus." He swiveled to look at Runyan. The two locked gazes and stared at one another for an extended moment. Then Fletcher broke off and waved a hand inviting Runyan to take the floor.

Runyan stood and made his way slowly to the blackboard, deep in thought. With a habit born of long hours in the classroom, he selected a moderately long piece of chalk from the tray before turning to face his audience.

"Let's forget the seismic signal itself and concentrate on the derived trajectory for a moment," he began, unconsciously slipping into a pedagogical tone. He turned to the board and sketched a circle representing the earth, with a curved arrow above it indicating the direction of rotation. Then he added a straight line beginning a third of the way from the equator to the North Pole which passed through the center of the circle and out the opposite side.

Watching the tip of the chalk, Danielson suddenly pictured a stiletto, piercing the earth. Her shoulders contracted in a brief shiver.

"The source moves like this," Runyan tapped the line with the chalk, "with a period of eighty minutes and thirty seconds. We can think of the earth as a sphere of roughly constant density which produces a certain gravitational potential. An object falling freely in that harmonic potential would oscillate back and forth along a line. To close approximation, the line would point to a fixed direction in space. The period would be eighty some-odd minutes." He looked at Fletcher, then at Leems. "Essentially the same as that of an earth-orbiting satellite."

There were scattered rustlings in the room as a couple more individuals began to see where Runyan's arguments were leading.

"Now, if we consider the real earth," Runyan continued, "there would be some differences. A minor factor would be that the density of the earth is not constant. An orbiting object would feel a somewhat different gravitational pull than the idealized case I've described. That would alter the period of the trajectory somewhat. There could also be precessional effects on the orientation, but all that's negligible for now."

He looked around the room, focusing briefly on Danielson. Her stomach tightened as if his gaze were a physical grip. His face was a sharp image against blurred surroundings. She could make out beads of sweat along his hairline.

"The significant feature," Runyan continued, "is that the path is anything like a free orbit since, as we all know, the earth resists quite effectively the attempt of any material body to move through it. If I'm on the right track, the orbiting body can't be ordinary material."

"Let me get this straight," said Gantt. "You're proposing that something is actually orbiting within the earth?"

"C'mon!" snorted Leems.

"That's the only picture that makes sense to me," Runyan replied, his voice tensing at the implied scepticism. He turned to the board and drew heavily, repeatedly, on the line that slashed through the circle. "Back and forth on a line fixed by the inertial frame of the stars, independent of the rotation of the earth. That's been one of the strangest features of the story Dr. Danielson has told us.

"The problem," he continued, "is to identify what the thing could be. It's apparently slicing through the earth like the proverbial knife through butter. That seems to call for something significantly denser than the densest parts of the mantle and core, denser than anything occurring naturally on earth or made in any laboratory."

"I don't see where you're going," said Leems sceptically. "Are you talking about some superheavy element?"

Runyan glared at him. He could see the answer so clearly. Was Leems being deliberately obtuse?

"In a sense," he replied, coolly. "My thoughts go to stellar examples, where high densities naturally result from huge gravitational fields." He glanced at Fletcher who gave a brief nod. "White dwarf matter, which is crushed until atoms blur into one another, exists at densities from a million to a billion grams per cubic centimeter. Neutron star material is even more extreme. Matter is squeezed until atomic nuclei dissolve at densities greater than a hundred trillion grams per cubic centimeter. If you could drop a chunk of either kind of matter on earth, it would meet virtually no resistance and plunge to the center and pass through to the opposite side as it performed an essentially free orbit."

"Are you suggesting a neutron star is orbiting inside the earth?" asked Gantt incredulously.

"No," Runyan replied, frowning. "A full-sized white dwarf would be as large as the earth and have as much mass as the sun. A neutron star would only be a few miles across, but again would have the mass of the sun. The earth's orbit hasn't been appreciably affected since the astronomers haven't raised an uproar, so whatever we are dealing with can't have much mass."

"Then you're talking nonsense, aren't you?" It was a statement more than a question from Leems.

Runyan ignored him. "We might consider a small piece of a neutron star or a white dwarf, but we understand the physical processes involved there reasonably well. Freed from the gigantic self-gravity, a small piece would explode under its own outward pressure. What we need is something which will remain at high densities even though it has relatively low mass. Although I can list reams of practical objections, I can only think of one possibility which fits the picture we now have."

Leems was exasperated. "Honest to god, Alex," he said in a disgusted voice, "you're not making any sense at all. What in the hell are you getting at?"

Runyan's resolve to proceed dispassionately dissolved. "Oh, for chrissake, Harvey!" he stormed. "Can't you see it?"

He was suddenly angry that the responsibility for the message was his. He aimed his fear and frustration at Leems.

"It's a black hole!" he raged. "The earth's being eaten by a goddamned black hole!"

Danielson recoiled back against the cushion of the sofa at Runyan's outburst, her face draining of color. Black holes? Her mind reeled at his vehemence, the radical leap of his argument. Black holes had to do with stars, space, galaxies! Not downtown Dallas, Nagasaki. What in god's name was he talking about?

"Oh, bullshit!" blurted Leems. He locked eyes with Runyan and then looked down and away to a neutral point in the room.

"What?" demanded Noldt. "What did he say?" Fletcher leaned over to him and began an intense reprise of Runyan's arguments.

Runyan continued to glare at Leems and made no attempt to respond to the commotion. He felt the first wisps of relief that the burden was no longer solely his to bear.

Good god! Have I blundered? Isaacs thought to himself as he sat upright in his chair. With a sinking sensation, he looked quickly from Runyan, to Leems, and back to Runyan.

Was coming to Jason a grievous error? Was his innate distrust of these far-out academics finally justified? He could feel his months of work and risk slipping away. What a disaster, if all he had to take back to Drefke was some harebrained idea. He turned to Phillips with a look of dismay.

Phillips saw the startled concern on Isaacs' face. As he stood and moved to the front of the room beside Runyan, he surveyed the others. Leems was red-faced, as if he'd picked up the color Danielson had lost. Fletcher was still explaining, waving a finger back and forth, tracing a trajectory in front of the nose of a bewildered Ted Noldt. Gantt and Zicek were attempting a disjointed analysis across the length of the room, their voices ringing with surprise. Phillips motioned for quiet.

"Gentlemen," Phillips said firmly, "let's see if we can have an orderly and objective discussion of this remarkable suggestion Dr. Runyan has made." Turning to Runyan he continued, "Alex, you'll have to forgive our collective scepticism, but this notion strains all credibility. From where could such a thing have come? What could it be doing in the earth? Surely, there's a simpler explanation."

When he answered, Runyan's voice was still too loud, his normally avuncular tone replaced by a hint of righteousness.

"Simple? What we all crave is a less radical solution. We've striven for that and come away empty-handed. I submit we won't find a simple solution in the sense you mean, Wayne. Only an orbit fits the odd trajectory. Only an orbit would have a fixed period and a direction anchored in space, independent of the earth's rotation about its axis and revolution about the sun. Can anyone deny that a simple orbit fits the picture?"

The rhetorical question was greeted with silence.

Runyan paced back and forth in a tight little orbit of his own. Danielson's thoughts were awash with the idea he had thrust upon them. Her eyes watched the muscles flexing in his sun-tanned legs. His tone became calmer.

"I ask myself what sort of thing can be orbiting through

the earth, and I see no alternative to the conclusion that it is very dense. Ordinary, even extraordinary matter can't exist in small quantities at extreme densities, so I'm forced to conclude that we are dealing with a small, but very deadly, black hole. Don't get the idea I'm happy with this idea. On the contrary. It scares the hell out of me."

He continued to pace, thinking.

"Here's more support for it," Runyan said. "Look at the holes drilled in solid concrete with no sign of searing or scorching. That's one of the singular pieces of evidence and very hard to understand any other way. It's just what a small black hole would do. A black hole will pull in matter from a volume much bigger than itself as it moves, the gravitational force sucking the material in from the immediate vicinity." He made a crushing motion with his fist. "A black hole will carve a tunnel as it goes, but leave no other sign of its passage, not like a laser beam or any other such device, as Dr. Danielson was quick to see." He smiled at her for a moment. "In fact, from the size of the holes left behind, I can estimate the mass of the thing."

Runyan paused and dug into a pocket of his cutoffs and brandished the napkin. The numbers blotched irregularly where the ink from Danielson's pen had run in the porous material. He did this more from a sense of drama than from a need to refresh his memory. He recalled the result perfectly well. He made an abbreviated OK sign with index finger and thumb and peered through the small hole at his audience.

"The holes drilled are about this size," he said, "a few millimeters to a centimeter. Depending on the tensile strength of the material through which the hole passes, I would guess the mass to be comparable to a small mountain and its size to be about that of an atomic nucleus."

"But would a small black hole do what we are observing?" Gantt asked. "That is, if it knifes through the earth as if it were butter, how does it generate the acoustic signal?"

Runyan pondered for a moment. "Well," he began, "as I've

said, it would exert a force sucking in matter from the immediate vicinity. It would carve a tunnel as it went. Does that suggest anything?"

"I suppose," replied Gantt. "At least in subsurface rock the ambient pressure would prevent such a tunnel from existing except momentarily. I can imagine the collapse of such a thing generating acoustic waves, depending on the size."

"That's a good point," Runyan aimed a blunt finger at him, "the size of the tunnel is related to the mass of the object and the rate at which the tunnel forms and collapses should give an estimate of the acoustic power—which we know! Can we check to see if the picture is self-consistent?"

Gantt joined Runyan at the board and they began a crude, but rapid calculation. They stood in front of their figures and symbols to the consternation of those in the room trying to follow the arguments. After a few minutes of gesticulation and occasional cursing, Gantt returned to his seat.

"With some uncertainty," Runyan announced, "the acoustic signal is consistent with the idea of a small tunnel continuously being drilled at the orbital velocity and then collapsing."

"I'm sorry," Isaacs said, his voice polite, but firm. "This is very important because you're talking about the basic data that led us to this thing." If Runyan were off base, Isaacs wanted to nail him quickly. He also recognized that the notion of a black hole and its implications were too foreign to him to be absorbed rapidly. If it turned out to be more than a crackpot idea, he didn't want to miss details that would aid his ultimate understanding. "Could you explain to me a bit more clearly what you just did." Isaacs gestured at the board.

"Oh, sure." Runyan was loathe to halt the flow of ideas, but recognized his responsibility to Isaacs. "The picture is that a small black hole will move without resistance through the rock of the earth's core. It's like a little vacuum cleaner, sucking up particles that it gets too close to. The mass of the black hole dictates the strength of the gravitational pull it exerts. Close to the black hole that gravitational force is overwhelming, but at larger distances the tensile forces of the rock which make it solid are stronger than the gravity of the black hole. The quantitative question is to determine the distance from the black hole at which the internal forces in the rock are stronger than the gravitational pull of the hole. Further than that, the rock remains intact. Closer than that, the suction of gravity is dominant. If you were somehow to hold the hole still, it would eat out a cavity the size of which is proportional to the gravity of the black hole and hence to its mass. If the hole has a mass comparable to a small mountain, as I said, then it will carve a hole of about the diameter that you've reported in the foundations of those buildings."

"Okay," Isaacs replied, "I guess I see that. And you get a tunnel rather than single hole if this black hole moves along a path sucking up everything out to a certain distance." He pinched an imaginary particle between thumb and forefinger and moved it methodically in a line at arm's length.

"Exactly," Runyan confirmed.

"Then where does the seismic signal come from?"

"Ah!" Runyan exclaimed. "Now picture this hole falling freely through the rock at a speed which is determined by the gravitational acceleration of the earth. That speed determines the rate at which this little tunnel is carved.

"But what happens to the tunnel?" Runyan proceeded to answer his own question. "After the black hole moves on, the tunnel can't just sit there. The huge pressure in the surrounding rock will crush it. So there's a continuous process by which the hole carves the tunnel and then moves on leaving the pressure forces to collapse it. The seismic signal is very plausibly the continuous noise made by the collapsing tunnel."

"That can't be the whole picture," Isaacs was thinking hard. "At the surface, in normal rock, you should just get a hole drilled, just as we've seen in these concrete foundations."

"Good, good. That's very perceptive." Runyan was a little condescending, but he looked at Isaacs with new respect. "In the mantle the pressure forces are not as great and the wound of the tunnel should remain unhealed. I remind you that the strength of your seismic signal falls as the influence nears the surface. Pat said there was no detectable signal from the upper mantle. This could be exactly the reason!"

"What about the acoustic signal in the water?" Isaacs inquired.

"Probably a similar idea with cavitation."

"Cavitation? You mean like with a motorboat propeller?"

"Right. The hole should consume a surrounding volume of water just as it does rock. After it moves on, the water will rush into the vacuum in its wake creating thousands of tiny popping bubbles. Cavitation, and acoustic noise."

"It looks to me," Fletcher pointed at the board, "as if you've assumed the hole moves subsonically. What if it moves faster than the material can respond. What if it moves supersonically?"

"I don't think that's a problem except maybe in the liquid iron core of the earth where the hole would be moving at its highest speed," Runyan replied. "Whatever this is seems to move relatively slowly at the surface—fast, but slower than the speed of sound in rock, water, or even air. There could be shock waves near the earth's center, though. I'll have to think some more about that."

"Gentlemen," cut in Phillips from the side of the room where he had been standing, "I'm impressed with the virtuosity of your arguments, but I'm still very disturbed at the nature of your conclusions. Doesn't anyone have an alternative suggestion?"

The question was greeted with silence. Runyan stood mute. His eye rested on, but barely registered, a dollop of coffee on the desk, spilled from a cup Gantt had brought in after lunch. His fixation was broken by Ted Noldt who stirred and said, "I have a question which bears on the possibility of a black hole."

Runyan lifted his eyes and looked at the speaker.

"I don't know much about black holes," Noldt said, "but I thought the small ones, about which you are talking, were supposed to radiate away their mass and energy at a great rate, causing them to evaporate and explode. Doesn't that rule out such a black hole?"

"We're going to have to consult a real expert on the subject, which I'm surely not," replied Runyan. "That question has been very much on my mind." He paused a moment and then continued. "Here's a possibility. The theory of evaporating black holes was worked out in the context of idealized, empty space, whereas this one's in the real world!" He caught himself. "Sorry. A grotesque pun. Unintentional. Anyway, maybe the fact that this one is surrounded by matter changes things."

"That may be right," mused Fletcher, picking up the argument. "If it's consuming matter, the infall may squelch the outflow. Let's see, didn't you and Ellison estimate the rate of consumption just now?"

"Right," said Runyan, turning to the board once more. "I don't remember all the formulae for the evaporation rate, but maybe I can piece something together." He doodled for a minute while the others looked on and listened to the scratching chalk. "Yes!" he looked up. "That's probably it; there seems to be a comfortable margin. As long as the hole bores through the earth, it will eat the matter and grow. You'd have to stop the consumption to get it to evaporate."

"Wait a minute," said Noldt, punching a finger in the air. "That's not really relevant, is it? This thing must have come from space somehow, so it must be massive enough not to have evaporated before it got caught in the earth. Isn't that right?"

Runyan beetled his brows at Noldt and paced along the narrow corridor in front of the blackboard a couple of times. Then he turned to face him again.

"No," he said, "I'm not sure that is right. It's true that the cosmologists have told us about the possibility of such mini-black holes created in the turbulence of the Big Bang. But there are two problems. In the first place, though my estimates are crude, I don't believe this object is massive enough to have survived since the beginning of time. Secondly, there is a great difficulty with the curious fact that it moves with the earth."

"What's that?" Noldt was puzzled.

"If this were a black hole born in space," Runyan explained, "there is little chance that it could get trapped in the puny gravity of the earth. For that to happen, it would have to be moving very slowly with respect to the earth. But what with the earth's motion around the sun and the sun's motion around the galaxy and the galaxy's motion off to god knows where, the relative speed between the earth and any random astronomical body would be much greater than the escape velocity from the earth. The earth could not possibly attract and hold anything moving past it so rapidly.

"Do you remember the Tungus event?" He asked Noldt.

Noldt had to think for a second. "Tungus? Russia. Siberia! Big explosion?"

"Right," Runyan replied. "Still rather mysterious. Some explosion in Siberia in 1919. Burned and flattened trees for miles around. But no crater. That ruled out a large meteorite. Any piece of space rock big enough to do the damage done would have to have left a crater rivaling the old one in Arizona. The best idea seems to be a comet. Comets are thought to be very loose filamentary icy structures. Such a thing could deliver a hell of an impact but be sufficiently diffuse not to gouge a crater."

"So?" Noldt did not see the point.

"Well, whenever something strange happens somewhere, someone is going to suggest a black hole." He broke off and looked at Leems scowling at him. "I know what you're thinking, Harvey. If the shoe fits. . . . But hear me out.

"There was a suggestion that the Tungus event was caused by a small black hole. Then it would just dig a small tunnel as I've described, not make a large crater.

"This idea was quickly ruled out though, for just the reason I said. Any black hole coming in from space would have to be moving at a huge velocity, at least a hundred times greater than we're dealing with here. The question Carl raised a minute ago is pertinent. Such velocities are supersonic and the hole arrives with a large shock wave. That's what was supposed to cause the Tungus blast itself. But then when the hole went through the earth it would have generated seismic waves that would have pinned seismographs all over the earth, and while the Tungus event itself was registered, nothing like the passage of a supersonic black hole occurred.

"Finally, you can trace the angle of impact from the pattern of flattening of the trees. Any such black hole should have reemerged in the Baltic Sea and blown Norwegian fishing boats out of the water. From all reports, they fished peacefully that day.

"So the hypothesis of a black hole from space ultimately made no sense there." Runyan looked directly at Noldt again. "And it makes no sense here either for the same reasons. The velocity would be too high. But whereas a low speed black hole would not have caused the Tungus event, a low speed black hole fits what we've seen here." He nodded toward Isaacs and Danielson.

Noldt thought for a moment. "Well," he said, "suppose the universe is littered with these things, and we just happened to have the bad luck to finally overtake one slowly, and it settled in."

"We don't know anything about the distribution of such holes in space, of course," said Runyan. "No evidence for them has ever been observed. To have enough small black holes to make the interaction you describe probable, I would think they would have to be so densely distributed that we would have noticed many other astronomical effects."

"I don't understand what you are saying," stated Noldt. "What is the alternative? Surely such a thing doesn't occur spontaneously on earth?"

"No, I don't see how it possibly could," agreed Runyan. "I don't see how it could have occurred naturally on or off of the earth." He paused, unable to avoid sounding portentous, and somewhat embarrassed at doing so. He was determined not to speak next.

After a moment, Leems spoke up with an edge in his voice. "If we accept your arguments up to this point, then we're forced to the conclusion that this thing was manufactured. Is that what you're saying?"

Runyan nodded, but remained silent as all eyes shifted toward him. At last he said, "That's the second conclusion I've reached. I think we must allow for the possibility unless it can be rigorously ruled out."

Again Runyan became silent as he exchanged glances with his colleagues, desiring to support, but not lead the discussion at this critical juncture.

"There are two possibilities then, aren't there?" asked Fletcher. "It's man-made or . . ." He paused and finally said in a flat voice, "Or it's not."

"Omigod!" exclaimed Noldt. "You mean this thing could have been manufactured by extraterrestrials and. . .and planted here?"

Several voices were raised in simultaneous protest.

"This is getting out of hand!"

"UFO's again! That's very hard to believe!"

Isaacs had a flash of memory of the AFTAC headquarters in Florida where he had first heard of the seismic signal. He couldn't believe what he was hearing. How could that simple little rattle in the earth be related to the insanity that was being expressed in this room! Then he thought of Zamyatin. Whatever was going on, he couldn't feature explaining black holes to the KGB chief, never mind trying to convince him they were being fired by nasty little green men from outer space. He shook his head and pinched his eyes with thumb and finger. This discussion just had no connection whatever with the real world of geopolitical confrontation with which he dealt every day.

Runyan cut in. "I'm sure we agree that the whole situation is hard to believe!"

"The energy requirements to make such a thing must be gigantic," said Leems. "Surely the suggestion that it's artificial is absurd."

"It would take a lot of energy," Runyan agreed.

"Don't you think it's fair to conclude then," Leems pressed, "that such a thing would be exceedingly difficult, if not impossible, to create? I have a strong suspicion we're on the wrong track altogether despite your argument here."

"I don't deny that point," replied Runyan. "It's very difficult to conceive how such a thing could be done."

"Still," argued Noldt, "it's not that it's impossible, just that we can't see how it could be accomplished technologically. Isn't that correct?"

"I think that's correct," said Runyan. "We're talking about very large amounts of energy, but not an infinite amount. In principle, it could be done. After all, we're fairly comfortable with the notion of it happening spontaneously in an astronomical context. Also, the large energy you're thinking about is based on brute force compression. There may be more elegant means to the end."

"Then," said Noldt with a barely suppressed excitement, "since we see no way to do it on earth, aren't we forced to consider the possibility that such a thing was made by extraterrestrials and put in the earth for some purpose?"

"Before we invoke some malevolent intent, terrestrial or otherwise," Leems said with scarcely veiled sarcasm, "I must say I'm not satisfied that we really know enough to rule out a natural origin. Even if we accept that we're dealing with a black hole, and I'm as yet far from convinced of the necessity, how can we eliminate the possibility that this thing started out exceedingly small a long time ago? Maybe the earth even condensed around it, and it took all this time, five billion years, for it to grow to its present size."

"I have two responses to that," Runyan said. "One is that the universe was already quite old when the earth was born.

There were no special conditions at the time to create small black holes, and any born in the Big Bang should have long since evaporated."

"Well then, figure out a way to prevent evaporation," Leems said harshly. "That still seems more likely than insisting on some intelligent plot at work."

"Maybe so, maybe so," Runyan said slowly. "The other thing that bothers me is that the growth time for this thing is relatively long. I find it peculiar that this phenomenon has only just been discovered, since the technology to detect it has been around for some time."

"Are you saying that this thing has just been put here recently?" asked Noldt. He half-glanced over his shoulder as if expecting to catch a glimpse of an alien presence.

After a moment's hesitation, Runyan spoke again. "I'm disturbed that we're skirting a bit close to the edge of reason here with too few facts to support us." He cleared his throat, then continued. "Perhaps we should set aside for awhile the issue of how such a thing could come to be and try to consider some other factors. We should discuss what we can do to learn more about this object."

"I've been thinking about that," said Fletcher, "as a remedy for incipient hysteria."

Pat Danielson had been following the discussion intently. She had felt herself becoming more edgy as the tension in the room increased. She had read some popular accounts of astronomy and their discussions of black holes and thought she was beginning to make some sense from Runyan's remarks, but the idea that he would leap from the evidence she had compiled to this conclusion still left her stunned. And now talk of manufacturing such a thing. That just couldn't be. She joined the nervous laughter after Fletcher's remark and could sense the more relaxed mood that spread through the room.

Fletcher continued, "There should be quite a bit one could do by adopting your hypothesis as a working assumption and constructing appropriate models. If we could predict the behavior of a small black hole, or whatever, orbiting through the earth, we could compare such predictions with the seismic data and other observations and perhaps get a much better idea of just what we are dealing with. Ideally, we should be able to prove your hypothesis true—or false."

"Ah, a voice of reason," said Leems, in a more lively tone. "I don't know much about seismic waves, but it still seems to me that they should be modeled as well, to see whether the data that have been reported can be accounted for as some natural seismic phenomenon. The data are admittedly quite bizarre, but surely our seismologist friends don't know everything about the workings of the inner earth. Maybe there are special fissures or lattice works that channel waves in this special way.

"I do concede, though, Alex," Leems continued, "that since you have let this particular genie of yours out of the bottle, it should be pursued."

"That's right," agreed Noldt, "if we are, in fact, dealing with a black hole and it originated on the earth's surface, then, if I have the picture correctly, it should return roughly to its point of origin."

"I wish you wouldn't assume it was made on the earth's surface," interrupted Leems.

Noldt gave him a befuddled glance and continued, gesturing toward Isaacs and Danielson. "We already have reasonably accurate predictive capabilities. We can predict when and where the thing is due to come up and, well, of course you don't just grab it, but surely we could learn more about it then."

"In fact," added Fletcher, "shouldn't an orbit tell us just where the origin was with respect to the surface?"

Leems frowned again, but did not say anything.

"Yes, exactly right," said Runyan. "If we compare the apogee, the point farthest from the center of the earth, to the earth's topography, that should give us some pertinent information. We already have an interesting indication from the Dallas event so nicely predicted by Dr. Danielson." He nodded at Danielson and she smiled quickly in return. "About forty seconds elapsed from the first episode in the bar to the destruction of the building across the alley. An object in free fall could not have risen and then fallen more than a few thousand feet. So apparently apogee is somewhat above sea level, but not far. The point at which the orbit peaks will occur deep under mountains of any height, the Rockies or the Himalayas. More precise information of this sort could be most useful."

"If we can tell where this thing comes out of the earth, what sort of tests can we run?" asked Noldt. "You can't see such a thing can you?"

"No," answered Runyan, "it's about the size of an atomic nucleus. You surely couldn't see it directly. It's most distinctive characteristic, of course, would be its gravitational field. That should be quite appreciable. Gravimeters set up in the vicinity should be able to tell us precisely what the mass of the object is, whether or not it comes to or through the surface. A simple seismic wave will have no effect on the local strength of gravity. A massive, orbiting object, on the other hand, should give a definite signature.

"I propose that this be our first move, and that since Gantt is our resident seismologist, he's the man to mount such an expedition." Runyan turned to Gantt. "What do you say, Ellison? If Dr. Danielson can predict where the event will approach the surface at a given time, won't you be able to measure or set stringent limits on the fluctuations of the gravitational field?"

"That's an excellent idea!" responded Gantt with enthusiasm. "I'll start planning immediately."

Runyan glanced at Leems and then inquired, "What do you think of that, Harvey?"

Leems clasped his fingers together and stared at them for

a moment. "The gravity seems to be an effective discriminant. By all means, let's put your idea to the test."

Gantt raised a finger and inquired, "How well can you predict the point of surfacing? Can Dr. Danielson's estimates be improved?"

"I think there's much to be done with computer models," responded Runyan. "I sketched a crude hypothetical orbit on the board. There will be many perturbations to an idealized orbit, but to work those out in detail can be done with sufficient effort. In addition, there may be some effect from the sun and moon, and perhaps the larger planets. With the exception of the effect of the structure of the inner earth, which is not known precisely, computation of a detailed hypothetical orbit should be possible."

"Who would do these orbit calculations?" inquired Noldt.

"The people with the expertise," replied Runyan, "are those who calculate satellite orbits. They've already developed techniques to handle inhomogeneities in the earth's gravitational field as well as perturbations of the sun, moon, and planets. The effect of irregularities in the interior of the earth have not, of course, been studied in that context. Incorporating the effects of structure on the orbit should be possible in some approximation, though. There will also be drag forces, since the orbiting object will be accreting and, if nothing else, losing energy into the seismic waves we are detecting."

There was a pause as these various practical considerations were pondered.

"At the risk of leading us back to the brink of insanity," began Fletcher after a moment, "I think we should at least touch upon one more item. I know we would all rather go after experimental results than to speculate with insufficient data, but I think we are charged here with exploring all avenues, at least in a preliminary fashion." He looked sharply at Runyan. "What should be done if you're correct, Alex?"

This query plunged the room back into an uncomfortable silence. The relief that had come with the discussion of the dispassionate collection of data was replaced with general discomfort. No one was anxious to contemplate what could only be a dreadful prospect.

Leems spoke first. "Surely it's premature, but, yes, let's play the game out."

"Perhaps I should lead off," Runyan spoke quietly. "Though I confess I have nothing definite, and certainly nothing positive, to say on the subject." He paused, collecting his thoughts, sensing again the yawning chasm.

"Black holes are notoriously one-way affairs. They get bigger. A black hole will eat and grow like a cancer in the bowels of the earth. Where it does orbit above the surface, it becomes accessible in a sense, but it's not clear that that does us much good. As Ted remarked earlier, you don't just load something the size of an atomic nucleus and the weight of a small mountain in the back of a truck and haul it off. We have two choices: destroy it, or remove it from the earth. The hell of it is, I don't see any way of doing either."

After a moment's quiet, Fletcher spoke. "There's a third choice, isn't there?" He looked around at his colleagues. "Evacuate the earth."

"Good lord!" ejaculated Leems. "Let's not get morbid."

"Carl's not trying to be morbid," said Noldt with some heat. "We need to explore all the possibilities, and he's just being honest."

Fletcher gave a quick nod of acknowledgment in Noldt's direction and then addressed himself to Runyan. "If it is a hole, Alex, how fast is it growing?"

"That depends rather sensitively on how massive it is and the structure of the material it passes through," Runyan replied. "The time to double in mass could be several thousand years."

"As short as that!" exclaimed Noldt.

"I could easily be off by a factor of ten. It could be longer."

He looked Noldt in the eye. "Or it could be shorter." He glanced around at the group. "This is a crucial point that Carl has raised. Any estimate of the time scale will require a knowledge of the mass, which makes the effort to measure the mass even more important. In any case, if we are dealing with a black hole, it will only grow at an ever increasing rate. We'll never have any longer to figure out what to do about it than we have right now."

"Do you have any idea how quickly it will become dangerous?" Fletcher wanted to know.

"Again, I can make some guesses as to what will happen," replied Runyan, "but I can't say just when without more information.

"If it is a black hole and we can't get rid of it, it will continue to consume the matter of the earth. We'll have to look at the details more closely. This will be part of the orbit calculations I just mentioned. It may, for instance, eat the liquid core faster than the solid mantle, although it's traveling faster in the core and that may mute the effect. In any case, it's riddling the mantle with small holes. Either consuming the core or weakening the mantle will induce earthquakes of increasing magnitude. The drag associated with its motion will eventually cause it to settle into the center of the earth. Not only will it then be irrevocably out of reach, but the core will be rapidly consumed.

"As the molten core of the earth is consumed, the earth will shrink. That in turn will remove the pressure support that holds up the giant continental plates. They will begin to rapidly shift and collide, in turn giving rise to another source of destructive earthquakes. All of this seismic activity will cause severe volcanic activity and tidal waves. As the hole gets to be near the mass of the earth, the earth will begin to oscillate in orbit, as it revolves around a common center of mass with the hole. This will drastically enhance the destruction.

"Finally, the hole will grow so large that it will rapidly ingest the last of the core and large chunks of mantle. The outcome will be a black hole with the mass of the present earth, but only the size of my thumb." He made a fist with extended thumb for illustration. "In the end there will be nothing but the moon orbiting a small black nothingness, maybe along with a ring of rocks that managed to avoid being pulled in."

The group of people in the room sat silently, mesmerized by this gloomy prediction. Caught up in the story he was spinning, Runyan paused, but then proceeded on an afterthought.

"I'm sure it's of only academic interest, but one can carry the story to its end. This small black hole and its moon would continue to orbit the sun. After several billion years, the sun will swell to become a red giant and will engulf the hole. If the earth still existed at that point it would be vaporized in the fire. But if the black hole has done its work, the tables will be turned. The process will begin again but with the sun the victim. The hole will slowly spiral down through the matter of the sun. It will settle to the center and consume the whole sun in the space of a few years. That black hole, now immensely massive but only a few miles across, and its remnant planets, if any, will then proceed through space until the end of time."

Chapter 12

Konstantin Naboyev climbed into the helicopter with a feeling of grim pleasure. It was not much of a revolt, but it was his, and he was so bored he could eat the hinges off a hatch cover. He had to do something to scratch this itch; there was nothing else in sight, so this was it.

He went through the pre-flight check quickly and lifted off the helipad as the control started to give him permission. The voice squawked that he had not maintained procedures. Up yours, he thought to himself. What are you going to do, send me back to Afghanistan?

He longed to return to that incredible challenging mountain terrain. There your ass was on the line every second of the day. Even when you were asleep, those tricky, fierce bastards could figure some way to get to you. In Afghanistan, you were either a man, or you were dead. In a way he loved those tough rebels who fought like stubborn terriers and kept him on the razor's edge, every nerve throbbing with awareness. But most of all he loved to find them scrabbling over the rocks in the high country, in places where it was impossible to fly, where the passes were too narrow, the air too thin, the cross winds too vicious. He would fly there anyway! He would find them, bring his great machine whining up over a ridge, catch them in his sights, and rip them to bloody shreds.

And so what was he doing now? Flying off a ship in the middle of the flattest, most boring god-awful expanse of ocean known to the mind of man. The mindless routine was driving him absolutely berserk. Stop in the ocean, lower the small boats, rig the large aluminum plate between them, sail around trying to see if something coming out of the sea would punch a hole in the plate. Naboyev, now he was really lucky. He got to take off, fly in a lazy circle about the small boats below, not see a goddamn thing, then land back on the ship, so they could sail a few hundred kilometers and then perform the same idiotic routine the next day. Well today, by god, he was at least going to find out a little about what was coming out of the ocean.

The rumors making the rounds were that they had gotten pretty good at positioning the plate so whatever it was came up and made the silly little hole. Since that was the only action around, Naboyev was determined to play the game and find out what they were all up to. He'd just kind of break formation at the right time and fly on over that plate and see what he could see.

He went into his standard circular pattern, listening to the radio traffic. He had learned to time the scattered information that came over his frequencies and knew when to kick the rudder and head for the platform. He wanted to get there in time to hover over the platform at a couple of thousand feet for thirty seconds or so before the hole got punched. That way he would have time to get stabilized and oriented before anything happened. With any luck there would be a circus. There would sure be one when he got back on ship. To hell with them!

Naboyev listened to signals being relayed to the small boats carrying the plate from some sonar installation in the mother ship. When he heard the call for them to hold position, he broke off and headed for the knot of boats. He took up position over the boats and peered down. He saw a small turbulence and a rising plume in the water next to one of the boats. If that's what they were after, he thought, they missed it today. He strained, but couldn't see anything else, nothing came up in the air toward him.

The helicopter bucked and Naboyev felt he had been hit by a shell. His craft began to shake as if caught in a gigantic paint mixing machine. Naboyev fought the controls of the ship like a madman. Out of the corner of his eye he saw a half-meter long slab of metal go arcing gracefully out and down toward the ocean below. Without knowing how it happened, he recognized that the tip of one of his rotor blades had been sheared, and that the vibration from the imbalance of the rotors would make it impossible to land even if the chopper didn't shake itself apart.

Naboyev throttled down to reduce the centrifugal force on the blades. He changed the pitch to decrease the lift and the machine dropped like a rock. The shaking was eased minutely, but the ocean came up with terrifying speed. At the last possible second, Naboyev restored the pitch and opened the throttle. The craft halted its plunge ten meters above the gentle swells, but began to vibrate more fiercely than ever. Naboyev kept a death grip on the stick with his right hand, and opened the hatch door next to him with his left. He took his feet off the pedals and stuck his butt out the door, leaning, straining to keep the wobbling ship on even keel with the stick. He got his feet on the rim of the hatch as the craft began to rotate, and then in one swift desperate movement, he released the stick, kicked it with his foot and used the leverage to eject himself out the doorway. The effect was to knock the stick to the right as he hurled himself to the left. The helicopter followed the lead of the stick and lurched to the right as Naboyev fell clear, hurtling to the water below.

He curled into a ball and felt the blistering blow as he smacked into the ocean. He uncurled and opened his eyes, struggling to orient himself as he heard and felt the great churning of his wounded, pilotless machine plunging into the water twenty meters from him. He swam for the surface and broke through to the pure sweet air, shouting to himself as he broached.

Death! You rotten bastard! I've looked into your putrid eyes. And I've won again!

Isaacs stood near the door, watching the mild confusion as some members of Jason tried to leave the room past the clutter of chairs and lingering people. After Runyan's projection of the destruction of the earth, if not the sun itself, by his hypothesized black hole, Phillips had called a halt to give time to think and evaluate. They would reconvene the next morning.

Isaacs recalled Runyan's fatalistic shrug when Phillips suggested their free time should be spent seeking a different solution to the problem. Isaacs recognized that Runyan was sincerely convinced he had the correct interpretation, however wild the idea, whatever the gaping questions left unanswered. But a black hole! Isaacs could see no immediate weakness in Runyan's argument; it made a certain sense. But it violated every professional instinct. Somehow, Runyan had to be wrong. Isaacs determined to have a quiet, serious talk with Phillips.

Danielson noticed that Isaacs was not moving to leave immediately. In attempting to get out of the way, she did a brief Alphonse-Gaston routine with Zicek before retreating into the cranny between the desk and the sofa. Runyan edged along the blackboard and then in front of the sofa to get behind Zicek, Fletcher, and Noldt. Out of a sense of propriety for his temporary quarters, only Gantt remained seated in the swivel chair at the desk.

As Danielson watched Noldt, the last of the first group to leave, she was startled to feel a grip on her elbow. She looked around to see Runyan, whose mood was transformed by an infectious smile of mirth and well-being.

"You see what you and your boss have done?" he asked merrily. "Put me through the wringer! What I need now is the company of a pretty lady for dinner. Do you have any plans?"

Her smile which had been spontaneously induced by Runyan's radiating good spirit brightened further. Runyan's revelation had left her shaken, the idea was too strange, too new for her to readily cope with it. Her immediate reactions were much more personal. She was exhilarated that her work and risks had paid off. These men of Jason had given her the ultimate accolade by taking her analyses seriously. Besides listening to her, Runyan had deeply impressed her with his mind-boggling explanation of her discoveries. She was delighted at the chance to prolong these feelings with an evening in Runyan's company.

"I'm not sure what Mr. Isaacs has in mind," she said.

"Well, let's just see," Runyan cut her off. Without releasing his grip on her arm, he led her around Gantt to Phillips and Isaacs.

"Gentlemen. I propose a few drinks and a good meal in pleasant company as therapy for our weighty problems. Will you join us?"

Isaacs noted with irony that Runyan had appointed himself and Danielson the core of the action, as if Phillips and he were the peripherals. Danielson had comported herself very well through everything today, thinking on her feet, picking up quickly on the lack of scorching, a point he should have stressed. More evidence of her good prospects in the Agency. His glance fell on Runyan's possessive hand on her elbow. Isaacs was still nervous about Danielson consorting with these academics, particularly Runyan, coming on fast this way. She was a grown woman, though, and deserved some recognition for her excellent work of the past few months. He looked at the expectant smile on her face and smiled himself in acquiescence.

"Of course, provided we're not out too late."

"I'd be honored to be in your company," replied Phillips, with a small bow.

As if remembering suddenly whose room they were in, Runyan spoke back over his shoulder, "How about you, Ellison? Can you join us?" His jovial tone dropped a note, a slight hint that Gantt was welcome to go his own way, which Gantt ignored or failed to notice.

"Sure, I'd like to join you if you don't mind," said Gantt, rising from his chair.

"I'm sure Dr. Danielson would like a chance to freshen up," Phillips nodded in her direction. "Let me show you and Mr. Isaacs to your rooms." Then to Runyan he said, "Let's meet in the lobby downstairs in forty-five minutes."

As Phillips escorted the pair out, Runyan turned to Gantt. "You brought your Thunderbird down here from Pasadena, didn't you, Ellison? Can you take all five of us?"

"Sure, I can manage that."

"Hey, good. I'll see you downstairs later."

Runyan left, pausing a moment to look down the corridor to his left where Phillips was showing Danielson into her room. He then proceeded up another flight of stairs to his own cubicle.

Danielson shut the door behind her and looked around the room which was markedly similar to the one she had been in all afternoon, but less cluttered. There was no desk and the dormitory bed remained in its position near the windows. Her overnight bag had been neatly deposited on the use-worn bureau by the marine chauffeur they had rated on this official trip. She peeked into the bathroom and then kicked off her shoes and lay back on the bed, her mind spinning with the events of the afternoon. She found herself thinking about Runyan, the way he had taken charge of the meeting, and of their plans for dinner. She felt a warm glow, twinged at the edges with fingers of darkness.

Phillips showed Isaacs into a very similar room across the hall and two doors down.

Isaacs looked in the door with scarcely concealed disinterest. He turned to address the older man.

"I know it's been a long afternoon, but there are a few points I would very much like to clarify. Could you possibly spare me some time now?"

"Of course," nodded Phillips with a hint of a smile. "I thought you might ask. Come," he said, gesturing down the hallway with his right hand as his left touched Isaacs' arm in invitation. "Let's go down to my office. We can be more comfortable there."

They retraced their steps down the hall and descended the stairs by which they had come up earlier in the afternoon. Phillips led the way to the end of the lower corridor and into the office which served the dormitory supervisor during term. A bay window looked out over a well-kept green lawn. Phillips crossed the room to a cabinet nestled among long rows of bookshelves.

"Would you have some sherry?"

"Why, yes, please . . . I would," Isaacs replied.

"I hope you don't mind cream sherry. I developed a taste for it as a youth."

"That would be fine."

Phillips extracted a decanter and two small cut-crystal glasses from the cabinet and set them on the desk. He poured carefully and handed one glass to Isaacs. They toasted one another in quiet salute, then Phillips moved a chair up along the edge of the desk for Isaacs so the expanse of the desk would not discourage intimacy. Phillips sat in the nicely upholstered chair behind the desk and watched as Isaacs seated himself.

Isaacs followed Phillips' motions as the physicist took a sip of the sherry, rolled it on his tongue and then swallowed. Isaacs felt too drained for preambles. "May I ask what your reaction is to Runyan's proposal?" he inquired. "It's so outrageous. Can he be serious? Surely there must be a more reasonable explanation."

"My instincts are the same as yours," Phillips replied. "I feel we need to seek some explanation in terms of more, shall we say, acceptable happenstances. But recall that it's the nature of the data Dr. Danielson has presented which boxes us in. Make no mistake; Alex is most serious."

Phillips pondered for a moment, then continued. "Yes, we must pursue any reasonable alternatives, but that includes Runyan's proposal. Outrageous or not, it's the only one which has been advanced which fits the facts as we know them. Perhaps with an evening to relax and think things over, someone will turn up other alternatives. Just now I believe the appropriate response is to adopt Dr. Runyan's proposal as a working 'worst case' hypothesis and lay out the appropriate course of action."

Phillips placed a palm on each knee and continued to address the younger man.

"May I put the situation in perspective as I see it?"

"By all means."

"There's currently no indication that the signal you report has any connection with a hostile country."

"That's correct."

"Or a friendly one for that matter," Phillips continued. "We may, of course, find that we're dealing with some heretofore unknown seismic phenomena with a few startling coincidences thrown in. In such a case, the whole problem will be dropped from our agenda, although not, I daresay, from Ellison Gantt's. If Runyan's proposal is correct, then the issue is most serious, even though it doesn't involve what would normally be thought of as hostile activity. At the risk of sounding melodramatic, the security of our nation, indeed of the entire world, would be very much in jeopardy."

"The problem, if I understand it," stated Isaacs, "is that if there is a black hole down there, it is actually slowly eating away the earth. Good lord, what a thought!"

"Quite right. And putting a stop to it will be a most formidable, if not outright impossible, task."

Isaacs stared out the window, trying to imagine Drefke's response to this. And McMasters. Maybe the old bastard would have a heart attack. How in the world did one approach the President with such an idea? Phillips, sensing his preoccupation, inquired, "I've had the pleasure of dealing with the Central Intelligence Agency before, as you know, but procedures have a way of changing. Perhaps you could refresh my memory as to the way a situation such as this is handled?"

Isaacs averted his gaze from the window. "There's never been a situation like this," he grinned ruefully. "But of course you're right, there are certain procedures." He straightened perceptibly in his chair. "As head of the Office of Scientific Intelligence, my first responsibility will be to draw up a summary of our discussions here for the Deputy Director of Intelligence."

"Yes, I've had the pleasure of meeting Mr. McMasters," said Phillips.

"I see."

Phillips noted the look of stiffness which passed over Isaacs' face.

"You're probably aware, then, that the DDI has control over the intelligence which is passed up to the Director for consideration by the National Security Council. For most problems we have the 'in-house' expertise to give the DDI a complete and self-contained summary. If Runyan is right, we'll be dealing with an area which is not entirely in our venue. Once the situation is well-defined, we can analyze its impact on the geopolitical situation, but we will undoubtedly need to continue consultation with your group until we have a thorough understanding of the problem. In the early stages, a close working relationship with key individuals in Jason will probably be necessary. When the time comes to present our recommendation to the DDI, you or some individual you designate should be prepared to act as technical consultant."

"I presume you'll apprise Mr. McMasters of the present situation on your return to Washington."

"That's correct."

"But a formal report is also necessary?"

"Yes, the DDI requires a formal presentation prior to his report to the Director. The Director then prepares an agenda for the NSC. The Director often takes the DDI, and sometimes me, along to the NSC meetings to make detailed presentations if they seem necessary. In a case like the present one, I can envisage your delegate attending any or all of these discussions."

"The real expertise to deal with this problem may not lie within Jason as it's presently constituted," Phillips noted.

"In what sense?"

"If we are dealing with a black hole, we have no one who is professionally acquainted with the intricacies of the subject."

"Not Runyan, then? I did want to ask about his qualifications. Minnesota doesn't really have the reputation of some of the universities represented here, does it?"

Phillips held up an admonishing hand. "Be careful about the prestige game. Good people are where you find them. In any case, Alex was a colleague of Gantt's at Caltech. He likes the outdoors though, an avid cross-country skier, if I remember correctly. Also, I believe his wife has a nice position at Honeywell."

"But he's not an expert on black holes?"

"No, Alex is broadly studied, but I'm sure he would be

the first to point out that others have a greater depth of knowledge."

"Yet you seem to put some store in his hypothesis?"

"Certainly. It's his broad background and cleverness at synthesizing which makes him such a valuable contributor to our group."

"In any case," continued Isaacs, "if we must, as you say, turn to others for expertise, that can be arranged. With due regard to security, of course."

Phillips nodded and took another sip from his glass.

Isaacs put his glass down to take up another of the items on his personal agenda. He leaned toward Phillips. "Let me ask you, in your own mind, how do you balance the immediacy of the problem against the lack of specific evidence?"

Phillips played his drink in a small circle, watching the fluid coat the sides of the glass. "You're concerned about whether to recommend immediate presidential attention?"

"Yes."

"Professor Runyan is more qualified than I to discuss the particular parameters of the problem. I deduce, however, that while we want to move with all dispatch, the magnitude of the problem will not be seriously increased by failure to take immediate action. We're not faced with a situation where we must invoke presidential authority to quickly resolve the situation. On the contrary, I fear no such quick resolution will be possible. I would sooner think that it's a question of marshalling resources over which the President has authority once we have some notion how to proceed."

Phillips swiveled in his chair and looked distantly out the bay window.

"Our first priority is proof. We must be satisfied beyond any doubt in our own minds." He was almost speaking to himself. "But I can foresee that an immense effort may eventually be required that would be a severe tax on this nation's resources. How to proceed will be a decision which only the

President can make. Our choices will be radical surgery or the slow death of the patient. Either way we would face a time of severe trial."

Phillips turned back to confront Isaacs. "If we are really in the dangerous situation Dr. Runyan describes, it's not a concern only for our nation. The whole world is in peril. A multinational approach to the problem may not only be proper, but necessary. One must then consider the political situation. That's your province. Under what circumstances do you foresee taking this problem before a world forum?"

Isaacs considered for a moment. There was an important asymmetry in his relation with this sharp, inquisitive old gentleman. Isaacs' responsibility was to learn all that he could about the current situation from Phillips and his colleagues. But there were limits to which the converse was true. He thought about Korolev and his interview with Zamyatin, but decided that only some general reply was in order.

"You understand that this sort of decision is out of my hands; it would be decided by the NSC. I have the same reservations you do about prematurely bringing this problem to the attention of the NSC and the President. Those reservations apply doubly to communicating with our allies. We must be very sure of our situation before spreading any possible alarm. I think we must proceed very cautiously. If, as you say, there is little prospect of immediate resolution by quick action, then we can afford to go slowly and carefully."

"I was thinking not only of our allies," put in Phillips. "From a scientific point of view, I have several colleagues in the Soviet Union who would make valuable consultants."

Isaacs stared at Phillips a brief moment, eyebrows raised. He could foresee a situation developing in which a cooperative effort with the Soviets at some level would precede notification of formal allies. He saw no point in raising this possibility with Phillips at this early stage.

"I believe that's out of the question just now."

Phillips pressed the issue.

"It may not be our prerogative to bring this problem to the attention of others. Don't the Soviets have the same capability as we do to monitor seismic activity? Or perhaps even the People's Republic, where there is a long history of interest in earthquakes and related phenomena. You mentioned this Russian aircraft carrier. Should we not move as soon as is feasible to forestall the possibility of further misinterpretation?"

Damn this sly old dog, Isaacs said to himself. He was strongly tempted to tell Phillips the whole story of Korolev and the Novorossiisk, but he thought of the uneasy truce Drefke had forced between him and McMasters. He had no authority to disclose the details of these geopolitically charged events. The last thing he wanted to do was to open another procedural dispute with McMasters. He was sensitive to the hypocrisy, but felt compelled to head off this line of discussion.

"I've considered such questions, Professor Phillips," Isaacs replied, forcing a trace of coolness into his voice. "I don't believe we disagree in principle, but the issue of when communication of intelligence to other countries becomes feasible or desirable must be weighed most carefully. You surely appreciate that such decisions cannot be made in the context of one isolated set of events. All possible ramifications must be considered simultaneously. The ultimate decision is not within your province, nor even mine. I can assure you that the points you raise will be given due consideration."

"Please!" said Phillips raising a hand in protest. "Don't think I'm trying to dictate your actions in an area outside my competence. It's just that I can foresee yet other situations developing which will prove difficult to contain. I'm sure you and your organization are most competent to take appropriate action."

Both men lapsed into silence, consciously attempting to

quell the mood of confrontation which had threatened to develop. They sipped their sherry quietly for a long moment, each pursuing private thoughts.

Phillips stirred and proffered the decanter once again. Isaacs smiled saying, "Just a little," and then flashed a halt sign as Phillips refilled his glass anyway. Isaacs followed the neck of the decanter encased by Phillips' deeply lined knuckles as it tilted up from his glass, crossed to the other and dipped to release more amber liquid. He spoke as Phillips carefully replaced the stopper in the decanter.

"There is one more point."

"Please."

"You mentioned the question of hostility a while ago, or lack thereof. There was some talk about the possible origin of a black hole this afternoon. Runyan seemed to feel such a thing must be artificially manufactured."

Phillips' eyes were half closed in concentration, but he did not speak. Isaacs continued.

"To my mind that raises two issues. One is whether we're endangered. If there is a black hole down there, the answer is yes, we are, although I gather the exact nature of the peril and the time scale remain to be worked out. The second issue is whether this dangerous situation was intentionally created. If that's the case, then it seems to me that is by far the greatest threat, and we mustn't lose sight of it."

Phillips swiveled again to look out the window. He cupped the glass of sherry in both hands in his lap and replied in a ruminative tone.

"Which is the greatest danger? The bullet streaking toward our heart—or the man who pulled the trigger?"

He was silent for a long moment and then said, "I cannot help you there, Mr. Isaacs. The discussion this afternoon was inconclusive because we don't know enough. I understand your concern. None of us will rest easily for a long while."

Phillips continued to gaze out the window. Isaacs studied his profile for a time and then broke his own reverie by throwing down the sherry at a gulp. Phillips made no move. After a moment Isaacs rose and crossed the room. As he closed the door behind him, he glanced one last time at the old man, his vision still locked on some distant point.

Danielson opened the door at the knock and smiled a greeting at Isaacs.

"Hi. Just a second, let me get my purse." She turned back into the room and reappeared shrugging into a sweater as she juggled her purse by the strap. Isaacs reached to help with the sweater.

"Thanks," she said as they headed down the hall. Her glance at him took in a bit of damp, mussed hair over his temple. Despite this evidence for a recent face washing and attempt to freshen up, she thought he looked tense and drawn. "You feel up to this?" she inquired. "Going out?"

His smile put some life back in his face. "Of course. Besides, I'm hungry as a bear. I always pick at that airline food I had for lunch."

Phillips, Runyan, and Gantt awaited them in the foyer. Runyan's attention immediately focused on Danielson.

"I've suggested a little Japanese place downtown. Not your flashy knife-juggling kind, but excellent sashimi and tempura. And not so expensive that it will do violence to our government per diems."

Danielson's eyes swept him quickly. He had swapped his beach clothes for loafers, dark slacks and an expensive Italian shirt unbuttoned to show matted grey hair on his chest.

"That sounds fine," she responded.

Runyan busied himself herding the group out. When they reached the car, he insisted that Phillips ride in front, in deference to his age. He ushered first Isaacs then Danielson into the back seat and then squeezed his own limber form in next to Danielson. He leaned forward to back-seat drive until Gantt had the Thunderbird safely headed southward on the interstate. Then he leaned back and drew Phillips into a good natured, if somewhat embarrassed, reminiscence of Phillips' encounter with a lady of the evening at one of their scientific meetings.

The meeting had been held in a hotel dominated at the time by a convention of salesmen. In the bar, Phillips had mistaken the woman for a waitress and the call girl had mistaken him for one of the salesmen with whom she had previously made an appointment. Runyan related both sides of the conversation which had proceeded at total cross purposes before the misunderstanding was revealed.

Gantt had seen Runyan use this tack before, relating a story with sexy overtones to check the reaction of a new female acquaintance. Seems to be working, he thought. He glanced in the rear view mirror and could see Danielson's broad grin as she followed Runyan's animated delivery.

"And do you remember that look she gave you as she was leaving and patted you on the head? I think she would have preferred you to her paying client."

"Now, Alex," Phillips chuckled with embarrassment.

"Whoops—here's Washington Avenue; turn off here," Runyan directed at Gantt, reverting to navigator. "Okay, now left under the interstate. There it is, on the left, just beyond. See it? I'm not sure where to park. You always have to scrounge a place here."

"Well, why don't I let you out here while I go find a place," volunteered Gantt.

They piled out of the car and then crossed the street. There was a small queue on the sidewalk, but they were admitted shortly after Gantt rejoined them, having left the car in the lot of a gas station which was closed for the night.

Despite the somewhat crowded space, Runyan managed adroitly to get them seated around a table intended for four, drawing up a fifth chair for himself at the end of the table by Danielson and Phillips.

The meal was all Runyan had advertised. Dish followed excellent dish and when they all felt full, a new and interesting plate would arrive, served by a quiet, cheerful woman in traditional geisha garb. Runyan ordered a steady flow of saki and Japanese beer and always ensured that Danielson was liberally supplied. He helped her with playful solicitation to mix the cube of mustard into the tiny dish of soy sauce to make the dip for the bits of raw fish. He was very adroit with chopsticks and insisted on feeding her a bite from every new dish as it arrived.

Danielson found herself basking in the attention Runyan lavished on her and greatly enjoying his company. She mused to herself that, although he was about forty-five, as close in age to her father as to herself, in terms of physique he reminded her of the beach bum whom she had thought of marrying so long ago. She realized she was greatly attracted to Runyan's radiant sense of well-being and self-confidence, the spirit that had drawn her to Allan. But Allan had no purpose in life, no goal beyond mastering the next wave. Runyan was completely different in that regard. He operated on an intellectual plane Allan would never even glimpse. She was also fascinated by the inner security she thought Runyan must possess which enabled him to range from the terrifying creative *tour de force* he had displayed that afternoon to the wellspring of *joie de vivre* presently at her side.

As they left the restaurant, Runyan tried to drum up enthusiasm to go dancing. Danielson was in a mood to go along, but quickly followed Isaacs' lead when he demurred.

The ride back to La Jolla was, nevertheless, made in good spirits. Danielson mostly listened as the men traded anecdotes about Washington politics. The perspective of the three scientists was similar, deriving from the National Academy of Sciences and experience with certain congressional liaison committees. They were highly entertained, therefore, by the different view Isaacs provided from his wife's exploits as a lawyer.

When they arrived back at the Bishop's School, their spirit of camaraderie spilled out of the car into the absorbing stillness of the campus. Runyan locked arms with Danielson and escorted her up the stairs of the dormitory to her door. Isaacs followed along behind. He had enjoyed the evening, but had continued to view with some jaundice Runyan's attention to Danielson and her ready response. He forced a grin as Runyan stopped with Danielson at her door and proceeded with comic formality to kiss her hand in farewell. Isaacs made sure Danielson was safely in her room, then walked on down to his.

Runyan climbed the stairs to his own room. He switched on the light and stood for a moment viewing the casual disarray. The desk was strewn with books. Many were opened face down, others were face up with any convenient object—calculator, coffee cup, pencil—used as a place holder. Soiled and clean clothes were intermingled in a pattern discernable only to the occupant.

The evening's look of merriment was gone from Runyan's face. He relieved himself in the bathroom and then sat at the desk. His first thoughts were of Pat Danielson. Bright woman. He unquestionably wanted to get in the sack with her. He pondered the dilemma of the modern age. How do you treat a competent woman professionally when your cave-man hormones are singing their atavistic song? In Danielson's case, he could sense she was ripe. If the circumstances had been a little different, a chance for some intimacy, one of them might at this very moment be sneaking down the hall toward the other's room. He pictured her face as he gently unbuttoned the blouse she had worn today. Whoa! He shook his head. Enough torture of that sort. Let's try another. He rummaged for a pencil and a pad of lined paper on which he began to scratch a long series of calculations. After an hour he rose and stretched and then moved to a softer chair next to a reading lamp. A journal devoted to astrophysics lay open on the arm, draped face down. He retrieved it and began to read. As he read, he half consciously waited for someone to come and explain where he had gone wrong in his thinking. No one did.

By three in the morning, his fatigue ran deep. He tried to replace the journal on the chair arm, but he was well over half through, and the unbalanced volume slipped to the floor. He swore, straightened the pages and marked his place with a dirty sock. Then he undressed, fell into bed, thought briefly again of Pat Danielson, and drifted into a fitful sleep.

Nine o'clock the next morning found the group reassembled in Gantt's room. Danielson and Runyan were talking in quiet tones on the sofa. Gantt had conferred his swivel desk chair to Phillips and taken the seat near the door. The others took their accustomed places.

Phillips broke off his conversation with Isaacs, who was seated next to him, as Noldt, the last to arrive, came in swinging the door against Gantt's chair and causing him to slosh some of his post-breakfast coffee into his lap. Noldt dithered in helpless apology while Gantt waved him off and dabbed the spot with a handkerchief. After Noldt took his chair, Phillips cleared his throat and began.

"We have no formal agenda this morning. Would anyone care to add to yesterday afternoon's discussions?"

"That is to say," broke in Runyan, "can anyone put a quick and merciful end to Runyan's folly?"

There were several chuckles which died away into silence as it became clear that no one was about to volunteer a viable counterhypothesis or cite an obvious failure in Runyan's logic.

"With all due respect to you as our resident astrophysical pundit, Alex," said Fletcher, breaking the silence, "if you're on the right track, don't we need to call in some expert help on this problem, someone who knows about this particular subject of small black holes?"

"Absolutely," answered Runyan. "There are several individuals whose advice would be invaluable, for instance, Korolev in Russia or Pearlby in England. I'd love to discuss this problem with Korolev over a glass of vodka."

Isaacs straightened perceptibly, startled by this sudden injection of Korolev's name. But of course, he thought, these people are probably old friends, cronies.

Phillips saw Isaacs start and took the lead.

"There is, ah, a question of security here, of course," Phillips said.

"Surely not in the classical sense," said Noldt with some bewilderment. "This isn't just a national issue. The whole bloody world is being sucked up."

"There's no proof of that yet, Ted," reproached Phillips. "In any case, there seems good reason to proceed cautiously at this point."

"What about a colleague of mine at Princeton," suggested Fletcher, "Clarence Humphreys?"

"Of course," Runyan enthused, "Clarence could be very helpful. I don't know about his stand on security matters, but he should be approached."

"There seems to be a consensus, then," summarized Phillips, "that we will proceed on the assumption that Alex has provided the correct explanation of the events reported. We will try to enlist the support of an expert on black holes, particularly the miniature variety—starting with Humphreys. We've already established that Gantt will set up a gravimeter experiment to seek direct evidence for or against the black hole theory. Alex, you mentioned the need for detailed orbit calculations. Can you see to that end of things?"

"The best way to proceed there would be to make use of the computer facilities and programs at the Jet Propulsion Laboratory," said Runyan. "I could move up to Pasadena for the rest of the summer. As for security, we can't simply ask them to calculate a black hole orbit inside the earth. I must have special personal access to the computers, but I'll need to consult with the experts on the relevant codes which require modification. Someone will have to do some arranging for me."

Phillips looked at Isaacs who nodded in confirmation. Phillips then addressed the group again. "Anyone have anything else to add?"

After a moment Zicek spoke up.

"Our course of action is just as you have outlined, Wayne—some straightforward steps to better define the situation. Last night I took a different tack and spent a good deal of time pondering Alex's basic premise. He not only wants a small black hole careening through the earth, but he led us to the brink of concluding that such a thing must have been artificially manufactured. Despite his logic, like many of us here, I found that idea *prima facie* absurd. And granting that absurdity, I questioned the whole scheme. My apologies, Alex."

Runyan shrugged and waited for the point to which all this was preamble.

"This morning," Zicek continued, "I am not so sure."

His eyebrows compressed together as he paused to formulate his words.

"I do not see how to create such a little monster, but I am no longer so positive that to speak of such a process is absurd.

"As many of you know, I am actively involved in Project Antares at Los Alamos. Our goal is to create controlled thermonuclear reactions by imploding a pellet of deuterium and tritium. The present scheme has six gas lasers the size of locomotives producing seventy-two laser beams which are brought to focus on the pellet. The pellet is drastically compressed, creating high enough temperatures and densities to trigger the fusing of deuterium into helium.

"This is only one of the projects currently being undertaken by our government and by that of the Soviet Union, which appears to me to bear on this problem. The others, given the current political situation, are related to weaponry. I speak of beam weapons of many kinds which unload their destructive power at the speed of light and will render normal missiles and aircraft obsolete and defenseless.

"I myself have had a role in developing the infrared chemical laser which the Navy is using in their Sea Light lethality verification program and the related Talon Gold pointing and tracking tests. The Air Force has its own parallel program with a carbon dioxide gas laser on an NKC-135 at Kirtland Air Force Base.

"While I'm not involved with them, except as a competitor for funding, there are several programs developing particle beams. The White Horse project at Los Alamos aims for a space-based neutral beam generator using a radio frequency quadrupole accelerator. The Advanced Test Facility at Livermore is producing an electron beam, and the RADALAC at Sandia can fire electrons, protons, or negative hydrogen ions at near the speed of light. Lord only knows what sort of gadgets the Russians have by now. Most of our ideas were stolen from them. We know they have developed techniques to use chemical explosions to drive magnetic flux compression generators. They have used stupendous electric currents generated by these devices to power rail guns—linear induction motors which can be used to hurl payloads into orbit or drive armor piercing bullets at hypersonic velocities."

Zicek leaned forward, resting his forearms on his thighs and interlocking his fingers. "Now my point is, any of these devices—lasers, relativistic electron beams, rail guns—can, in principle, be focused inward to achieve implosions. So far the goal of implosion studies has been to achieve high density and temperature and produce nuclear fusion. Such processes cannot achieve extreme densities because the energy expended to raise both the temperature and the density is too high. Alex and Harvey discussed that yesterday.

"But suppose our goal was not high temperature, but just high density— very high density. It is true that I cannot see how to reach densities where self-gravity plays a role and a black hole becomes feasible. I can, however, imagine a few tricks in principle to keep the temperature relatively low even as the density rises."

He unlaced his fingers and gestured with open palms.

"I'm sorry to be so long-winded. What I am trying to say is that our technology is moving even now in a direction where such a thing becomes imaginable. Technological and scientific advances are growing exponentially. Who knows what comes next?"

Zicek looked around the confines of the small room, eyeing his colleagues.

"Are you inviting us to conclude," asked Fletcher in a voice of deliberate calm, "that, while we cannot now do such a thing, perhaps a society only somewhat advanced from ours could?"

"Never mind a very advanced society," put in Noldt more excitedly.

"Oh, hold on," said Leems disgustedly. "Granted, Vlad, we're inventing a cornucopia of implosion machinery. There is still an immense jump to making black holes. Just because we've launched a space probe out of the solar system doesn't mean that intergalactic space travel will be possible for us or for any advanced civilizations which might be out there. Sometimes practical limits can erect just as solid a barrier as physical impossibility. You damn well can't strike a match on a wet cake of soap. I still find the whole black hole business preposterous."

"Perhaps you're right, Harvey," admitted Zicek, "but I feel we should not jump to a conclusion either way. No one has really thought seriously about how hard or how easy making a black hole might be if one really tried. I'm just saying such a thing may be possible. Our knowledge of the behavior of matter at only slightly greater than nuclear density is very sparse."

"Well, what we don't know, we can't use to reach any conclusions," said Leems, still sounding disgusted.

"Of course, of course," placated Zicek. He addressed himself to Phillips again. "My thoughts in this direction lead me to one concrete suggestion you may want to consider."

"Yes, what is that?" inquired Phillips.

"We have discussed bringing in other experts to help us deal with the particulars of this problem. Carl suggested Humphreys," he waved toward Fletcher. "I think we should consider more carefully this question of how such a thing might be made. One person comes to mind who would be uniquely qualified in terms of both experience and creative insight."

"I'll bet you're thinking of Paul Krone," said Runyan.

"Yes, in fact, I was," replied Zicek.

Isaacs looked up sharply at this reference. He had heard of Paul Krone, and he was not the kind of man Isaacs would be keen to bring into this effort. Not exactly stable.

Leems made clear where he stood.

"That horse's ass? Surely you don't want to set that bull loose in this china shop?"

"You're being unfair," Zicek replied tensely. "I know there are people jealous of Paul's successes because they don't understand his methods, but he has great insight which could serve us well and he's currently deeply involved in these questions."

"Jealous?" Leems waved a hand in dismissal. "He can't even keep a job. Half his ideas are fantasy—sheer gibberish. And who knows what other troubles he would bring."

Isaacs thought Leems probably was jealous. Krone had worked his way through a couple of universities, private industry and various government labs, a maverick always on the move, but he had a midas touch. A dozen times during his career he had started a little company on the side, working on some development or other. If the idea worked, Krone would keep a controlling interest, but turn the company over to professional managers and never look back. The scientists he worked with were always suspicious because he made so much money. Businessmen couldn't understand how he could throw it all over and go back to tinkering in some laboratory or doodling equations.

Krone was a man of great appetites as well as great talent. There had been some trouble getting him a security clearance for one government consulting job, and the case had come to Isaacs' attention informally through an acquaintance with the FBI. There had been questions of drugs and women, a year or two ago he had taken up with an expatriate Russian of all things, and legal entanglements concerning the proprietary rights to some of his developments. In looking over the file, Isaacs had been amazed to see the number of well-known companies, three of them on the Fortune 500, that Krone controlled, directly or indirectly.

Runyan laughed to take the sting out of Leems' words.

"C'mon, Harvey. It's true Paul can be hard to take when he starts ranting. There's no question he's a raving egomaniac with a penchant for hiding his ideas until he can spring them on the world. And maybe half his ideas are nonsense, but half of them have some real insight, and half of a lot is a lot."

He addressed himself to Phillips.

"It strikes me someone like Krone who's familiar with both theoretical physics and engineering developments might be useful to us."

Runyan turned to Zicek.

"What's he doing now? Didn't I hear he was consulting at Los Alamos?"

"That's right. He started another company and has a consulting contract with the Lab to explore just these developments I was describing—laser implosion, relativistic beams—both experimentally and theoretically. That's why I thought he would have a general grasp of the situation which would be useful to us."

Isaacs saw there might be some merit to the arguments Zicek and Runyan made, but his sympathies were more with Leems. He spoke up. "I wonder whether the questions Dr. Zicek raises, and perhaps Dr. Krone's involvement, might be of secondary importance just now. It seems that our critical task is to confirm or deny Dr. Runyan's suggestion. I would like to ask Dr. Gantt whether he has considered the requirements of the proposed experiment. I'm sure your seismology lab at Caltech is well equipped, but I wonder whether you will need any help which my agency or some other government agency can provide?"

"I've not had time to plan any details," replied Gantt. "We'll want to go someplace which is seismically inactive—away from the California fault system, perhaps Arizona. I might use some help with transportation and some support equipment. I'd like to use an on-site minicomputer for analysis. I have one, but it's cumbersome to move."

Isaacs nodded. "We can help with that."

Gantt continued, "We must, of course, know where to look. From Dr. Danielson's present data it appears that the activity comes near the surface at about twelve-hundred-mile intervals. The trick is to be in the right place at the right time. You've said you can predict the surface location at any particular instant to within a kilometer or so." He looked toward Danielson for confirmation, and the young woman nodded.

"With updated sonar data, we should be able to do better than that," she said.

Gantt turned to Runyan. "What gravitational perturbation did you estimate for a distance of a kilometer, Alex?"

"That should give you a fluctuation of a part in a million," replied Runyan.

"We can do that," asserted Gantt.

"I'm going to be busy with things in Washington," Isaacs said, "but I'd like to have someone on the site with you. Would you mind if Dr. Danielson joined you?"

"Not at all," Gantt replied. "I think her knowledge of the background to this situation could prove most useful." He smiled at the young woman and got a brief appreciative one in return.

"You wouldn't mind joining Professor Gantt, would you, Pat?" Isaacs asked.

She thought of her urge to go to Dallas to be where the action was. Nothing would keep her from being on top of it the next time.

"I would like to very much."

Oho, Runyan thought to himself, now there's a trip I'd like to make, too. He looked at Isaacs' stern visage and decided now was not the ideal time to press his petition.

"Excellent," said Phillips, with an air of summary. "Perhaps we should leave it at that, then. I know Mr. Isaacs has a plane to catch, and I don't believe further discussion would enhance the situation at this point. I suggest we adjourn."

He rose to emphasize his decision and watched as the others stood and filed out. He joined Isaacs in the hall and they waited a moment for Danielson and Runyan, who were the last ones out.

Isaacs and Danielson gathered their things from their rooms while Phillips called for a car. They caught a noon flight back to Washington.

They spoke little until the plane was in the air. When the no smoking sign was turned off and the attendants began to move around the cabin, they turned as if at a signal, and looked at one another. Each read in the other's eyes the special camaraderie of a shared, shocking experience. Impulsively, Danielson leaned over and gave him a quick peck on the cheek. Surprised and pleased, he patted her hand on the armrest, in what he hoped was a fatherly manner. Danielson leaned back in her seat.

"Wow!" she exclaimed quietly. "I feel like I'm trying to work an idea into my head that's a hundred sizes too big to fit." She turned to him. "Thanks for the opportunity to go with Gantt. I really want to do that."

"You've done an excellent job all along," Isaacs told her. "We need you to follow up."

"Thank you," she replied, "but you're the one who deserves congratulations. I know what you risked to bring us this far."

The rolling chaos of the serving cart appeared in the aisle next to them, and they each ordered a bloody mary.

Danielson took a sip of her drink, then stared into it, probing on the lime slice with the swizzle stick. "Who would have thought that that faint signal would lead to this?" she asked herself as much as Isaacs.

She turned to him. "You certainly were right about the effectiveness of Jason. What did you think of Alex Runyan? Wasn't that amazing the way he so quickly drew everything together?"

"That was quite a show he put on," Isaacs replied neutrally. "We do have to remember that for all his arguments we have no direct proof. Perhaps we should reserve judgment until Gantt performs this experiment."

Danielson was surprised at his coolness. She shot a sideways glance at him, with a sudden flash of intuition. Was it possible, just possible, that Bob Isaacs was the tiniest bit jealous of Alex Runyan? At the attention he had shown her? She took another sip of her drink. There were a number of things, big and small, to savor about this trip. She added that notion to the list.

Chapter 13

Ellison Gantt glanced at the naked sun high over his shoulder, wiped sweat from his forehead and dried his hand on the seat of his pants. He checked the date on his watch. Tuesday, August 10. Hot in this part of the world. The Jason meeting with the CIA people had catalyzed a week of exhaustive activity. He had assembled an impressive array of seismological data monitoring equipment and made what modifications he could to suit the mission at hand. They had been encamped for two days in this remote part of the Lechuguilla Desert, thirty miles from Yuma, a little southwest of Welton. Despite the debilitating, blistering August heat, they had managed to set up the equipment and to repair the minor damage done in transit. Gantt still marveled at the speed with which the transportation had been mobilized once a suitable site had been selected and the equipment was ready. Isaacs had arranged for an Air Force cargo jet to fly them to the Yuma Marine Corps Air Station, then for a helicopter ferry to this remote site.

The basic location had suggested itself naturally enough. Gantt had briefly considered a shipboard experiment in the ocean west of San Diego, but he concluded that the delicate measurements he hoped to make would be virtually impossible with the present equipment on board a pitching ship. Even on this solid land where he now stood, the natural tremors of the earth could mask any small effect, and he did not really know what effect to anticipate.

He mentally surveyed the layout. Arrayed over several miles of barren rolling desert were a series of seismometers to measure the ordinary activity of the earth, and the special seismic waves that were due to be superposed. There were also the special instruments designed to detect any accelerations which might occur if a significant gravitational pull, in addition to that of the earth, were to occur. All these instruments were connected to a small but powerful computer energized by the portable generator whose noise disturbed the otherwise quiet early afternoon. This computer would provide an instant analysis of the data. It not only recorded the strength of the signals but, using information from instruments spaced at a distance, it could also triangulate and determine the direction and distance to the source of the waves or gravitational acceleration.

All was now in readiness. Gantt felt a small chill despite the heat. In a little over an hour the seismic waves should broach the surface about two hundred miles away in eastern Arizona, registering on the seismometers but perhaps only marginally on the accelerometers even with Runyan's most extreme estimates. Eighty and a half minutes later the source of the waves would again approach the surface but a thousand miles to the west, over seven hundred miles off the Pacific coast. Since the incommensurate period of rotation of the earth made the surfacings appear to shift one hundred ninety miles every twenty-four hours, tomorrow at nearly the same time the waves should impinge on the surface very close to their present location.

Gantt turned his back on the encampment and looked out across the shallow hills. He had great difficulty accepting the picture proposed by Runyan, and yet he could not resist a morbid temptation to imagine what was proceeding if the hypothesis were correct. A small speeding object was now plunging down through the deepest basalt layers of the earth's crust. In fifteen minutes it would enter the molten core, picking up speed as it went. Sensing the change in gravitational pull as it passed the earth's center, it would begin to slow as it shot back toward the surface, where it would peak with majestic slowness before crashing back into the dirt and rock.

Gantt shook his head and strode back to the main tent of the encampment. The interior of the tent was a little cooler because of the air conditioner installed to service the computer, but it was still stifling. Gantt became too engrossed to notice.

At five minutes before the appointed time, he focused his attention on the needles of the seismometers. They jiggled steadily but with nearly constant amplitude, tuned to the basic constant sounds of the earth. In a couple of minutes he saw the effect he was looking for. The swings of the needles on all three seismometers began to slowly grow in amplitude. Danielson's seismic waves were real enough all right. The question was what caused them. Even to Gantt's trained eye the signals on the three instruments looked identical. Only the computer could distinguish the minute differences due to the slightly different distances of the instruments from the source of the waves. Gantt turned to the computer, typing rapidly on the keyboard and then scrutinizing the screen in front of him as the printer to one side began to roll out the same data on a chain of paper sheets. The distance was about one hundred ninety miles, a little closer than their best guess, but within the expected errors. Gantt's gaze then swung to take in the readings from the accelerometers which might detect some variation in gravitational force. He thought he could make out the briefest fluctuation, but could not be sure. Again he keyed the computer and found his impression confirmed. There might be an effect, but it was only marginally above the noise level. A more sophisticated analysis that could only be done with time and a bigger computer might dig something out, but for now there was no firm conclusion to be reached. Still, he mused, an effect of the size Runyan predicted could not be ruled out. If the minute fluctuation were real, then something massive had just surfaced two hundred miles away, and in three quarters of an hour it would do so again on the far side of the earth.

Gantt stripped the printed computer output off the machine and examined it more carefully. He swore quietly as sweat dripped off his brow onto the paper, obscuring a few numbers. He stopped to wipe his forehead and neck and then returned his attention to the rows of numbers. The seismic waves stopped several miles below the surface. After a minute or so, the source of the waves began again, moving nearly vertically down into the earth. Gantt felt a nervous tightening across his abdomen. An ordinary seismic wave could be reflected, but it did not wait a minute while making up its mind. Such a delay might occur if the source of the waves moved up into light surface layers which were not conducive to the production of waves and then fell back again. Runyan's hole could do that. Deep in thought, Gantt sat for some minutes striving for an explanation in terms of the normal behavior of the earth as he knew it. Nothing occurred to him, but he told himself that Runyan need not be right on that basis, perhaps it was just his own lack of imagination or lack of sufficient information. The mysterious interior of the earth had surprised him more than once and might be doing so again. Taking solace from that thought, he proceeded to a close study of the data acquired during the event.

Wednesday morning Pat Danielson clambered down from the rear seat of the jet-black F-16 which was rigged for tactical reconnaissance. She was aided by the pilot and a ground technician. Her legs were a little unsteady from the excitement of the Mach 2 flight from Washington—over two thousand miles to the Yuma Air Station in an hour and a half. She followed a young marine to a waiting helicopter and stood there while he went into a nearby utilitarian terminal building. He reemerged in a moment followed by Alex Runyan. Runyan was halfway across the tarmac when he looked up and saw her. The look of surprise and pleasure on his face was delicious to her.

"Pat!" He ran forward, grabbed her hand in both his and gave her a spontaneous peck on the cheek, oblivious to the watching servicemen. "What a delight. I didn't expect to see you here."

"After you pleaded with Bob Isaacs yesterday," Danielson said gaily, "we decided to coordinate the trips, save a helicopter ride."

"That's great. When did you leave? It's a long way."

She laughed with obvious glee. "Crossing three time zones helps, but so does that," she pointed toward the fighter. "We landed before we took off."

"Holy cow!" Runyan exclaimed. "Now I know who has the real clout. I thought I was Mr. Big with the puddle jumper your boss arranged for me this morning. Well, let's get on with the adventure!"

He helped her through the passenger hatch in the side of the helicopter, handed up her light bag, then his and finally swung himself up and in with a single easy motion.

"What did you think of Gantt's preliminary report?" Danielson shouted over the whine of the cranking engine, as they buckled themselves in.

"Too soon to tell," he shouted back, "but I'm afraid there was nothing to prove I was wrong."

After they took off, the flight noise made conversation difficult. Danielson watched the country flash by the open hatch, vividly aware of Runyan's long lean thigh next to hers.

Gantt was engrossed in making some changes in the computer analysis routines when he heard the chopping roar of the approaching helicopter. He approached the landing site and stood a hundred yards off as the machine circled once around the area and then settled slowly to the ground. As the rotor speed decreased and the whine of the turbojet ceased, he saw a man get out and then turn to help his companion. Gantt squinted into the sun and then finally waved a greeting as he recognized the approaching figures.

"Hello!" shouted Gantt. "Alex! What a surprise. I didn't expect an extra guest at our little party here."

He shook hands with Runyan and then with Danielson. He grabbed the young woman's hand with both of his and gave an extra shake. He suddenly wanted Danielson to feel welcome as a colleague, rather than a visiting government official.

"Do you have baggage to unload?" he inquired.

"Just a couple of bags," replied Runyan. "Lord, it's hot here! What's the temperature?"

"About a hundred and fifteen in the shade," Gantt laughed. "Cools off in the evenings, though. Not so bad then."

Gantt looked back and saw the pilot unloading two small cases from the passenger compartment. He called to one of the young marines who had been recruited for the project to lend a hand and then ushered the pair into the mess tent.

"Can I get you something? Coffee? Iced tea? Lemonade? Lunch won't be ready for a while, but we might scare up a snack."

Both declined anything to eat. Gantt got a cup of coffee for himself and showed the others where to help themselves to iced tea. They sat at a table under the outstretched flap of the tent, shielded from the sun but open to the fitful breeze.

"Well, Alex, I needn't ask what brings you here, but it is a pleasant surprise."

Runyan wiped his brow with the back of his hand and scratched his hot beard.

"I've been living with the computer at the Jet Propulsion Laboratory, adapting their orbital programs to calculate the path of a black hole through the earth. When you radioed your results from yesterday to CIA headquarters, Isaacs relayed the essence of it to me. I'd calculated so many orbital eccentricities that I was getting a bit eccentric myself. I'm afraid I was rather obvious about my desire to be out here where the action is, even though that wasn't on the program. Lord knows I'll just be a fifth wheel.

"In any case," continued Runyan, "I was picked up by an Air Force plane this morning and, much to my pleasant surprise, met Pat here in Yuma."

"Well, I'm glad to see you both," admitted Gantt. "I confess I've been bothered by not having anyone here to talk to about this business. How are your calculations going?" he asked Runyan.

"The model basically fits the data. But there are lots of loose parameters. We don't know enough about the detailed structure of the inner earth and how a small black hole would interact with it to predict small subtle shifts in the orbit with any degree of confidence. A little extra rock, like the roots of a mountain range, can perturb the orbit slightly, depending on angle of approach, a bunch of things. You can get slow cumulative effects, or an occasional finite perturbation. Hard to pin down. The data you're collecting now should allow us to fix some of those parameters. That still won't be the same as proving my picture is right."

"Actually," interjected Gantt, "if we are going to discuss this matter, and I surely want to, we should move over to my tent. It's a little less public there."

They picked up their drinks and moved off to Gantt's tent which was set off somewhat from the main compound. Gantt went off to gather up two more folding chairs and returned to arrange them in the small patch of shade available.

"Have you learned anything new?" he inquired of Danielson.

"I've collated some more data from the Large Seismic Array and various other monitoring stations. There have been some refinements in our estimations, but nothing qualitatively new." She took a sip of her tea. "In fact, there's been one major frustration. We had hoped to get the Navy to make systematic measurements of the sonar signal. That would have given us much better positions. Unfortunately, their old data isn't much good now, and they couldn't or wouldn't respond fast enough to get any new data this last week. As a result, the measurements of positions you got yesterday are probably the best we have."

"Did you explain Alex's hypothesis to the Navy?" Gantt wanted to know.

"No," replied Danielson, "the decision was made not to spread that notion any further than necessary until the results of this expedition are in." She leaned toward Gantt. "What about this cessation of the signal below the surface which you reported yesterday? My data have never shown a signal from the upper mantle, but you reported a definite time delay. That would be a small effect in my data which has poor time resolution, but it might be present. I didn't have time to look carefully before hopping the plane. Don't you think it's reminiscent of the sonar signal stopping at the surface of the ocean, just that it starts earlier and lasts a bit longer?"

"Yes, that's my impression," said Gantt. "It's strange behavior for a normal seismic wave, but it might be consistent with Alex's beast as we discussed in La Jolla." He paused to scratch his head and shuffle his toe in the dirt. "Still, I can't help wondering whether we could be dealing with some special fissuring that focused normal seismic waves, and those fissures could terminate below the surface."

"But that wouldn't explain the delay in the return of the waves," Runyan pointed out, "nor the holes drilled in Nagasaki and Dallas."

"Well, maybe the energy is temporarily stored as a mechanical stress in the rock and then released. I admit I don't have a real physical picture of such a process, but neither do I see how to rule out the possibility. The holes? Well, you're right; I can't account for them easily either. Coincidental imperfections in the concrete?"

This rhetorical question went unanswered. There was silence for a moment, broken by Runyan. "As I understand from Isaacs, you had a marginal detection of an abnormal acceleration?"

"Yes," replied Gantt, "there was some indication in the first event. It could be real, or just an accidental accumulation of noise."

"From the distances you got yesterday," Runyan continued, "what do you estimate for the location of this event coming up today?"

"My best guess is that the epicenter, if you can call it that, will be about a quarter of a mile to the northeast of here, but there's an uncertainty of a few hundred meters."

"Hmmm, too bad we don't have that Navy sonar data," Runyan muttered. "I'd hate to have this thing fly up my ass." He caught himself and turned to Danielson, patting her on the arm. "Pardon me, hon, excuse my language." She suppressed a smile. He turned back to Gantt.

"And you expect it at about 2:03 this afternoon?"

"Give or take a few seconds."

"So it surfaced almost half an hour ago in northwest Louisiana," mused Runyan. "It's passed through the core and is now headed up to a point in the East Crozet Basin in the southern Indian Ocean. And, after another quick pass through the core, it will soon be here." He stared down at the brown dirt and scrubby grass beneath his feet, as if by concentrating he could peer into the depths of the earth in reality as he could by imagination and thereby witness this rogue particle at work.

"You think you're right, don't you?" Gantt inquired.

"I'm *afraid* I am," Runyan answered.

Gantt stared at Runyan and then removed his glasses and wiped sweat from his eyes. "Let me give you a tour," he said and led his guests to the main tent where he explained the function of the arrayed instrumentation.

At fifteen minutes before two, Gantt had Runyan and Danielson stand aside while he made final preparations. Danielson glanced at her watch at two minutes after the hour just as Gantt turned to announce:

"Come and look—I'm getting a signal on the seismometers." Runyan and Danielson approached and peered over his shoulder. All three seismometers were showing a definite increase in activity. Gantt turned to the computer, fingered the keyboard, and examined the screen.

"I'm getting a good reading on the distance, but I'm having some trouble determining exactly where it's heading since, as predicted, it seems to be right beneath us."

They turned their attention back to the seismometers which were by now showing great activity.

"Look at this!" exclaimed Gantt. He pointed to the readings on the gravimeters. All were showing a definite and growing anomalous acceleration. Once more, Gantt swiveled in his seat toward the computer, but before he could key in his instructions, confusion erupted.

Runyan first saw the needle of the seismometer in the camp go off scale, slamming against its restraining pin. Before his mind could quite absorb the implication of that occurrence, his body recorded a rapid, bizarre set of feelings.

First, he had the definite sensation that the floor of the tent had accelerated upward suddenly like an express elevator. This feeling was terminated by a sideways impulse as if he had been hit with a sudden, strong gust of wind. Just as quickly, that sensation was replaced by a familiar fearsome tickle in stomach and gonads. Runyan was reminded of a roller coaster as it begins its first terrifying descent, leaving tender organs in the grasp of inertia. His ears registered a sucking whistle, rapidly diminishing in amplitude as if someone had turned on a vacuum cleaner just outside the tent and then whisked it rapidly away.

As these sensations passed, Runyan became aware of chaotic shouts beginning to echo around the camp and of Danielson half sprawled, grasping the back of Gantt's chair. Danielson had taken a step toward Gantt and had been caught with one foot in the air when she was bumped sideways and knocked off balance. Runyan helped Danielson regain her feet. She collapsed against him, weak-kneed and pale with shock. Runyan held her shoulders gently.

The whistling noise returned, this time not quite so loud and at a higher pitch. Danielson stepped back from Runyan, her hands on his chest, her eyes searching his for explanation, confirmation. After a moment, Runyan looked toward the instrumentation. Danielson's gaze followed his and they simultaneously swiveled to look at the seismometers. All needles had fallen to rest, tracking a straight line down the center of the strip charts. In the same instant as the faint whistling stopped, the needles twitched and once more the one on the camp instrument slammed against its restraining pin. As they watched, the needles began to swing, first entirely across the chart and then with gradually diminishing amplitude.

The hoarse voices outside the tent died with the swing of the needles, and Runyan spoke first.

"Goddamn!" he said with measured stress. And then again, "Goddamn!"

As the reaction began to sink in, he felt his legs begin to shake. He moved uncertainly to the nearest chair and collapsed in it. He looked at Gantt, whose face was ashen, and at Danielson who, by contrast, was beginning to regain some color. Her eyes now showed the intensity of contained excitement. She suddenly had an idea, turned and rushed out of the tent. The two men sat in silence until one of Gantt's assistants burst in.

"Dr. Gantt," he shouted, "what'n hell was that?"

Gantt turned and looked at him for a long moment before replying, "I don't know, an earthquake, I suppose."

"Hell, that wasn't like any earthquake I've ever been in," replied the other, his voice barely quieter. "Two fellows just outside the tent got knocked on their butts. I was a hundred yards away and didn't feel a thing. And that noise, I've never heard a quake make a noise like that!"

"It was somewhat irregular," Gantt conceded. "Why don't you check out the camp and the other sites to see if everything is all right. I'll see what I can figure out from the data we collected."

The man knew he was being put off, but could see nothing to do about it. He paused a moment until it was clear that Gantt had nothing further to say, then departed with an aggressive stride, nearly colliding with Danielson, who rushed in as he left.

She hurried across the tent floor and pulled up a chair to sit at right angles to Runyan. His arm was draped on the chair. Danielson grasped his hand in both of hers and gave it a strong, almost painful, squeeze.

Barely aware of Danielson beside him, squeezing his arm, Runyan was caught up in a maelstrom of fragmentary thoughts. He couldn't grasp the details; they moved too fast, too lightly, wafted away like floating cottonwood seeds if he tried to grab at them. Somehow, though, he caught enough glimpses through the swirl. Us? Them? He couldn't see who, but he knew the answer.

"You were right, Alex," Danielson said in a tense hissing whisper. "I don't see any sign of a tunnel outside the tent, but I know you were right. That force! It could only have been the gravity! It *is* a black hole!" As she said the last words she raised his hand in hers and banged it back down on the arm of the chair. Runyan winced slightly.

Danielson had been looking at his face without seeing. As the grimace passed briefly over Runyan's features, she suddenly became cognizant of the black desolation reflected there. She stared at his impassive face as her own tenseness and excitement abated. She turned her head to look briefly at Gantt and read the same feeling of devastation on his face. Her mind spun with conflicting emotions as she released her grip on Runyan's slack hand and slumped back in her chair.

My god, she thought, it's like being torn apart, elation and terror at the same time. She recognized that she had been completely committed to this project, that she craved for her passion to be justified. The frightening encounter had been so real, so visceral, she felt—vindicated! But something in her mind cowered like a timid creature, beset by a raging beast. Her mind froze, resisting the full implications of what had transpired here. Where had it come from? What were they going to do? They had done what they had come to do. But were they better off, or worse?

She grabbed at a straw. Take a step, a small step. We've got to move on.

"Professor Gantt?" she inquired. "I've got to call Bob Isaacs."

Chapter 14

The satellite, square-rigged with solar panels, sailed a smooth, circular, polar orbit every hour and a half. The rotation of the earth beneath it brought every square inch of the surface within viewing range in a twelve-hour period. Its eye was a large, finely-honed mirror, bigger than most earthbound telescopes. This eye, like many cousins, would never witness the stark glories of the universe. It was dedicated to peering at the human scurryings below.

Normally, the twenty minutes spent passing from the north pole down over Canada and the continental United States to the equator were downtime devoted to signal relaying and reprogramming. This orbit, the gyros hummed and locked the telescope on several spots in a dead east-west line running through the high mountains of southern New Mexico. If the computer knew slang, it would have called this operation a piece of cake. The signal carrying orders from the ground had not called for highest resolution, the capability to distinguish letters on a license plate, only enough detail to discern a car from a house.

Light from the sun scattered in the earth's atmosphere, bounced off the New Mexico landscape and was reflected upward. The mirror in the satellite gathered a tiny portion of this light and focused it as an image on a photocathode. A sweeping electron beam converted the lights and darks of the image into electrical impulses and the on-board computer converted the impulses to immutable numbers. A beam of radiation, modulated and encoded with those numbers, shot to a receiving station on the ground at the speed of light. This signal was relayed to the National Security Agency at Fort Meade, Maryland where it received routine preliminary computer processing to decode the signal and remove the worst of the spurious electronic noise. Without pause, the signal was then relayed by special laser-driven glass fiber cable, immune to interception, to receiving equipment and a computer in CIA headquarters. This computer produced an electronic signal which reproduced a picture of the mountainous terrain on a special TV screen. A hard-copy photograph was taken of the screen, suitable for humans to scan and bicker over. Scarcely half an hour had passed from the time the special order had been sent up to the satellite to the time the camera shutter clicked.

As the photograph moved through the automatic developing process, the satellite coasted over the equator above the eastern Pacific Ocean. It would rest over the Pacific and Antarctica except for occasional records of ships. Things would pick up as it tried to collect data on the movement of the Soviet fleet in the Indian Ocean. There would be several frantic minutes in the vain attempt to monitor troops and rebels in Afghanistan, then the well-established routine over mother Russia herself. As the Arctic ice cap slipped underneath, the cycle would begin again.

Wednesday evening Isaacs sat in his study, the smells of supper beginning to romance his nostrils.

"Dad!" Isabel's young girl volume resounded down the corridor. "It's for you!"

He reached for the extension.

Even before she came on the line, from the long-distance hollow echo, broken by occasional radiophone static, he knew.

"Bob?" her voice was tense, excited.

"Pat?" His flat reply.

"Bob, he was right! It's got to be a black hole! It almost hit us, came up right outside the tent. You could *feel* it, Bob! The pull, from its gravity, it knocked me over. Ellison is starting to analyze the computer records, but I just don't see how there can be any doubt."

Silence.

"Bob?"

"Sorry. That's——good work." He was suffused with a bone-weary fatigue. "It's just so hard to accept. I was trying to think of what to do next." How was he going to explain this to Drefke, to the President? Damn! Why had he brought the Russians, Korolev, into this? He certainly didn't want to hassle with them now.

"Have you started the site survey?"

"Yeah," he confirmed. "We got the satellite time on an emergency basis, shots of every site on the trajectory, north and south latitude, at the right altitude. The satellite should be working now, and we should have the first cut tomorrow morning. Then we can go back to anything that looks promising."

"I wonder what we'll find?" she asked the question slowly, rhetorically.

"Pat, right now I haven't the faintest damn idea. Let me know if Gantt's analysis turns up anything interesting. I'll get hold of the Director tonight and see if I can explain all this to him."

"Okay, good luck. You'll let me know what the site survey turns up?"

"Right."

"Bye."

"G'bye."

He hung up the phone and stared at it, unseeing. He knew he should eat before calling Drefke, but his appetite had vanished.

Pat Danielson slipped back into the tent and took a chair next to Runyan who leaned over Gantt's shoulder, watching numbers do formation exercises on the terminal.

"Did you get him?" Runyan swiveled his neck to look at her.

"Yes. He didn't sound too happy."

"Not the kind of thing you get happy about." Runyan paused a moment, contemplating. "I guess I feel relief. The peril is real and immense. I don't think any of us really appreciate in our guts the danger we're in. But I'm relieved that it's out in the open now so we can deal with it head on." He turned back to the terminal. "Ellison's finding out what our friend is really like."

Danielson maneuvered her chair so she could see. Gantt pointed to the luminescent figures. "You see the seismometers saturated when it got too close, so they stopped giving any useful information." He played with the keys some more. "The gravimeter here in camp also went off scale. They're meant to measure fluctuations of a part in a billion, and this one was at one percent before it pooped out. The outer stations were fine, though; here's the mass they detected, a bit over ten million metric tons. That's just about what you guessed, wasn't it, Alex?"

"Pretty close," admitted Runyan. He thought for a while and then asked, "How long were the seismometers inactive?"

Gantt consulted the computer and then replied, "Twenty-eight point— well, call it an even twenty-nine seconds, why?"

"Maybe we ought to go back to your tent where we can talk this over," Runyan replied.

They left the equipment tent and walked toward Gantt's.

Wary glances followed them. All over the camp men stood in groups of three and four, discussing the strange event in muted and not so muted tones. Runyan and Danielson occupied the chairs they had first sat in upon their arrival, only a few hours ago. Gantt disappeared inside the tent and returned with three styrofoam cups and a bottle of bourbon.

"A bit early in the day for normal circumstances," he said, "but I could use a little bracer. Will you join me?"

The other two nodded their acceptance and received their cups in turn. Runyan took a fairly healthy slug and looked on with mild surprise as Danielson drained hers in one quick motion and held it out to Gantt for a refill.

Danielson caught Runyan's look, grinned, and said in a voice hoarsened by the liquor, "All us Virginians are bourbon drinkers, suh!"

Gantt smiled at the quip and raised his cup to gesture a toast, "Well, here's to the future; may it not be entirely black." He continued with a shake of his head, "I must say that was the most god-awful feeling. I had the definite impression that you people had snuck up on either side of me and lifted my chair and then dropped it. All this instrumentation and electronics are well and good, but they're no substitute for being grabbed and shaken to let you know you're up against the real thing. The idea that that thing actually came up within, what, two or three yards of the tent? Jesus!" He drained his cup and poured another dollop.

"Did you feel a sideways pull?" inquired Danielson. "That's what bowled me over. I had one foot in the air when someone raised the floor and then gave me a shove."

"I guess maybe I did," answered Gantt, "but I was sitting down, so that took some of the edge off."

"You're right. The thing must have come up just outside the tent," Runyan joined in. "Must have been one of those times when it got jarred off course somehow. Actually, in spite of the low probability, it's lucky no one was hit. I was thinking, Pat may have had a good idea; it might be of some interest to find the hole it made coming out and the other falling back in. Apparently that occurred just a bit further to the east, near the edge of camp. I think we may have learned something important here, in addition to having the wits scared out of us."

"What's that?" asked Gantt.

"Well, there are three things that come to mind. First, we've confirmed the fact that it comes down near where it went up. That's significant."

"I thought of that. It's the same as Dallas," said Danielson, her eyes shining. "It must be moving with the same tangential velocity as the surface of the earth as it comes up."

Gantt looked puzzled, and Danielson explained to him, "Remember that, because it rotates, the surface of the earth is actually moving at about a thousand miles an hour. If this thing were literally moving on a line pointed at a fixed direction in space, then as it reached the surface we would move out from under it at just that speed. How long did you say it was up? About a half of a minute? Let's see, the earth's surface rotates about twenty miles in a minute or about ten in the time the thing was up."

"Closer to seven," said Runyan with unconscious pedanticism, "but clearly the relative motion could have been much greater than it actually was."

"I guess I still don't quite see," began Gantt.

"The point is," explained Runyan, "that when it comes to the surface of the earth it's virtually at rest with respect to the local terrain. That can't be an accident. It must have begun that way. We can rule out the idea that it's a naturally occurring black hole. To have it moving at precisely the earth's orbital velocity so that it could be trapped was asking a lot. To insist that it also move in consonance with the rotation of the earth is out of the question. I could never put any store in the idea anyway, but now I think we can really lay it to rest.

"Let me put it another way," he continued, "if you were to

imagine taking a black hole and holding it in your hand so that both you and it were moving along with the surface of the earth, and then you were to drop it, and let it orbit freely, the result would be just what we have seen. It would drop down, pass to the far side of the earth and return. It must return to precisely the same altitude as that from which it was dropped, and at its highest point, when it momentarily has no velocity toward or away from the earth's center, it must have precisely the same sideways motion as when it was released. To someone moving with the same motion, that is, with the velocity of the earth's surface, it would seem to come momentarily to an exact standstill."

"But it didn't stand still," objected Gantt, "that is, it continued on up."

"That's my second point," replied Runyan. "One we kicked around in La Jolla. We know how far up it went. It took about fifteen seconds to go up and an equal amount to return. At one gee, that's a distance of about three thousand four hundred feet. What's the altitude here?"

"About twenty-three hundred feet," said Gantt.

"Then apogee is about five thousand seven hundred feet above sea level. A bit over a mile. That must be the altitude from which it was originally dropped."

Before either Danielson or Gantt could comment, Runyan was on his feet. "Let me get something out of my luggage." He tossed off the remaining bourbon in his cup, set the cup on the chair arm, and strode purposefully over to the mess tent where their luggage had been placed. The cup blew off, and Gantt rescued it from the ground. Runyan rummaged for a moment and then returned with a stack of computer output. He regained his seat and balanced the paper on his knees so he could easily riffle the accordian-folded sheets.

"Another little project of mine," he explained. "Pat, you said that in Dallas your agents thought about forty seconds elapsed from the time you first heard the noise to when it returned. That gives an estimate of the altitude to which it rises. I figured they could be off by ten percent either way. The Seamount event gave a more accurate estimate. I narrowed down the maximum altitude to within three hundred feet. What I've got here is a list of every point on earth which falls along the locus of the orbit and within three bins in altitude, each spanning a hundred feet. With this new precise data of yours, Ellison, we can throw out two-thirds of the possibilities. There are surprisingly few left. Few enough that they can all be checked in a finite time. There are a couple in California, a few in Arizona, a small batch in New Mexico and that's it for the continental United States." He looked on down the list, "There's a couple of places in Morocco, one in Algeria, some in Iran, Afghanistan, and Pakistan, none in Tibet, it's all too high, and finally, in the northern hemisphere, several places in China." He flipped to another sheet. "The southern hemisphere is even more sparse. A few places on either side of the Andes, in Chile and Argentina. That's about it. Everything else is lower, mostly ocean."

Gantt's brows knitted in concentration.

"We're ahead of you there, Alex," Danielson smiled slightly, her voice touched with pride. "I made up a similar list of sites after we got back from La Jolla. Bob Isaacs had ordered up a photomontage along the trajectory several months ago. The problem was we didn't know what to look for, and there was too much area to cover. He just told me that we are collecting new satellite photos of the spots on my list; they'll be ready tomorrow morning."

She craned her neck and looked down his list, flipping the pages back and forth.

"I think I've got everything you have here, and a few more. Here in Chile, for instance, north of Santiago. There's a shallow valley there and actually two points, not just one, a few kilometers apart."

She looked up at Runyan, and he locked her eyes with a long, cool stare. Then he gave her a broad, friendly wink, and her heart jumped.

"You said you had three points?" Gantt prompted him to continue.

"This may be a bit more subtle, but just as important." Runyan leaned forward and put his stack of computer print-out on the ground. He retrieved his cup from Gantt and poured himself a small bit of bourbon. Resting his upper forearms on both knees and rotating the cup between his palms, he looked up at Danielson from beneath his brows. "Let me ask you, why is there such a small motion with respect to the surface?"

"But you just answered that!" objected Danielson. "Its motion at its highest point is set by the initial conditions with which it's released. If it moved with the surface at first, it always will."

"Always?"

Danielson stopped and stared at the bewhiskered scientist, her eyes shifting back and forth between his. Finally she said, "You said earlier there must be perturbations, friction. The orbit can't be perfect, it must shift slowly with time."

"Now I'm with you," broke in Gantt. "The orbit must shift slowly with time, but it hasn't shifted much." He looked at both of them. "So it hasn't had time."

"That's just the sort of thing I've been trying to compute," said Runyan. "My model isn't perfect yet, but I have some feeling for the scale of things. I would have to say this thing couldn't have been around for more than ten years, and probably less."

"What you're saying," said Danielson, "is that we only picked up a record of it recently because it's only been around recently."

"Let me get this straight then," Gantt said slowly. "You're arguing that someone or something, somehow, made a black hole of about ten million tons not more than a few years ago, releasing it at rest from a point on the earth's surface about six thousand feet above sea level." His forehead wrinkled in consternation.

"When we examine those places," Danielson said, pointing at the computer paper at Runyan's feet, "do you expect to see something definite?"

"Maybe not," said Gantt, looking at Runyan. "Granted that we're dealing with a small black hole, and that it was created artificially, which seems to follow."

Runyan nodded assent.

"Then," Gantt continued, "we're also talking about something beyond our technological feasibility. Suppose the only thing remaining at the 'launch site,' if I may call it that, is a burned spot and the impression of three round pods—I believe that's the classical imprint of a UFO."

"If we know where to look, we can find that too," said Danielson, "if not with satellites, then a direct fly-over."

"I suppose we must keep an open mind," said Runyan, "but I have a feeling that the clues will be more definite."

They lapsed into silence. Gantt broke it with a shake of his head. "I'm sorry," he said, "but despite the evidence, I find the whole thing too incredible to believe. An artificial black hole planted here in the earth—I mean, my god!" He raised his hands and eyes in an imploring salute to the skies.

"Alex," he continued, "you said a while ago you were relieved the issue was now out in the open. I must say I don't feel that way at all. After all, proving that we are dealing with a black hole is only the tip of the iceberg. Until we know who and why, we've barely begun to plumb the mystery. The most stupendous, terrifying, and profound aspects of this situation would seem to be before us."

He was silent for a moment and muttered, "Christ," and poured himself another jigger of bourbon and drank it off.

Runyan had slumped in his chair, chin on his chest. "I suppose you could be right, Ellison," he said. "I have a hazy idea of what's going on that suggests to me that, conceptually anyway, we're over the hump."

"How could we be? What in the world are you thinking?" Gantt demanded.

Runyan waved him off with a hand. "It's too vague. I'm probably being naive or stupid or both."

Gantt glared at him, uncomfortable with this dismissal.

At last he said, "Well, I don't know about you, but I'll go nuts if I just sit here and think about it. I've got to *do* something." He stood up and looked around impatiently.

"Should we have another look for a hole in the ground?" asked Danielson. "I really wasn't very thorough."

"We could do that," agreed Gantt. "We don't really want to attract too much attention to what went on here. On the other hand, if we don't look now, any sign may get covered up by people shuffling around."

The moment of tenseness forgotten, they discussed the problem of security for awhile and finally decided they would stage a reenactment. This would show who was knocked down by the passage of the hole, thus showing where to look without giving away their object. Gantt would then order some rearrangement of equipment which would occupy most of the members of the entourage. This would give Runyan and Danielson a chance to search the ground for signs of penetration without drawing notice.

They put this plan into action with Runyan noting the vicinity where the hole had come up and Danielson several hundred feet away locating where it had descended.

Then Gantt gave orders to set up a fourth instrumentation site outside of camp and prepare accommodations for Runyan and Danielson, a legitimate task postponed earlier. Danielson joined Runyan. For the next few minutes they assiduously searched the several square yards just outside the main tent, Runyan erect and Danielson in a low crouch.

"Let's try something else," Runyan finally said. He directed Danielson to stand against the tent wall.

"Now I'm going to jump and stamp—you look for some sign of settling dirt."

He launched himself upward and came down with a satisfying thud. He looked at the ground as Danielson peered around. They looked up at one another and shrugged. Runyan repeated the faintly ludicrous operation, working systematically across the suspect area.

On the the fifth try, Danielson pointed, "There, just by your left foot."

Two small stones were wedged in a depression, but as they looked a trickle of loose dirt sifted beneath the stones and disappeared.

Runyan crouched and carefully plucked away one of the stones in each hand. Beneath them was a hole in the sun-baked clay soil the size of a finger. Danielson jogged over to Gantt's tent and returned with a coat hanger under her arm and another she busily untwisted. When she straightened the hanger, she lowered it slowly into the hole. It met only minor resistance and sank to the hook which remained on the edge, marking the spot.

They walked to the second location and after a brief search found another hole. Again, they straightened a coat hanger and embedded it to mark the spot. Runyan rummaged up a tape measure he had spotted in the main instrumentation tent, and they marked off the distance between the two holes, which Runyan recorded in a small notebook in his pocket.

"Alex," Danielson asked as they headed back to Gantt's tent, "is there a special significance to the fact that it came down a bit further to the east? Is that related to the earth's rotation from west to east?"

"That's one of many effects," he replied as they settled into their chairs, "but you have to be careful to treat all the irregularities, all the perturbations."

"How does the rotation come in?" she asked.

"Well, here, I'll show you." Runyan retrieved his computer output from the ground where he had left it and turned it over on his lap to write on the blank side. He pulled out a pen and carefully blocked out a set of equations. Danielson scooted her chair around close to his so she could see.

Gantt returned an hour later and found them in an animated discussion of orbit perturbations. He did not follow the details, but it was clear to him that Danielson was holding her own with Runyan, giving him pause with penetrating questions and occasionally adding a twist of her own. Although the discussion was purely intellectual, Gantt could sense the electricity between the two. Alex is well into stage two, he thought, black hole or no. Then a question of the generation and propagation of seismic waves arose, and Gantt pitched into the discussion as well.

They were still at it when the dinner bell sounded. Runyan and Danielson lagged behind as they headed for the mess tent.

"Listen," Runyan said quietly, leaning over toward her, "there's not much to do here in the middle of god's country, but how about an evening stroll after things cool off. The desert can be quite beautiful then."

Danielson turned her head to look up into his eyes, light flashing within the dark aura of his hair and beard. She wanted to be alone with him.

"That sounds very nice," she said, holding his gaze for a moment. Then, with a new energy, they moved to catch up to Gantt.

After supper Runyan and Danielson joined Gantt at his tent in the fading evening light. Despite the lingering heat, they went inside the tent where Gantt switched on a generator-fed bulb. They discussed their current position and laid plans for the immediate future. Although the major point they had sought to check seemed well settled, they agreed that Gantt's station should remain in operation to compile a precise record of the behavior of the object. Danielson would return and report to Isaacs and redouble the effort to discover the hypothesized point of origin. Runyan would report to Phillips and resume his orbital calculations. Gantt again proferred his bottle of bourbon, and they drank a nightcap to seal their arrangement. Danielson excused herself. Runyan followed a few minutes later.

Runyan pushed aside the tent flap and stepped out. The acrid aroma of tarpaulin mingled with the wafted delicate fragrance of greasewood. The clean dry air was warm and enveloping, as if you could shuck your clothes and drink it in through every pore. Runyan waited for his eyes to adjust, then turned toward Danielson's tent, a sense of anticipation beginning to tickle his loins. He peered through the darkness toward her tent, some forty paces away on the other side of the one erected for him, but could only make out the vaguest outlines. Then he saw her, waiting for him in the deepest shadow. The familiar feeling of sweet power flooded him, and his mind filled with images of her warm curves, putting flesh to the dim silhouette he could barely perceive as he approached.

Danielson watched the figure picking his sure way in the dark. She had the irrational feeling that the ground would open up and swallow him before he reached her. It didn't. He stopped a pace from her, his strong presence palpable even at the distance. She felt an urge to reach out and touch him, but he made no motion and neither did she.

He lingered a moment savoring the invisible aura between them, then whispered, "Let's head out this way."

He pointed to the rudimentary road that led to one of the outlying sites. They walked carefully out of the campsite and onto the road. The moon was nearly full, casting faint shadows. Danielson found that at their strolling pace she could walk easily, with only part of her attention on the rocky roadbed. She looked around and up. Away from the moon the pure desert sky was almost a solid blanket of stars.

"It's so lovely," she whispered.

As she looked upward and outward the trauma of the afternoon receded and an overpowering expansiveness filled her. She reached for Runyan's arm and hugged it in both her hands, pulling him close to her. After several paces he freed his arm and encircled her waist. She slipped her arm across his back and leaned her head on his shoulder.

They walked on, speaking little, each lost in thought, awash in awareness of the other. Runyan estimated they had walked a half hour when he said, "I think we better head back."

"I suppose we should," she replied, her voice hinting regret. She felt something slipping by, something she didn't want to lose. As they turned around in the darkness she tugged at his sleeve to halt him. He turned toward her, and she gripped his other sleeve as well, facing him, arms open, body exposed.

He raised his arms to encircle her shoulders, drawing her into a gentle embrace. She cradled her head against his chest, arms around his waist, and stared down at the earth beside them. She thought again of the shattering event of the earlier afternoon, of the miniscule horror hurtling beneath their feet. Somehow, she felt this man was her protector, the sole barrier between her and the ferocious void. She lifted her head to look into his eyes. The shadows on his face were portals to a vast emptiness which she had to keep at bay. She moved her face closer to his so his features were clear, the shadows muted. She opened herself to a feeling she knew had been growing. She wanted this man. The world seemed large and empty. She needed to be with him, to hold to his firmness and strength.

She stretched to kiss him, feeling the prickle of his mustache and beard as he responded. Their lips brushed. A cool current raced through their bodies at the touch of sensitive flesh on flesh. He cupped her jaw and neck, fingers lightly tangled in her hair, kissing her deeply, drawing a dormant passion up and out.

They walked as quickly as they could back to the camp, pausing for another prolonged kiss when the interval grew too long to bear. The camp was dark and quiet when they returned.

Outside her tent she embraced his neck and stood on tiptoe for one more lingering kiss before crossing the threshold.

An image of the ludicrously narrow cot flashed in her mind. They could throw the thin mattress on the tent floor. She broke their kiss, found his hand, and brushed her lips across his palm. Then she pushed aside the tent flap and, still holding his hand, led him in. Runyan stooped to follow her, a small smile playing on his lips.

Chapter 15

Viktor Korolev forged down the sidewalk with long solid strides, his black mood radiating ahead, parting grumbling pedestrians like the bow wave of a ship. They had offered him a ride, but he needed to walk to work off his frustration.

So the Americans had done it! This inconceivable thing. He'd had to lay his proof before the generals. After that, none of his bellowing power could dissuade them from narrow thoughts of retribution. Granted the Americans were formally at fault, this thing was too different to be handled with old-fashioned polarized modes of behavior. Good arguments, to no avail.

Korolev thought of his message to Zamyatin, a meager return for gifts received. The American would rue the day he had proffered his insights, seeking help. Korolev sighed. Had this Robert Isaacs not catalyzed events, the day of reckoning would only have been postponed.

Korolev slowed his pace, frustration waning, pushed aside by the need to develop a constructive response. He began to mentally list others in the power structure to whom he could take his case for moderation, cooperation. Whatever the generals plotted now, he hoped it would involve no loss of life.

On Thursday morning, Isaacs studied each one of the photographs as Vincent Martinelli handed them over. He set one of them aside. All the others ended up in a neat stack of rejects. He picked up the special one and peered at it closely again.

"These are all the possible sites?"

"Every one Danielson gave us."

"And this is the only one that shows anything but natural terrain and vegetation?" He flapped the photo in his hand.

"The only one."

"Okay, so I'll bite. Where is it?"

"New Mexico."

"New Mexico! Good god! Then this thing may have begun in the United States?"

"Looks like it. We took five shots of New Mexico. That one is in the Guadalupe Mountains to the east of the White Sands missile testing range."

"Hmmm. Some connection there, you think?" Isaacs asked. "What is the place?" He waved the photo again.

"Hey, don't ask me." Martinelli protested. "You're the smart guys that figure 'em out."

"No idea?"

"No, seriously. I came up here as soon as they came out of the print machine. All I've got is the coordinates. They're on the back."

Isaacs turned the print over. The numbers meant nothing to him.

"I'll get Baris on this."

"Anything else from my side?"

"Not until we know what we're dealing with here."

"Okay, give a holler if you need something."

"Right, thanks for the quick work, Vince." Isaacs waved a salute as Martinelli let himself out.

Mid-morning was slow time. Esteban Ruiz sat in the guard house at the front gate of CIA headquarters trying to pick a rim of varnish from under his fingernail. A quiet smile reflected his thoughts. Tonight he would put the final coat on the new desk and shelves, and by tomorrow they could permanently set up the small computer he had scrimped and saved to buy his children. It was not the biggest, but it had been on sale, and when he lugged it in the door the children had shouted with surprise. Carlos, the oldest, had grumped a bit that it did not have enough memory, but Esteban's heart swelled with pleasure that his son even knew to question such a thing. Esteban did not know computers, was more than a little frightened of them, but he did know wood. The new shelves, the product of his hands, mind, labor, and love, looked good. He was proud of them and proud of his children who yearned to embrace a world he would never know. Ruiz was not aware of the black limousine until it slid to a quiet stop in front of him. Without quite focusing on detail, he knew what it was.

Holy Mary, Mother of God! he exclaimed to himself. Russians! He stepped quickly from the gate house, right palm on the butt of his service revolver, and tried to adopt his most gruff manner, but his voice shook, betraying his shock.

"Hold on there! Where do you think you're going?"

He addressed himself to the stolid faced driver, but received no reply. Instead, the rear window whisked down in response to an inner button.

"We don't intend to go in, Sergeant," Grigor Zamyatin used his most appealing tone. "But I have an urgent message for Mr. Isaacs, your Deputy Director of Scientific Intelligence."

He put a core of steel in the next words. "I must see that he receives it." Then he spoke smoothly again. "Could he possibly come here to the gate and receive it directly?"

Ruiz could not help the edge of respect that crept into his voice. His hand slipped off his pistol butt. The driver of the limousine surreptitiously shifted his body and relaxed slightly as well.

"Sir, I can't comment on specific personnel. If you have a message, I'll take it."

Zamyatin smiled slightly at this expected, but cumbersome subterfuge. No one knew who worked at the CIA except every spy in the world, and anyone else who cared to check. He reached into his jacket pocket and extracted the sealed envelope with Isaacs' name carefully handwritten across it. He extended it to the guard, but kept his grip as Ruiz reached for it. Zamyatin locked eyes with him.

"This is extremely urgent. It must be delivered to Mr. Isaacs, and no one else."

"I'll see that it is put into the proper channels," Ruiz said noncommittally, but his voice rang with sincerity.

Zamyatin would have preferred to deliver the envelope personally to Isaacs, but this was the most he expected. He was confident Isaacs would have it within the hour. He released his grip on the envelope, and the window swished shut. Ruiz stepped back as the limousine backed up, performed a U-turn and accelerated out of the entry drive toward the Washington parkway. He stepped back into the gate house, placed the envelope gingerly on a shelf, and grabbed the phone.

"Ralph? This is Steve at the east gate. Damn car full of Russians, embassy types, just dropped off an envelope they say has to be delivered to Mr. Isaacs. I think you'd better send somebody from the bomb squad down here. Right. You bet your ass I won't!" He punched the button disconnecting the phone and cradled the receiver on his shoulder while he flipped through the directory and ran his finger down the page until he came to the Office of the Deputy Director of Scientific Intelligence. Then he dialed again.

Bill Baris left the document section with as much material as he could conveniently carry in both hands. He walked rapidly down the corridor, intent on his destination. Baris was in his late forties, sharp-featured with thinning blond curls. He rarely stopped to ponder the fact that he was good at what he did. He just continued to do what felt right. This felt right, he thought of the material in his hands. Isaacs had nailed it.

He passed through Kathleen Huddleston's office giving a nod to her and barged into Isaacs' with a familiarity born of long comfortable association.

"Here you are, Bob." He deposited the files on Isaacs' desk.

"What have you got?" Isaacs inquired.

"It's a private lab, about two years old. Strictly devoted to weapons research subcontracted from the Los Alamos National Laboratory."

There was something very familiar about that description. Isaacs couldn't quite place it.

"Who runs it?" he asked.

"Guy name of Krone."

"Paul Krone!" Isaacs slammed his fist on his desk, remembering Zicek talking about Krone in La Jolla, suggesting he be brought in. Looks like he was already in, Isaacs thought grimly.

"Sir?" Kathleen spoke over the intercom.

"Yes! What is it." Isaacs was more abrupt than he intended.

"Sir, I just got a call from the guard at the front gate. Apparently a car from the Soviet embassy dropped off a note they insisted be delivered to you. It's being processed through security."

Isaacs' mind raced through the possibilities.

"From the embassy, you say. Did the guard recognize anyone?"

"Not specifically. The car was an embassy limousine. There

was a chauffeur and some official in the back seat who handed over the note and did all the talking."

Isaacs had a vivid mental image of looking out through his rear window and seeing nothing but the grill and long hood of Zamyatin's limousine.

"Ask security to have him check some mug shots of embassy personnel. Make sure one of Colonel Grigor Zamyatin is among them."

"Yes, sir." Kathleen rang off.

What could Zamyatin want? Isaacs asked himself. Why would anyone else in the Soviet embassy hand-deliver a note to him? He put these questions aside and picked up the pile of material Baris had brought in.

"Let me see some of that," Baris requested. "I only took time to skim it." He riffled through the pile of folders looking for some specific ones; then they settled down to read. Isaacs paused occasionally to make notes on a pad. Ten minutes passed in silence broken only by the shuffle of paper in the folders. Then the intercom buzzed again.

"Sir, Sergeant Ruiz, the guard, identified Colonel Zamyatin. He, Colonel Zamyatin that is, was very adamant that you get the note quickly and personally."

"Where is it then?"

"Sergeant Ruiz said someone from the bomb squad picked it up."

"The bomb squad!"

"Well, yes, I suppose they were concerned about letter bombs, that sort of thing."

"Letter bombs are anonymous. Not likely that the Colonel would drop by in his official limo to deliver one. Tell them to get that note up here. On the double!"

"Yes, sir!"

Isaacs waved his arms at the ceiling in a gesture of desperation. "What a world," he exclaimed.

"So what kind of picture do we have here?" he asked rhetorically, addressing Baris. "Krone Industries set up this lab to do research on contract to Los Alamos. They've done work on particle beams and lasers, particularly using them to implode material to high density and temperatures, just as Zicek said. That could be directly relevant."

"It's not just Krone Industries," said Baris. "I've been reading quarterly reports the lab submitted to Los Alamos. Krone himself is chief man on the spot, devoting himself one hundred percent to the effort.

"And not just his time," Baris continued. "Out of curiosity, I got a list of the companies in Krone Industries and looked up their financial reports." He hefted one of the folders he had selected. "That lab is not just running on its consulting contract with Los Alamos. Every one of these companies under Krone's thumb has diverted significant portions of their resources to the lab. There's an immense effort going on there. Far more than required by the government contract."

Isaacs leaned back in his chair to digest this information and looked up at a rap on the door. Kathleen opened it and ushered in an energetic young man with close-cropped hair. In his hand he clutched a mangled envelope.

"Mark Burley, sir. From counteractivity. This is the note delivered to you half an hour ago. We processed it as quickly as we could." He handed over the envelope.

Isaacs took it and raised a sceptical eyebrow. The envelope was crudely ripped open and both the envelope and the portion of the enclosed note, which was exposed through the ragged flap, were wrinkled.

"You opened it?"

"Yes, sir," Burley replied with deep sincerity. "We determined it was not a letter bomb by certain physical tests, but we wanted to check the contents for contaminants. Contact poisons. If we'd had time we could've opened it so you'd never have noticed." A small, proud smile came and went quickly. "As it was, we did the most thorough job we could, in the shortest time."

"I'm sure you did." If Burley noticed Isaacs' facetious tone, he gave no sign.

"Thank you, Mr. Burley. I appreciate the fast work."

"Anytime, sir. That's our job." The young man spun smartly on his heel and marched out. Isaacs exchanged an amused, wry smile with Baris.

"Boy Scout. Place is crawling with them," said Baris.

Isaacs' smile faded as he extracted and read the hand-scrawled note. It was very brief.

I know. I have to tell them. You must hurry.
Korolev

Isaacs had briefed Baris on his interchange with Korolev. He handed the piece of rough, light brown Russian paper to Baris.

"Know?" he asked. "Know what?"

"I'm afraid damn near everything we do," Isaacs replied. He thumbed the intercom.

"Yes?"

"Kathleen, get me Martinelli."

Isaacs put a hand on the phone in anticipation and looked at Baris.

"At the very least Korolev knows everything we did when Pat and I first went to talk to Jason because of the synopsis I sent him. There's a very good chance he followed the same line of reasoning as Runyan. As wild an idea as a black hole was, it has a certain inevitability in hindsight. Korolev didn't have direct access to our physical evidence from Nagasaki and Dallas, but he had his own from the Novorossiisk."

The phone buzzed and Isaacs jerked the receiver to his ear.

"Vince? I want to know about Soviet ship deployment. Particularly along thirty-two degrees forty-seven minutes, both north and south longitude." He listened for a moment. "Anytime in the last six weeks. I'd rather have that now and fresh stuff when you can get it." He listened again. "That's just the ticket. Thanks, Vince."

He hung up and looked intently at Baris. "We have to assume Korolev also guessed we were dealing with a black hole. I sent him my memo in late June. He's had six weeks to ponder it and move to do something about it. I also tipped off Zamyatin to watch Nagasaki. We can also assume they have at least a rough idea what went on there. If they have penetrated the Japanese with any efficiency, they probably have the full report. Korolev could pick up quickly on the parallels between the holes drilled in Nagasaki, and those in the Novorossiisk. For that matter, they may know about Dallas.

"In any case," Isaacs continued, "we lost three weeks sitting on our duffs waiting for Dallas to happen, three more before we got back to Jason, and Gantt got the real dope. That's six weeks when Korolev could have been pushing for some monitoring program in Russia. The trajectory doesn't pass through Russia, so they'd have to mobilize somewhere else. It makes most sense to me to use their Navy. We would have moved faster if ours hadn't been so recalcitrant.

"I don't know what their response time would be, but I certainly got the idea from Zamyatin that Korolev has clout at high levels in the Kremlin. If they put properly instrumented ships on the trajectory, they could learn everything we have."

"I see what you mean," Baris said. "If Korolev suspected a black hole, he'd have a gravimeter put on board to measure the mass."

"Seems obvious enough," Isaacs agreed. "Gantt considered a shipboard experiment, but elected to put his apparatus on dry land to make it as stable as possible. We know now it wouldn't have made much difference. They'd have to be a bit careful, but an inertially mounted device, isolated from the worst pitching of the ship, would do the job.

"Accurate timing would be easy," Isaacs continued. "With sonar monitors and some regular data acquisition they would know how long the thing hovered above sea level and could figure out the altitude to which it rose, just as we did."

"So they'd look along the trajectory at that altitude, just as we did," said Baris following the logic.

"And they would find this lab," Isaacs slapped his palm on the stack of folders in front of them, "just as we did. I think that must be what Korolev's note means. He's found Krone's lab, and, having raised a ruckus, he has to report his findings to the boys at the top."

The phone rang and Isaacs jerked it up.

"Yes? Right."

He reached for a pad and scribbled some numbers.

"Yes. Yes. Got that." He listened, then spoke again. "How far is that? Yes, damnit, no question. They're onto it. Sure, when they come in, but this is just what we needed. Thanks for the quick work. Great. Right."

He hung up and relayed the message from Martinelli to Baris.

"There are five small flotillas in the Pacific, three along thirty-two degrees forty-seven minutes north, two south. Each has a research vessel, a tender, and a destroyer. They're spaced 1170 miles apart, sailing steadily westward, about 190 miles per day."

"So they're tracking it," Baris summarized.

"They're tracking it," Isaacs confirmed.

"How long?" Baris inquired.

"Seven to ten days. Some got on station earlier."

"That's plenty of time to collect a good timing record," said Baris.

"I think there's no doubt now that Korolev has followed the same path that Runyan led us on," Isaacs said. "We've got to get to that lab and find out what's going on."

"And damn quickly," Baris said. "If you've got this right and Korolev reports to the top brass in the Kremlin that a black hole was made and released at a secret US government lab, oh, boy." Baris leaned back in his chair. "Can you imagine what the chest-medal crowd will do with that? We'll be right back to square one when they thought we'd zapped their carrier. Damned if they weren't right!"

Isaacs stood up and moved to the window. He clasped his

hands behind his back and stared out over the trees, rocking up on his toes. He could feel the mid-August heat which smothered the tree tops.

"We've got a powder keg already up there in orbit," Isaacs mused. "I don't know whether we can possibly move quickly enough to neutralize this situation. We've got to hope we can find an explanation that will satisfy the Soviets that this wasn't an intentional, government sanctioned plan."

He spun suddenly.

"It wasn't, was it?"

"Whoa," said Baris thoughtfully. "There's no clue in any of the files here." He pointed at the material on Isaacs' desk. "But that's pretty clean stuff. I just pulled it out of our library. Our job's to know everything the bad guys are up to, not everything our team does, so maybe there's an outside chance. Still, if I read this guy Krone right, he's the kind who would tackle something like this on his own. Remember these were Krone Industries resources being squandered. Unless there was some heavy-duty laundering, there wasn't much government funding. I'll check more deeply, but I think we're clean."

"We've got no choice but to get the whole story on Krone and that lab as fast as possible," said Isaacs, regaining his seat. "Bill, I want you to keep digging here. Track down everything you can going in and out of that lab that could be related to the manufacture of a black hole.

"Someone's got to go out to the site, though, and under the circumstances, I think I'd better take that one on myself.

"I'll call Pat and get her there too. And I might as well bring Runyan along. He knows Krone and is on top of the scientific aspects. I want you to get a team busy working up a reaction estimate. As things stand, how will the Soviets react if they're informed of Krone's lab? What will it take to keep them under control? Okay?"

"Right."

"Any questions?"

"A procedural one. Before you go, have you told the Director yet?"

"I spent three hours with him last night. Trying to explain about the black hole. Left him numb. I'll have to see him now and report on Krone and the message from Korolev. I guess we'll see what kind of stuff he's really made of."

"Is he going to want to go to the President? Or expect us to draw up a national intelligence estimate to circulate? The black hole is one thing, and perhaps an emergency in itself, but potential Russian reaction is a key issue now."

"We're in a bind. We've been waiting to get all our facts straight before dumping something like a black hole in the President's lap. Of course, until this morning we didn't know that it was made here, nor that the Russians were on to us.

"There's no time now for a formality like an NIE," Isaacs continued. "We've got a real crisis. We must get the story from that lab and then pass it to the President directly. I think the DCI will see it that way, but that's why I want you to get on that reaction estimate. We'll want that as part of the package."

Isaacs looked at his watch. "It's 10:45 now, 8:45 in New Mexico. I should be able to catch something at Andrews that will get us out there by mid-afternoon, local time. It'll take a few hours to check out the lab. I might make it back here by midnight.

"I'll suggest to the DCI that he lay the groundwork for an emergency meeting of the National Security Council about then. And just hope the Russians don't push the button for twelve hours."

"All right," said Baris, rising to leave. "I'll get on it." He strode quickly across the room and out the door.

"Kate?" Isaacs called, and she appeared in the doorway, attuned to the emergency atmosphere.

"Tell the DCI I'm on my way to see him. Top priority. Order a helicopter to Andrews Air Force Base. Forty-five minutes from now, maximum. Half hour better. Arrange for a flight out of Andrews for me and two agents. Call Boswank and get him to assign me two of his people. Call Danielson and Runyan in Arizona and arrange for a flight for them. Destination for all of us is Holloman Air Force Base near White Sands, New Mexico. Arrange ground transportation there. We're headed for a laboratory about forty miles away, up in the mountains. Better yet, see if you can get another chopper to take us from Holloman to the lab. Here's the name of the lab and of the guy in charge." He scribbled on a memo pad and handed it to her. "I'll want to talk to him when I get back from seeing the DCI. And call Phillips in La Jolla and talk to Gantt while you're on the line to Arizona. I want Phillips here this evening prepared for an NSC meeting. They may want to get together in Pasadena to assemble the relevant information."

"Yes, sir." Kathleen finished making notations on her pad and bustled back into her office.

Isaacs steeled himself and then headed off to hand his boss the second shocking revelation in less than twelve hours.

Danielson awoke in her tent in the waxing Arizona heat with the smell of Runyan about her. Over breakfast she felt as if she were two people. One of her talked business with Gantt as if nothing had happened. Her other self was full of Runyan and jolted every time he seemed to give her a special knowing glance. Gantt displayed no reaction, just smiled discretely to himself.

The call from headquarters came as they were finishing breakfast and galvanized them into action. They barely had time to throw their things together before the whupping of the Marine helicopter from Yuma broke the desert stillness. At the Yuma Air Station Danielson chatted casually with Runyan for the benefit of the strangers around them and continued to shout her secret messages until the transport was warmed up, ready to ferry them east to New Mexico.

Back in the desert, the camp settled into busy routine. Late that morning, one of the Marines relaxed in front of his tent, waiting for lunch. He didn't understand the technical functions of the camp and didn't expect to. He was assigned his job and did it. Nevertheless, he thought it strange that the chief of the operation would take time out to squat, motionless, at the edge of the camp with his index finger thrust past the second knuckle into a small hole in the ground.

Chapter 16

A faint rush of electromagnetic waves carried the orders from a Soviet ground station on the Kamchatka Peninsula. On the hunter-killer satellite a switch popped shut, releasing the latent energy in a battery and generating a healthy blue spark elsewhere in the circuit. The spark jostled and heated the fragile molecules of a volatile material. The heated matter expanded violently, its force focused by a tough surrounding casing. A detonation wave raced outward in a fury that shot in a narrow arc into space.

A few hundred yards away, a sleek white cylinder decorated with a small red, white, and blue emblem floated with deadly grace. It was directly in the path of the onrushing explosion. Then the onslaught was full upon it, the pressure soaring ferociously, the outer wall crumpling, the shock wave engulfing everything within. With the shock came heat, heat which triggered circuits in the cylinder.

In a repeat of the pattern played out only instants before, switches tripped, power surged, tiny sparks crackled and carefully designed chemical explosives imploded upon a finely machined, slightly warm sphere of metal, violently squeezing it.

The shock from the first explosion arrived at the same instant. The sphere was warped; the focus of its compression altered. It existed for a brief moment, teetering on the edge of consummation. Each part of it fed neutrons into the others. Deep in the dense nuclei of its atoms, reactions were triggered splitting the nuclei apart, releasing vastly more energy than the penetrating neutrons possessed and more of the catalyzing neutrons as well.

Then the moment passed. The wracking shock and the partial release of nuclear energy amplified the distortions of the sphere. The chain reaction damped, and the sphere of radioactive metal dissolved into harmless shards. In a heartbeat, the cylinder was gone.

Nearby, another cylinder, larger, ungainly, stirred into menacing wakefulness. Ports slid open in its sides. It rotated and slurred. Taking aim. Awaiting instructions.

By shading his eyes from the midday sun, Isaacs could make out the town of Alamagordo as the military transport continued its descent toward Holloman Air Force Base. He glanced around at his companions, Pat Danielson and Alex Runyan whom they had picked up on a quick stop at Kirtland Air Force Base in Albuquerque, and the two Agency men. Although the need was remote, they could provide security backup. The hollow feeling in his gut reflected his anticipation of the significance of this venture. They were headed for the source, the key to the myriad tangled events. He thought back to the simple anomalous seismic signal he had toyed with while on leave last March, over four months ago. His thoughts strayed to Runyan's voracious beast rifling through the earth and to the paranoiac escalation threatened by the note from Korolev.

Maybe not so paranoid. He played a game of role reversal he had often found useful. How would the President of the United States and his military and civilian advisors react to being informed that the Russians, deliberately or otherwise, had created a menace so hideous that it would eat away the substance of the earth? Even with the damage done, the urge to retaliate, fed by hatred and fear, would be strong, visceral. An image of a battered child who finally takes an ax to his tormentor slipped into his mind. He knew there were Americans who would argue that if the Russians had been the perpetrators, the time would have come to rid the world of them, before going on to face the ultimate menace. Could this development be the final straw for the Soviets, the one that pushed them over the brink in an attempt to eliminate their prime antagonist, despite the consequences? And role reversal, hell, he thought. How will the President react when he's informed this evening that his own team has committed this inconceivable atrocity?

The reality was overwhelming. They had a few scant hours to find the keys to defuse the crisis. They needed incontrovertible proof that the incredible event had actually occurred, that a small black hole had been forged on the mountaintop forty miles away. They must discover how and why and then hope the President could use that evidence to convince the Russians that the affair was not an overt act against them. They would also look for any dim shred of evidence that what had been done could be undone.

Already there was a hitch, an aggravating note of uncertainty amplified by the tension surrounding their mission. Where in the hell was Krone? Their flurry of phone calls had only succeeded in contacting some administrative head at the lab. Isaacs had worried about a confrontation with Krone. He might bluster, cover up, delay them. Worse, he might destroy evidence. Isaacs had dissembled with the administrator, told him that they were an inspection team under the auspices of the executive branch. Only a small lie. It would be presidential business soon enough. In any case, Isaacs knew the power of the vague reference to the Oval Office and he had invoked it unashamedly; there was no time for more complex explanations.

Isaacs looked over once more at Danielson, her face in profile as she stared out the small window. She and Runyan had been in good spirits when they met. Was there something between them? Would they both be at top efficiency as matters reached their crux? Isaacs was not sure he should have succumbed to Runyan's pleadings to go to Arizona.

For the second time in as many days, Alex Runyan had found himself catching a military plane on short notice and heading for a remote corner of the southwest. He and Danielson had taken a military flight for Kirtland and then had transferred to the plane Isaacs had commandeered out of Andrews. Isaacs had filled them in on the progress the Russians had made in duplicating their efforts which gave special urgency to their mission. That had surprised him, but the general chain of events was proceeding as he had foreseen.

Having convinced himself that a black hole was running rampant in the earth, Runyan had found a man-made origin more plausible than other preposterous possibilities. Still, a stunning technological feat was demanded, and he was keenly interested in discovering the details which this trip promised to reveal. His instinct told him that their only hope for salvation lay in fathoming the secrets of creation. Paul Krone. Runyan shook his head. He'd done it this time.

Runyan, too, glanced over at Pat Danielson. This trip promised no chance to renew the relationship started in the warm Arizona night. On the contrary, she seemed to be getting a little withdrawn. When they lay on the mattress, comfortable, chatting, she had confessed to having no close male relations for some time. Could she keep an affair casual, friendly, the way he wanted? Was she the type to suffer second thoughts if no permanent relation was in the offing? Now he'd have to watch his step.

Pat Danielson's mind was in a turmoil. On the noisy flight from Yuma she nearly forgot their mission, as she repeatedly thought of Runyan, buckled into the hard utilitarian seat next to her. She relived their undressing in the moonlight that bathed the tent, their tender precarious coupling on the narrow mattress, his successful, unhurried manner, the quiet conversation after, cramped cooperative attempts at sleep and his half-comical departure at dawn as the camp came to life.

Then in Albuquerque when they met up with Isaacs the enormity of the situation rushed back upon her. To all the fear and fascination she felt toward the object of their quest, now the burden of keeping the Russians at bay was added.

In Isaacs' presence, all business, she felt pangs of guilt for allowing her personal urges to come to the fore. With guilt came questions. Was it a one shot affair? Had he gotten what he wanted? Did he really care? He had spoken briefly of a wife and described, honestly it seemed, his estrangement. But was he honest? And even if he was, had he really said anything that implied a commitment to her, to Pat? The more she thought, the deeper became her guilt and embarrassment.

She looked out of her portside window now as the plane flew west, parallel to the main runway below. She made out a sprawling complex of runways, hangars, and military aircraft. That disappeared behind them until the plane went into a left bank which took them perpendicular to the runway, affording a clear view of the base and the Sacramento Mountains rising in the east. She thought she caught a glimpse of their ultimate destination on one of the far ridge tops. Again the plane banked for its final approach, and the only view was the desert plain and bounding mountains stretching endlessly to the north.

The aircraft bumped and twisted slightly in the mild cross-wind at landing. They taxied up to a hangar, the engines were cut, the hatch thrown open, and they scrambled out. They were met by a young lieutenant who handed Isaacs a message. Isaacs read it, crumpled the paper angrily in his fist and then hustled Runyan and Danielson aside. He spoke to them in an intense whisper.

"The Russians have moved already. They triggered one of the hunter-killers a half hour ago and took out our nuclear satellite that was on station with their laser."

Danielson felt as if she had been shocked out of a state of half-trance.

"It didn't detonate? The nuke?"

"No," Isaacs seethed. "They took the chance and pulled it off cleanly. The laser is free to operate with impunity."

"And what does that mean?" Runyan inquired, leaning over to catch Isaacs' words.

"It means," Isaacs spat, "that they can pick off all our early warning and military communications satellites. We've evolved to the point where we are absolutely dependent on that technology. We'd be blind to a first strike!"

"I thought we had backups stored in high orbit."

"Yes, but there's a good chance they could knock them off as they're brought down. Besides, if they go for a first strike, they could pull it off before we could adjust for our losses."

"Would they go for a first strike, risk retaliation?" Danielson asked, her eyes searching Isaacs'. "Maybe they just want to assert their authority to have the laser up there."

"Maybe. But now they have every reason to think we deliberately manufactured and released a black hole and then lied to them about it. A whole new level of escalation."

"Escalation of what?" Runyan demanded. "Surely they know we're as imperiled as they are."

"The cool heads, yes. It's the hot ones I'm worried about," Isaacs replied. "Theirs and ours!"

"In any case we have no choice but to push on," Danielson said. "If they pause now to assess our reaction, we can get to the lab and back to the President so he has all the facts to negotiate with. If they choose the insane path, well, those mountains will be as good a place as any to be." She gestured to the slopes rising to the east.

Isaacs was pleased that her common sense, though grim, was asserting itself again.

"Okay, let's go." He gave her upper arm a squeeze as he guided her toward the waiting helicopter. Runyan hurried forward to help her climb in. Danielson noticed him and paused. With her mind freshly cleared by the heightened air of crisis, she decided a show of independence would be healthy for both of them. She turned to the lieutenant who had delivered the message, smiled at him and offered her arm. The young man leapt quickly to her side and helped her to clamber in, leaving Runyan standing nonplussed on the tarmac. Isaacs watched this quick tableau and then climbed in himself, jaw muscles knotting as he clenched his teeth.

The flight up to the research complex headed by Paul Krone took only fifteen minutes. As they approached they could tell that Krone commanded a huge authority. There were six or seven large buildings linked by a maze of roadways. They landed on a pad in front of one of the buildings and were met by a small, jaunty man of about sixty. He wore a plain white shirt, green and white checked pants, and white patent leather shoes. The shirt was anchored at the neck with a large silver and turquoise string tie which clashed with his nineteenth hole outfit.

"Hello," he bubbled. "I'm Ralph Floyd, executive site manager here. We're so pleased to have you. We don't get attention from the top levels here very often." Behind his facade he was troubled, sensing a threat to his conspiracy of silence over Paul Krone's attempted suicide. Who were these people with their peremptory visit, vague credentials?

Isaacs recognized the type. Quintessential bureaucrat, delighted with the sudden interest which this delegation purported to represent, but fearful because he didn't know exactly who they were or what they wanted. Isaacs eyed the man impatiently. An ominous image formed in his mind—the Russian laser gathering power for an imminent onslaught. He gritted his teeth and determined to play out the cover story until he could get a firmer feel of the situation. Where in the hell was Krone? Isaacs introduced the members of his party, and they followed Floyd into the nearby administration building. Floyd led them to his office and seated them. Just the right number of chairs had been brought in.

"Now, what can I do for you gentlemen—and lady," Floyd corrected himself. Danielson returned his smile with a blank stare. The smile faded and he turned to Isaacs.

"This is very short notice, but of course, we are all at your disposal."

"The President keeps tabs on all the crucial components in our research and development program," Isaacs began, bluffing his way. "He has heard good things about the work Dr. Krone and all of you are doing here, and he wants to be brought more directly up to date."

Floyd beamed possessively, but there was a wariness behind his smile.

"We understand this complex is autonomous," Isaacs continued.

"Oh, yes," said Floyd, "our mandate comes from Los Alamos, and our budget from there and from Krone Industries, but we are self-contained and Dr. Krone has a free hand to do as he wishes." He leaned forward and assumed a frank look. "Dr. Krone is an authentic Genius, you know."

Isaacs could hear the capital G, but something in Floyd's tone suggested that being a genius was not something proper folk did.

"He does need some help in practical matters," Floyd continued with a self-effacing smile. "I do what I can to make his job easier."

"I'm sure," replied Isaacs with an answering smile that did not quite reach his eyes.

"We were hoping to see Dr. Krone."

"Ah," said Floyd, his face drooping mournfully, "Dr. Krone has not been well for some time. We have not seen him at all for a few months. But," he brightened, "all our programs are proceeding actively."

Isaacs divined that Floyd was in manager's heaven—all programs routinely active and no boss to foul things up with new ideas, directions, and suggestions. Managing the affairs of a genius would be trying. He fixed on the time Floyd mentioned. A few months. What did Krone's absence imply? That was about as long as they had been tracking the black hole. Could that be coincidence?

"Is Krone available if necessary?" Isaacs persisted.

"Well, that would be difficult," answered Floyd. "He has a house up off the road a few miles back. A quite nice one actually, built with money from his patents, a product of his mind, he likes to say. He has always demanded his privacy there and has no phone. I'm afraid he's not in a condition to accept visitors personally."

"May I ask what the problem is?"

Floyd was silent for a moment, then made a futile gesture with his hands.

"I've been led to understand it's nothing serious, that is to say, nothing organic. The stress, though—Dr. Krone carries many responsibilities."

Isaacs caught the implication—cracked up, occupational hazard for geniuses, not the kind of thing that happens to proper folk. Isaacs fought down a wave of despair. He could feel the mission slipping away, sabotaged, inconclusive, leaving them at the mercy of the deadly laser, on the precipice of war. There were still the facilities to check out. Maybe they would learn something of interest. They had to move on.

"Well," he said, with forced conviviality, "perhaps you would care to give us a look around."

"Certainly, certainly," agreed Floyd, anxious to prove that all was in working order and, despite a suicidal boss, fit for presidential approval.

Floyd led them to a waiting van and played tour guide as the driver steered around the maze. There was a small section of simple tract homes and apartments for the personnel. A powerful nuclear reactor supplied the prodigious energy needs of the various experiments. They stopped at several buildings with Isaacs fuming inwardly with each passing minute. They were treated to a zoo of fantastic devices that shot, banged, sizzled, lased, fused, fried, evaporated, imploded, and exploded. Despite his growing frustration, Isaacs was impressed with Floyd's acumen in his own area. While no expert on the basic scientific and engineering principles, Floyd knew the origin and use of every nut and bolt and their price to the penny. Apparently Krone was good at picking people, as well as at creating new inventions.

At last, Runyan drew Isaacs aside.

"This is a waste of time. What the hell are we doing on this two-bit tour?"

"Goddamnit, we had to start somewhere!" Isaacs replied just as hotly, in a fierce whisper. He was not sure what they were looking for, but he was sure they hadn't seen it. He had been ticking off the various buildings mentally. As they climbed into the van once more and Floyd began to make noises about the end of the tour, Isaacs stopped him.

"We haven't seen that farthest building, out near that large cleared area."

"Oh," Floyd seemed nervous, tentative. "These experiments I've shown you are all basically mission oriented, and each has its own project scientist. That building contains Dr. Krone's own special experiments."

He leaned closer to Isaacs and lowered his voice.

"Frankly, we regard that set up as part of the overhead. It has been frightfully expensive, but it has kept Dr. Krone occupied and happy when he was not working directly on one of the other projects."

"I'll need to see it."

"Oh, but it was shut down when Dr. Krone became—ill." Floyd could see visions of presidential commendation vanishing with the opening of the door to that boondoggle building.

"Just the same," Isaacs insisted.

"Very well." Floyd gestured to the driver, and they were deposited in the drive of the far building. Perhaps, he thought, this will finally distract them from the condition of Krone himself.

Floyd dawdled over his keys, but finally accepted the inevitable and opened the door. The small group stopped immediately inside the door and craned their necks upward. The building was essentially one immense room, ten or eleven stories tall and somewhat larger in length than width. What arrested their attention was the behemoth construction which dominated the room, towering almost to the ceiling. It had the complex unfinished look of a research project as opposed to some of the production prototype devices they had just seen. An array of massive tubes projected radially from a hidden core, giving the whole structure the look of a giant monstrous hedgehog.

If Isaacs had any doubts that this was it, the look on Runyan's face banished them.

Runyan stood transfixed as his brain catalogued the components he vaguely recognized and wrestled to identify myriad paraphernalia which were foreign to him. Then he slowly moved toward the device, circled it and within a minute was scrambling up ladders and around catwalks in a furious desire to lay hands on the machine.

Ralph Floyd jittered from foot to foot, aware of the change in mood which had come over his visitors, but unable to comprehend it.

Isaacs turned to him.

"Do you know what the purpose of this thing is?"

"Only very vaguely," replied Floyd. "I believe Dr. Krone was studying states of matter at very high density. I believe he had some goal of generating large amounts of cheap energy in a new way."

He snickered behind one hand.

"To tell you the truth, the technicians who worked in here had a private name for it—Gravel Gertie."

Isaacs raised an eyebrow.

"Well, when the thing was working, if that's what you could call it, it consumed vast amounts of material. Lead bricks! My god, you don't know how he had me scouring the whole country for lead bricks. He'd feed them in over there at a whopping rate—"

Floyd pointed to an extension of the machine at the far side.

"They would vaporize and disappear. And at the same time he'd feed it granite from that hopper up there—vaporize that too. At one point about a year ago he hired fifty dump trucks. Fifty of them! And he kept them working around the clock for a month dumping gravel into that hopper. That's where the name came from. Just the overtime alone I had to pay! My head still spins.

"That's where that clear area out back came from, by the way. Disappeared into that hopper."

Isaacs looked at the little man and refrained from asking him where he thought all that rock went to. Instead he said, "My companions and I would like to look around here a little. Would you mind waiting outside?"

"Oh, no, of course not. I'll, I'll just be outside." Floyd dreaded the thought of leaving his visitors alone, unable to make convenient excuses and explanations, but he turned to leave, pulling the door shut behind him.

Isaacs looked at his watch. 3:40, local time, twenty till six in Washington. The world was still in one piece. Apparently rationality reigned, if only for a little while, and global catastrophe was held in abeyance. He hadn't really expected a first strike, yet some small fatalistic corner of his mind would not have been surprised to see a mushroom cloud rising in the distance as they walked between buildings. Now he could be confident their mission would not be a total disaster. If they could learn nothing from the machine that loomed before him, others would follow who could. With this the Russians could be stalled, if not convinced. There was time to look a bit here, he thought, try to see Krone, and still get back in time to lay the whole story out for the President. He stood and watched as Runyan scrambled around the device like a kid on a city park playscape.

A call from Pat Danielson came from the far side of the room.

After a minute of staring at the gargantuan, incomprehensible device, Danielson had looked around the room. Along its perimeter individual cubicles had been partitioned off. Although dwarfed by the looming device in the center, they were normal sized rooms, some even fairly large. She walked the perimeter peering into each through their large glass windows and discovered they were shops. The first was crammed with oscilloscopes, amplifiers, power supplies, and other electronic accouterments. Next was a machine shop with a multitude of drills, lathes, and saws, and a carpet of coiled, oily shards on the floor.

After wandering past several more rooms, one housing a late model large capacity scientific computer, Danielson found a small windowless room just opposite the door from which they had entered. She tried the door and stepped in, groping for and finding a light switch. There was a small but comfortable desk, shelves filled with books and computer output. What caught her eye, however, was a bound laboratory notebook resting alone on the desk. She reached for it and thumbed rapidly through. The book was three-quarters empty. She found the last entry, read briefly and then walked to the door.

"Mr. Isaacs," she shouted, "Bob? I've found something!"

Isaacs rounded the device looking for her and hurried across the intervening space, stepping over cables strewn on the floor.

Danielson watched him approach with an air of excitement. "Look here! I've found a lab book describing the experiment." She twisted to let him read over her shoulder where her finger marked a place. "The experiment has been a tremendous success," Danielson read aloud, "much has been learned about the properties of matter at ultrahigh densities and the transition to the final state of that matter. The experiment is not over, but it is no longer in my hands."

There was a gap and then other entries in a more hurried, scrawling manner.

"How could it have gone wrong!" Danielson read. "The sudden loss of containment is shocking, some instability, something unexpected in the containment process. The principle is now established. Must 1) study containment 2) study implications 3) retrieve them."

The two exchanged a long glance.

"That's the last entry?" Isaacs wanted to know. Danielson nodded.

"Are there any more of these?" Isaacs inquired, turning to examine the shelves.

"Not in here," Danielson replied. "There is a computer. It may have files of interest, but this book seems to be where he records his personal insights and reactions."

"Let's keep looking," Isaacs said.

They toured the rest of the perimeter, but found only shops. There were no more lab books. Isaacs went outside and spoke briefly with Floyd who was fidgeting in the driveway. He returned and explained to Danielson.

"Floyd says anything connected with this experiment should be here, unless Krone has other books at home. He worked at home a lot."

He raised his voice.

"Alex? Time to move on. We've got to go see Krone."

Runyan was near the top of the device. His voice carried faintly.

"A little longer. I've hardly explored a tenth of this thing."

Isaacs allowed control of his temper to slip a little.

"Goddamnit, Alex, we're on a tight schedule. You're never going to understand that thing poking around by yourself. It's not going anywhere, and we've got to talk to Krone if we can!"

Runyan muttered something unintelligible at the height, but began to climb down, feet clanging on the scaffolding steps. When he reached the bottom, his eyes still contained a glow of passion.

"That thing is fabulous! Do you see those immense particle accelerators?" He pointed at the hedgehog protrusions. "And apparently a gigantic superconducting magnet. Inconceivable that one man did that!"

Danielson clutched the lone lab book to her chest and felt a pang of jealousy. Jealous of a machine! Damn him! she thought.

Back at the administration building, Isaacs gave Floyd a receipt for the lab book.

"We'd like to try to see Krone. Perhaps we could borrow your van."

"I'm really afraid that won't——" Floyd said, then halted, stopped by the steel in Isaacs' eyes. He thought desperately, but could see no recourse. He could try to stymie this group, but others would follow. Silence had been his only defense, and now that silence would inevitably be shattered. Why had these people come?

"Yes, of course," he conceded. "I'll give instructions to the driver."

"That won't be necessary. The pilot who flew us up can drive. I don't want to cause you excess trouble." Or let you in on any more than necessary, Isaacs finished to himself.

"Fine, if that's what you wish. I'll give directions to your man, it's just a short drive, perhaps fifteen minutes."

"Is there anyone else in the house?" Isaacs inquired.

"There is a, ah, woman. She's lived with him in the big house for, well, I guess about two years now. I believe she's been taking care of him while he's—incapacitated. There is also a Mexican couple who come in to help, but they are only there for half a day. They wouldn't be there at this hour."

Isaacs herded his team into the van and made sure they had the directions straight. A woman. He remembered the stories of the Russian refugee he had heard from his contact in the FBI. Of course, she could be some old peasant lady who changes his sheets.

Chapter 17

Maria Latvin opened the door and knew the dreaded visit had come at last. The two men wore conservative western business suits, but she recognized the type and, despite herself, felt as if she had been suddenly yanked eight thousand miles back to the home she had fought so hard to leave.

The taller man stepped forward and reached into his inner jacket pocket for a small leather identification folder. He flipped it open and Maria stared at it. Not his papers, but photographs. Her mother and younger brother still trapped in Lithuania. Fighting the growing feeling of numbness, she stepped back and held the door open for them.

The tall man spoke quietly in Russian.

"We must see Paul Krone."

"He's not well," Latvin replied, slipping into the same language.

"We know that. We must see him anyway and judge his condition for ourselves."

"You know who I am. Why are you interested in Paul?"

"This is not necessary for you to know. You will take us to him."

The woman led the two Russians into the study.

"There, you see," she pointed to a figure seated before the fireplace, "he is very ill and cannot talk to you."

The two men approached the figure in the chair slowly. They crouched next to the chair, then began to whisper animatedly to one another.

Finally the taller one stood and walked back across the room to where Maria Latvin stood.

"You take care of him?"

"He responds to me a little. Enough for me to feed and wash him, to see to his basic functions."

"His research?"

The woman merely raised an eyebrow in a deeply sceptical look.

"What do you know of his work?" the man demanded.

"Nothing. I am no scientist. I know nothing."

"Notes. Does he keep notes of his work?"

"If he does, they are at the lab. He never worked here."

A faint crinkling cracked the frost around the man's eyes. "I must report for instructions. He will stay with you," he said, gesturing to his companion.

The woman's face betrayed no expression. The man shot a glance at his companion, a silent order, and left the room rapidly.

He had been gone five minutes when they heard a car coming up the drive. Maria Latvin looked questioningly at the remaining Russian. He shook his head and slid a hand toward the bulge under his jacket.

"Quickly," she said, "you can hide in a rear bedroom. I'll see who it is."

"Get rid of them. Immediately!" he demanded, as she hustled him down the hallway.

Isaacs scanned the house as they approached. It was a large, multi-level adobe structure, graceful despite the characteristic thick walls and solid projecting beams. It faced the southwest with a glorious view of the plains and the oncoming sunset. Isaacs spoke to the agents and the pilot who had driven them up to the house.

"This is a private home, and we don't want to come on like an invasion force. We're just going to try to speak with the man who runs the complex up the road. I'd like you to sit tight here."

The agents nodded.

Isaacs, Danielson, and Runyan walked up the flagstone walk to the massive carved front door. Not seeing a doorbell, Isaacs used his knuckles.

After a moment the door swung open. Runyan was not sure what he expected, but it was certainly not what he saw in his view over Isaacs' shoulder. A lovely young woman stood there, one hand on the knob of the door. She was of medium height, dressed in a dark hostess gown. She had a smooth brown complexion, thick black hair in a longish page-boy cut, and high cheekbones. Her black eyes sparkled behind gold-rimmed eyeglasses, but registered no surprise at the three strangers in the doorway of her redoubt. Runyan saw her take in Isaacs and then swing her gaze to him. After a moment she looked past him to Danielson and raised one eyebrow in a slight quizzical gesture.

Isaacs displayed his badge and said, "We are here by authority of the President of the United States. May we come in?"

The woman seemed to instantly understand and accept the situation. She stepped aside and said, "Come in," in a lilting slightly accented voice.

Inside the door was a foyer, high ceilinged and about eight feet across. There was a closet door on the left. On the right was a small stand holding a lamp and fronting a mirror which ran nearly to the ceiling and added even more width to the area.

The woman led them from the foyer to a large living room. The room was decorated in Spanish style. A massive fireplace dominated the wall directly across from where they entered. A thick Navaho rug lay on the dark tile floor in front of the fireplace. Bordering the rug were two heavy leather sofas at right angles with a high-backed overstuffed leather chair filling the gap on the right side of the fireplace. On the wall on either side of the door through which they had entered were floor to ceiling shelves of dark mahogany which contrasted with the whitewashed walls. The shelves were filled with books and excellent specimens of Mayan and Incan relics. To their left a large archway led to a dining room dominated by a great mahogany table, surrounded by twelve ornate chairs, but set, Isaacs noted, with only two places—the right end and the position to the immediate left of that, such that the diner would face away from the living room. To the right of the fireplace a hallway disappeared from view.

The woman stepped around the sofa which faced the fireplace and sat back in the chair, tucking her legs beneath her. Without taking his eyes off her, Runyan followed her and perched unbidden on the corner of the sofa nearest her chair. Danielson watched him with the closest scrutiny, but remained standing behind the central sofa with Isaacs. Isaacs asked the key question.

"Is Paul Krone here?" The woman looked back at Runyan and then at Isaacs.

"Yes," she replied simply.

"May I ask who you are?"

"I am Maria Latvin, his companion."

"I would like to speak with Dr. Krone."

"Certainly." She arose without further comment and proceeded down the hallway to the right of the fireplace.

Runyan rose with the woman as she led the three of them down the corridor. They passed a closed door on the right, but she paused before a door somewhat beyond that to the left. Opening that door, she stood aside and gestured for them to enter.

The room was a study, extending down to the left and ending in another large fireplace which backed up to the one in the living room.

The other three walls were lined with shelves completely filled with books. A large desk dominated the middle of the room. Its surface looked well used, but was currently empty save for a pencil holder and a couple of mementos. Two high-backed large chairs, mates of the one in the other room, flanked the fireplace. Unlike the other fireplace this one had a small flame flickering in the grate. A figure was seated in the chair to the right of the hearth. From their vantage point just inside the door at the far end of the room, they could only see extended legs, and the left arm draped on the armrest.

"Paul?"

Runyan jumped slightly and turned at the sound of the voice behind him. Her tone had been gentle, but faintly condescending, as one might address a child. The figure gathered itself slowly and rose from the chair.

Isaacs had never met Krone personally, but he recognized him immediately from photographs. He also saw more. Krone was in slippers and a dressing gown, incongruous attire for a physicist, but it was his face which arrested Isaacs' attention. The jaw was slack, the eyes glazed and unfocussed, his whole visage one of lifelessness. Isaacs stepped forward.

"Krone? Paul Krone?"

The eyes shifted slowly to the speaker, but there was no sign that the words registered.

Isaacs stepped up to Krone and lightly grasped his arm above the elbow. The eyes maintained their original focus. Isaacs waved his other hand in front of Krone's face. The eyes blinked about three seconds later with no apparent regard to cause and effect.

Isaacs released Krone and spun around to face the dark figure in the doorway. "He's virtually catatonic! How long has he been like this?"

Her face was nearly as expressionless as Krone's except for her eyes which, by contrast, still sparkled with life. "Since last April," she replied succinctly.

"Has he been treated?" Isaacs' voice betrayed more strain than he intended.

"Three experts have been called in. They have been of no use."

"Do you know what happened to him?"

She unwound slightly, moving around Runyan and Danielson to the desk and extending the fingers of her left hand until they rested lightly on the surface. She turned her face to speak directly to Isaacs. Her voice dropped in pitch.

"He was doing experiments in his laboratories. He was very excited, totally engrossed. Then the excitement left. He became withdrawn, more and more. Very late one night he tried to commit suicide. I called the doctor at the laboratory. He was in the hospital for a month. They saved his life, but since then he has been like this."

She moved to the motionless figure beside Isaacs and took his arm in much the same manner that Isaacs had.

"Come, Paul," she spoke gently and led him to the chair where he sat as if by instinctual response. She saw that he was arranged comfortably and then turned and proceeded directly from the room without a glance at her visitors.

During this interchange, Danielson's eyes had been scanning the bookshelves. When Maria Latvin departed, she moved over and touched Isaacs' sleeve. He followed her pointing finger to a shelf behind the desk. There was an array of lab books identical to the one they had found at the complex. Isaacs and Danielson stepped around the desk and began to examine them. They took turns lifting down a volume, checking its contents briefly and adding it to a growing pile on the desk. All the books seemed to be related to the experiment which led to the creation of the black hole. Although it became clear they were in chronological order, they continued to spot-check to make sure that all dealt with the same subject.

Maria Latvin hurried along the corridor to the room where she had left the Russian agent.

"They are from the Central Intelligence Agency," she whispered. "They also came to see Paul. I could not make them leave. You must warn the other. He must not come in."

"What are they doing?"

"I left them in the study."

"They cannot talk to him. Perhaps they will leave."

"I do not think so." She had lied to the Russians. She knew the lab books were on the shelf, but resolved to tell them as little as possible unless forced. She had seen that Danielson carried one of the books and knew they would spot the others. "I think that they will want to take Paul away." That was a stall, but also the probable truth.

"Show me a back way out," the man demanded. "I will head my compatriot off, and find out our orders. You must learn the intentions of the American agents. Keep them in the front of the house, and meet us back in this room in ten minutes. If you are not here—."

He reached under his jacket again, his meaning crystal clear.

Isaacs was rapidly evaluating the situation. Krone was useless for their immediate needs. The machine itself would speak to experts, but not to them. The lab books were a treasure, but was there something else they should know about? They could grab the books and head home, but if they quickly perused them they might find other valuable clues as to what had gone on in this remote place. He grabbed several books at random.

"Let's spend a little time looking through these," he said. "See if there is any hint that we should try to dig up something other than these books themselves."

He went over to the second high-backed chair and swiveled it to face the room. He kept one book to read and put the others on the floor. Danielson sat at the desk and began to look at another, the last she had taken down from the shelf. Runyan rummaged through the stack to find some of the earliest tomes. He looked around, realized all the chairs were taken, and moved to the wall near the door where he plopped himself on the carpet and leaned back against the bookshelf.

Some time passed in a silence broken only by the crackling of the fire and an occasional rustle of a turned page. Danielson suddenly became aware of a small motion in the doorway. The woman, Maria Latvin, stood there looking at the chair in which Krone sat. Her hands were clasped softly in front of her, perhaps that was the motion that had caught Danielson's attention. Danielson was sure the woman had been there for some time, quietly watching.

The same motion must have caught Runyan's attention, too. Danielson watched him as he sat a little more than an arm's length from the doorway.

Danielson could see his eyes as he scanned the lovely, composed face, down the curves of her body to her feet in open, tastefully designed sandals. She turned to go and Runyan bent over and craned his neck to follow with unabashed interest her passage down the hallway. When he could see her no longer, he straightened up and looked over to catch Danielson's eyes upon him. Danielson looked quickly down at the book before her with blurred eyes. She felt ice in her stomach and warm fire on her face.

Maria Latvin opened the door to the bedroom. At first she

thought only one was there, but then the tall one stepped out from behind the door.

"What do they do now?"

"They look at books in the study and talk among themselves." A mix of truth and half-truth.

"We are taking Krone. And you. To care for him."

God! To go back. She felt the wave of despair again.

"And what of them?" She gestured toward the front of the house.

"If you cooperate, they need come to no harm. Where is Krone now?"

"He is still in the study. With them."

"You must bring him here. We will escape out the back to our car which is hidden down the road."

"And if they resist?"

"You must find a way. If they discover our presence here they will die."

"If we get away, they, and soon many others, will follow," the woman argued.

The tall man thought for a long moment.

"You must make it look as if it is your idea. If they look only for a woman on the run, our job will be easier."

Now Maria Latvin thought deeply. She could go to the agents in the study and reveal the Russians, but at the risk of death or worse for her mother and brother. She could make off with Paul herself and to hell with them all, but the Russians, at least, would exact the same penalty. She wanted no harm to come to those in the other room, least of all Paul. She dreaded the idea of going back, but she would be with Paul, and surely the Americans would do everything to have him released. Staying close to him was her best chance of survival.

She needed some way to distract them. She thought of the lab books. Paul had been working with them when he had drifted from her. The Americans were keenly interested in them. She supposed the Russians would be too, if they only knew how near they were. She hated them!

She spoke to the tall one.

"I will get him out in the car. You can wait to see us leave. We have a hunting lodge higher in the mountains, I'll draw you a map. I will head in the opposite direction and then double back on another road. We can switch to your car there."

"I don't like it," said the other man. "We shouldn't let her or Krone out of our sight."

The tall man turned to speak to him, keeping his eyes locked on Maria Latvin.

"I don't think there will be any problem." He smiled an unpleasant smile and patted the leather folder in his breast pocket.

Isaacs closed another book and checked his watch. He had found no reference to other useful material beyond an occasional technical journal. The lab books seemed self-contained. There was no reason to delay further.

"It's time to get back to the base and radio a report," he said. "How are you doing?" he inquired of his companions.

"This is amazing stuff!" Runyan replied enthusiastically. "The man is really incredible. He has developed a whole series of innovative techniques to accomplish things I would have said were impossible. Apparently, he deliberately set out to make a black hole. He wanted to use it as an energy source, utilize the power emitted as material is swallowed. Vast power from anything, dirt, water, air. He started by investigating how great a density he could create in the lab. Just a question of pure basic science with no practical application in mind. Then he got the idea of creating a black hole. He imploded pellets of iron with his standard beam techniques—iron so that there would be no nuclear reactions. The problem is that it requires vast energies to overcome the internal pressure of the compressed matter. Krone seems to have developed a way to neutralize the electrical charges in the pellet and the beam which compresses it. That reduced the pressure and allows much higher densities. I haven't gotten to anything about black holes yet, but if I'm any judge his studies will advance our knowledge of the behavior of nuclear matter by a decade."

"Could be," replied Isaacs. "I was just looking here somewhere in the middle of the story," he checked a date, "about a year and a half ago. Apparently, he has had some success at reaching high densities, but trouble maintaining them. He's describing here the development of a magnetic confinement configuration which can support the compressed pellet while he continues to focus the intense neutron beams on it. The discussion is highly technical. I'm barely getting the gist of it."

Isaacs paused to rub his eyes.

"The real question is whether we are going to learn anything from these that will tell us how to undo the damage. Are you getting any sense of that?"

"He's done the impossible and recorded it in meticulous detail," Runyan replied. "Only time will tell, but I can't believe there won't be some new knowledge, some hints. I know this, as long as the original knowledge is locked up there," he glanced at Krone's still figure, "these books are invaluable."

Danielson had not seemed to pay any attention to this interchange. She had swiveled her chair away from the desk and was staring at the fire.

"Pat?" inquired Isaacs.

She turned to look at him with a vacant smile. "I was thinking about Shelley."

"The poet, Percy Bysshe?"

"No, his wife, Mary Wollstonecraft."

"Oh, right, Frankenstein. Well, our scientist has created a monster all right."

"Four of them."

"What's that?"

She pointed at the book she had abandoned on the desk.

"He thinks he made four of them. At first the suspension

system was ineffective. He cites evidence that he managed to start three seeds, but then they disappeared from the system. There was no sign that they had evaporated, no unexplained release of energy. He suspects they fell into the earth, but are too small to detect. By the fourth time, he made significant improvements to the magnetic suspension and managed to force-feed and grow the one we know about. Eventually, the suspension failed again. This time he detected it seismically and knew for sure what was happening."

"My god!" gasped Runyan from his seat by the door. "Didn't he know what he was doing? Why didn't he stop after the first disaster?"

She looked at him coolly.

"The journals are pretty clinical so his state of mind is only implicit, but I get the feeling that he was totally caught up in the scientific and engineering questions and driven by a powerful megalomania. Apparently, he was so consumed by his quest that he didn't question the failures in that way, just what had become of them. When the fourth got away from him, he finally thought seriously about the implications of what he had done—and it destroyed him." She waved a hand toward the quiet figure in the chair by the fireplace.

"But if he's right about the other three," said Runyan, "then even if we find some solution to the big one we're still in danger from the others. Drag on them is going to act more quickly to cause them to settle into the earth where they're unreachable. They may take a much longer time to grow to a dangerous size, but it's still just a matter of time."

He exchanged a long glance with Isaacs. Isaacs broke it off, gathered up the books he had been reading and stood.

"Well, let's see if we can get these books to someone who will understand them better than we do."

Danielson stood up from the desk, and Runyan gathered his long legs under him and shoved himself to his feet.

Maria Latvin appeared in the doorway. She gave Runyan a

cool look and then addressed herself to Isaacs.

"I must put Paul down for his rest. Then I would like to talk to you, if I may. Would you please wait in the living room?"

"Certainly," replied Isaacs. "We have a couple of issues to discuss with you as well."

They filed out of the room and down the hall as the woman bent to help Krone from the chair.

Isaacs deposited the books he had been holding on the table in the foyer. He walked over next to Runyan who had settled in the chair next to the fireplace. Danielson examined the artifacts on the shelves.

"What next?" Runyan inquired.

"We'll explain to her that we need the books and that we'll have to send someone for Krone. Something tells me she's not going to take that news too well."

Runyan's face clouded over. "I don't believe I fathom that lady. Surely she realizes that we represent some threat to upset her isolated but rather posh applecart here, yet she doesn't seem at all perturbed."

"I'm not sure of her role, either," Isaacs answered. "She does seem to be devoted to Krone. If he returned the consideration, he may have set her up for life, regardless of what happens."

Runyan smiled an impish grin. "Or maybe Krone's not as incapacitated as he seems. That's one good-looking woman there."

"Oh, for heaven's sake!" Danielson turned, exasperated. "You can see what shape that man is in. Can you imagine what an effort it must be to care for him? All by herself?"

Runyan leaned toward Isaacs and said in a stage whisper, "Touchy feminist."

"Mr. Isaacs," Danielson's voice was cold with fury. "I don't believe you need me here anymore. I'll wait in the car." She paused to pick up the lab books Isaacs had left in the foyer and then swept out the front door.

Runyan gave a half shrug as Isaacs fixed him with a stony stare.

"That was completely unnecessary, Alex. I don't know what you've done to upset her, but I want a lid on it."

"Hey, it was a little joke."

"There's more to it than that. Something's going on between you."

"Well, to hell with you," Runyan scowled. "My personal life is none of your business."

"It is if it keeps one of my people from performing at top efficiency, or distracts us at all from what we're doing here."

"Horse shit," seethed Runyan. "Don't tell me I'm not on top of what's going on." He stood up and looked down at the slightly shorter man. "You wouldn't even be here if it weren't for me."

"I know what you've contributed, and I'd like to keep you on the team, but if you get in my way, you're out!"

The two men glared at one another, then Runyan broke off and looked at the carpet, scuffing his toe, then finally back at Isaacs.

"Look," he said, "this thing is too big for us to lose sight of it fighting over some girl."

"Girl! She's a damn fine worker. Let me remind you neither of us would be here if it weren't for her early work."

"She's a bright lady, I know that. She's also attractive, in case you hadn't noticed. We got a little friendly out there in Arizona. Didn't mean anything."

"I think it did to her."

They were silent a moment. Then Isaacs spoke.

"We've got to get a move on here. The woman's had plenty of time to put Krone to bed or whatever she was going to do. See if you can find her. I'll get the two men in the car to start carrying out the books."

Runyan headed down the hallway. He heard a noise, turned into the study, and was rooted with shock. A huge fire roared in the fireplace. In disbelief, he watched Maria Latvin pick up an object, squirt it with charcoal lighter, and toss it into the fireplace where it ignited with a FOOMPF! and added to the blaze. He looked more carefully and realized that the grate was filled with burning books. The lab books!

"What the hell are you doing?" he shouted, rushing toward her.

The woman swiveled quickly, the fingers of her right hand deftly sweeping up a bone-handled knife as she turned. I wish no one hurt, she thought, but I'm too close to let this one stand in my way. I must get to Paul!

She faced Runyan in a half-crouch, the position they had learned when planning the escape. She felt the rush of irony that she should use this skill to fight her way back in. She spread her feet wide, wielding the weapon in the classic offensive position, point out, not down from her fist like a dagger. Runyan registered her savage, determined look and the wicked tip of the blade. He tried to brake, off balance.

The knife whipped in a deadly arc toward his face. He jerked his head back and threw up his arms for protection, stumbling backwards. He felt his jaw go numb as the blade went by and then a deep agony flashed through his right forearm. He crashed onto the floor. The woman's knife hand had completed its vicious cycle, instantly ready to strike again. Runyan's fall on his back, legs sprawled, had taken him just out of reach. He saw her look at his exposed crotch and draw back the knife. Panic seized him. He shuttled backward, crab-like, then flipped onto all fours. He screamed as his right arm gave way, and he fell on his face. He crawled awkwardly with one arm, flailing, splashing blood, then finally got his feet under him and lurched out the door and down the hallway.

Isaacs was on the front step when he heard Runyan shout. He raced into the living room just as Runyan, frightened and bloody, ran from the hall.

"Burning the lab books!" Runyan shouted hoarsely, as he

collapsed onto Isaacs who lowered him to the floor. The two CIA agents pounded into the room. Danielson and the pilot followed them, breathing hard, eyes wide.

"The woman! Get her!" Isaacs directed the agents. "And watch out— she's got some kind of weapon. Pat, see to him, will you?" he said standing, pointing to Runyan's sprawled form. "You!" he said, fingering the pilot, "come with me."

He raced down the hallway. At the end of it, the two agents were putting their shoulders to a locked door. Dimly, Isaacs heard the roaring start of a high performance engine.

"A car!" he shouted. "Out the front way. See if you can stop her! If she's got Krone with her, for god's sake don't do anything to harm him."

Isaacs turned into the study as the agents ran back down the hallway past him. He fought down a sense of dismay at the sight of the hearth full of burning books, then grabbed the fireplace tongs and began to frantically pull them from the grate. The pilot backed into the room watching the two CIA field men disappear into the living room. Then he turned and stopped transfixed, watching as Isaacs threw book after burning book about the room.

"Get your jacket off!" Isaacs shouted over his shoulder. "Smother those!"

The carpet was starting to smoulder in a dozen places. The young pilot stripped off his jacket and began to extinguish the flames, covering the books with his jacket, kicking them away from areas of smoking carpet.

Isaacs pulled the last book from the grate, a half-consumed block of char. He removed his jacket and methodically worked on the flames nearest him. After a frenetic minute, the last of the flames died. Isaacs, breathing in huge gulps of air, smiled gratefully at the young man. His proud grey-blue jacket was a scorched tatter. He was covered with soot and his hands were red with angry welts. Isaacs felt his own hands begin to puff and sting with burns he had ignored.

"Sorry about your hands, and clothes."

The young man shrugged.

"Would you make sure these are all out?" Isaacs asked him. "I'll check the others."

Isaacs left the soldier gently kicking the books into the hallway, checking for those still smouldering.

Pat Danielson had run over to Alex Runyan and then stopped, weak-kneed. He lay on his back, staring pale faced at the ceiling. His shirt was slashed just below his right elbow and a dark stain spread into the cloth, but it was his neck that held her attention. His beard below the chin line dripped red blood. She paid no attention to the two CIA agents who tore through the room and out the front door. My god, she thought, dropping to her knees, his throat's been slashed!

Runyan rolled his eyes to her and smiled weakly. "I'll never look at another woman again."

Danielson forced herself to look at his neck. With relief, she realized the wound was just along the jaw bone. It was deep, with pink bone showing, but not life threatening.

"She—she nearly cut your throat."

"I certainly got the impression that was her goal," Runyan croaked.

"Let me look for something to stop the bleeding," Danielson said. She ran through the dining room into the kitchen. She slammed through the cabinets until she found a stack of dish towels. She turned to go, then stopped and pulled open drawers until she found a large, sharp kitchen knife. She trotted back to Runyan who was struggling to sit up.

"Lie down, crazy," she said, pushing him in the chest with the butt of the knife.

Runyan spied the gleaming blade. "You're going to finish the job," he groaned. "Make it quick."

Danielson put the knife and towels down and gave him a pained look. She rolled one of the towels up and aligned it with the cut on his jaw.

"Hold that!" she said sternly, grabbing his good left hand

and putting it on the towel. She laid his right arm slowly, gently, straight out from his body. Then she picked up the knife and carefully inserted the tip in the hole in his shirt and slit the gash to the end of the sleeve. She reversed the knife and extended the slash to his upper arm so she could curl the cloth away from the wound. It was also deep, with sliced tendons exposed, bleeding steadily and profusely. She wrapped a towel around the forearm and it promptly turned a bright crimson. She slit another towel in several places with the knife and then tore it into strips. She knotted two strips around the towel on the wound and another just above the elbow as a tourniquet.

She felt Isaacs crouch at her side.

"How is he?"

"Not as bad as he looks, I thought his throat was cut. He's lost a lot of blood, though."

"I'll send the pilot in the van for his chopper. There must be someplace he can set down around here. We'll get him down to the base hospital at Holloman as soon as possible."

Isaacs headed quickly for the door. Outside the two agents were jogging back up the driveway.

"Missed her?" Isaacs inquired.

"No way," one of them replied. "Damn Ferrari, or some such thing. But she didn't head for the lab; she took off in the opposite direction. Shall we take the van after her?"

"No, we need it to help get medical attention for Runyan. Was Krone in the car?"

"Didn't get a good look, but yeah, I thought I saw a passenger."

"Can't be too hard to find such a car in these parts," Isaacs observed.

"Nah," the agent agreed, "it's bright red and goes two hundred miles an hour. Should be a snap from the air. It'll be dark soon, though. That could give her an edge."

"Let's get on it then," Isaacs said. "You go with the pilot to the lab. Radio from the helicopter for a search team."

"Right," replied the agent, heading for the van.

Inside the house, Runyan had closed his eyes. Pat Danielson looked at his face, nearly as white from shock as the plaster on the adobe walls. Slowly, she reached out and put a comforting hand on the pale forehead.

"Damn you," she whispered. "Damn you."

Chapter 18

From his helicopter seat, Robert Isaacs looked down on the lights of the ellipse, the thrust of the Washington Monument, and the illuminated sheen of the White House. His exhaustion ran so deep that the sight barely stirred him. His hands stung from burns and his belly ached from the cold, greasy, hastily packed box lunch that he had grabbed from the commissary at Holloman Air Force Base and shared with Pat Danielson on the flight back to Andrews. With luck, he thought, the car would be depositing Danielson at her apartment about now. He, on the other hand, had to face the most important meeting of his career with scarcely the energy to hold his head up. There would be shock, a lot of heat, a search for scapegoats. He knew he would be a target if his collusion with the Russians were revealed.

He hoped he didn't look as bad as he felt. The clean jacket that an aide had picked up from his home and delivered to

Andrews helped, but he could see singe marks where the shirt cuffs showed. He looked at his watch as the helicopter settled onto the pad on the White House lawn. 11:37. A helluva time to decide the fate of the nation. He thought he might prefer to change places with Runyan, trussed up in a hospital bed, or the two agents who had gone chasing a Ferrari through the mountains of New Mexico. Isaacs wondered whether they had gotten anything to eat. He steeled himself as the door swung open and climbed down into the rotor's wash. He supervised the unloading of the precious footlocker, keeping one of the lab books to show the President and then headed for the nearest door of the White House.

Inside, a White House guard escorted him to the cabinet room. Isaacs thanked the guard, opened the door and stepped inside. Seventeen people were seated around the large table which filled the room. Isaacs nodded to the Vice-President, several cabinet officers, the Chairman of the National Security Council, and various others he knew. He recalled that the Secretary of Defense, smart enough to beat the August heat in the capital, was absent on a tour of European defense installations. Some of the faces displayed excitement at the state of emergency, others, blasé and disgruntled at the lateness of the hour, glanced at him long enough to ascertain that he was not The Man and returned to desultory conversations. The President's chair, halfway along the table, its back to the window, was still empty.

Howard Drefke rose from his seat at the far end of the table in front of the unlit fireplace. Wayne Phillips, who had been seated next to him, also stood as Isaacs walked the length of the room to join them.

"Bob. How are you?" Drefke's voice was low in the hush of the room, but warm.

"I'm fine." Isaacs grimaced slightly at the pain of the handshake, but offered his hand as well to Phillips. They sat down, Isaacs taking a spare chair next to Phillips. He placed the scorched lab book carefully on the table. "Sorry to call you back here so suddenly," Isaacs said to the physicist.

"No problem at all. I'm so happy to be of service."

"You brought the slides from Gantt?"

"Yes, they're in the machine."

Phillips gestured at a projector sitting on the waist high table next to Drefke in front of the fireplace. Isaacs checked the alignment of the screen at the other end of the room, next to the door through which he had entered. He confirmed that Drefke had brought the satellite photos. All seemed in place.

"I caught one of those commuter flights from La Jolla to Burbank just after you called this morning," Phillips continued, "and Ellison was ferried over from Arizona. We had several hours in Pasadena to assemble the data and make the slides before my flight east. I'm sorry that Ellison isn't here to help with the presentation, especially since poor Alex is hurt. His condition is not too serious, they tell me?"

"No, he lost some blood, and he'll be in a bit of pain for awhile, but he'll be fine. In any case, you're the head of Jason, the man the President will want to hear from."

The door banged open and the President barged through. Isaacs immediately perceived that the individual normally so bluff and hearty on television press conferences was thoroughly steamed. He strode to his chair and sat down so quickly that no one had a chance to stand. There was a momentary bobbing of bodies as several of the people started to rise, thought better of it, and resettled themselves. The President had a piece of paper partially crushed in his tight grip. He slammed it on the table.

"The goddamned Russians have gone berserk! This is the third hot line message from them today. This morning they wiped out the nuclear device that was our protection against their laser. All afternoon they've been methodically picking off pieces of space junk, showing what they can do. There are rumors in every major capital that our surveillance system is compromised and that one side or the other is on the verge of a preemptive strike."

He poked a rigid finger at the paper.

"If we so much as blink we'll be at war and our NATO allies are panicked to the point where any one of them could push the wrong button."

He looked around the table. "The Russians are mad, and they are scared, and they are blaming us. I want to know what the hell is going on!"

The President paused and forcibly composed himself. He continued with a quieter but still strained tone. "They seem to think that we have developed and are testing some fantastic new kind of weapon which can be fired through the earth."

He turned toward the Director of Central Intelligence at his far right. "Howard, you indicated you could shed some light on this. I hope you don't mind sharing one or two of your secrets with me before the whole world goes up in a goddamned nuclear war!"

A look of anguish passed over Drefke's face. The sarcastic attack from his old friend pained him, and he knew the President was not going to like the story he had to tell.

"Mr. President," his voice quavered, but then grew stronger, "the case I have to present is highly unorthodox. My associate, Mr. Isaacs, has only just this moment returned with the evidence to confirm that we are faced with a peril of unprecedented proportions. Through a bizarre set of circumstances, the earth itself has become mortally endangered."

"I've always considered nuclear holocaust dangerous," the President said, his irritation still plainly evident.

"I don't mean war, but something far more insidious," Drefke pressed. "If our understanding is correct, the issues we currently regard as crises, including this exaggerated light sabre rattling of the Soviets, become nearly irrelevant."

Drefke could sense that his strong statement, coupled with

the ire of the President, had created a profound air of discontent around the table. He rushed on.

"Our current understanding has been developed by the Office of Scientific Intelligence under Mr. Isaacs with the collaboration of the Jason group chaired by Professor Wayne Phillips who is here to answer questions of a technical, scientific nature which may arise."

Phillips nodded at the array of severe faces which surrounded the table.

"I will give you a brief overview," Drefke continued. "Mr. Isaacs will then provide details of the present situation." He paused and looked at some notes before him.

"In late April, analysis of seismic data from the Large Seismic Array showed a peculiar signal. Closer examination by members of the OSI staff revealed this signal to be quite regular with a period of eighty and a half minutes. Attempts to relate this signal to a man-made origin were unsuccessful. On the contrary, the source of the seismic waves moved along a line which always pointed to the same direction in space."

"Hell's fire!" The expletive came from the representative of the Office of Naval Intelligence, a man of stern military bearing. Several people in the room, including the President, flinched at the outburst. Drefke, who had been anticipating it, looked at him stonily.

"You're talking about the same thing the Navy has been monitoring on sonar," the Navy man continued. "Fixed orientation and all that. We lost a ship on that mission. What the hell's going on?"

Drefke looked coolly at the President, confident of his special relationship.

"If I may continue?"

The President nodded and Drefke proceeded to ignore the hot glare of the naval officer.

"It is true," he said, "that the phenomenon generates an acoustic signal in water which is the counterpart of the seismic signal within the earth."

His voice took on a slight condescending note. "My colleagues in the Navy are aware of the phenomenon I'm discussing. They chose not to pursue the matter in a manner which would give any useful insight." Drefke knew that this simple statement on his part would eventually cause heads to roll in the hierarchy of naval intelligence, including, perhaps, that of his obstreperous colleague at the table. He proceeded with the matter at hand.

"The Navy lost a ship, the Stinson, with tragic loss of life, while monitoring this phenomenon. That relates to another important point. At the same time, also beginning last April, another chain of events was set in motion, which are well-known to all of you here." Drefke hunched forward, leaning on the table, and looked intently at his colleagues. "I am referring to the Soviet carrier, the Novorossiisk."

There was a rustle and exchange of glances around the table. Drefke continued.

"You all know what transpired from that seemingly minor incident. The Soviets unveiled their first laser and demolished one of our surveillance satellites. We captured that satellite, thanks to the brave action of our shuttle crew, but that led to the launch of a new laser satellite and our nuclear weapon in a standoff which was broken this morning, leaving us in our current state of emergency. We now have reason to believe that the object which damaged the Novorossiisk and, in sad fact, sank the Stinson, was the very thing the Stinson was sent to monitor, the source of the odd seismic and acoustic waves.

"Mr. President," Drefke faced his commander-in-chief, "we now believe that all these events and several more peculiar happenstances are intimately related, although it was difficult, until very recently, to see the common thread. It is very much to the credit of Mr. Isaacs and his team that the crucial connection was made. The seismic information was used by the OSI to predict that the source of these waves would appear in Nagasaki and Dallas on specific dates last summer, July 7 and July 26, respectively. In each instance, there was some relatively minor, unexplained damage. In each case there was also a death, but neither was directly attributable to the source of the seismic waves. This much information was presented to Jason by Mr. Isaacs in early August. A possible explanation was forthcoming."

Drefke leaned back in his chair, took a deep breath, looked at Isaacs and Phillips, and then exhaled. He looked keenly at the President.

"Mr. President, I know you have heard the term 'black hole.'"

"Yes," the President answered with a note of questioning in his voice, "some sort of gravitational trap, I believe. Supposed to be formed by a collapsing star, if I have the picture right."

"That is the basic idea," Drefke assented.

"So what's the point?" the President demanded. "Are you going to tell me that in addition to the Russians threatening to blow us to kingdom come, we are about to fall into a black hole?"

"Apparently, Mr. President, we are doing so at this very instant."

This statement brought outbursts of protest from around the table. Drefke looked pained again and raised his voice.

"Mr. President! Mr. President! I beg your pardon! If I could be allowed to explain."

The President quieted the group. "Russians I can deal with somehow, Howard, but what the hell are you feeding us now?"

"Please consider my position," Drefke pleaded in the most dignified tone he could muster. "I sympathize with your incredulity, but you have not heard all the arguments. Understand that there is no way to introduce this idea without surprise and shock."

"All right, all right," said the President with protesting hands in the air. Then he dropped his elbows to the table and supported his head in his hands muttering, "Jesus Christ!"

"At the Jason meeting the suggestion was made that, despite the seeming impossibility, the only explanation consistent with the facts was a very small black hole. In addition, a suggestion was made for a definitive test of this hypothesis. Such a thing should have a precise and measurable gravitational field. The meeting with Jason was on the second and third of August, nine days ago. An expedition was mounted a week later, and results were obtained only yesterday.

"Mr. President, the answer is unambiguous," Drefke continued. "An object with a mass of about a hundred million tons and of very small size is oscillating through the solid matter of the earth as if it did not exist. The conclusion seems inescapable that the object is a black hole and that it is slowly consuming material from the inside of the earth. Left unmolested, that process will proceed to completion."

A stillness had fallen on the room as Drefke spoke. It continued for a few moments, then was broken by the President.

"And now you are going to tell me the Russians are onto this thing and think we have done it?" he said in a forlorn voice. "Why wasn't I apprised of this before I had World War III dumped in my lap?"

"Sir," Drefke pleaded, "as I said, the results confirming the hypothesis only became available yesterday, and even then there were important unanswered questions. You must understand that the notion was so incredible that we had to be absolutely sure before bringing it to your attention."

Drefke paused to collect his thoughts. He had always been comfortably frank with this man before and after he became the President, but he did not care to confess in front of this group his culpability in delaying Isaacs' investigation. He chose his words carefully.

"Besides drawing us into a confrontation in space, the Soviets have been pursuing their own investigation of the damage to the Novorossiisk." He could not suppress a quick glance at Isaacs. He also did not want to expose Isaacs' role in tipping the Russians to the nature of the black hole. "We are not sure of the details, but with their extensive naval deployment in the Mediterranean and the Pacific, they have evidently also discovered the regular sonar pattern associated with this thing. We have recently found that they have a series of vessels deployed precisely on the path that the, uh, black hole follows as it punches through the earth's surface."

"May we deduce then," an abrupt voice broke in, "that the Soviets have the same information that was available to our Navy?" The forceful baritone belonged to the Secretary of State, a diminutive man whose tone belied his physical stature. "But they have gone ahead to reach the conclusion that this thing is a great danger?"

"I believe that is a fair statement," Drefke replied. In his peripheral vision he could see the jaw muscles of the naval intelligence officer clinch and bunch.

"And they have concluded as you have," the Secretary of State continued, "that it is a black hole and have further concluded that we are responsible?"

"That seems to be the best guess," answered Drefke. "They have individuals with the necessary insight and imagination. Often their highly compartmentalized system keeps the people with the data from the people with the insight. In this case, however, one of their very best scientists has been in on it from the beginning, starting with the analysis of the events on the Novorossiisk. Academician Viktor Korolev."

There were several nods of recognition around the table. Korolev's defense-related work was known to many of them.

"We think," Drefke continued, "that it is very likely that, faced with the same data, Korolev would come to the same conclusions that we have."

"Where did this thing come from then?" the chairman of the National Security Council demanded. "Outer space?" He glanced at the Secretary of State. "Why do they think we had anything to do with it?"

"Those questions are closely related," Drefke said. "I want you to follow the logic so that you can see that the Russians, Korolev, have probably done the same thing. I would like Bob Isaacs to lay that out for you and report what he found today."

"Very well," said the President, "Mr. Isaacs, why don't you proceed?"

Isaacs stood, fighting the fatigue of his hectic day, images flashing: the discovery of Krone's lab, the race to New Mexico, the machine, the encounter with Krone and the woman, Latvin, the flight back. He had to admire Drefke's presentation, a politician who'd scarcely heard of the phrase black hole a day earlier. He moved behind Drefke to the projector, switched it on, and picked up a laser pointer, as the officials swiveled in their chairs toward the screen.

"I'm going to leave out some of the background details for now," he said, pushing a button to advance through a number of the slides Gantt and Phillips had prepared, until he came to the one he wanted.

"This," he said, "is an illustration of the path the black hole takes when it comes out of the earth, rises to a peak, and falls back in. It will then go through the earth and come out the other side. For now, I want you to concentrate on the fact that it rises to a fixed height each time. We can determine the amount of time it is above the earth's surface, and that tells us how far up it goes. The answer is fifty-seven hundred feet. The simplest hypothesis is that it was formed somewhere at that altitude and always returns to that height as it swings in orbit through the earth."

He pushed the button and advanced the projector to a map of the earth centered on the western hemisphere. He used the laser pointer to mark twin red horizontal lines.

"Here you see the path where the orbit intersects the earth's surface, one line in the north through Dallas and Nagasaki, another in the south. As you have heard, we obtained hard evidence that we were dealing with a black hole only yesterday. We immediately did an orbital survey of every point on those two red lines that was at an altitude of fifty-seven hundred feet. You can see there are not many, because of the broad expanses of ocean and low terrain, but it still took some time. You can appreciate that with the orbital path and timing data, the Russians can follow the same procedure. All the locations of interest were empty save one."

Isaacs paused and looked at the floor as he gently cleared his throat. He looked up and found, not to his surprise, that he was the center of undivided attention. He pointed to the map.

"That exception is here in New Mexico, east of the White Sands proving grounds and just south of the Mescalero Apache reservation in the Sacramento Mountain Range."

"Wait a minute now," the President said excitedly. "New Mexico? You're claiming this thing was made in New Mexico?"

Isaacs flipped through several more slides to reveal a blown-up photograph.

"This is a satellite photograph of the point of interest taken late yesterday afternoon," he explained.

All around the table the members of the council peered intently at the complex of buildings perched on top of a mountain range.

"We found out this morning that it's a private research laboratory, subcontracted to the Los Alamos Scientific Laboratory, two hundred miles to the north. The man who runs it is Paul Krone."

"Krone? Of Krone Industries?" the President inquired.

"Yes, sir," answered Isaacs.

The President exchanged a glance with Drefke. They both knew that Krone had heavily financed his opponent in the last election.

"And now you're going to tell me he made a black hole? There?" The President extended a pin-striped arm and pointed a finger at the slide without removing his eyes from Isaacs. "At a government sponsored laboratory? Right in our own backyard? Without our knowledge? Without *my* knowledge?"

"Yes, sir, that seems to be the case. When we discovered the site this morning, I took a team for an emergency visit to confirm our suspicions.

"There is a machine in this building," Isaacs said, using the pointer on the screen, "the details of which we do not understand. But it is of gigantic proportions and appears to have consumed the rock missing from this ridge." He pointed to the bare patch of mountain top bordering the lab. "That's about a hundred million tons of rock, and the strong circumstantial evidence is that it was compressed by this machine to produce the black hole.

"We then proceeded to a home which Krone maintains near the lab. We found him in a semi-catatonic state. He attempted to commit suicide about four months ago and has some brain damage. We recovered from his study a set of laboratory notebooks, of which this is one."

Isaacs stepped around behind Drefke, picked up the lab book from his place and walked half the length of the table to set it by the President's elbow.

"We haven't had time to study them, but they seem to contain a complete record of Krone's experiments which led to the creation of the black hole. There may also be important computer files."

"It's burned!" exclaimed the President.

"Yes, unfortunately. A woman who lived with Krone attempted to burn them. It was a ruse on her part to distract us while she smuggled Krone out the back door. Some were badly damaged before we could stop her."

"She smuggled him out? While you were there?" The President was incredulous. "Where are they now?"

"The woman got away with him, at least temporarily. They're somewhere in the mountains. We have air and ground search parties after them."

"Who is this woman?" the Chairman of the NSC inquired.

"Her name is Maria Latvin. She's apparently a refugee," Isaacs explained. "From Lithuania. Krone met her in Vienna after she escaped, and she's been living with him ever since."

"A plant?" the Chairman asked.

"Not that we can tell," Isaacs answered. "We're still looking into her background, but the escape from Czechoslovakia seems genuine enough. It's in Krone's character to take up with such a person, to flaunt the possible security risks."

"Why would she run off with Krone?" the Chairman pressed.

"We haven't come up with any motive yet."

The President slumped back in his chair.

"All right, let me summarize this." He shook his head in dismay. "Krone somehow eats a mountain at government expense and makes a black hole. That black hole punches a hole in this damn Russian carrier?" He looked at Drefke, who nodded his assent. "The Russians from some perverse instinct, which turns out to be right, assume we are at fault, and start our first space war.

"I thought we had everything fought to a standstill up there," he jerked a thumb at the ceiling, "eyeball to eyeball, and all that, and all of a sudden they don't just blink, they haul out a baseball bat and crack me upside the head. And turn all our low orbit stuff into a damn shooting gallery with their laser. God knows what else they've got in mind.

"Now, Howard," he turned to look at his Director of Central Intelligence, "you seem to be saying that what's happened is that the Russians have followed the clues and deduced that we made a black hole there and are more convinced than ever that we're out to get them."

Drefke straightened in his chair, his thoughts equally divided between the crisis before them and the years of friendship with the man at the center of the table. Those years would be swept away if he didn't handle this properly.

"We have no final proof, although we are working through our contacts in the Soviet Union to find out just what they know. The circumstances strongly suggest that they reached the conclusion at virtually the same time we did, that we manufactured a black hole there. Blowing up our nuclear satellite was apparently their way of letting us know that they're on to us."

"Mr. President."

All eyes turned to General Whitehead, the Chairman of the Joint Chiefs of Staff. He was a large man with bristly close-cropped hair and, at this hour, stubble on his stern jaw to match.

"I've been out of my element with this black hole stuff, but now we are beginning to get into my territory. As I see it, we need to get the Russians back into their corner while we sort all this out. First of all, we need to make crystal clear to them that they've absolutely got to put a cap on any escalation of the current situation. All this skeet shooting they've been doing is one thing, but if they so much as scorch a surveillance satellite, they had better put their population on alert. I also recommend we go after that laser again, to give ourselves some breathing room."

Drefke ignored the General and spoke to the President again.

"The immediate task before us is to defuse the anxiety of the Russians, not to scare them further. I think that candor is the best policy here. I recommend you tell them everything we know, give them all our data and let them reach their own conclusions. Yes, there is a black hole. Yes, it was made at that site," he gestured at the slide. "That should add to our credibility. We must convince them that it was an accident, not an offensive act."

"I agree with that sentiment," the Secretary of the State firmly announced. "Mr. President, the problem we face here is a unique one. We must bear in mind that, although a U.S. Government lab is involved, the threat is a universal one. I believe it is incumbent upon us to share the information we now have not just with the Soviet Union, but with all our major allies, the People's Republic, and the Third World."

There were outbursts of protest. The National Security Advisor finally gained the floor.

"Mr. President, I sympathize with the desire of the Secretary for openness and candor, but it seems to me premature to broadcast this problem until we fully understand all the ramifications. At all costs, we must avoid the widespread dissemination of this information and the panic that would ensue."

"We already know the basic nature of the problem," protested the Secretary, "and we may very well need to call on the resources of other countries to devise a solution."

"This country has plenty of resources on its own," rumbled General Whitehead, "and in any case I don't like telling the Communists any more than we have to." He shot a glance at Drefke. "There's no way they won't twist this around and throw it in our face, or somehow use it as a lever against us. We should keep the Russians on a short leash and the Chinese should certainly be kept out of it."

"I don't disagree that the Chinese have very little to offer us in the current context," the Secretary appealed to the President, "but for the sake of our future relations with them we must keep them apprised of a problem of this magnitude and of such universal concern. The same argument applies even more strongly to our allies."

"If these fellows are right," replied the General, gesturing with a thumb toward Isaacs and Drefke, "we may not need to worry about future relations."

"And if that is the case," rebutted the Secretary, "there is certainly no point in maintaining your cold war mentality toward the rest of the world. On the contrary, we can throw out the historical constraints and solicit the aid of the world community to tackle this common menace."

"Rot!" said the General, heatedly. "If knowledge of this

situation becomes widespread, it will just put more pressure on everyone. There will be an every-man-for-himself scramble, and the world political situation will go to hell in a handbasket."

"If we sit on this until it is too late," the Secretary insisted, "and then spring the problem on the world, something like you describe may well occur. That is why it is of the utmost importance to proceed immediately and discretely to inform others of the situation so that a cooperative and measured response can be orchestrated."

"Mr. President," the Security Advisor cut in, "I think we must make a guarded release of information to the Soviets. We must make them understand we are aware of the problem and taking active steps to explore the facts. I believe we must also inform our closest allies of the basic situation. They deserve to know what has caused the Soviets to react so dangerously. I confess I would proceed gingerly in spreading this information any further than absolutely necessary. I would suggest holding off with the Chinese and the Third World countries."

While the Security Advisor was speaking, an aide came in and handed the President a message.

"Hold it!" he said, cutting off the Secretary of State, whose mouth was open to reply. The President read the message through again, then looked around the table.

"We may not have the luxury of designing our response to the Soviets. I have here a message from Colonel Grigor Zamyatin, head of Washington KGB." He turned to fix first Drefke and then Isaacs with a steely glare. "It says that fifteen minutes ago Paul Krone and Maria Latvin were put on an Aeroflot flight from Mexico City to Moscow."

Isaacs felt the room spin and his hurriedly consumed meal congeal into a knot.

"Colonel Zamyatin would like an audience," the President continued. "He's waiting at the front gate."

"You can't have him in here," General Whitehead protested.

"Show him in," the President addressed his aide.

The room was deathly quiet as they awaited the arrival of the Russian. Isaacs strained to understand what had happened. Had Latvin been a spy? How could she have known what Krone was up to when his own government didn't? Or was she put onto Krone on general principles and just happened to hit the jackpot?

The door opened and the aide ushered Zamyatin in. He walked to his left along the wall until he was directly across the table from the President. The President nodded and there was some shuffling to vacate that chair. Zamyatin sat in it with deliberate calm.

"Colonel." The President greeted him. "I'm rather surprised Ambassador Ogarkov is not bringing whatever message you bear."

"When the river reaches floodtide, new channels are carved," Zamyatin replied. "I assure you my authority comes from the highest levels."

"That will, of course, be checked," the President responded. "Am I to understand, Colonel, that you have openly confessed to the abduction of an American citizen?"

"Ah, you attempt to seize the initiative," Zamyatin replied, unruffled. "But you have a weak hand. Of course we have taken him, and the event pales next to the heinous act the individual committed, the one for which you are ultimately responsible."

"What act are you talking about?"

The Russian left the question hanging for a long moment. "If you are going to be stubborn," he finally said, "this discussion can be carried on in a more public forum."

The President met his hard gaze, and again there was silence.

"Why did you take him?" the President asked.

"We intend to know everything there is to know about this crime against humanity. Paul Krone is the ultimate source of that information."

"He must be returned to us."

"Ah," said Zamyatin, "precisely what we had in mind." He enjoyed the look of surprise that flashed on the President's face. "We would like to return Dr. Krone to you along with his charming companion."

"You just kidnapped him; now you want to return him," the President said, with mild scorn. "What's the rest of the deal?"

"The deal," Zamyatin said carefully, "the deal is an exchange. The two people for the complete set of those." His eyes went to the charred lab book that still sat, momentarily overlooked, beside the President. "Krone is of no use to us in his present state. We want those lab books and any other written or computerized records."

"Mr. President," General Whitehead said in a low warning voice, "we don't know what sort of valuable information may be in those."

"Of course you don't," Zamyatin snapped, his gaze fixed on the President, "not the way you have bungled this affair. Mr. President, there is undoubtedly information in those books that would be considered priceless for defense matters under ordinary circumstances. We are not concerned with that now, nor can you afford to be.

"Mr. President," the Russian's voice turned cold and hard, "you have delivered a mortal blow to my country, your country, the very planet itself. There is the merest wisp of hope that the peril can be removed. The Soviet Union is prepared to take any steps that may rescue us from the monumental insanity which you have visited upon us.

"First," he continued in a matter-of-fact tone, "we must understand the problem in minute detail. That means knowing what is in those books and other records, and in the mind of Paul Krone. We have Krone, you have the records and the sophisticated medical techniques that may restore Krone's health. We will swap."

"You must return Krone," the President said firmly, "but we do not need your spy; you can keep the woman."

"Spy?" Zamyatin cracked a small smile. "Yes, she is one of us, an illegal escapee, but no spy. Let us say she was merely susceptible to persuasion, a family in the old country, you understand? And you do need her. She is the only contact with the man. Yes, we could keep her, exact the usual punishment, but we believe her presence will hasten the day that Krone becomes rational and useful. You see we are trying to be reasonable.

"Of course," the Russian shrugged, "we will also send a more reliable representative to monitor your progress with Krone. We expect you to relay to us every scrap you learn from him."

"That's outrageous," the President said, "you can't expect us to put one of our citizens under a microscope for your pleasure."

"The outrage has already been committed," Zamyatin replied, coolly. "You will put Krone under that microscope to serve your own ends. We are merely asking you to share the proceeds.

"Mr. President," Zamyatin continued, his voice suddenly friendly, "I think you do not adequately appreciate the spirit of the offer we are making. There is no shrinking from your ultimate responsibility here, but the problem is immense and complex. We do not demand Krone and his records. You will have Krone and his machine, and, of course, you will keep a copy of the records. We must share this information and seek a common solution to our common peril.

"The seeds of cooperation on this problem have already been planted." The Russian glanced for the first time at Isaacs. Although no one else seemed to notice, Isaacs felt as if a spotlight had just been turned on him. His heart raced, and he could feel his face flush.

"To further this spirit," Zamyatin continued, "we will make

the following additional offer. Mr. President, you know Academician Korolev, our distinguished scientist?"

"Yes, of course I do," the President replied tentatively.

"Academician Korolev took an early and active interest in this problem. You know that he is crucial to our defense effort and has never been allowed to travel to the West. Mr. President, as a gesture of good will and of our intention to hasten the day when a solution may be devised, we are prepared to place Korolev at your disposal as our scientific ambassador.

"Mr. President," Zamyatin continued, cordial and reasonable, "I do not expect a reply to our offers just now. I deduce you have only just learned of the problem. You will need some time to fully appreciate the situation, and the generosity of the proposals I have presented. I would remind you that there are factions in my government that are not amenable to such a cooperative approach. There are some who would advocate immediate public exposure, an attempt to wrest full propaganda value from your predicament. Others would contemplate far more serious and direct reprisals.

"Before I go, there is one other thing. I stress that we have proposed a cooperative approach to the problem at hand. We presume that you do not want the situation and your role in it to become widely known. We will follow your lead in such matters if you will but cooperate with us in one other regard. The problem with which we are now faced arose from a certain line of investigation."

The Russian paused, holding the eyes of the President.

"We ask that you immediately cease all research and development on beam weapons and related technology."

The room filled with a crescendo of outrage. General Whitehead was among the loudest, shouting, "I knew it, I knew they'd turn this against us."

Zamyatin rose and departed, as if oblivious to the uproar his demand had caused.

"Mr. President," General Whitehead continued to shout,

"we cannot even think of responding to that crap. If we make the slightest concession there, they'll come after our nuclear arms."

The President cracked a loud palm down on the table, resulting in a rapid, strained silence.

"It's nearly one a.m.," the President said. "I'm going to adjourn this meeting. I want you all on call by six. In the meantime," he addressed his National Security Advisor, "I want to know precisely the line of authority Zamyatin represents and the makeup of the other factions he mentioned." He turned toward Drefke. "Howard, I want you, Isaacs and Professor Phillips to stay. I need a little more perspective on this."

The President led them to an upstairs study and poured brandy all around. They sat in silence for awhile, each man trying to assimilate the rush of events in his own perspective. For Isaacs, the shock of Zamyatin's announcements had waned, and he could feel the deep fatigue again, but he carried a burden he knew he must unload. He appreciated Drefke's attempt, not completely altruistic, to avoid mention of Isaacs' communications with Korolev. For that matter, Zamyatin could have roasted him, but chose not to. He knew, though, that the President could not reach a cogent decision without knowing all the background. From a strictly personal point of view, he would be better off confessing his involvement with the Russians rather than having the President discover it, as he surely would. He broke the silence.

"Mr. President." The eyes of the three men swiveled to him. "I have been in on this affair from the beginning. There are some things about Zamyatin and Korolev you need to know."

Drefke lifted his eyebrows in surprise, but remained silent.

"Let's hear what's on your mind," the President said.

"I have been aware for some time," said Isaacs, searching for the right words, "that there is a contingent in the Soviet

Union which has some sympathy for our situation. I believe Academician Korolev is a key person in that contingent. I think that he has led them to the understanding that we are dealing with a black hole and that it was made here, but I think he recognizes the true nature of the problem, that it transcends geopolitics. Korolev is under pressure; he had to tell them what he knew. But he is sympathetic to us, and he had influence there. I believe the offer to have him work with us is highly significant, both scientifically and politically. Mr. President, I think it is crucial that we reach out to the people Korolev represents."

"Even though they demand we abandon our research on beam weapons, giving them full head to develop an anti-missile technology unilaterally?"

Isaacs had no reply to that.

The President looked sharply at Isaacs. "How can you be so sure that this one man can and will be of help to us?"

Isaacs knew what was coming. He looked at the floor and then back at the President. "I've been in touch with him," he mumbled.

"What was that?" the President demanded.

"I said, I've been in touch with him," Isaacs replied.

Phillips stared at Isaacs in surprise. Isaacs vividly recalled his private conversation with the physicist in La Jolla, his suppressed desire to confess his communications with Korolev.

"You mean the Agency has?" the President asked.

"No sir, it was a personal correspondence."

"Personal?" the President blurted. "You mean to say you've been communicating with Korolev directly? On the most sensitive issue of the decade? Goddamnit, Howard," he turned to Drefke, "don't your people know what channels are for? I've got black holes in my back yard, laser cannons in the front, and hired hands sending post cards back and forth discussing policy!"

"At the time there were extenuating circumstances," Isaacs attempted to explain.

"Extenuating?" the President exclaimed. "May I ask just what you and Korolev were discussing behind my back, that you didn't care to have me know?"

"I knew that Korolev was in charge of the Novorossiisk investigation, that he was puzzled and frustrated by it. That much was clear from official communications. Our effort was bogged down after the Stinson was sunk.

"Frankly, sir," Isaacs continued, "I was frightened. I thought something was sinking ships, triggering a global confrontation. For a variety of reasons, my efforts were stymied. I thought that Korolev might have more luck getting to the bottom of things."

Isaacs rolled the brandy snifter in his hands. "I told Korolev about the seismic signal and my suspicion that it was related to the damage to both ships."

"You told him that?" The President was angry and bewildered. "You gave us away? Virtually inviting him to look for and find the black hole and pin it on us?" He rose and paced to a window, peering into the dark outside.

Isaacs spoke to his back, trying to explain more than defend his actions. "I had no idea we were dealing with a black hole at the time, certainly not that we were in any way responsible."

The President turned from the window and spoke to Drefke. "My god, Howard, you sandbagged me! Did you know your man had been talking to the Russians? This borders on treason."

"Jim," implored Drefke, falling into old, first name habits, "it was a lot more complicated than that. Yes, I did know it, and I had already had it out with him. It's not what it seems. You can't take it out of context."

"Why don't you just put it into context for me then?" The President was still angry, frustrated at events that had spun so rapidly out of his control.

"The simple fact is that we wouldn't be anywhere on this thing if it weren't for Isaacs here," Drefke continued his appeal. "The black hole would still be there, eating away, and we wouldn't have the faintest idea. This thing was bound to blow up in our face one way or another. We know that after the Novorossiisk, one thing led to another and we've gotten into a fine jam over it, but we would still have no idea why. Isaacs broke every rule in the book to reach out to Korolev, but I agree with him that that contact is probably our only way out of this problem. Without Korolev, we could be dealing with a bunch of generals ready, anxious, to finger the button.

"As it is," he continued, "there is some evidence that the Russians have been calmer to react than they would have been if Isaacs hadn't been in touch with Korolev."

"Calmer?" The President was incredulous. "They just blew our nuke out of the sky!"

"They were on the verge of it six weeks ago, when they first put up the hunter-killers. Cooler heads prevailed, and we have reason to believe that Korolev was instrumental."

"How do you know that?"

"We got it from Zamyatin."

"From Zamyatin? What the hell is his role in all this?"

"We don't fully understand. His appearance this evening was a total surprise to us. But he does seem to be in Korolev's camp. He's been the liaison between Korolev and Isaacs."

"Oh, for crying out loud!" The President returned and dropped back into his armchair, slopping brandy over the side of his snifter and onto the carpet. "Honest to god, Howard, how am I supposed to run this country if things like this are going on behind my back."

"Jim, this has been a complex and rapidly changing situation. We have only begun to appreciate the stakes in the last couple of weeks, to see how it all ties together. You've got to look at the signals," Drefke implored. "There are people over there trying to understand, trying to keep a lid on things. Sure, they're trying to get some advantage from it; they have to cover their own asses internally. But we still have to seek them out, appeal to the rational ones who see the common danger if we're going to keep the crazies in check. We need to pacify the Russians and figure out what to do with this damnable black hole, but we must tackle both problems together. We've got to open up and work with them on this thing. If we don't, they'll cram it all down our throats, the black hole, their laser, everything."

Drefke stared at the familiar figure, unsure whether his arguments were effective.

Isaacs had scarcely breathed during the intense discussion. He appreciated Drefke's stout support and thought that the Director had established his moral motivation as well as possible. Still, his breach was massive. There were immutable political forces once such things came to the attention of the President. Without seeing the specifics, Isaacs numbly recognized that his career at the Agency was over.

The President got up and went to the serving cart. He put down the sticky glass and poured some more brandy into a fresh one. He sat and took a reflective sip. After a moment he said, "Let's put aside the political factors for now. I need to get some feeling for the broader perspective.

"You say," the President continued, looking at Drefke, "that this black hole is consuming the earth, that the earth is falling into it, as you remarked previously. But apparently there is little directly noticeable effect now. How soon before we have an emergency on our hands? That is to say, a public emergency?"

"That's a difficult question to answer," Drefke said, glancing quickly away from the President to Isaacs and Phillips and then back. "The ultimate danger is apparently many generations away. But let me stress that although that is farther in the future than we are normally used to dealing, the threat is real and implacable."

"But what is the future course of this thing?" the President asked. "Professor Phillips, I haven't heard from you. What is your prognosis?"

Phillips set aside his brandy and clasped his fingers in his lap before replying.

"If it continues on its course," Phillips said, "there will be a phase of increasingly violent earthquakes. As the object grows bigger it will be able to trigger large earthquakes by releasing stress already stored along fault lines. At a somewhat later stage the tunnels themselves created by the passage of the object will be so large that their collapse will engender a continuing series of major earthquakes. As the hole grows even larger, the earth will begin to orbit it. The oceans will be sloshed from their basins by huge tides. The earthquakes will grow in magnitude until the whole earth is rent by them and totally uninhabitable. In the final stage, all the material of the earth will be consumed, and only the black hole grown to about this size will be left orbiting the sun." He made an OK sign for illustration.

Silence filled the room as Phillips finished his description. The President stared into his glass. He gave his head a small shake and looked up toward Phillips. "I must ask again how long it will be before this thing becomes overtly dangerous in the way you have just described? With the earthquakes and tidal waves?"

"Such a thing could happen now," Phillips said, "particularly in the Far East or along the coast of California where the orbital plane intersects regions of tectonic activity."

"But when will such things begin to occur with regularity?" the President inquired.

"Very difficult to answer," Phillips shook his head, "perhaps a hundred years, maybe as much as a thousand."

"In a sense then, we have that long before we must cope with this thing directly," the President asserted, "that long before massive deaths begin to occur."

Phillips thought for a moment. "Yes, the hole will become a deadly menace at some point, but that may not be a measure of our grace period in terms of taking active steps against it."

The President raised an eyebrow in question. Phillips unclasped his hands to draw an elliptical path in the air with his finger. "As the hole follows its orbit, it is subject to drag forces as the inevitable adjunct of its consuming the matter of the earth. These drag forces will slowly cause the hole to spiral to the center of the earth. After a certain period of time, the orbit of the hole will no longer carry it above the surface of the earth. After that it will be totally inaccessible to us and our fate will be truly sealed. Right now it is difficult to say whether the hole will disappear beneath the surface before or after the massive earthquakes begin. We will not have to rely on theoretical estimates for long, however. Observations currently underway will tell us directly how fast the settling is occurring even if we have no accurate way of predicting when regular extensive damage will begin."

The President rested his forehead against his hand, leaning on the arm of the chair. He rotated his head from that position and once more inquired of Phillips, "There remains one more major question then, doesn't there?" He looked straight into Phillips' eyes. "What can we do about it?"

Phillips returned the President's gaze forthrightly. "Mr. President, on this issue I must be perfectly candid. So far none of our discussions have produced a glimmer of cause for optimism."

Phillips glanced at the other two men and then returned his attention to the President. "Understand that I do not mean that we must accept defeat. We have only just begun to study the problem, and it would be foolhardy to suggest that because a possible solution is not apparent now that one will not be forthcoming in the future, if enough ingenuity and manpower are brought to bear. But it would be equally foolhardy to minimize the magnitude of the problem. This object is so tiny and so massive that it cannot be moved except by the most titanic of forces. My colleagues and I are far from ready to give up on the problem, but we must all be prepared to concede at some point that there is no solution. It certainly is conceivable that the earth is doomed."

The President absorbed the gloomy assessment. "Well, we can't give up without a fight. You spoke of manpower and ingenuity, Professor. What can this office do to provide the resources necessary to find a solution to this problem, presuming one exists?"

"Just now the stress must be more on ingenuity than brute manpower," replied Phillips. "At the present stage we need an idea, or set of ideas, some hint of a useful program. Then I imagine that a massive engineering program such as the Manhattan Project or the Apollo program would be called for."

"From the scientific point of view," the President rubbed a hand over tired eyes, "can we proceed without the Russians?"

Phillips pondered his answer. "I appreciate the dilemma you are in. You cannot lightly submit to coercion. We have many great scientists in this country, men and women who would gladly give up careers of research to work with you on this. Perhaps, no, we don't need the Russians in that sense. But you ask me as a scientist. I will tell you this. I do not know the depth of Korolev's political connections, although I have every reason to believe that he has great influence. But I do know that there is no brain on earth that I would rather have working on this problem than that of Viktor Korolev."

The President nodded, then spoke. "Gentlemen, I have much to think about. Please keep yourselves on call."

They left the White House by a side exit and climbed into Drefke's waiting limousine which whisked them away through the quiet Washington streets.

Chapter 19

On the evening of January 5th, a taxi made its way from Logan Airport, skirting the Charles River along the edge of Boston. Eventually, it came to Newton and slowed on the tortuous suburban streets. The air was noticeably colder outside the city, and the snowflakes fell more thickly. The passengers huddled in the corners of the flat Checker seat listening to the wheels plow through the slush. The smaller figure tried to ignore the stream of frigid air which came from his window which would not quite close. He wore a topcoat, but shivered from lack of natural insulation. The man was in his early forties, of average height, thin to the point of frailness. His head was round in profile, but thin so his face was a flattened oval. His sparse hair was combed straight back; a trim Vandyke adorned his chin. He wore old nondescript horn-rim glasses, the temples of which showed the grey corrosion of long exposure to facial grease.

The other passenger was a large, hulking man. His coarse slavic features were broken by a relaxed smile as he looked out at the snow. His bulky winter coat was undone to display a grey suit of plain utilitarian cut. His mind spun with the excitement of his first visit here, and his eyes had captured all the details—from the gross flashing signs atop Kenmore Square to the fine old houses with large yards they now passed by.

The taxi finally pulled up in front of a large white house on which the porch light signaled welcome. The cabbie flicked the plexiglass partition open without looking back, disgruntled at the thought of the long trip back to the airport without a fare and scheming for a way to cover that loss. The slim passenger grimaced at the figure on the meter despite it being covered by his expense account and shoved some bills through to the driver, waving for him to keep the change. The driver showed his gratitude by remaining immobile while his passengers worked the doors open and stepped out. The smaller man's left foot landed ankle deep in water in the gutter. He uttered a quiet exclamation of dismay, shoved the door shut and stepped gingerly to the plowed walkway leading to the front door. He navigated the cleared path, waited for his companion, then pushed the button as he stomped his wet shoe.

Inside Wayne Phillips rose quickly from the couch and got to the door just before his wife who had come in from the kitchen. He opened the door and greeted the men on the stoop.

"Clarence! Viktor! Come in!"

He turned to his wife, "Betsy, you remember Clarence Humphreys from Princeton? And I would like you to meet my good friend and colleague, Viktor Korolev, from the Soviet Union. They've been working together in Moscow on our project."

"Of course," she nodded, "how are you? I'm afraid we've welcomed you with rather dismal weather." She spoke with a

British accent, being a lifelong cherished companion from Phillips' youth at Oxford.

Helping Humphreys off with his topcoat, Phillips was too close to notice the soggy shoe. From her vantage point a few feet off and blessed with an eye for such things, his wife saw it and gave a small gasp.

"Oh, my! You've stepped in a puddle!"

Humphreys acknowledged this misfortune sheepishly.

Betsy Phillips immediately took complete control.

"Here. You sit down before the fire and get those wet, cold shoes off. Professor Korolev, won't you sit here? I'll fetch a pair of Wayne's slippers and fix you both a nice hot toddy." She guided her guests toward chairs in front of the fireplace. Alex Runyan arose from the couch, his right arm encased in a sling.

"Viktor, welcome to the United States." He pumped the Russian's hand awkwardly, backward, with his left hand. "After all these years—such a delight to have you here. When your name came up in La Jolla, I never actually thought I'd see you working with us." He turned to the other scientist. "Clarence, how are things in Moscow?"

"Hello, Alex," Humphreys returned the greeting. "Well, it's snowing there too, but the rivers are still in their banks." He lifted his wet foot and both men grinned.

Humphreys sat and with a disdain for propriety which belied his academic standing, quickly removed his shoes and socks. He extended white, blue-veined feet toward the fire and wiggled his toes. Korolev looked around the room. It was large and tastefully decorated, mostly in colonial, in keeping with the house which dated back to shortly after the Revolution. The floors were original, wide planks held down with wooden pegs. He was admiring a large heavily decorated Christmas tree in the corner when Betsy Phillips returned with a pair of faintly scruffy slippers and a tray upon which she balanced two steaming concoctions in tall glasses. Humphreys slid his feet into the slippers and smiled gratefully.

The Russian toasted her with his glass and smiled his broad smile.

"I'm glad you could stop over before we have to go to Washington," Phillips said, after his wife had discreetly retired. "That is when the real work will begin, but Alex and I are anxious for a chance to hear your ideas while there is still a little peace and quiet. I understand Krone's notes have been useful?"

"Absolutely! They're invaluable," said Humphreys enthusiastically. "The man understood an incredible amount, and there's an even greater wealth of information implicit in the computer data that will require years to completely analyze. We've only had time to scratch the surface."

Humphreys looked at his Russian colleague.

"Things have been so hectic. We've been under tremendous pressure to digest those notebooks."

He spoke to Phillips and Runyan.

"I want both of you to know what an immense help Viktor has been. More than that, most of the time I have foundered in his wake."

Korolev nodded in silent sober acquiescence at the praise.

"I don't know what bolt of enlightenment hit the Soviet hierarchy," Humphreys continued, "volunteering his services for this project when he was not even allowed to attend a conference before. Anyway, we should all be grateful."

"Ho," said the Russian in his deep rumbling baritone. "I explain certain facts to them. Sometimes they understand. But this is a complicated thing. Your government. My government." He waved a hand in dismissal and tossed down a healthy slug of his drink.

"The fire was unfortunate," Korolev said. "Some important things are missing."

"Viktor has filled in most of the missing parts," Humphreys explained, "but there are a couple of awkward gaps. The books weren't the only casualty. I'd heard you'd been hurt, Alex. How's the arm?"

Runyan flexed his fingers slowly. "I had surgery again a month ago," he said. "Damn tendons are tough to heal." He leaned back and fingered his beard to show the scar on his jaw. "Got me in the chin and arm with one blow. Tough lady, let me tell you."

Humphreys shook his head in sympathy.

"Where is this man Krone now?" Korolev inquired. "I must talk with him."

"Unfortunately, he's in no condition to talk even yet," Runyan explained. "He's in Walter Reed Hospital, and they're doing everything they can to bring him around."

"How about the woman?" Humphreys asked.

"Well, under the circumstances, I didn't press charges. Everything she did was under coercion. She's got an apartment in Washington I hear and visits Krone daily. The doctors think she is a beneficial factor." Runyan stared into the fire, recalling his encounter with Maria Latvin, and shivered slightly.

"Listen," Runyan brightened, shaking off his reverie, "we want to hear more about this idea of yours. You think you have some way of attacking the hole?"

"Well, it's not fully worked out yet," said Humphreys, "but we do have a proposal. I wish we had a bit more time. I'm not so sure how we will fare trying to convince the President and his advisors of its workability."

"Try it out on us," encouraged Phillips. "You suggested in your letter that stimulated emission was involved?"

"That's right. You know how the principle works in lasers. Atoms are energized and ready to emit a photon of light. Then if a seed photon is sent in, it stimulates one of the atoms to emit an identical photon. The two photons then induce the emission of two more identical photons, the four become eight, the eight, sixteen and so on, leading to a chain reaction.

"The same process can be made to work on any system which radiates. If a thing emits photons spontaneously, then it can be induced to emit photons on cue under the proper circumstances. Viktor pointed out that, in particular, this applies to black holes. We know that because of the quantum mechanical uncertainty principle, the event horizon of a black hole is slightly fuzzy and that light leaks out. Every black hole slowly radiates away its substance. The question is, can our black hole be stimulated to radiate away its mass and disappear faster than it would ordinarily?"

Humphreys stopped and took a sip of his drink. Runyan, his mind churning, fixed him with a stare.

"You would need an intense source of light then," said Runyan, gesturing with his good left hand as if trying to conjure up such a source on the spot.

"Yes," answered Humphreys, "and it needs to be focussed since the target is so small."

"A laser then," said Phillips quietly.

"Right," Humphreys addressed him. "We think a super powerful laser could be fashioned which could siphon off some of the mass of the hole. Even more," he paused, "there are hints from Krone's notes that such a process could be even more efficient than the basic first order theory would indicate. We haven't worked it all out yet, but certain of his data suggest the existence of nonlinear effects which could improve the efficiency of the stimulated emission dramatically."

"Just how dramatic is that?" asked Runyan. "You don't want to liberate too much energy too fast—Mc^2 for that hole is a lot of E."

"There is no way to eliminate the hole in one step with any foreseeable technology, and, indeed, we would not want to if we could, as you rightly point out," replied Humphreys. "If what I'm suggesting works at all, the best we can hope for is to peel a little bit of mass off at a time and to repeat the process many, many times.

"Viktor has also devised an interesting variation on that

theme. A properly shaped initiating blast may cause the bulk of the energy to be liberated in one direction. We might be able to guide the impulse in such a way to offset the drag and keep the hole from settling prematurely completely into the earth. Our hope is to boost the orbit so that it is totally outside the earth. Then little by little we could widen the orbit and eventually set it adrift into interstellar space.

"If the process must be repeated a thousand times to gain control, we have hope. A million times? Well, we should begin looking for a new home."

"Do you have any idea how effective the process will be?" inquired Phillips, maintaining his quiet demeanor.

"It depends on the relative efficiency for the production of photons and particles with mass: electrons, protons, neutrons. There will also be neutrinos. The particles are the most efficient repository for mass and momentum, from our point of view. The neutrinos can in principle carry off a large amount of energy. If the process works at all, there should be a large explosion.

"To answer your question, Wayne," Humphreys continued, "our current estimates are that the hole could be nudged out of the earth with about a hundred thousand repetitions, each releasing about the explosive energy of a ten megaton bomb. Those numbers are very tentative. They could be off by a factor of a hundred either way."

"Your recommendation then?" Phillips wanted to know.

"Put every talented scientist available on the analysis of Krone's notes, and begin the design and engineering of the necessary laser. The first goal is to run a field test to see whether it works. Then go into full scale mass production. The lasers will be immense and expensive, and, if the process works, you'll destroy them every time."

"We must also worry about the others," rumbled Korolev, "the three he made first."

"As I understand it," Runyan said, "our government and

yours are analyzing every scrap of seismic and sonar data available. I think one of them has been found."

Phillips swirled his drink and took a reflective sip of it.

"Viktor," he said, "I think there's no question that you and Clarence are to be congratulated for coming up with such a clever and positive sounding approach. What about the practical problems, though? It strikes me that what you have suggested is going to be fiendishly difficult to accomplish in reality."

Korolev gave Phillips a long frank look devoid of the self-effacing geniality he had been displaying.

"This frightens me," he said. "I can think of no other way to proceed, but what we ask, to hit a rapidly moving, vanishingly small particle in just the right way—this is very difficult. By comparison, the moon is huge, your Apollo program a trivial exercise."

The Russian paused to rub his chin. "The stakes are very much higher now," he said in a ruminative tone. "If we fail, it is not just the prestige of a country that is at risk, but the future of all life." His head sunk on his chest, and he lost himself for a moment in the flicker from the grate. "We must try," he continued, "but some projects are too complex, too difficult, to be solved by any number of talented people, any amount of resources."

He was silent again for awhile. Then his head came up, and he leaned forward with a more earnest air. He gestured with an extended forefinger.

"Here are some of the problems we face. How do we make a laser which works at the energies most destructive to the black hole? The lasers must be huge, but they must swivel rapidly while maintaining infinitesimal accuracy. How do we do that? The operation must be computer controlled, but the task is monumental. I fear a new generation of computers must be invented just for that purpose alone."

The four men talked late into the night, analyzing the strengths and weaknesses of the plan and solutions to unprecedented engineering problems. The next morning they caught an early shuttle to Washington.

Four months later on a Saturday afternoon, Pat Danielson shouldered her way through the door of her new condominium, kicked the door shut with her foot, and set the bulky box of kitchen utensils down in the middle of the disarray. The room was piled with cardboard boxes pilfered from liquor and grocery stores. The only piece of furniture was a sofa bed which would have to do double duty until she could buy more furniture. She walked down the hallway to the left, sniffing the acrid, clashing odors of new carpet and paint, past the small bedroom she would use as a study and the bathroom opposite, and into the larger bedroom with its own bath and dressing area. She walked the length of the room to the curtainless window which faced the front of the complex and opened it to the fresh spring air. Looking straight down six stories, she could see the security guard structure at the front gate. Craning her neck to the right she could see, just past the small balcony jutting from her front room, the swimming pool sauna complex, and the tennis courts beyond. What a swinger, she kidded herself.

"Coffee's on!" she heard Janine shout from the kitchen.

Coffee? "How are you making coffee?" she called back as she retraced her steps down the hallway. Her old coffee pot was in the box she had just carried in. As she entered the front room she inhaled the delicious aroma and followed it into the kitchen. The cabinets were bare except for a new automatic drip coffee maker and a bag of freshly ground mocha java.

"Where did that come from?" Pat marveled.

"House present," Janine said. "From Alex Runyan. He stopped by while you were gone. He tried to call the apartment, but I guess you weren't there yet, or had left. Did you know he was in town?"

"I'm not too surprised. There's a meeting next week that I

thought he'd be involved in, but he's not a great one for advance notice."

"He said he had some business this afternoon, but would call you later."

"Great, and I'm supposed to hold my Saturday open until the last minute in case he shows up."

Janine was embarrassed by her friend's predicament and covered up by grabbing a couple of glasses off the counter.

"Well, at least we can drink his coffee. I couldn't find the cups. Can we make do with these?" She brandished the tumblers.

"Sure," Pat conceded. "It smells marvelous."

Janine filled the glasses three-quarters of the way to the top. "Watch out," she warned, "they'll be hot with no handles. Hold the top." She handed one to Danielson, and they moved through the tableless dining area into the living room.

Pat looked around at the piles of boxes, the sofa heaped with clothes, laughed, and sat on the floor, leaning against the wall, crossing her legs in front of her. Janine perched on the edge of a box. She lifted her glass, held gingerly by the upper rim.

"Here's to your promotion and new home, ex-roomie; may it become the den of iniquity you've always wanted."

Pat chuckled, "Fat chance of that."

They sat quietly, sipping the rich coffee, each lost in her own thoughts.

"Pat?"

"Um?"

"What's the matter between you and Alex? He's always seemed so charming to me."

Pat was silent for a moment.

"Would you go out with him?"

"Sure, I guess so."

"That's the problem. He'd take you up on it. Roommate or not. The truth is, of course, that I still find him fascinating. He knows so much about so many things. He's warm and engaging and can focus some sort of personal intensity that makes it easy to fall into the illusion that you're the only interesting person in the world."

Pat stopped to take a drink of coffee. "I think he really does like me. But he's got enough 'like' to spread it around pretty liberally. He separated from his wife, but, as they say, the chances of him settling down are between slim and zero."

Janine took a sip of her coffee and rolled the glass between her palms.

"Is he good in bed?"

"Hey!" Pat laughed. "What kind of question is that?" She leaned her head back against the wall staring at the white ceiling. She could feel Runyan's hands on her waist, his lips near her navel. "Yes, damn it," she said with resignation, "he's pretty good."

"Well, then," said Janine, with an impish sidelong glance at the sofa, "I suggest that we prepare yon piece for its proper initiation."

She drained her glass, set it down, and went to grab an armload of clothes off the sofa.

Pat laughed again as Janine disappeared down the hall.

"Thank you, lord," she said in a loud stage voice, "for delivering me at last from nosey, interfering roommates."

Then she stood and looked around. The last shall be first, she decided. She hefted the box of utensils she had most recently deposited and headed for the kitchen, bent on the task of imposing order in her new abode.

The following Friday, Robert Isaacs put the finishing touches on his report to Drefke as the setting sun sent lances of light through the blinds of his office windows then dropped below the wall of trees. He was tired, but exhilarated. The report concerned the epochal meeting which had begun early Monday and wound up after lunch Friday, a complete success. A small coterie of scientists from both sides of the Iron Curtain and a larger group of diplomats had come to unprecedented, unanimous agreement. The public confrontation would continue, but driven to a close and desperate cooperation, the two countries would, in complete secrecy, launch a massive joint effort to rid the world of Krone's creations.

If all went according to plan, in three or four years an international armada of ships would form a circle a hundred miles in radius in the expanse of the north Pacific. In the center of the circle would float an artificial, portable island. On the island would be an immensely powerful and complex piece of machinery designed for a suicide mission. The product of a dedicated, cooperative effort between the superpowers, it would produce intense beams of laser light, finely tuned and aimed by the gravitational pull of the black hole itself. Since there would be no way to control the orbit of the hole, the device would be located where orbit perturbations by irregularities in the earth were minimal. The position of the device would be precisely fixed by accurate orbital calculations to be steadily refined over the years.

In addition to settling on the basic engineering attack, there had been a host of ticklish political problems to resolve. Paramount had been the continuing demand by the Russians that the United States cease work on beam weapons. Isaacs had admired the consummate skill of the team from the State Department. They had pointed out how item after item which the Soviets wanted banned was, after all, related to the massive effort before them. Other projects they discarded spontaneously, activities that had to take second seat to the main effort anyway. Neither country had the resources to devote to full scale development of beam weapons when faced with the resource-devouring assault on the black hole. In the final analysis, the Soviets had enough concessions to feel they had accomplished their goal, and the United States did not feel significantly weakened politically in the process.

Another issue had been the manner in which to treat the

results of the test. If the project were successful, an explosion of considerable violence would ensue. Technically, it was not in violation of the Nuclear Test Ban Treaty, but in certain quarters all doubt must be forestalled, and that in turn called for an explanation of the predicament which demanded the undertaking. The NATO allies and Japan would be notified and sworn to secrecy and certain aid would be solicited from them. All would be allowed observers stationed at the site.

Dissension over the role of the Chinese had nearly split the meeting, but a precarious accord had been reached. When the time came, the Chinese would be informed of the test, but the underlying reason would only be hinted. The Soviet Union had chosen to inform none of the countries in its orbit, and the U.S. had not demurred.

Isaacs gathered up the report with its final corrections and headed for the outer office. His eyes skimmed the brass letters on the doorway—Deputy Director of Scientific Intelligence—and the ones below—Robert B. Isaacs. The report was virtually his last official act in that capacity. There had been no scandal, no public condemnation, just the gentle irrefutable suggestion. He thought of his new position with the Georgetown University Center for International Studies, amused at the irony. After years of suspicion and mistrust of academics, he would join their ranks. He was actually looking forward to it. Time to do some thinking. Some writing. "Forget it," Martinelli had said. "You'll be as busy as ever."

Kathleen Huddleston was in the outer office. "Here's the last of it," he said to her. "I sure appreciate your staying late."

She acknowledged his gratitude with a smile and flipped expertly through the pages. "This will just take a few minutes. It'll be on Drefke's desk when he comes in in the morning."

"Great," Isaacs replied.

He locked his office for the night, waved goodbye to Kathleen who was busy in front of the screen of her word processor and headed for the stairs. As he walked, his mind whirled with images of the fateful moment, the target of the gargantuan effort outlined in the report.

At zero hour the lasers would be triggered and the tiny hurtling particle would be immersed in a carefully designed cocoon of photons. In lightning response, the hole would emit a corresponding burst of particles and energy in rapid cascade and shrink a fraction in size. From the distance of the monitoring flotilla, this unprecedented set of events would look similar to another man-made holocaust.

Information of the blast would be fed nearly instantaneously to nerve centers around the world. Within hours it would be known whether the experiment was a success, whether the energy released and the shrinkage of the hole were as expected. Only then would they have some concrete basis for the hope that the mass of the hole could be peeled away, little by little, that the orbit could be shifted until the menace was free of the earth.

As Isaacs descended the stairs, he thought of the arguments he had heard from Runyan, Humphreys, Phillips, and Korolev. He trusted these men and believed them when they argued that this was the only rational approach, but their descriptions of the possible pitfalls were deeply troubling. The response of the hole was predicated on deductions from Krone's data concerning previously unknown effects. Great effort would be put into developing theories to interpret the Krone experiments, but these theories could not be tested except by the ultimate event itself.

If the current expectations were overoptimistic, the experiment could be a dud, the black hole continuing on its rapacious path. They could err in the opposite sense. If too much mass were liberated from the hole, too much energy released, the explosion could be catastrophically powerful, threatening the Pacific basin with deadly tsunamis and perhaps the whole earth with climactic changes.

Even if the expectations were correct, the required engineering feats were enormously complex. If the aim of the laser were not perfect, the black hole might be kicked inaccessibly beneath the earth's surface rather than boosted further above it.

Uncontrollably, Isaacs brooded on the implications if the experiment should fail. The warp and woof of human affairs were woven on a tapestry of time, comfortably stretched by geologists and astronomers to billions and billions of years. How would humanity change if the future were known to be abbreviated, longer than a single human life, but grimly truncated? Isaacs began to think of the future in its possible shortened version. Earthquakes beginning in several hundred years, growing ever stronger, more devastating. Then in several tens of thousands of years—nothing. A sun, eight planets, and a small, dark marble.

Isaacs found himself in the foyer, headed outside. It was early on a spring evening as he pushed out through the door. No one was around as he paused at the head of the steps. The glass door swung shut behind him and the rubber, steel, and oil smell of man was replaced by the sweetness of growing things. The warm, heavily scented air engendered a feeling of being tugged gently but firmly downward, as if by a languid lover, but his eyes rose to the multitude of stars winking on in the deepening dusk.

An oasis, he thought. There must be another.

His eyes searched the bright points for a sign of welcome.

EPILOGUE: Three Years Later

Alex Runyan responded groggily to the rap on his cabin door. I'm getting too old for this, he thought to himself. Then the significance of the day awoke in him like a spreading spark. He sat up, fumbled for the light, switched it on and fell back on the bunk, eyes in a tight squint, the light filtered blood-red through his lids. He lay for a moment feeling the gentle roll of the ship, to which he had never gotten quite accustomed. The USS Bradford, a Navy frigate, single shaft, displacing twelve hundred tons and rigged for research duty, had been his home for six weeks. He estimated he had logged a total of eight months of sea duty in bits and pieces since the project had gotten into full swing. He still preferred a floor that stayed where you aimed when you took a step. He swung his legs over the side of the bunk, grabbed his pants off the floor where he had discarded them only a scant few hours before and stood up. He leaned over and picked up one foot, preparing to thrust it into the trouser leg, but the slow tilt of the deck threw him off balance. He braced himself with one arm on the bulkhead and struggled awkwardly, failing to get a foot in the floppy denims while he held them with just one hand. He grabbed the trousers with both hands, lifted a foot, and was tilted off balance again. This time he was slow to drop the pants and reach for support. He smacked his head against the shelf over his bunk.

"Goddamnit!" he swore at the offending protrusion. Chagrined, he sat down on the bunk to put the pants on like any landlubber. Everything's tougher at sea, he laughed to himself as he stood to hoist the pants, zip the fly, and fasten his belt. Then he sat again to shove his feet into sneakers and lace them up. That was one of the first things the Navy types told him when he came aboard. More the miracle that they were ready a bit ahead of schedule, if not on budget. He looked at his watch, 4:07, shrugged a light jacket on over his T-shirt, scratched his beard mightily with both hands, ran fingers quickly through his hair, then opened the door and stepped into the passage.

He made his way toward the galley, his eyes feeding him the jumpy images of sleep deprivation. He joined the small queue at the urn, grabbed a cup, filled it with steaming black coffee, scalded his tongue, and carried the cup out, swearing to himself, alternately blowing on the coffee and trying to sip as he walked. He negotiated the steep stairs with one hand on the railing, then walked back on the main deck toward the stern. The chopper was already warming up on the pad, lit by spotlights, harsh grey and shadow, its rotors driving cold moist air down along the deck. Runyan shivered and clasped the neck of his jacket with his free hand. He spied Viktor Korolev in the small knot of scientific advisors and lifted the cup in salute. Damn Russian, he muttered to himself, doesn't he know what it means to run out of steam?

Korolev met him with a smile, jacket open, oblivious to the prop wash.

"Ho, Alex! So today is our big day, eh?"

"You look disgustingly chipper for someone who's about to seal the fate of the world," Runyan grinned, "particularly at this ungodly hour."

"Ungodly?" Korolev's smile faded a bit. "Not at all, in fact the whole thing is now in God's hands, don't you think, and those of all these superb engineers we've worked with. Certainly not mine."

"You don't want your government to hear you invoking deities at this stage, do you?"

"Maybe they won't arrest me for a little generic prayer, you think?" Korolev chuckled and slapped Runyan on the shoulder, causing him to slosh coffee on his hand.

"Time to get on," Korolev said, jerking his chin toward the helicopter where people were starting to clamber aboard.

Runyan transferred the cup to his other hand, licked his fingers, dried them on his jeans, took a last, long swallow of coffee and then handed the cup to a young ensign.

"Run this stolen property back to the galley for me, won't you?" he asked the young man and then jogged to the hatch of the helicopter as the rotors began to pick up speed.

The last one in, Runyan sat near the small port. They lifted quickly and the Bradford rapidly disappeared beneath them, but as it did Runyan could see the faint lights of other ships come into view, scattered sparsely over the ocean as far as he could see in any direction. He did not bother to count them; he knew it was pointless since there were over a thousand, ranging from small craft like the Bradford to a handful of hulking carriers. He settled in for the familiar, minimally comfortable half-hour ride.

They did not approach it on a direct line, probably because of other air traffic, Runyan mused, and he could begin to make it out when it was still some ten miles away—a floating behemoth extravagantly lit, a sparkling diamond, a cross section of L.A. from Mulholland Drive. They hovered nearby while another helicopter landed and took on a load of people.

Runyan marveled again at the structure below. It was patterned after an oil drilling rig, but was specially constructed in almost every detail. It spanned a hundred meters on a side and was covered with a complex superstructure dominated by the central dome, two and a half billion dollars of floating technology. The helicopter spun and settled toward the pad, a white circle surrounding a stark black letter K, the only hint of the prime contractor: Krone Industries.

Runyan jumped out and walked off the pad, thankful for the firmness beneath his feet. The platform was anchored by a dozen telescoping floodable legs that extended deep down to the stable layers beneath the ocean swells which rocked the Bradford. It felt as solid as St. Paul. Here was a place where a man could put on his pants in civilized fashion, thought Runyan, rubbing the bruise on his forehead. Behind him the helicopter filled with departing personnel and lifted off.

Korolev assembled the small group of men.

"Okay," he said, "you know your tasks. You are to oversee the last minute checks and then, most importantly, make sure every member of your crew gets off the platform. You all know your scheduled departure times?" He looked around the group, satisfied at their affirmative nods. "Okay, I will see you back on the Bradford."

Runyan knew that he should go immediately to the computer room, but he was confident that his people would have everything under control, and he wanted a last look. As he made his way through the corridors, he noticed how empty they felt. The platform had bustled with a thousand souls for a year, but now was down to a skeleton crew. He stepped into the central dome. The wave of *deja vu* was stronger than ever, amplified by the tension of this last morning. The device which loomed in the center of the room was more polished, but resounded with echoes of the machine Paul Krone had constructed which had brought them to this pass—a hedgehog array of gigantic lasers all focussed into a central chamber where the hole would make its appearance in a little over two hours.

Unlike Krone's original, this one was designed not to create and support, but to track and destroy. It was mounted on powerful hydraulic gimbals which allowed it to lift and settle, rotate and track. Each laser was individually aimed, controlled through an elaborate computer-driven feedback process. Although it weighed hundreds of tons and should have been ponderous, it was quick as a gunfighter. Runyan watched in awe as the device was put through its final paces, leaping and slurring with blurring speed. In principle it could follow the hole even though the platform were buffeted by gale force winds. This day was carefully chosen, however, the weather monitored for weeks, and all the device needed to do was follow a simple parabolic trajectory. Runyan shook his head as one would at the imminent death of a magnificent animal.

He left the dome and descended to the computer complex. He paused inside the door of the operations room and glanced through the window of the cubicle where the central computer stood. It was not much bigger than two men back-to-back, but was the state of the art parallel processing machine. In turn, it communicated with twenty-odd smaller dedicated machines scattered about the platform. Runyan made a silent tour of the room, pausing behind each of the half dozen operators at their terminals who made final cross checks before turning the whole operation over to the central computer. Signals from special seismic and sonar monitoring stations throughout the world were fed by satellite relay, so the computer could register the location of the hole instant by instant. Any perturbation in the orbit was translated into a signal to the powerful turbines in the bowels of the platform. These could drive the platform at a maximum speed of ten knots and represented the coarse guidance adjustment. Peering at one terminal, Runyan saw that the turbines were engaged to combat a small drift due to ocean currents. Another operator was checking the program that predicted the precise path of the hole as it rocketed up a reinforced shaft into the dome so the device there could anticipate how to move. Yet another tested the operation of the gravity detectors that would enable the lasers to focus their blast in the precise fashion to stimulate the hole to emit an even greater rocketing burst of energy. That release would reduce the mass of the hole and boost it, however minutely, further out of the earth, closer to the sanctuary of space.

Everything looked in order, but Runyan felt a sickening knot in his stomach anyway. He and hundreds of others had worked very hard to determine the orbit of the hole. This site in the mid-Pacific had been selected with careful attention to the sub-mantle rock distribution to minimize any final perturbations to the hole's orbit. He was too close to this aspect of the project, though, and knew that despite all their care, this was the weak link. A small last second nudge, a drift in the orbit, one that was a bit too large for the huge turbines and the snake-fast device overhead to accommodate, and the whole gigantic enterprise could backfire, sending the hole deeper into the earth, beyond reach. Everything had seemed to function perfectly in half a dozen dry runs in which they had ambushed the hole, but allowed it to pass through their floating trap unmolested. This time they would pull the trigger. Their aim had to be true.

Runyan watched quietly for several minutes and then announced, "It's 5 o'clock. Our ride leaves in ten minutes. Let's button it up."

The operators glanced at him and then finished their tasks, logging out, turning their functions over to the computer and the remote monitors. One by one they sighed, pushed back from their terminals and left the room. The last one leaned over and gave his terminal a perfunctory kiss and a pat. Runyan smiled, clapped him on the shoulder in sympathy, and followed him out.

They gathered by the pad and the helicopter dropped down out of the dark sky right on schedule. Runyan knew each of the men intimately, but went through the formality of checking each off on a list as they boarded the helicopter, attesting that they were safely off the platform. Then he climbed aboard himself and didn't look back.

Back on the Bradford, Runyan stopped in the galley to choke down a doughnut and sip another cup of coffee. Then he joined the gathering crowd on the deck, their backs to the rosy dawn, their eyes on that which they couldn't see, a hundred miles away across the flat ocean expanse. Runyan sought out Korolev. The Russian turned to face him, and they shook hands mutely, somberly, and then leaned on the rail staring like all the others.

After a while Korolev grumbled.

"I saw a report the other day."

Runyan listened in silence.

"Seismic activity along the trajectory," the Russian continued. "Just statistical. Not a strong signal. But real, I think."

He took a sheet of note paper from his pocket and slowly and methodically tore it into strips, and the strips into bits. When he finished, he spoke again.

"A definite increase in earthquake activity. No big quakes, but a larger number of small tremors. A weakening of the earth. The first small signs."

Runyan nodded.

"Nervous?" He asked, gesturing at the scraps in the Russian's gnarled fist.

"Yes," Korolev smiled, "but no, this is something else. A little trick your Mr. Fermi taught us years ago. The Manhattan Project. If we see nothing, we have a dud. If it works," he lifted his fistful of confetti, "we have a little hint of how well."

At a pre-arranged time they put on dark goggles. All was silent on the Bradford. Runyan thought briefly of his wife.

Then a new star was born.

After the initial flash, Runyan whipped off his goggles.

The fireball grew rapidly, expanding along the horizon, blasting upward. Outward it rushed, silently, painfully white, looming, violent, menacing. No, Runyan heard himself telling it, no, that's big enough. He had to crane his neck to see the top. No. No. It was impossibly big, and still it spread, implacable, ravishing the sky. They were safe at a hundred miles, Runyan thought, they had to be. But in a detached way he could feel a primal force gathering in his belly, forcing a scream toward his throat.

Then it paused, sated, halted its outward rush, and began to billow even taller.

They watched quietly, all diminished by the horrifying splendor. After long minutes, Runyan could make out the shock ripping toward them at unbelievable speed across the surface of the water.

"Hold on," he heard Korolev mutter.

The Russian grabbed the railing with his free hand. His lips moved as he counted to himself, watching the shock front and tracing its path. Then he threw the shards of paper in the air between himself and Runyan. The shock arrived with the roar of an express train, and the bits of confetti leapt sideways. Korolev watched them continue their wafting fall to the deck.

"It was a big one, Alex," the Russian growled over the continuous rumble, "a very big one. Pray the recoil was in the right direction."